Michelle Smart's love when she was a baby a in her cot. A voracious found her love of roman stumbled across her first Mills & Boon book at the age of twelve. She's been reading them— and writing them—ever since. Michelle lives in Northamptonshire, England, with her husband and two young Smarties.

Annie West has devoted her life to an intensive study of charismatic heroes who cause the best kind of trouble for their heroines. As a sideline she researches locations for romance whenever she can, from vibrant cities to desert encampments and fairytale castles. Annie lives in eastern Australia with her hero husband, between sandy beaches and gorgeous wine country. She finds writing the perfect excuse to postpone housework. To contact her, or join her newsletter, visit annie-west.com.

TO HIRE
AND TO HATE

MICHELLE SMART

ANNIE WEST

MILLS & BOON

First published in Great Britain 2025
by Mills & Boon, an imprint of HarperCollins*Publishers* Ltd,
1 London Bridge Street, London, SE1 9GF

www.harpercollins.co.uk

HarperCollins*Publishers*, Macken House, 39/40 Mayor Street Upper, Dublin 1, D01 C9W8, Ireland

To Hire and to Hate © 2025 Harlequin Enterprises ULC

Greek Boss to Hate © 2025 Michelle Smart

Forbidden Princess's Billionaire Bodyguard © 2025 Annie West

ISBN: 978-0-263-34490-5

12/25

MIX
Paper | Supporting responsible forestry
FSC
www.fsc.org
FSC™ C007454

This book contains FSC™ certified paper and other controlled sources to ensure responsible forest management.

For more information visit www.harpercollins.co.uk/green.

Printed and Bound in the UK using 100% Renewable Electricity at CPI Group (UK) Ltd, Croydon, CR0 4YY

GREEK BOSS TO HATE

MICHELLE SMART

MILLS & BOON

CHAPTER ONE

DRACO MANOLIS STRODE through the main entrance of Tsaliki Shipping with his entourage following in his wake. Nodding greetings at the reception staff, he ignored the elevators and took the stairs to his office on the top floor. Having come straight from the airport after a fourteen-hour flight from California, climbing the stairs was an excellent way of getting his leg muscles working and his blood flowing. That Grace, Theodore and Stav huffed and puffed their way behind him was not his problem; they were perfectly at liberty to take the elevator. It didn't occur to him that his closest staff were all so used to following his instructions to the letter that independent thought had been lost, much like when humans lost the need for their appendixes.

After a week away from his newest and most important acquisition, one headache Draco didn't need was to reach the eleventh floor and be ambushed by what felt like every member of the finance team. He could tell by their expressions what they were going to complain about: Athena Tsaliki. In the month since his buyout of Tsaliki Shipping and the attendant deal that he employ all of Alexis Tsaliki's siblings for a minimum of three months, Athena's name had come up on a daily—often hourly—basis, and never for complimentary reasons. There had been no respite from the complaints during his week in Silicon Valley.

'She strolled in an hour late again.'

'She refused to photocopy the Druman report.'

'She told Christos to make his own coffee.'

'She asked Evangeline if she'd dressed in the dark.'

At the last one, Draco had to bite his lips to control an unexpected swell of amusement. His inherited finance director had what could only be described as a unique sense of style.

Holding his hands up for silence, he caught the eye of every complainant before saying, 'Leave it with me. I'll deal with her.'

Except how to deal with her, that was the question. He was fast running out of options.

Buying out a multi-billion shipping company was never going to be plain sailing, but he'd never imagined the biggest headache would come in the form of a five-foot-seven blonde. In just one month, Athena had worked—and he used the term in its loosest sense—in six different Tsaliki Shipping departments. Staff mutinies had forced him to move her on each time. Four days ago, at the end of his tether, Draco gambled and ordered that she be placed in finance in the hope the staid, calm atmosphere would rub off on her. Judging by the racket blaring out at the far end of the floor, this was a gamble he'd lost.

With a deep sigh, he headed to the open-plan section where the finance department's administrative team worked.

Three of the administrators were diligently working on their computers. One was photocopying documents. One was peering through a ledger and cross-referencing figures. One was playing on a hot-pink phone that perfectly colour-matched her hot-pink spaghetti-strapped Lycra top, her slender shoulders, face and the tight bun she'd tied her streaky-blonde hair into jiggling to the dreadful excuse for music blaring from the large speakers on her desk.

Without a greeting or any fanfare, Draco plucked the phone from her hand and looked at the screen. Instead of doing whatever job she'd been tasked with, the bane of his life had been reading an online fashion magazine. He looked at her and raised an unimpressed eyebrow. Luckily, he didn't expect contrition because none was forthcoming. No, the bane of his life flashed her perfect teeth and cheerfully said, 'Morning, boss. What do you think of the dress in the feature article I've been reading? Do you think it matches my skin tone or would I need a deeper spray tan to pull it off?'

Long past asking God to give him strength where Athena Tsaliki was concerned, he merely pursed his lips and gave a jerk of his head. It was a gesture he'd given so many times she didn't need it translating, and with the docile obedience she'd proved herself an expert at faking, got to her feet.

Ignoring—for now—that she was wearing a hot-pink tutu in lieu of a skirt, he handed the phone back to her with a pointed, 'Music off.'

She gave a little pout. 'You don't like grime?'

'No one with any taste likes grime.'

Her pretty straight nose wrinkled, and in a theatrical aside she said, 'Seeing as I'm the only person in this whole company with an ounce of taste, I think I'm the best qualified to be the judge of that.'

If she was bothered by the heads of her colleagues all turning sharply to her and the daggers they all aimed at her, she didn't show it. In fact, Draco would be willing to bet she didn't even notice, never mind care. She pressed her pretty fingers with the hot-pink, diamond-studded nails to the screen of her phone and a beat later merciful silence reigned.

'There,' she said with another of her wide beams. 'All done. Anything else you want me to do before we go to your office and you give me what I assume is going to be another bollocking?'

'You could try turning your computer on.'

She wiggled her finger at him, then wiggled it at the computer before finally pressing the button. 'Ta-da!'

Only when she skipped out from behind her desk did he notice that she was wearing hot-pink tights and hot-pink ballerina shoes. Genuine ballerina shoes with pointe toes and pink ribbons tied around her calves. He could only be grateful that she didn't pirouette up the last flight of stairs to his office.

The top floor of Tsaliki Shipping's headquarters consisted of a large reception area filled with comfortable seating and coffee-making facilities, a sprawling board-room and various private offices, the largest of which was occupied by Draco. His entourage dispersing to their work spaces, Grace, his PA, took her seat at the horseshoe desk that guarded Draco's door, flashing disappointment when Draco closed it, thus excluding her from the forth-coming fireworks.

While he sat at his newly installed cocobolo desk, Athena threw herself onto one of the leather sofas. 'I see you finally changed the décor and furniture,' she said, wriggling and stretching herself out. 'It's nice to be able to lie down and not have to think of my father having sex with one of his secretaries in here.'

Used to Athena's outrageous comments, he gave no

reaction other than to say, 'This isn't a therapy session. Sit up.'

'It would be much more fun if it was a therapy session as we'd be discussing my favourite topic—myself!'

'Don't worry; this conversation will be all about you, specifically your attitude and behaviour. Now sit up. And that's an order.'

'Yes, boss.' Instead of swinging her long legs around like a normal person would, she kicked them high into the air and then, with perfect grace, scissor split them as she twisted her hips. A moment later she was sat demurely with her hands on her lap and a beatific expression on her beautiful face.

One thing Draco had discovered about Athena in the long, long, long month she'd worked for him was that she hated silence, and so he took great pleasure in making her sit in it.

She managed five seconds. 'Well? What specifically do you want to bollock me about?'

'Let's start with your time-keeping. I hear you were an hour late today.'

She held her hands up. 'I was having a manicure.'

'I've told you this before, Athena—manicures, like all personal grooming, are to be done in your personal time, not work time.'

'But my nails were electric blue, which didn't go with my outfit,' she said earnestly, 'Also, I'm really busy in my personal time. Swamped.'

'I know, you've told me before.' Many times. 'Moving on, I hear you refused to photocopy the Druman report.'

Her hands rose again. 'I'd only just had my nails manicured.'

'And refusing to make Christos a coffee?'

She waved her manicured fingers.

'You are an administrator. Making coffee for the directors and other senior members of the finance team is part of your job description.'

'Do you have any idea how much this manicure cost me?'

'Do you have any idea how many of your colleagues want to shoot you?'

Her mouth formed a perfect O, the rest of her beautiful features forming the perfect expression of shock. 'People can be so cruel.'

'Speaking of cruel, I also hear you asked Evangeline if she'd dressed in the dark.'

'That wasn't cruelty, that was curiosity—honestly, Draco, have you *seen* what she's wearing today?'

'No, but you are in no position to judge, sitting there dressed as the Sugar Plum Fairy. I thought I'd made it clear—no more fancy dress or inappropriate attire in the office.'

Her long, thickly mascaraed lashes fluttered. 'What's inappropriate about this outfit?'

This woman was going to be the death of him.

Two more months. That was how much longer he had to keep her employed.

But this was the deal he'd made. Alexis Tsaliki had been immovable about the condition his siblings be employed and the penalties that would be invoked if any were sacked before the three months were complete. Any other deal and Draco would have walked, but this was Tsaliki Shipping, the company he'd coveted for decades. In eight sweet weeks, Georgios Tsaliki, the unconscionable Tsaliki patriarch who'd already experienced the ignominy of having his own company wrested from his control by his eldest child—how Draco had enjoyed observing that from afar—and then sold without his input would experience the ultimate humiliation of knowing everything he'd worked for his whole life was gone. The Tsaliki name, for decades considered one of the greats in shipping, would no longer exist.

How Draco would enjoy watching Georgios and his equally unconscionable wife's faces when the new name was revealed. As far as revenge went, this was minor in terms of the damage Draco could have done, but fate had already played its hand and taken its revenge for him. Georgios and his wife now lived at the mercy of Alexis, the only Tsaliki sibling to have made anything of himself. Taking away the Tsaliki name was simply Draco putting the icing on the cake of revenge Georgios's own actions had caused.

It wasn't just Georgios and Rebecca now living at Alexis's mercy. All Alexis's siblings were too. Alexis controlled everything, and it was with this power that he'd set the terms of the deal with Draco and forced his siblings to comply.

Draco had fully expected to despise all of Georgios's children. The last thing he'd expected was to feel sorry for them. Alexis, he grudgingly admired. Alexis had his shit together and had long let go of his father's coat-tails to make his own way in the world, but the others were collectively famed for being a bunch of useless, work-shy wasters. Credit where it was due though, they were trying. Whether that was because they took their oldest brother at his word that failure to complete three months of work would see them cut off financially for good didn't matter. They were trying. All except the family princess, Athena.

Alexis had warned him Athena would be the trickiest

sibling to integrate into the workforce, and Draco had duly prepared himself…or so he'd thought.

He'd had no idea what he was letting himself in for.

Resting her elbows on the tulle tutu, she placed her knuckles under her chin and sweetly murmured, 'I know you don't want to admit defeat, but why don't you just give in and sack me?'

If only.

Athena Tsaliki was a chameleon. An outrageous, rude, bitchy, beautiful chameleon who left a trail of destruction and tears in her wake. Slender and in perfect physical shape, with her pretty green eyes and wide mouth she had the face of an angel and the tongue of a viper. The staff he'd inherited in the buyout all hated her. Her siblings, all brothers, hated her. The few members of staff in his other business ventures who'd had dealings with her hated her.

But sacking her would cost him. That had been the deal. A one hundred million penalty for any Tsaliki sibling sacked before the three months was up. Athena, the trickiest of the lot, came with a premium. If he sacked her, he would have to pay a billion-euro penalty, and while it would definitely be worth taking that financial hit, Draco had never admitted defeat about anything in his life and he wasn't going to start now. A man didn't become a self-made billionaire before he hit his thirties by turning down a challenge. Draco thrived on challenges, and in Athena he'd found his biggest challenge yet.

'I'm not going to sack you, Athena,' he said. 'But you are welcome to do everyone a favour and quit.'

She pulled one of the many faces that made her so mesmerising, this particular expression a cross between rueful and sad, and with a voice pitched to match it, said, 'We both know I can't do that. My darling brother will cut me off forever if I quit…' She suddenly brightened. 'Unless you want to support me? I wouldn't ask for much—just a townhouse with a minimum of six bedrooms and views of the Aegean—can you believe the apartment Alexis has stuck me in doesn't have a decent view of anything?—an island of my own in the Seychelles, a private plane of my own, all the upkeep and maintenance and staffing costs paid for all this, of course, a clothing allowance of a hundred thousand a week and an additional allowance of a hundred thousand a week, index linked to rise with inflation. Oh, and a couple of cars. Those Baby Bentleys are really cute. What do you think?'

Not for the first time, Draco had to bite back amusement. Athena's green eyes were sparkling, not with hope or expectation but with mischief.

Leaning back in his seat, he steepled his fingers, shook his head and suppressed a smile. 'As tempting as your suggestion is, you're way past the age of being supported.'

Her eyes widened in fake outrage, mouth dropping open. 'Are you calling me *old*?'

'Hardly. You're a decade younger than me.'

'Ooh, so you're thirty-one, then?'

Biting back yet more laughter, he raised an eyebrow. 'You know damn well I'm thirty-eight.'

'That makes you eleven years older than me…just.' She covered her mouth and leaned forward to whisper, 'I won't tell anyone your real age if you don't tell them mine.'

'Ageing only bothers those who trade on their looks,' he said pointedly.

'I know! You have to feel sorry for those people. If they would only cultivate a personality, they might not feel the need to inject their foreheads every other week.'

She pulled a rueful face and shrugged in a 'but what can you do?' fashion.

'As entertaining as this conversation is…'

She beamed.

'… I'm supposed to be in a finance meeting, so let's get this wrapped up—you're now going to work directly for me.'

She wriggled her shoulders in mock excitement. 'Ooh, a promotion! My family will be so proud!'

Draco had no idea how he kept a straight face or how he was able to keep his tone stern. 'For the next two months you will work your contracted hours, and in those contracted hours you are going to do some real, actual work. You will be at your desk by eight-thirty a.m. and leave no earlier than five p.m. When I travel, you will travel with me and if that involves working late or over weekends then you will work late and over weekends. You will not go for lunch and then decide that having a bikini wax or highlights in your hair is more important than returning to the office.'

She was nodding along as if agreeing to every word.

'You will dress appropriately for the office. No more tutus, no more Elsa costumes—'

'What about Ana?'

'The red wig doesn't suit you.'

She gasped as if affronted.

'No more ripped jeans, no more leather, no more mini-mini-skirts—no one needs to see the colour of your knickers.'

She fluttered her eyelashes again. 'Yes, but that's why bikini waxing is so important.'

He *would not* laugh or respond in any other fashion. 'The next time you come to the office wearing anything

I deem inappropriate I will personally dress you in one of Evangeline's dresses.'

'Ooh, will you strip me first? That could be fun!'

He gave her the look that made every single other employee quail. 'Appropriate attire, Athena. Business attire. Do you understand?'

In the short—but excessively long—time he'd had to suffer Athena Tsaliki, Draco had trained himself to ignore her innocently delivered suggestive and flirtatious comments. Athena was one of Athens' most notorious socialites. She was used to wrapping men around her little finger, using sex as her weapon of choice. Not that he had an issue with that, and if he were to meet her again in one of the nightclubs he'd occasionally seen her dancing at until the early hours and they were to catch each other's eye before she found another man to fall out of the club with and there was no risk of anyone finding out—Athena might not care about her reputation but Draco cared about his—he'd gladly take her home and see if she was as spectacular in bed as the grapevine suggested.

However, Athena was trouble with a capital T, and she would have no qualms in weaponising any sex between them while she remained in his employ, so until the three-month mark passed, Draco would keep his hands to himself and his thoughts far away from imagining those long limbs wrapped around his waist.

Most definitely not quailing, she huffed a sigh. 'Yes, boss, I understand. And I understand why you were named Draco. You're a right dragon.'

'Actually, I was named for the first lawgiver of ancient Athens.'

'That's just as fitting, seeing as that's where the word draconian originates.'

He stared at her meditatively. 'You're not as stupid as you like to pretend, are you.'

'I assure you, I am. I failed every single school exam. Not even Daddy's suitcases of cash were enough to get me into one of the Ivy League universities. He even offered to fund a new library for one of them, and they still said no.'

'Athena?'

'Yes, boss?'

'Go home.'

'What, now?'

'Yes. Now. You're giving me a headache. Use the afternoon to buy some appropriate attire. Tomorrow, we will work on your attitude and we *will* see an immediate improvement with it.'

She jumped up from the sofa and gave another beaming grin. 'I love your optimism! See you in the morning.'

'Eight-thirty sharp. No excuses—you will be on time, and I don't care if the colour of your nails clashes with your outfit.'

She bounced out of his office without a backward glance. As the door closed, he heard her calling out to the staff, 'See you in the morning, suckers!'

CHAPTER TWO

SOMEONE HAD PUT a drill to Athena Tsaliki's head. Opening one bleary eye, her dream dissipated enough for consciousness to tell her it wasn't a drill but her doorbell. Someone had their finger on it.

Opening her other eye, she focused enough to see her bedside clock telling her it was seven a.m. And still the ringing continued unabated.

Muttering curses under her breath, she crawled out of her lovely warm bed, padded to the front door and put her tired eye to the spy-hole.

Her heart slammed against her ribs, and she went from half-asleep to fully awake in a blink.

She didn't know who she'd expected—in the month she'd been living in this dump of an apartment, she hadn't had a single visitor—but the last person she'd imagined was Draco, suited and booted and ready to embrace another boring day of work.

For a moment, she debated ignoring him and going back to bed. She would never show it, but she found his presence increasingly disturbing. She didn't know why; he was just a man. A good-looking man for sure, but her world brimmed with good-looking men. She didn't think he'd had the surgery so many of them had started dabbling in though. If he had, he needed a new surgeon because his face was too lined to justify the cost. A manly, lived-in, rugged face with a firm mouth, straight nose tipped up at the end and a dark brown close-cropped beard, all topped with a thick head of dark brown hair worn short at the sides and slicked up at the top. He was also tall and muscular, but her brothers were tall and muscular so that couldn't be it either.

He let go of the doorbell to rap loudly on the door. 'I know you're there, Athena,' he called before putting his finger back to the bell. 'I can do this all morning.'

Muttering another curse, she yanked the door open. 'What do you want?'

'Not a morning person, I see,' he said, stepping uninvited into her temporary home, bringing in the winter air and a cloud of the cologne her nostrils always twitched to inhale deeply. 'I thought as much.'

'I am a morning person when it's the morning. This is the middle of the night.' And she was in her pyjamas. Embarrassingly, they were her oversized red and black checked pyjamas, the ones she wouldn't let anyone see her dead in. Terrible reputations like Athena's didn't maintain themselves; they needed cultivation. 'Why are you here?'

'To get you to work on time.'

She groaned. 'I will get to work on time. I just need another hour in bed.'

'No, you need to do your Pilates and take a shower.'

'How do you know I do Pilates? Have you been spying on me?' She stepped backwards and feigned fear. 'Are you secretly stalking me?'

He gave her the unimpressed face she'd been on the receiving end of more times than she'd had birthdays. 'Athena, you sat in the middle of a warehouse the other week and did half an hour of Pilates and refused to move when people told you that you were in the way.'

'Sometimes the mood just takes me.' And she'd known it would get her, if not sacked, then moved to a different department. Of all the departments she'd been assigned to, the colossal warehouse in Inland Services had been the worst. It had been so cold in there that her hands had become all dry and she'd needed daily manicures to fix the terrible state they'd got into. At least, that was what she'd told her immediate boss all the times she'd failed to return after lunch. That boss had ended up threatening to resign if Athena wasn't moved somewhere far, far away. Result!

She had a feeling that this boss, her ultimate boss, would prove much harder to wear down. Unlike the other bosses she'd been lumbered with—and the colleagues she'd been forced to work alongside—this one was proving a tough nut to crack. He hadn't even raised his voice at her! Still, Athena was nothing if not tenacious, and the sooner she made Draco crack and fire her, the sooner she'd get her life back. Just look at what she'd achieved in a month! Six different departments, and now he'd run out of options for where to place her because no one else would have her and so he'd lumbered himself with her! He'd be throwing the billion-euro penalty at her brother before the week was out, possibly even the end of that very day if she played her cards right.

'Just get yourself sorted. We leave in an hour.'

'It takes that long to dry my hair.'

'Don't wash it then.'

She feigned horror. 'Are you mad?'

There was a slight crinkling of the lines around his eyes, but his voice remained stern. 'One hour, Athena. If you're not dressed and ready in that time, I'll dress you myself.'

She pouted her lips. 'Ooh, I love it when you're all masterful.'

He folded his arms across his impressive chest and pulled another unimpressed face.

She gave an exaggerated roll of her eyes. 'Okay, okay, I'll go get ready.'

Bed hair swishing, she sauntered back to her bedroom figuring that as she'd been caught in unsexy oversized pyjamas, she might as well own it.

When the door closed, though, she stilled and let out a long breath. Her heart was beating even harder than it usually did around him. Probably latent embarrassment at the state of her apartment. Not that she would allow embarrassment to show. Athena didn't do embarrassed. People could take her or leave her; she didn't care. Most chose to leave. Actually, make that *all* chose to leave. Which was fine by her because who needed people? Not her. Best to push them away before they got too close because the closer people got, the more it hurt when they left, and Athena did not do hurt, not since she was six when, as fate's quirk would have it, Draco's mother had been driven out of her life.

Athena hadn't allowed herself to think about Cora Manolis for years, not until Draco Manolis made the business headlines with the billion-euro sale of his tech start-up company founded on a ten thousand euro investment. Since those headlines a good decade ago, their lives had skirted around each other, which was the way of the Athens society scene—everyone knew everyone even if they'd never been introduced—but the first time she'd voiced her belief that he was their old housekeeper's son had been when Alexis announced he was selling Tsaliki Shipping to him. The scorn that had been heaped on her for this would have wounded if she allowed herself to feel pain. None of her family remembered Cora having a son and, as more than one of her brothers patronisingly reminded her, Greek women kept their surnames on marriage and Greek children took their father's surnames. Rebecca, her English stepmother, had been the most scathing, saying, 'If that cheap slut had a son, he would never have amounted to anything.'

'Don't you think due diligence means you should check if I'm right?' Athena had said, addressing Alexis directly. 'After all, why would a tech giant want to go into shipping?'

'He wants to diversify. Draco has the funds and is proving himself receptive to my conditions, so stop trying to cause drama where there is none.'

'What conditions?' she'd asked, immediately suspicious.

Alexis had smiled, and not in a kindly way. 'You will find out in due course.'

Well, due course had come about and here she was, evicted from the family home, stripped of her allowance and installed in this poky apartment with the order to work and fend for herself for three months so she could *appreciate the privileges of her life*. And she was still convinced Draco was Cora's son. He looked nothing like her—for which Athena was grateful as she didn't think her stony-cold heart could bear it if he did—but there was something about him that felt so familiar, and if the others wanted to bury their heads in the sand about it then that was their problem. Whatever Draco's real intention behind the purchase, it would come out, as her brother would put it, in due course, and if that due course should bring humiliation to the family then they couldn't complain they hadn't been warned. If she wasn't so intent on getting herself sacked at the soonest opportunity, she'd use the fact she'd now be working at his side as a means to get sleuthing.

Athena was ready to go in forty-seven minutes. Not wanting Draco to think he'd got the better of her or that she had any intention of complying with his directives, she lay belly down on her bed for the next thirteen minutes drawing. Trying to draw. Draco was in her apartment, a fact that had made her shower and apply her make-up much more quickly than she usually did and was distracting her now.

Maybe, she mused, he disturbed her because he didn't react to her antics in the usual way. His reactions were thoughtful. Calculated. He didn't shout or show exasperation or even look as if he secretly itched to raise his hand to her. Maybe that was it—the way he looked at her. Draco had the brightest, bluest eyes she'd ever seen, and when they fixed on you it was like they pierced right through you. She remembered catching his eye once in a nightclub and experiencing that pierce. She'd turned away and continued dancing, but the sensation had lingered. Anyone would find that disturbing. Luckily, Athena was an expert at not letting her inner feelings show, and even more luckily, she'd be fired soon and would never have to be disturbed by him again.

Exactly one hour after she'd gone for her shower, there was a loud rap on her bedroom door and a rough, gruff voice called, 'Are you ready?'

'Nearly,' she called back. 'Two minutes.'

The door opened.

She looked up from her drawing book while hastily closing it. 'Oi!'

Not stepping over the threshold, he pulled the familiar face. 'Move.'

Huffing, she climbed off the bed.

'What on earth are you wearing?'

'Clothes. Work attire. Exactly as you ordered.'

'Hot pants are not appropriate work attire.'

'They're not hot pants, they're shorts.' Very short shorts that she'd made even shorter by rolling the hem up. 'And they *are* work attire, see?' She did a twirl. 'See, they match.' It had taken her hours to find this outfit, and she'd blown the last of her credit buying it. A tight, prim white shirt and brown waistcoat with tight shorts and tie a shade lighter, all complemented by white knee-high socks. 'How can they not be appropriate? You can barely see my cheeks, and there is nothing in the company dress code that forbids women from wearing shorts, only men, which is a bit sexist when you think about it, but there you go.'

The rugged face she found far too disturbing for comfort was going through varying contortions, but the blue eyes she found even more disturbing were piercing her skin with the clear message that she might have beaten him at this particular game but that he'd be the winner of the next one.

An expert at smiling through discomfort, she bestowed on him her best coquettish beam. She'd worked on the edges of Draco's law and beaten him at his own game. One nil to Athena. Hopefully she'd soon be able to make it two nil.

First, though, she needed to leave her room. If it was anyone else blocking the doorway, she'd barge past them. It wasn't Draco's size that stopped her doing this—the only girl in a family of eight boys, she'd learned to use her elbows before she'd learned to use cutlery—it was some instinct warning her not to get too close, the same instinct that had made her turn her back to him in that nightclub all that time ago. Athena knew men. She knew how to play them and manipulate them and knew when to back away before things got out of hand.

Instinct and experience told her Draco Manolis posed danger to a girl like her. This was not a man who'd allow himself to be manipulated and toyed with. Teasing and flirting with him were fine in the office, but she wasn't in the office, she was in her bedroom, and he was standing on the threshold, a place no man who wasn't a Tsaliki had stood before, and he was the most ruggedly handsome man she'd met in her life, a real man, not a boy-man like the men she chose to play with.

She knew he wouldn't make a sudden move on her, but that didn't stop her heart from pumping hard to imagine it, and it wasn't the pumping of fear that had happened a couple of times when she'd misjudged the boy-man she'd been toying with and found herself with a predator. Luckily, she'd been able to extricate herself from those situations without any harm being done—at least, not to her—but this was a whole new situation and a thousand times more frightening because, for the first time in her life, her skin was tingling and sensation was stirring between her legs, a sensation that excited, sickened and terrified in equal measure.

Suddenly the silence that had formed from nowhere between them had become deafening, the piercing sensation from Draco's blue eyes gaining in strength, and she tore her stare away so she could breathe...for some reason, her lungs had stopped working...and tugged at the edges of her bedsheets more for the distraction while she tried to pull herself together than to straighten them.

'So you *can* keep something tidy,' he observed, a strain in his gruff voice as he broke the silence. 'I'd assumed from the state of the rest of the place that your hands didn't work.'

She snatched at the open goal he'd just presented her with. 'We can't all be born poor and have to muck in with the chores. I'm sure your mother did an excellent job passing on her cleaning skills to you.'

The sharpening of his stare sent a burst of triumph through her. She'd known it! She was right and the rest of her family was wrong!

The triumph dissipated as quickly as it had risen, and not just because of the danger now ringing in his sharp, piercing stare or the ice that echoed in the warning of his gruff voice. 'What the hell do you know about my mother?'

If there was one thing Athena was a pro at, it was her ability to keep talking and smiling whatever turmoil was occurring beneath her skin, and she smiled now as she met his dangerous gaze. 'Know about her? Draco, I *remember* her…well, I should say I remember when she was sacked. She wasn't the first or the last person to be fired for screwing my father. Her bad fortune was that she didn't screw him when he was married to my mother. Rebecca is a different breed. She turns a blind eye to most of his affairs but, unfortunately for your mother, she gets her claws out when he screws the domestic staff.' She wrinkled her nose. 'I think she finds it extra humiliating.'

She knew the moment her tongue shut itself up that she'd gone too far. Her heart thumping harder than ever, the silence that followed filled with a thick tension different to the tension of moments earlier, one that posed a different kind of danger. It took all her strength to hold her nerve, hold her smile, hold Draco's stare and stop the guilt curdling in her guts from showing, not just guilt for what she'd said but guilt for weaponising the woman who'd once been like a comfort blanket to her and who had shown Athena nothing but love. It took even more strength to maintain all this when he stepped off the threshold towards her.

Loath though Draco was to stand anywhere near the poisonous *femme fatale,* he moved his face close to hers so Athena could feel as well as see and hear his contempt for her. 'I was warned you were a grade-A she-devil when I made that deal with your brother,' he said slowly. 'But you're worse than that—you're like your father. He gets his kicks from screwing women; you get yours from screwing with people's heads.' Enjoying the way the golden colour of her face paled and the barely-there flicker in her green eyes, he pulled his lips into a cruel smile. 'Still, the whole of Athens knows you also get your kicks from screwing anyone desperate enough to have you, so that makes you even more like him.'

Still smiling, he stepped back, needing to be out of the poisonous orbit of Athena Tsaliki and the soft scent of her perfume being that close to her soaked into his airwaves. 'I don't care what you think you remember; my mother did nothing wrong. She is worth a thousand of you and a thousand of your father, and if you think taking bitchy potshots at her means I'm going to sack you…' He shook his head. 'You need to do better than that, Athena. Much better.' He left the room, shouting over his shoulder, 'I've made coffee. Yours is getting cold.'

In the small kitchenette, Draco tightly cupped the coffee he'd made for himself and closed his eyes.

How the hell had Athena Tsaliki of all people made the connection that he was Cora's son? She could only have been a small child at the time his mother was sacked, an incident that would have been consigned to ancient history by a family continually seeped in scandal. Ancient history to them but not forgotten by him. Draco would never forget or forgive Georgios and Rebecca Tsaliki for what they'd done to his mother.

For five years she'd worked as the Tsaliki housekeeper, bearing witness to a chaotic household ruled by a stinkingly rich patriarch who played harder than he worked. Serially married, no woman expected Georgios to be faithful; his wives expected to turn a blind eye and hope his current passion wasn't the one to oust them. Ousting, though, wasn't a great hardship as being an ex-wife meant being installed in a grand home and having all your expenses paid and still being included in all the fun family stuff, all without having to share Georgios's bed any more.

No woman was safe from Georgios's advances—Draco's mother had personally caught him in the act with two maids—but for five years Cora Manolis had maintained a cordial, professional relationship with Georgios and wife number three. Wife number four, Rebecca, as Athena had pointed out, was of a different breed to wife number three, and took an instant dislike to Cora. Six months after usurping wife number three, she got her chance to get rid of her and grabbed it with both hands. Her chance came when Cora's father died unexpectedly. Cora received the call at work. Vulnerable and distraught, she'd accepted Georgios's comforting embrace. Never one to miss an opportunity for a taste of female flesh, Georgios had taken full advantage of the moment and Cora's grief-stricken weakness, and kissed her, a full-blown French kiss that was, unfortunately, observed by one of the maids, who went running off to tell Rebecca. When Cora returned to work the next day, she was unceremoniously fired in front of all the other staff, with no severance pay and no references, her name blackened.

Over twenty years later, Rebecca Tsaliki's ruthlessness meant she was still to be usurped.

Draco had never thought it possible to despise a Tsaliki more than he despised Georgios and Rebecca, but Athena had just achieved that accolade, and he hated that when he'd been putting her in her place and giving her a verbal taste of her own medicine he'd experienced the strong compulsion to give himself a taste of *her*.

Maybe he would, he thought moodily. Treat her the way her father had treated his mother. Taste her, discard her and humiliate her.

He tossed his coffee down the sink without drinking it. If Athena had touched it, it was probably poisoned, and God, what was he thinking? To taste her would be to poison himself—she was already poisoning his mind—and there was no humiliating someone as narcissistic as her. To feel humiliation, you had to feel shame, and Athena had none. Athena didn't need to wear the armour and spear of her goddess namesake: her skin was so thick it was its own armour, her tongue more pointed than any spear.

Footsteps approached.

He dragged a breath in through his nose, inhaling the soft scent of her perfume, and braced himself before turning to face her.

'You've tidied up,' she said brightly, as if nothing had happened, as if she hadn't just cruelly insulted his mother and he hadn't cruelly rammed some home truths down her throat.

'Someone had to.' Her small open-plan apartment had been strewn with unpacked boxes. He'd stacked them together in the living area, noticing how she hadn't even put any photos of the people she loved out. But then, to love, you needed to have a heart, and any heart Athena had been born with had long blackened. He'd also loaded her half-sized dishwasher with what he estimated was a week's worth of chipped dirty cups and glasses, and wiped the surfaces down. His question of why there had been no dirty dishes had been answered when he'd looked in the bin and found it crammed with takeaway containers.

She shrugged. 'Not much point in keeping it tidy or unpacking. I'll be out of here soon.'

His mind unwittingly zipped to her bedroom. If he'd had to imagine it, he'd have pictured it like a witch's coven, not the soft, feminine, spotlessly clean room that it was. 'Not for another two months.'

'You'll have sacked me by then.'

'No.' He drilled his stare into her. 'That is not going to happen. You are going to spend the next two months tied to my side. By the time you're released from the contract, you'll be as sick of me as I am of you. Now, drink your coffee. We need to get going—we've got a long day of work to do.'

For once, she didn't make a quip, flirtatious or otherwise. Instead, she drank her coffee, grabbed her handbag and sashayed to the front door. Only when she turned back to see if he was following did he notice she'd replaced the too-short shorts with a black skirt that fell to mid-thigh and the knee-high socks with sheer but respectable black tights.

CHAPTER THREE

ATHENA'S FIRST JOURNEY in a plush, chauffeur-driven car in a month was spent fighting her thoughts and her senses. Her thoughts kept wanting to take her to a past she couldn't forget although she'd spent over twenty years blurring the emotional impact. A therapist or psychiatrist would probably say the times she'd blurred had shaped her into the woman she was today, but they would be wrong—she'd forged herself into the Athena everyone loved to hate.

Being the Athena everyone loved to hate meant never apologising because apologising was a sign of weakness that showed you cared, and when people knew you cared they knew they could hurt you. Best not to care at all.

Being the Athena everyone loved to hate also meant holding your head high and brazening out the awkward moments that came after you'd said or done something your stony heart knew had crossed a line. While her stony heart didn't care if people liked her or not, it did feel heavier in those times, lasting until whatever she'd said or done was forgotten and things returned to normal. It had happened many times with her stepsister Lucie. Athena's feelings for Lucie were the most complicated of all her feelings for everyone. Or had been.

Enclosed in a luxurious but small space with Draco

Manolis as she currently was, her stony heart was feeling heavier than it had in as long as she could remember.

She wished she could take back what she'd said about his mother. She'd never had any intention of mentioning her to him, but she'd been so frightened of the tension that had suddenly grown between them and all the sensations firing inside her that she'd snatched at the open goal to get herself fired he'd provided her with.

Cora Manolis was entwined with her blurred past and so was a door she'd never wanted to open, loving her as much as Athena had once done. Compartmentalising feelings was easy until it wasn't, and Draco's furious defence of his mother had been an unwelcome reminder of just how much Athena had loved her.

Funny how life turned out, she thought bleakly. For the first time in so long, she remembered being a little girl and asking Cora all about her son. Remembered, too, Cora showing her a photo of him, and deciding Draco was the most beautiful man—to five-year-old Athena, any boy over the age of fifteen was a man—in the world and that she would marry him when she was all grown up because if she married him, she'd be able to live with Cora.

And then Cora had been fired and Athena had never seen her again.

And now here she was, sitting beside the man her younger self had wanted to marry, and her senses had never felt so sharp. It wasn't just Draco's fresh, citrusy cologne she was breathing into her lungs with each inhalation, it was his shower gel and shampoo and the way it all interplayed with the underlying essence of his skin, coming together and combining into a scent she found as beautiful as she'd found his face all those decades ago. It wasn't just his gruff voice diving into her ears as he conducted a long business call, it was the staccato of each consonant and the short breaths he took in the pauses, a voice that was contrarily exciting and soothing.

The car stopped outside the Tsaliki Shipping headquarters. Draco carried on talking into his phone. He fixed his piercing eyes on her and indicated with a sharp turn of his head for her to follow him.

The Athena everyone loved to hate produced her widest smile and did as commanded.

If Draco had to admire anything about Athena, it was her chutzpah, and when they reached the top floor and she strode beside him as if she'd been promoted to Chief Executive Officer and said, 'So which office is mine? I assume I get one with its own shower-room,' he came close to cracking a smile.

'The office you'll be contained in certainly comes with a shower-room, but you're banned from using it—you're sharing my office.'

'Ooh, I get to be the keeper of your secrets. Exciting!'

Only her restraint from making a quip about sharing a shower with him convinced him that she really was experiencing a modicum of contrition for weaponising his mother the way she had. Which was just as well as after that journey together the last thing he wanted was to imagine himself sharing a shower with her.

Twenty minutes alone in a car with Athena Tsaliki, her presence filling the space as much as her perfume filled his nostrils, had been much harder than he'd envisaged, even with business calls to distract him. Even with his loathing for her still thick in his blood. It was those damned sheer black tights. He kept catching glimpses of them. They were the most modest item of clothing he'd known her to wear and it was all he could do to stop himself from imagining ripping them off and running his hands over the golden skin beneath. He'd been half-tempted to tell his driver to take them back to her apartment, and make her change back into those ridiculous socks and shorts. And so he'd tried to train his glances to her feet, but she was wearing a pair of sexy black stilettoes and damn if he ever normally noticed or gave a damn what shoes his staff wore.

Athena wasn't staff. Not under any rules of what staff meant. She was his burden to bear until their contracted time was up, angel face and viperous tongue and all.

Her contrition did not extend to Grace. She whisked past her on those sexy stilettoes with an airy smile and a, 'Nice suit. Brings out the colour of your eyes.'

Gritting his teeth, Draco closed the office door and tightly said, 'Did you have to be rude to her?'

'I paid her a compliment!' she refuted indignantly.

'She's wearing red.'

'Exactly! See,' she added, 'I'm already working on my attitude.'

'You need to work a million times harder than that.' Grabbing at his hair, he reminded himself that this was the reason he'd decided to install Athena in his office, to stop her spreading her poison anywhere else. Although she did have a point about Grace's eyes. The whites were definitely more red than white. 'There's your desk. Turn your computer on.'

'Yes, boss.' She sashayed to the desk he'd had put in the corner of the room by the entrance door, as far from his own desk as it was possible to get. The office rivalled the boardroom for size and he'd have to raise his voice to be hcard when he spoke to her, but already her presence made it feel perceptibly smaller.

'Phone away,' he said when he watched her swipe it on.

'Yes, boss.' She put it on the desk.

'Face down and to the right of the desk where I can see it.'

'Yes, boss.' Obeying, she then clasped her hands together and looked at him with such fake avid expectation that he couldn't stop himself from envisaging clasping that beguiling face and kissing those poisonous lips so thoroughly that when she next looked at him she wouldn't have the sense left to fake or mask anything.

Breathing away the frisson racing through his veins, he folded his arms across his chest and perched on the edge of her desk. He would not allow his unwanted attraction for her distract him or allow himself to recall the way her green eyes had darkened in her bedroom in that split second when the chemistry he preferred to pretend didn't exist between them had flickered to undeniable life. Before she'd turned her tongue on his mother.

'Here's how things are going to work,' he said roughly. 'You are going to be my shadow. You will do everything I tell you to do without complaint. When you accompany me to meetings, you will sit in silence—your input will not be required. You will treat other members of staff with courtesy—in fact, let's make it a blanket rule that you will treat each and every person you encounter in the course of your work with courtesy and respect. On the occasions you're left in this office alone, you will stay at your desk and continue with whatever task I've set you. You will not use your phone for any purpose or use the landlines to make personal calls. Is this all clear or do I need to repeat myself?'

'Crystal clear, boss.'

'Any questions?'

'How soon can I go on a break?'

Close to biting her head off, he caught the flash of mischief in the green eyes and came within a whisker of smiling. Maybe he would have done if she hadn't then stretched and gathered her blonde hair and piled it on top of her head, only to immediately let it go, releasing a cloud of her shampoo as the silky tresses tumbled over her slender shoulders.

He knew then that she wasn't just his burden to bear but his curse.

When Athena's doorbell rang five weeks later, she dragged herself out of bed without even bothering to swear, padded to the front door, unlocked it, opened it, yawned, 'Morning, boss,' then shuffled back to her bedroom.

Before getting in the shower, she checked her phone for messages. Nothing. Lips tightening, she threw it on the bed, then reminded herself it was still the middle of the night and all her family would still be asleep.

Draco didn't feel the need to make sure her brothers got out of bed, she thought resentfully. Or tie them to his side. The bastard had been as good as his word in that regard. The office that had once belonged to her father and then her brother Alexis and now belonged to Draco also belonged to her. Sure, the office was huge and she was at the far side of it from him, but he'd arranged it so she had to face him and had taken to strolling over with varying degrees of frequency to check she was actually working on the tedious tasks he set her and not scrolling through social media. She even had to ask permission for bathroom breaks!

She'd never been so bored in her life. The tasks he set her were so mind-numbingly tedious that a trained monkey could do them. Her hopes had been raised slightly when he'd informed her he had a job for her to do from one of his other business ventures, but then dashed when he'd given her a printout of email addresses thicker than her arm and told her to go through them one by one and strike out those who'd unsubscribed. She was one hundred per cent certain it was a task without any meaning and that once she was done—probably when she reached the age of ninety-eight—the printout would be shredded with no further action.

So yes, she was bored out of her skull and yet… The work itself was mind-numbing but there was a fizz in her veins that sustained her through the long working hours. Draco was so focused and serious that distracting him had become a thing of joy. She knew perfectly well he woke every morning cursing her name and probably cursed her under his breath an average of five times an hour, but the times he wasn't quick enough to stop his eyes crinkling or his lips twitching at something she said never failed to accelerate the fizz.

As incredible as it was to believe, she would step into her apartment after another long working day and her spirits would plummet. She supposed the novelty of living alone after a lifetime living in a household filled with people and noise had sustained her the first month in her dingy flat, but since Draco the Dragon had decided to tether her to his side she was finding the solitude of her new life harder to endure. The childish art she'd long ago created as a way to switch her mind off enough to sleep was now being used to stave off this new loneliness. She was reaching for her drawing book and charcoal tin earlier and earlier.

She told herself it was this secret loneliness that meant

she increasingly liked that Draco had turned himself into her personal human alarm clock. He had no idea his was the first and last face she saw each working day. He had no idea that the weekends she'd spent since being tethered to him had been spent entirely alone.

She liked, too, that she got to share her first coffee of the working day with him. Liked that he always made it while she showered and dressed. Liked that he would always raise an unimpressed eyebrow at whatever boundary-pushing outfit she was wearing.

Obviously, she would never share any of these likes with him because what she didn't like was the way her fizzing blood heated those times their gazes would inadvertently meet across the vast office space, times when it didn't feel that he was looking at her to ensure she wasn't procrastinating. She would tease and flirt with him—often outrageously—and he would give her 'the look', but that was all fun and meaningless. The inadvertent gazes didn't feel meaningless. Sometimes she would do some actual work just to distract herself and drive away the feelings they induced.

'Just so you're prepared, we're flying to California on Sunday evening,' he told her when she joined him in the kitchenette. 'Pack enough clothes for a week.'

She picked up the coffee he'd made her. 'Why?'

'Because that's where the North American headquarters of Manolis Technology is located.'

'I know that, but why am I going?'

'Because I don't trust I'll have any Greek staff left if I leave you behind. If you don't think you'll be back from Sephone in time, I'll arrange for a helicopter to collect you...on second thoughts, I'll send the helicopter anyway.'

Athena's fingers tightened around her cup. That evening, her entire family were flying to Sephone so her brother Alexis and his wife Lydia could have their baby baptised in the private island's chapel. This was the same chapel where Thanasis had married Athena's nemesis, her stepsister Lucie. 'No need, I'm not going.' Just as she hadn't gone to Thanasis and Lucie's wedding.

Surprise furrowed his forehead. 'You're not going to your own nephew's christening?'

She smiled breezily to prove she didn't care. 'My malevolent presence has been deemed unwanted.' Or, translated, Thanasis and Lucie had refused to let Athena set foot on the island. As Thanasis, who was Lydia's brother, owned the island, his word was law there, and none of the Tsalikis had cared enough to argue for Athena's inclusion.

She didn't care. Sephone was the most boring island in the whole of Greece, and if Alexis wanted to put his stepsister over his blood sister then she didn't care about that either. Her family had been putting Lucie's feelings over Athena's since Athena was five.

'I think they're worried I'm going to curse the child like Carabosse in *Sleeping Beauty*.' Her nephew was three months old. She'd been allowed precisely one visit. In that visit, she'd been allowed to hold the baby for less than a minute, both her brother and sister-in-law staying close and watching her like hawks as if worried she was going to deliberately drop their precious bundle.

'You mean they haven't invited you?'

'More accurate to say I've been ordered to stay away.'

He stared at her with disbelief. 'Don't you *care*?' Contempt laced his voice.

She pulled a face. 'What's there to care about? Babies are incredibly boring so it's not as if I'm going to be missing out on anything, and I wouldn't be able to go even if I had been allowed—I'm going clubbing tonight and intend to spend tomorrow in bed catching up on all the sleep I've missed since my dragon boss decided it was acceptable to wake me in the middle of the night every day just to get me to work on time.'

Contempt was no longer confined to his tone, etching itself in the lines of his face. It was a contempt she hadn't seen since that first early human alarm clock morning when she'd so angered him, an incident that had never been mentioned by either of them since. Seeing it cut her deeper than she could have imagined. 'That's you all over, isn't it—putting your own pleasure above your family and everyone else.'

She dredged her best Athena-everyone-loved-to-hate smile. 'Life is short, and a girl needs to get her kicks where she can.'

'The rate you're going, the only kicks you'll be able to get soon are from people you have to pay to take them from you.' Disdain positively dripping from him, he turned sharply and strode to the door.

Athena had to swallow hard to loosen her throat enough to drink her coffee. Clutching her bag tightly to stifle the tremors in her hand, she lifted her chin and straightened her spine, and then followed Draco out to the waiting car.

After a drive conducted entirely in silence, Athena trudged up the twelve flights of stairs in her purple stilettoes without a single one of her usual complaints, and it wasn't because Draco was impervious to her complaints. Everything inside her felt all tight, as if all the cells in her body had wound themselves into a coil.

The coil loosened a little when her phone buzzed in her hand. Heart skipping, she took her seat at her desk and swiped it, only to see that it wasn't a message from any of her family or friends but a bank deposit notification. She'd been paid. Well, that was one good thing. She'd actually have money to spend that evening. Despite telling Draco she was going out clubbing, she'd worried she'd be forced to stay in due to lack of funds. Her credit card was maxed out and when she'd called Alexis the night before, asking him to increase the limit, he'd laughed and told her to get a second job. As if she had the time for a second job!

Her phone pinged another message. Hope rose then was dashed, finding it was from her favourite beauty store, emailing a discount code.

'Are you planning to turn your computer on any time soon?'

She looked across the room to meet Draco's baleful stare, smiled, and made a big deal about putting her finger to the on switch.

'Well done. Now go and make us a coffee.'

'Yes, boss.'

'And leave your phone on your desk.'

She smiled through her scowl, then disappeared to the kitchen area and fixed the coffee in the exact way Draco liked it, which handily was the same way she liked it. When he'd first ordered her to make it, she'd deliberately made it too bitter, thinking it would stop him asking her to do it again, but all it had resulted in was him demanding she make it again and again and again until she got it right. When she carried the cups back into the office, she set his down carefully, having learned her lesson not to deliberately slop it everywhere when he'd forced her to clean his entire desk as punishment.

'Thank you, Athena,' he said, his voice deliberately edged with politeness.

'You're welcome, boss,' she said, mimicking his tone.

She had to wait until he left the office for a party planning meeting before she could snatch another look at her phone. Draco was throwing a huge party to celebrate his acquisition of Tsaliki Shipping but, despite the whole of Greece knowing Athena was the queen of parties, she was excluded from all planning. They were the only meetings he attended that he didn't drag her along to, which was incredibly unfair as all the meetings he did make her attend were as exciting as watching vegetables grow.

No new messages. The coil inside her tightening a little more, she impulsively called Stelios, the only one of her brothers she shared a mother as well as a father with. He was working in the company's logistics department and no one had demanded he be fired!

'I'm about to go into a meeting,' he said tersely when he answered.

'Poor you. Fancy meeting for lunch?'

There was a beat of silence that was a beat too long. 'I've already got plans.'

'Can I gatecrash?'

'The others won't want you there.'

'Then dump them and come out with me,' she half-joked.

'I'm not going to do that.' There was another too long beat of silence. 'How about lunch one day next week?'

'The dragon's making me go to California with him, but we can definitely do that when I get back. Are you flying straight to Sephone after work?'

'You know I am.' Yet another too long beat of silence. 'Are you okay?'

'Of course! Glad it's Friday—this has been a long week!'

'Good… I need to go.'

'So do I! Don't get too bored this weekend, and don't miss me too much.'

She ended the call to find Draco standing in the doorway, glaring at her. Her heart made the familiar jump. She was glad she hadn't let the smile she'd maintained throughout that whole wounding call drop.

He strode to his desk to collect a file he'd forgotten to take into the meeting with him. 'Next time I catch you making personal calls in work time, I'm going to put you on toilet cleaning duty.'

Somehow, she managed to widen her smile. 'Yes, boss.'

CHAPTER FOUR

DRACO GOT OUT of his car feeling like he'd lived a life-time in five weeks. It was all Athena Tsaliki's fault. She was the most selfish, lazy and subversive person, man or woman, he'd met in his life. Installing her in his office might protect the rest of the workforce from her viperous tongue and malign influence, but it meant he got no respite from her. Minute after minute, hour after hour, day after day spent in her beautiful, sexy, infuriating presence. He was aware every time she coiled a lock of hair around her finger, of every bite of food she ate, of every tap of her keyboard when she ran out of ways to procrastinate and actually did some work.

Hard though it was to believe it possible, she'd been even more subversive than usual that day, constantly checking her phone whenever she thought she could get away with it. He'd even caught her reangling the screen of her desktop so she could try and hide what she was doing. It was getting to the point where every sweetly delivered *yes, boss* made him want to throw her out of the window.

But, as infuriating and fury-inducing as she was, there was something about her attitude that day that troubled him. Her breeziness had been just a little bit too forced, her quips lacking a touch of their usual sweet bite, everything just a touch more brittle. If it was anyone else, he'd think they were upset about something, but this was Athena. Rhinos were envious of the thickness of her hide.

He let himself into his mother's home, determined not to think of Athena Tsaliki for the rest of the evening. She'd infected enough of his world as it was without letting her infect his time with the most important person in it, the person whose past she'd deliberately, cruelly twisted and weaponised.

Of all the things Draco's wealth had allowed him to splurge on since he became rich, nothing had given him greater pleasure or pride than when he'd bought this villa in one of Athens' most exclusive districts for his mother. Finally, he'd been able to repay the woman who'd given him life, loved him fiercely, taught him to always be the bigger person and worked her fingers to the bone to provide for him. Being able to move her out of the cramped narrow home—an image of the apartment Athena inhabited like a graceful swan in a pigsty came to his mind, an image he immediately blinked away—she'd been forced to move into with her sister when they'd lost their home after her sacking had meant more to him than everything else combined.

Despite having enough money to employ a fleet of staff to take care of her every need, Cora Manolis preferred taking care of her own needs and was a better cook than half the Michelin-starred chefs Draco knew. That evening, he walked into her kitchen to the welcome aroma of his favourite slow-cooked lamb tagine and tried not to imagine what take-out Athena was dining on that night.

Embraces and kisses exchanged, Draco poured the wine and then they sat down to eat. As usual, the conversation mostly revolved around family—Draco was an only child but had plenty of cousins—and gossip about friends, interspersed with a little about work. He'd just poured them both a second glass of wine when her voice softened and she said, 'Tell me, how is Athena getting on?'

His surprise at the question turned into an automatic grimace. Since telling his mother about the deal he'd made to employ all the Tsaliki offspring, they hadn't touched on the subject of them. His mother had always wanted to put her years as the Tsaliki housekeeper behind her, especially the way it had ended. It was Draco who'd been unable to forgive or forget.

'She's a pain in the arse,' he answered flatly, before taking a drink.

She gave a sad smile. 'Bless her heart.'

He choked on his wine.

'She was always such a little angel,' she said wistfully.

He thumped at his chest. 'Whatever she was as a child, she's now in league with Lucifer.'

His mother gave him one of her rare disapproving looks and then sighed. 'I'll never forget how that little girl screamed when Penelope left. She was such a mummy's girl, and it was cruel—*cruel*—the way she was forced to stay with her father when he moved Rebecca in.' She shook her head, lost in memories. 'Georgios always kept the children when he changed wives, but I never thought he'd insist Athena stay too. That little girl needed her mother, and Rebecca was never going to be a mother to her. They handled it so badly. Georgios had to physically restrain Athena from running after Penelope. I have never heard screams like it. They broke my heart.'

Draco's heart was thumping. His adolescence had been littered with stories about Georgios's ever-evolving love life and procession of new wives, but this was a story he had no memory of. 'How old was she?'

'Five.'

Something twisted in his chest.

So he'd been sixteen, a time when he'd first discovered girls and his life had revolved around trying to lose his virginity.

His mother met his stare and sighed again. 'I've thought about her many times over the years. After Penelope went, Athena became my shadow. Her brothers were all older than her, but they were boys and their relationships with their mothers were very different to Athena's. They didn't understand.'

'And Georgios?'

Her deeply lined face twisted into something ugly. 'Rebecca had a daughter who was even younger than Athena. She became his new toy to dote on, and he spent so much energy trying to make Lucie feel at home that poor Athena was pushed into the shadows. I think that's why she latched on to me. Wherever I went in that house, whatever I was doing, she would follow me and hold my hand and wrap her arms around my waist whenever she could. She needed comfort, and I was the one she trusted to give it to her.' She gave another shake of her head, blinking back tears. 'I've always suspected that Rebecca hated how much Athena loved me. They sent her to her room when they fired me and wouldn't let me say goodbye, but I remember looking up at her window when I was getting in my car and seeing her there. She was banging on it, trying to get my attention. She was crying. I cried too.' She wiped away tears. 'I would have left when Rebecca moved in, but I loved Athena too much to leave her when she was so vulnerable, and it breaks my heart to remember that sweet little angel—and she was sweet, Draco. Whatever she's become as an adult, she was the sweetest little girl in the world.'

She pulled her napkin off her lap and blew her nose. And then she smiled. 'Forgive me for being maudlin. I always think about her more when it's her birthday, and now that she's working for you it all feels much closer than it has in a long time.'

There was a deeper, even more painful twist in his chest. 'It's her birthday?'

'You didn't know?'

He shook his head, remembering her brittle, almost hurt demeanour and the way she'd continually leapt on her phone. Remembered, too, the flash of dejection he'd seen in her eyes when he'd caught her using her phone for a personal call. 'She didn't mention it.' No one had. Seven of her brothers worked for Draco, five of them in the same building as Athena.

She'd eaten her lunch alone at her desk.

His mother gave another wipe of her nose and spluttered a laugh. 'Then she really *has* changed. I've never known anyone so excited for their birthday.' The brief laughter died away. 'Will you do something for me?'

'If I can.'

'If ever it feels right and appropriate...please tell her I've never forgotten her and that I'll always love her.'

Draco's driver opened the door for him. He put a foot out of the car and then stopped. His front door opened, his butler welcoming him home.

He put his foot back in the car. 'Take me to The Playroom.'

The Playroom was one of the most popular nightclubs in Athens. Draco had learned recently that its biggest rival was owned by Alexis Tsaliki. Gut instinct told him Athena would avoid her brother's club, even though he was with the rest of their family in Sephone, preparing for his child's christening.

The Tsalikis had gone away en masse on Athena's birthday for a weekend of family celebrations she was excluded from.

Assuming she would be in the VIP section, he checked that out first, but there was no sign of her. Beer in hand, he stood at the curved balustrade that overlooked the main dancefloor below. It was packed, dancing bodies everywhere.

'Draco!' A hand slammed into his back. It was Tobias, one of his closest friends and partner in a number of business ventures. 'What are you doing here? I didn't think clubbing was your thing?'

Draco had been clubbing a few times over the years but he found it such a waste of his time that he'd stopped bothering. 'A spur-of-the-moment thing.'

'Come and join us—I'm with the usual crowd.'

Still scanning the dancefloor below, he said, 'Another time.'

'Who are you looking for?'

He mentally braced himself before saying, 'Athena Tsaliki.'

Tobias laughed. 'I didn't know you were that desperate.'

For some inexplicable reason, Draco's immediate instinct was to punch his friend in the face. Possibly he would have done if Tobias hadn't then followed with, 'There she is. At two-o'clock.'

Draco looked to two-o'clock and a moment later spotted her and, now that he'd seen her, couldn't understand how he'd missed her, considering she was the only person there wearing a short sleeveless canary-yellow jumpsuit and thigh-high pink stiletto boots. Her dance moves had what could only be described as a frantic quality, her long blonde hair flying in all directions, arms waving, slender body slinking, twisting and shaking, oblivious to the other dancers surrounding her.

He'd seen her dance before, but it hadn't been like this, and he had to swallow a ragged breath into his lungs. If his mother's tale wasn't so fresh in his mind, he would be thinking Athena's moves her usual attention-seeking abandon but with added zest. He wouldn't be seeing the desperate unhappiness behind it. But he could see it, and seeing it meant it was all he could see.

The track she was dancing to changed. She wiped her forehead with the back of her hand and wound through the other dancing bodies to head towards the bar…which was when Draco realised he wasn't the only man to have noticed her. Falling in step behind her, two men whose body language set Draco's antennae to immediate alert.

From Draco's vantage point, he saw them join her at the bar, flanking her, and start talking to her. A moment later, one of them shouted their order to the bartender. Three bottles were placed before them. The man who'd bought the drinks said something that made her turn and lean into him as if to hear more clearly. Whatever he said made her laugh, even as she shook her head and took an unsteady step back, and while all this was happening, the other man dropped something into one of the bottles, swirled it quickly, and then, when she turned back to him, handed it to her.

Draco's blood turned to ice, his body recognising what he'd just witnessed a split second before his brain did.

The three of them clinked their bottles together. Athena brought her bottle to her lips and drank deeply.

Fuck…

* * *

This was the best night ever! Athena's new friends were amazing. She was having the best time. Who cared that her family had all forgotten her birthday? Not her! Who cared that Lucie still hated her? Not her! Who cared that the only birthday messages she'd received were from on-line retailers she'd given her birthdate to? Not her! She'd received loads of discount codes from them, so that was something to celebrate and made up for not having a birth-day cake, plus she'd managed to wangle her way into The Playroom for free on the back of it being her birthday and got her first drink free too! Oh, and she'd just been bought a drink by her new friends!

She took another sip of her beer. Her brain was start-ing to feel fuzzy. She must have drunk more than she'd realised. Time to stop. After all, she didn't have her driver to get her home. She didn't *have* a driver any more! Or bodyguards! Alexis had taken them away from her as part of his drive to turn her into a responsible, self-sufficient adult, and being a responsible, self-sufficient adult meant she had to get herself home. She would take the Metro...

What time was it? Not wanting to miss the last train back, she looked at her watch, accidentally elbowing one of her lovely new friends. He put his arm around her waist to keep her steady.

She really must have drunk more than she'd thought because she couldn't read the hands on her watch.

Twisting round to shout, 'What's the time?' in her new friend's ear, she didn't like it when he tightened his hold around her. Didn't like it at all. Didn't like the feel of his body pressed to hers or the smell of beer on his breath or the smell of his aftershave. In fact, she found it repulsive. The only man's smell she liked was Draco's. She liked that very much. She liked him, even though he was a bastard and made her do stuff like work. But he made her coffee. Every morning. She didn't even think he spat in it! And he made sure she ate lunch, going so far as to have Grace, his senior PA whose nose had been so pushed out of joint by Athena sharing his office, deliver fresh food to her desk. He made sure, too, that she was safe in her apartment after work each day before telling his driver to leave. She would close her front door and he'd still be there, and then when she looked out of the window he'd be gone.

Her new friend still had hold of her. 'Let me go,' she said...slurred. He couldn't have heard her. She tried to repeat herself, but the connection between her brain and mouth had become alarmingly disjointed.

Her other new friend took her hand. She tried to pull it out of his hold but his grip was too tight, and she became aware that her feet were moving, that she was being dragged away...

Panic and confusion gripping her, she looked around wildly...tried to look around... The world was starting to blur and spin around her.

She needed help, but the disjoint between her brain and mouth prevented her from calling out. The panic accelerated and she blinked hard to clear her vision, to keep hold of herself.

The panic faded when his face swam before her. Rugged. Gorgeous. Furious.

Safe.

She reached out her arms to him.

For the second time that evening, Draco's driver delivered him to his front door. For the second time that evening, Draco's butler opened the door to welcome him. This time, two female members of staff stood with him, ready to take care of the woman asleep in Draco's arms.

He rubbed her shoulder and pitched his voice to wake her without frightening her. 'Athena, we're here. You need to wake up.'

'I don't feel very well,' she whispered into his chest, her mouth the only part of her body that moved. At least she was talking now. She'd been mute for hours. He'd never have believed a mute Athena wouldn't be a cause for celebration.

'I know you don't, but we need to get you inside so we can get you to bed. You'll feel better after a good sleep. Come on, work with me. I'll help you in.'

Her, 'Okay,' was a barely audible mumble.

Keeping his hold around her, Draco swung his legs out then gently coaxed Athena into following suit. When he finally had her standing on her bare feet, she slumped like a deadweight into him, would have fallen to the ground if he didn't have such a firm hold of her.

'Listen to me,' he said quietly. 'I'm going to carry you inside, okay?'

Her cheek moved against his chest in assent.

Using the car to prop himself steady, he slid a hand beneath her bottom and scooped her into his arms. She nestled into him, cheek to chest, like a trusting child.

He carried her carefully into his home and up the stairs, carefully because he was afraid too much clunky motion would agitate the sickness that had already led to her vomiting twice, and laid her gently on the turned-down bed of the guest room his staff had uncomplainingly got themselves out of their own beds to prepare for her.

The duvet covering her, she curled onto her side and reached a hand to him.

He took it between both of his and rubbed it sooth-ingly. 'Zoey and Rhea are going to take care of you now.'

She gave the tiniest shake of her head, the pads of her fingers making a weak compression of protest in his palm.

'I gave my word you wouldn't be left alone tonight.' A promise he'd made to the medical team he'd called out to the club when he'd needed to satisfy himself that The Play-room's medical staff and the police were right, that any danger had passed and that sleep was the best thing for her.

'You stay,' she mumbled.

'They'll take good care of you, I promise.'

Her eyes opened and searched for his. They filled with tears. 'Don't leave me.'

His heart thumped, whether at the sheen of tears or her plea he didn't know, knew only that this was a request he could not deny. Gently squeezing her hand, he nodded.

There was the tiniest twitch of thanks at the corners of her mouth before her eyes closed again and her hand went limp.

Draco turned the bedside light out. He'd left the light in the en suite bathroom on so Athena would know where to go if she woke. The angle its golden light cast gave her blonde hair a halo effect.

Removing only his blazer, shoes and socks, he settled himself on top of the duvet at the edge of the bed and hooked his arms above his head.

Gaze fixed on the ceiling, he took deep breaths, not wishing to relive the experiences of the last few hours but unable to stop them replaying.

He'd never experienced a shot of adrenaline like the moment comprehension had hit him that Athena's drink had been spiked. He'd raced down the curved stairs in seconds. As hard as he stretched his memory bank, he had no recollection of what he'd done with his beer, but his hands had been empty by the time he'd fought his way through the packed dancefloor to her. Which had been just as well as the punch he'd landed on the predator who'd dropped the pill into Athena's drink might not have landed so well.

He would never forget her expression when she'd recognised him. The wild fear that had been etched on her face...it had vanished in a blink. She'd fallen into his arms and then refused to let go, clinging on even when he'd got her to the medical room and the police had arrived.

He pinched the bridge of his nose. He must not let his imagination take him to what would have happened to her if he hadn't acted so quickly. If he hadn't been there. If he hadn't learned it was her birthday.

'Draco?' His whispered name cut through the night's silence.

He swallowed. 'I'm right here.'

Slowly, she turned over and shuffled over to him. When she reached him, she nuzzled her nose into his side before lifting her head to lay her cheek on his chest and curl into him.

He closed his eyes and took another deep breath before wrapping his arm around her. Her slenderness felt very fragile.

It was a long time before he was able to fall asleep.

CHAPTER FIVE

THE DRILLING IN Athena's head was different to the drilling of Draco incessantly ringing her doorbell to wake her. Had she changed the tone, she wondered blearily before she blinked her eyes open and memories flooded back, at the same moment she realised her pillow was a human chest and that much of her warmth came from the arm hooked around her.

Draco.

Her heart ballooned into her tightening chest, and she closed eyes suddenly filled with hot tears. Chin wobbling, she concentrated with all her might on breathing, the only way she knew to stop tears from falling, unable to think of anything but that she was in bed with Draco and that he'd saved her.

Oh, God, what must he think of her? If he'd hated her before, he must despise her now, and in her weakened state she didn't have the mental strength to tell herself she didn't care what he thought of her.

She couldn't stay here like this. She needed to find a way to thank him for taking care of her that didn't sound pathetic and didn't make his disdain for her rise even higher, and then go home and clean herself.

She wished she could clean her soul too.

If she could extract herself without waking him, she

would write a note of thanks and leave without a scene. Or she could message her thanks to him. He'd programmed his number into her phone and made her send him a message so he had the right number for her, for the sole purpose that if she did a disappearing act in the office he could contact her and demand she get her backside back to her desk.

Extracting herself proved harder said than done. Somehow, she'd managed to cocoon herself in the section of duvet that wasn't trapped beneath him, and she had to wriggle away from him and use her hands to dig herself out of its confines.

Her head had never pounded with such strength. Clutching it, she eased herself upright. On the bedside table facing her sat a large glass of water and two painkillers. She looked at them, blinking back more tears at this unexpected kindness.

It was as she was shakily putting the empty glass back down that he spoke. 'How are you feeling?'

She closed her eyes and summoned the breeziest smile she could muster and hoped it sounded in her voice. 'Like I need to go home.'

'I'll take you back later. When you're feeling stronger.'

'I feel fine,' she lied, 'and I wouldn't dream of putting you out any more than I already have. What you did for me last night...' She swallowed a breath, swallowing tears with it. 'Thank you.'

She felt the mattress move as he sat up. She couldn't bring herself to face him. Didn't think she'd ever be able to look him in the eye again.

He hauled himself over to sit beside her, his feet resting on the porcelain floor a safe, respectable distance from hers. 'You remember?'

Gaze locked on the now empty glass, she nodded. 'Some of it's hazy, but I think I remember most of it.' Her voice dropped. 'I know how lucky I am that you were there. I'm sorry for ruining your night.'

His gruff voice was heavy. 'You didn't.'

'I did. You probably wanted to carry on partying after it all happened, but I clung to you like a limpet. I guess it's because you appeared when I needed you.' And the moment he'd put his arms around her she'd felt protected and safe, feelings she hadn't felt since she was a child, feelings she'd been too weak to resist or fight. She extended her neck and lifted her chin. 'Anyway, now's your chance to get it over with.'

'Get what over with?'

'The bollocking for being stupid enough to have my drink spiked.'

She heard him exhale a long breath. 'The only blame for the spiking goes to the men who did it. That wasn't stupidity on your part, that was all them. They had those drugs with them for a reason. If it hadn't been you, they would have fixed on someone else.'

'But they chose me for a reason. They knew who I was. They thought I was easy prey.'

After a long silence, he said, 'Would you blame a rape victim for being raped?'

She whipped her stare to him. His gaze was fixed on the wall. 'Of course not.'

'Then why are you victim-blaming yourself?'

She turned her gaze back to the glass and whispered, 'Because everything is always my fault.'

His voice became even heavier. 'I don't know about everything, but I know about this, and this was not your fault, not even a little bit.'

Oh, God, she was having to swallow back even more tears.

'I didn't know how dangerous it was out there,' she quietly admitted once she had control of her tears. 'I should have known. I should have been better able to protect myself, but I've always been protected from predators and, in many ways, protected from myself. Whenever I've gone clubbing before, I've always known that, whatever happens, I will get home safely because my father paid people to keep me safe.' She finally mustered a laugh. 'Do you think this was what Alexis meant when he said he wanted me to spend time in the real world so I could appreciate the privilege of my life?'

'Absolutely not.' On this, as with everything else, Draco was firm. He didn't believe for a second that Alexis had wanted his sister to be endangered. Unwittingly, though, that was what his drastic action of cutting all his siblings off, installing them in poky flats and leaving them to fend for themselves had brought about. If Draco lost everything overnight, he'd survive, because he'd grown up poor and so he knew how to survive. Athena had never had to survive. She'd never had to manage her own finances or clean up after herself, and she'd never had to worry about her personal safety. Always there had been people to do those things for her.

However noble Alexis's intentions, setting Athena loose without any backup had been cruel. You wouldn't set a mollycoddled, pampered pet out in the wild and expect them to survive.

What a damned family, he thought darkly. The whole bloody lot of them.

'How steady are you on your legs?' he asked, needing a change of subject.

'I don't know. I haven't tried to stand up yet. Why?'

'Because I was going to suggest a shower. You'll feel more human for it. I've clothes you can change into.'

'I...' Her voice caught. 'I can shower at home.'

'Stay here a while longer. Shower and get some food in you. Then we can look at taking you home. Okay?' he added when she didn't respond.

'Okay,' she whispered.

Shyness was not something Athena had suffered from before, but she entered Draco's dining room feeling tongue-tied and hot of cheek.

The time spent showering had been time spent thinking and remembering, and what she'd remembered made her want to hide under a rock. Although she'd remembered everything when she'd woken, it had all been a little hazy and abstract. Standing beneath the shower had cleansed her mind as well as her body, rinsing away the haziness and allowing her to remember in clearer detail how she'd clung to him as if he represented a form of sanctuary. How she'd begged him not to leave her.

The last person she'd begged anything from had been her mother when she'd closed her ears to Athena's screams and left without her. Her mother purported to love her, but still she'd left.

Draco didn't even like her, but he'd stayed. He'd stayed with her the whole night when he must have wanted to be anywhere else. He was under no obligation to her, but still he'd stayed.

Decency without an agenda was in short supply in the Tsaliki world, and she didn't know how to respond to it or how she could ever repay it. Probably the best way to repay it would be to get out of his hair and leave him to enjoy the rest of his weekend without her malign presence poisoning it.

Strangely, she felt more naked being fully clothed in front of him in his tan workout joggers she'd had to roll the waist and heels to vaguely fit and black sweatshirt than she did when half her body was on display. It didn't help that her face was bare of the make-up she always wore as a form of armour.

He rose in greeting. He'd showered too. She could smell the clean freshness beneath his cologne: those scents that all enhanced the natural smell of Draco she'd spent so many car journeys trying to block out of her senses. The glance she allowed herself told her he'd trimmed his beard and shaved his neck. The light navy sweater, sleeves rolled to his elbows, and black jeans he wore was the first outfit she'd seen him in that wasn't a suit.

The maids who'd hovered outside the bathroom while she'd showered and escorted her down the stairs helped her into the chair facing Draco's before melting away.

The table was laden with pastries, bread rolls, toast, fresh fruit, dried fruit, yoghurt and varying condiments.

'Please, help yourself,' he said. 'Coffee?'

She shook her head. Her stomach still felt a little too fragile to manage anything but the blandest food. 'Just water, please.'

The butler poured her a glass from a jug and then he, too, melted away, leaving the two of them alone.

'Feel better for the shower?'

'More human,' she agreed, not looking up from her empty plate. She was still having trouble looking at him.

'If your stomach's feeling tender, toast should help.'

As she reached for a slice, she noticed a black cherry blossom tree with what appeared to be some form of Asian symbol beneath it tattooed on the inside of his forearm, something she'd never seen before. It was after she'd finished her toast that curiosity got the better of her and she asked, 'What does your tattoo represent?'

'The symbol is my mother's name in Japanese,' he answered steadily. 'When I was growing up, her dream was to go to Japan in spring to see the cherry blossoms. I had the tattoo done when I was eighteen as a tribute to her and for what it represents—the hope that comes with the new beginnings of spring.'

Athena, her throat suddenly tight, had a sip of her water. Hardly able to raise her voice above a whisper, she said, 'Did she ever see the blossoms?'

'She has visited Japan every spring for fifteen years.'

She closed her eyes. Athena had watched Cora drive away, knowing she would never be allowed to see her again, and then spent the next twenty-one years doing her best to forget. Twenty-two years now, she supposed.

'I'm glad.' She pulled in a long breath and forced herself to meet his piercing stare. 'What I said about her that time... I'm sorry. It was cruel of me.'

The piercing eyes held hers. 'It was,' he agreed in a far more reasonable tone than she deserved.

'She was always...' she swallowed '...very good to me.' Suddenly, she couldn't stand the tension or the memories or the feelings churning inside her a moment longer, and pulled herself to her feet. 'I'm sorry, Draco, but I can't eat any more. I can never thank you enough for what you did for me last night, but I need to go home. If you can tell me where my bag and boots are, I'll get out of your hair.'

'You're not in my hair and you don't need to leave.'

'That's very nice of you to lie to me, but I do need to leave. I've encroached on your time quite enough.'

'Athena, you haven't...'

'I have.' If he could be firm then so could she. She *needed* to be firm, not for him but for herself, otherwise she'd allow herself to take words intended to soothe and read more into them than was there. No one in their right mind ever wanted her to stay, but this was the first time in over two decades her heart had tugged with a wistful hope that could never be realised.

Draco Manolis was a good man, possibly the best man she'd ever met, and he would no more throw an injured sparrow out of his home than he would a broken Athena.

And she was broken. She knew that with a clarity she'd never allowed herself to acknowledge before, and she suspected those piercing blue eyes could see it, too, which made her feel a thousand times more vulnerable for reasons she would never be able to understand.

'I thank you again, but I'm going home. I promise you, I feel much better. I don't need any more nursing.'

The piercing blue eyes held hers a fraction too long before he bowed his head in agreement. 'I'll take you back.'

'No. This is your weekend.' She dredged up a smile and managed to inject a modicum of breeziness into her tone. 'You have to put up with me all week without having me gatecrash your weekend, too, but I'll gladly take a lift off your driver—I bet he really misses my scintillating company at the weekends.'

His gaze held hers for another long moment before his handsome rugged face broke into a half-smile. 'Okay, you win. I'll get Deacon to drive you home. But I want you to promise me you'll take it easy and that you'll call me if you start feeling worse.'

She saluted. 'I promise on my honour.'

He feigned amazement. 'You have honour?'

'When it suits me,' she confirmed, her airiness driven by and laced with relief that the weighty tension had lifted. 'But don't tell anyone. I have a terrible reputation to protect.'

Lying on her belly drawing, Athena was lost in her own little world when the incessant ring of her doorbell penetrated her consciousness and sent her heart into a triple salchow.

There was only one person who rang her doorbell like that—okay, only one person who'd ever rung her doorbell—and she'd slammed her book shut and bounded to her feet and was halfway to the front door before sanity could ask what she was playing at and tell her to slow down.

He was probably here out of some warped sense of duty. He'd saved her from those awful predators and now felt the same sense of responsibility to her that he'd feel at the sparrow who flew into his window.

Her heart thumping so hard it was painful, she fixed her brightest smile to her face and yanked the door open with a flourish. 'Hello, boss. Are you lost?'

'I think I must be,' he riposted drily. 'Can I come in?'

'Yes, but only for a minute. I'm *extremely* busy.'

'I'm sure you are.' Firm lips twitching, his gaze flickered over the pyjamas she'd already dressed herself in after a bath that hadn't helped her melancholy, especially when the hot water ran out whilst filling up so the long, lovely warm bath she'd been looking forward to had turned into a short, crap, tepid one. She had no idea how to fix the hot water situation. Her call to the building's maintenance man had gone to voicemail with the message that he'd be back on duty on Monday. Which was no good as she'd be in California with this man.

'You're looking better,' he observed.

Standing aside to let him in, she smiled, lifted her chin and swished her hair. Might as well get the practice of normal Athena behaviour in. It was the only way to build herself back up. She might not have had the bath she longed for, but physically she felt much, much better.

'Where are you off to dressed up like that?' she asked, sashaying to the kitchenette to fix him the coffee he was bound to want: she was quite certain that if you cut Draco Manolis he would bleed coffee. He'd changed out of the casual clothing he'd been wearing when she'd left his home into a sharp charcoal suit paired with a white silk shirt he'd left unbuttoned at the throat.

'Dinner. And you're coming with me.'

She whipped her head round to stare to him. 'What are you talking about?'

'I'm taking you out to dinner.'

'You are not.'

'I am. You had a horrific experience last night, and this is my way of putting something good back in your life—a good memory to counter it.'

How she maintained her smile was a mystery to be solved in another life. 'That's very sweet of you, but I'm not a charity case. Go and take your girlfriend out.'

'I don't have a girlfriend, but if I did she could take herself out. I'm taking you out for dinner and I'm not taking no for an answer, so take yourself off to your bedroom and get changed into something more Athena—not even my grandmother would wear those pyjamas.'

'They are *extremely* comfortable.'

'They are extremely ugly. Now, do as you're told.'

Suddenly she found she didn't have to do any work to

maintain her smile. Grinning, she saluted, 'Yes, boss,' and practically danced to her bedroom.

Draco watched her dance away, shaking his head with a smile.

He'd known the moment she opened her door that she was feeling better. He could see it in her posture and the strength with which she held herself. If he'd had any doubt she was up to going out he'd have ordered a delivery for them.

What he did have doubts about was her emotional recovery, and it was this aspect that had seen him pacing his home for what had felt like hours, resisting the growing urge to call her oldest brother and tell him to get his backside back to Athens and take care of his sister. But, as strong as the urge had been, what good would it have done? If Alexis or any of the other Tsaliki offspring gave two shits about Athena they would have remembered her birthday. Yes, she was an acerbic madam, but they'd left her all alone on her birthday. They'd forgotten her. Even her mother, who, despite not having been a Tsaliki for over twenty years, had flown to Sephone with the rest of the Tsaliki family and forgotten her daughter. When it came to Tsaliki family gatherings, everyone, even ex-wives, was included.

Everyone but Athena.

Athena was all alone and far more vulnerable than she wanted anyone to believe.

Draco had needed to satisfy himself that she was as fine as her replies to his messages made out. Whenever he remembered how she'd walked out of his home barefoot, hugging her knee-high boots to her belly, his heart constricted. He didn't see her as a charity case as she'd suggested, but he'd developed a weird sense of protective responsibility to her, and responsibility, too, to his mother and her insistence that the acerbic, quick-witted, vivacious nightmare called Athena had once been a sweet, angelic, loving child.

She'd clung to him like a trusting child. She'd cuddled into him in her sleep like a child. But she was all woman. Beautiful, sexy woman. Beautiful, sexy, vulnerable woman.

The longest night of his life had been spent hardly able to breathe.

It was only as the long night had gone on that it had come to him that there had never been any physical contact between them before. Not even a brush of an arm or the brush of a finger when cups of coffee were exchanged. They'd both maintained that distance, he realised. The woman who flirted like she'd taken a master's degree in the subject and who was forever picking off bits of fluff from the clothes of colleagues brave enough to go near her had never allowed her flirtations with him to become the slightest bit physical.

Athena had been keeping her distance as he had, wary of the attraction that flickered between them. Which begged the question, though he knew he shouldn't let it, of why. He knew why he had to keep her at arm's length, but Athena's affairs, incredibly short though they all were, were legendary. She was never shy about showing off her latest lover. If she wanted someone, she pursued them until she got them.

There had been no paparazzi shots of her falling out of nightclubs either alone or with a lover since she'd started working for Tsaliki Shipping.

None of his business, he reminded himself firmly. Theirs was an attraction that would forever go unacknowledged, and whatever reason Athena had for refusing to acknowledge it would forever remain a mystery, because that was how it had to be.

She'd cleaned the kitchenette, he observed as he made them coffee. Spotting a pair of rubber cleaning gloves, his heavy mood lifted and he grinned, picturing Athena wrinkling her nose as she slid her pretty hands into them. This was better. Think of Athena as she was, not as the vulnerable woman she'd been asleep in his arms.

Still grinning, he took his coffee into the living area. The boxes were exactly where he'd stacked them that first day. He'd come to the point of thinking she never used the living area because it never changed from day to day, but that day there was an A4-sized book and a pencil tin on the floor.

Curious, he picked up the book and flicked through it. Then he blinked, closed it, and reopened it at the beginning.

Taking a seat on an ancient sofa that almost sagged to the floor under his weight, he went through the book carefully, page by page, filled with an emotion like nothing he'd felt before.

When he heard the door handle turn, he quickly placed it back where he'd found it with a thumping heart, suddenly certain that what he'd been looking through was intensely private to her, and then when she appeared before him his chest managed to tighten and swell all in one motion.

There was a faint stain of colour on her cheeks as she did a twirl for him. 'Better?'

'Much.' He swallowed a lump that had formed in his throat. 'Much more Athena.' Inimitably Athena. Only Athena could get away with wearing a hot pink jumpsuit with red, purple and white swirls covering it in paisley fashion. But unlike the canary yellow one she'd worn the night before, this jumpsuit was neck-high and long-sleeved, the short shorts displaying her fabulous legs but with more modesty, the hem an inch longer than she normally wore. She'd kept her honey-blonde hair loose but had brushed it until the silky tresses shone, her make-up lighter and fresher than she usually applied it, enhancing her beauty all the more.

She might not be an angel but she had the beauty and glow of one. And, God, she could draw like one.

CHAPTER SIX

USUALLY WHEN ATHENA shared the back of Draco's car with him she spent her time dreaming up ways of annoying him and ingenious ways of skiving off doing any work. The times Grace and any of his other minions joined them, she had a marvellous time annoying them too. She didn't even need to speak. Literally, all she had to do was open her mouth, and their lips would purse and their faces pinch in on themselves. Unlike Draco, who rarely showed disapproval or annoyance with anything stronger than a raised eyebrow, they made no bones about despising her.

She'd never shared the back of the car and found her brain turn to goo or felt such awareness of him. Not like this. Since that first morning he'd decided to become her human personal alarm clock, she'd made a studious effort to deny those strange sexual feelings, to not let them even flicker. Her efforts had mostly paid off, but then Athena was an expert at turning off unwanted feelings. She couldn't seem to turn them off now, though. It wasn't just Draco she was so hugely aware of but herself, the strength of her heart and racing pulses, the sensation, almost like electricity, dancing through her skin.

As the day had passed, more of the haziness had passed, memories clarifying. Draco punching the man who'd refused to let go of her hand. Draco breathing into her hair when her blood sample had been taken. Draco coaxing her into drinking water. Draco holding her hair when she'd been sick into a bucket. She thought that might have happened twice.

And now he was taking her out to dinner. And he'd confirmed he didn't have a girlfriend, a confirmation that shouldn't have made her heart leap. In the five weeks he'd kept her chained to her desk in his office, she'd often had to stop herself pondering too deeply about his love life. She'd never once asked about his plans for the evening or asked when they shared their early morning coffee in her kitchenette how his evening had gone or how he'd spent his weekends.

He never asked about her evenings or weekends either, a realisation that made her heart thump.

'You know, I should be the one taking you out to dinner,' she said, breaking the thick silence that had developed between them. 'To thank you.'

'You've already thanked me.'

'I know, but it feels so inadequate after everything you've done. I should pay. Where are we going?'

'Zeus.'

The swankiest, most expensive restaurant in the whole of Athens.

'In that case, I take it back…unless you want to give me a pay rise so I can afford it?'

'I'd consider giving you a pay rise if you ever did any work.'

She gave a mock gasp of outrage. 'I'll have you know I worked so hard last week that my forefinger feels bruised from inputting all that stupid data.' She lifted the finger and waved it in front of him. 'See?'

He gave the unimpressed face she so adored.

'I think I might have repetitive strain injury too. And possibly tennis elbow. I should see a doctor and see if I can be signed off work for the next three weeks.'

Draco couldn't help but laugh. Athena was the most incorrigible person he'd met in his life, but she amused him, and he admired how she refused to let the awful incident in the nightclub hold her down and was forcing herself to bounce back from it. He didn't think it had occurred to her that what she'd been through would have most people needing a sick note, just to recover emotionally.

Athena didn't allow herself emotions. He recognised that. But she had them. He recognised that too. She was just better at hiding them than other people. Especially, he suspected, from herself.

Their car came to a stop in the underground car park.

'Come on, you,' he said, grinning. 'Time for dinner.'

She matched the grin. 'You do know that people will talk, don't you? You being seen with me in polite society on a Saturday night…people will put two and two together and make five. Mr Serious and Miss Trouble…both our reputations risk being ruined.'

'I'll risk it,' he said drily as the driver opened Athena's door.

Draco had already considered this. He knew from his mother's experience at the hands of Georgios and Rebecca Tsaliki how easily a reputation could be destroyed, but the whole of Greece knew he currently employed the Tsaliki siblings, and he had no doubt the whole of Greece knew he'd taken Athena under his wing and had guessed why. So long as he maintained the professional distance they always kept between them, there would be no need for anyone to talk. Taking the underground entrance cut the risk of being spotted by the paparazzi to zero.

He'd avoided the paparazzi at the nightclub by leaving through a private exit. Hefty bribes had ensured nothing of the previous night's incident would make it into the press.

She brought her beautiful face close to his as she swung her long legs out of the car and practically sang, 'Don't say I didn't warn you.'

Athena had dined at Zeus a couple of times before. Located on the eighth floor of the exclusive Dionysus Hotel, the pretty terrace they'd been seated at had the requisite spectacular views of the Acropolis and the Aegean, clever heating staving off the winter chill of the evening. If a tourist wished to experience a traditional Greek meal and ambience, Zeus, despite its name, was not the place to come, the food contemporary, the atmosphere rarefied. The last time she'd dined there had been a date with yet another rich plaything who'd believed she was easy pickings and who'd returned home barely containing his anger when she'd kept her legs closed.

Draco, she was certain, wouldn't end the meal expecting her to put out, and it was partly because she wasn't already thinking ahead as to how she was going to brush off his advances that she found herself relaxing in a way she was so rarely able to when dining out with a man. This was despite the none too subtle glances being thrown their way.

Let them stare. She didn't care. Well, maybe a little, but not for herself. For Draco. She would hate for any of their fellow diners to think less of him for dining with her. Athens was a city where everyone knew everyone. Draco, a serious, focused, discreet man, had one of the best reputations in the city. She had one of the worst. Actually, make that *the* worst.

After they'd finished their appetisers and their main

course had been served, she inhaled the delicious aroma of the chilli pepper oil-infused citrus beurre blanc encircling her cod and steamed lobster, and happily dived in. It was the first evening meal of her adult life that she didn't have a glass of wine with—she didn't think she'd ever be able to face alcohol again—and it touched her immeasurably that Draco, without making anything of it, had eschewed alcohol too.

'Can I ask you a personal question?' she asked.

'Since when have you needed permission to ask anything?'

She grinned. 'Have you ever been married?'

'I *am* married.'

In the time it took her to blink in shock, her heart had turned to ice. Fingers tightening their grip on her cutlery, she had to swallow to say, 'You're *married?*'

He raised his glass of water. 'To my business.' He smiled wryly. 'That's what a number of girlfriends have told me.'

The ice melted, warmth rushing to her head, almost dizzying her. She laughed reflexively. 'And are they right?'

He lifted a meaty shoulder in a shrug. 'Probably. In the early years, definitely. I knew I had the brains to make a success of the software I'd developed, but I didn't have the money or connections.'

This would be the tech start-up he was talking about, Athena thought. An inbuilt safety device for computers that made them unhackable.

'Making it work took seven years of twenty-hour days and most of that was spent teaching myself English and trying to get my foot in the door of investors and then buyers,' he continued. 'That left no time for romance. Once I'd made it a success, I knew I could lose it all if

I took my eye off the ball. The next big thing can easily become tomorrow's forgotten thing. I wasn't going to let that happen to me.'

'But surely you're worth so much now that you don't need to work?'

'I could sell everything and live like a prince until the end of time,' he agreed. 'But I'd be bored out of my skull in days.'

'So why not marry? Even I know you don't work twenty-hour days any more.'

'While you're filing your nails in the evenings, I'm usually holding conference calls with my Californian team.'

'That's defamatory. I've never filed my own nails in my life.'

His face creased and he gave a low rumble of laughter.

Athena had never heard him laugh before. There had been many times she'd been certain he'd come close to it, but this was the first time she'd heard it and it sank into her skin like a sunbeam.

'Workaholic tendencies aside, I'm fussy. If I'm going to marry, I want a woman who's going to slot seamlessly into my life and understand the business comes first and that she can't make demands on my time. I want a wife who's going to be an asset to me and the business, not a noose around my neck.'

'Have you considered using technology to create an android of this paragon? Because I hate to tell you, she doesn't exist in human form.'

He shook his head with another rumble of laughter. 'Then I shall live out my existence married to my business. I've studied your father enough to see how marrying the wrong woman can be fatal. He built his own business like I did, but he was too intent on having a good time and maintaining that pointless vendetta with the Antoniadises to protect it. If your brother hadn't stepped in and taken control, you could all have lost everything.'

'I can't argue with that,' she agreed with an easiness she no longer felt on the inside. 'But marriage wasn't the cause of it. I hate Rebecca as much as anyone, but she's not to blame. Life has always been one big party to him. My father thinks with his cock—when he's not screwing it into any woman who catches his eye, he's waving it at his rivals...' Her voice trailed away, and she whispered, 'But you already know that.'

The lightness that had sparkled in Draco's eyes throughout their conversation had vanished. 'The day it happened, my mother's father died. Your father took advantage of her grief but he never screwed her. It never went that far, and yet it was she who lost her livelihood and her home and had her name blackened.'

She felt the last of the lightness drain out of her, her heart tightening the way it always did whenever she thought of Cora Manolis. 'I'm sorry. Rebecca spoke so vilely about her, and my father has had so many affairs and flings over the years...' She shook her head to clear a sickening image that had flashed in her mind, of the time she'd gone to the spa of their yacht when they'd been on a family holiday and caught her father with one of the crew. He'd barely broken his stride, telling her to come back in five minutes.

Her appetite gone, she put her cutlery down and finished what she'd been saying. 'I assumed the same thing happened to your mother as it did to all the others.'

Athena, Draco knew, was an expert at faking contrition. There was nothing fake about the remorse evident in her green eyes now.

'You were a child,' he said evenly, speaking through a rock that seemed to have lodged itself in his throat.

'I know, but that doesn't excuse how I spoke about her that time. I really am sorry for that.'

'You've already apologised.'

'I just felt it needed saying again.'

'Put it behind you. I have.'

Her stare, so much more intelligent than she wanted people to believe, intensified. 'Have you really?'

There was an unbearable impulse tingling in his fingers to cover her hand. He could still feel the imprint on his skin from where her hand had slipped into his while she'd slept. 'Yes.' He took a heavy breath. 'My mother would want me to put it behind me. She still thinks the world of you.'

Her eyes widened. 'Really?'

He nodded, would have passed on the message his mother had asked of him if the rock in his throat hadn't expanded.

'I...' Now it was as if the same rock had lodged in her throat. 'I still think the world of her too.'

He cleared his throat. 'I'll be sure to tell her that.'

'Thank you.' Her lips pulled together before forming a tremulous smile. 'She must be so proud of you.'

'Probably the proudest mother in Greece.'

'I knew it.' Her smile softened into something so beautiful his heart clenched. 'She used to tell me about you. Lamb was your favourite food.'

'You remember *that*?' Of everything she'd said to shock him, this rose straight to the top. Draco's early memories were like snapshots taken with an out-of-focus camera. He couldn't remember any conversations below the age of seven, maybe even eight, let alone the favourite food of someone he'd never met, and it came to him that not only did Athena have a prodigious memory but that she really had loved his mother.

'I don't know why, but that always stuck with me. And...' she hesitated a moment '...that your father died before you were born.'

Dumbstruck, it took a beat for him to respond. 'Yes. There was an accident at sea—he was a fisherman.' But he could see from the expression in her eyes that she already knew this. That she remembered his mother telling her.

'Is that why you have her surname?'

'Yes. She made that choice when I was born because she knew the two of us would be a unit until I became an adult.'

Her head made a slow inclination, the green eyes that saw much more than she wanted people to believe flickering with her thoughts. 'Why did you buy my father's company, Draco? It's so far apart from your other businesses that it might as well be from the moon, and from what I've read it's the only business in your portfolio you haven't built from the ground up. Did you buy it to destroy my father?'

He could lie or refuse to answer but there was something in the atmosphere of honesty cloaking them that forced his tongue to speak the truth. 'I wanted to. Destroying your father was my prime motivator in those early years. I used to dream of having enough money to force a buyout of Tsaliki Shipping. I was going to dismantle it so everything your father had built would be gone and his legacy no longer existed.'

'Do you still intend to do that?'

'Those were dreams fuelled by fury and bitterness. I'm not going to put tens of thousands of people's jobs at risk for revenge. I'm still going to erase his legacy, but in a way that will only injure him.' He smiled at the thought. 'And injure his wife.'

'How?'

He narrowed his eyes meditatively. 'Can I trust you?'

'No.'

Her reply was so immediate and sparky and decisive that amusement burst free. 'Then you will have to wait like everyone else.'

The creasing of Draco's eyes lifted Athena's spirits straight back up and loosened the tightness that had been coiling her insides again, the creasing a signal that she could move on from a conversation that was heavier—much heavier—than she ever allowed. As wonderful as she was starting to admit to finding Draco, this was unfamiliar territory and she was struggling enough pretending her whole body wasn't alive with awareness of him and that if she moved her foot two inches it wouldn't brush against his, without wishing a plague on her father and Rebecca for the way they'd treated Cora and without trying to decipher how it felt to be exchanging confidences with someone because she never, ever exchanged confidences.

It was disconcerting how badly she wanted to know even more about Draco, how there had to be a dozen questions about his life queueing on her tongue, and she bit them all back to produce a wide smile and airily said, 'I can wait until the launch party, no problem.'

The expression on his face was the giveaway and she laughed, a laughter that came from her belly and not her throat like her laughs normally did.

'What else could it be?' she giggled when she had better control of herself. 'I thought you were excluding me from the planning meetings out of spite but it's because

you don't want me to know what you're up to, isn't it—
don't tell me!' she hastened to add when he opened his
mouth. 'I'm terrible at keeping secrets. And don't confirm
or deny about the party, even though I know it has to be
that, seeing as anyone who's anyone is invited, including my father and Rebecca…' A thought occurred to her.
'When you say injure…'

He gave a rueful half-smile. 'Injure their pride. Nothing more.'

'You promise?'

Sincerity rang from his eyes. 'I promise.'

Satisfied, she grinned and picked up her cutlery.

'You don't care?' There was none of the contempt he
usually showed when he asked if she cared about something, only curiosity.

Appetite regained, she piled the dissolve-on-the-tongue
cod onto her fork. 'After the way they treated your mother,
they deserve whatever it is you're planning to throw at
them.'

His piercing stare held hers, the intensity of it sending
electricity through her skin. And then he smiled. 'You are
constantly full of surprises.'

She winked. 'I like to keep people on their toes.'

'You certainly keep me on mine,' he murmured.

The tingles of electricity increased.

They finished their meal with light, easy conversation
that steered well away from anything else that was re-
motely personal, Athena doing her best to entertain him
so she could hear that wonderful deep rumble of laughter again, whilst also doing her best to pretend her heart
wasn't racing and that there wasn't a heated charge flowing through her veins. When their waiter appeared to clear
their table she experienced a pang of mingled relief and

regret that their meal was coming to an end. The pang deepened when she caught Draco indicating something with his eyes which the waiter nodded at before carrying their plates away without asking if they would like to see the dessert menu.

She lifted her chin and squashed the undeniable disappointment. She had nothing to be disappointed about. This wasn't a date—she would never have agreed to it if it had been. Draco had taken her out to cheer her up out of a sense of duty and now his duty was done he...

A sparkling flame caught her eye and cut away her despondent thoughts. One of the waitresses had stepped onto the terrace carrying a plate with a chocolate bomb on it, one of those sparkler candles in its centre. To Athena's astonishment, the waitress placed it in front of her.

Gobsmacked, she met Draco's stare.

He smiled and softly said, 'I know it's a day late, but Happy Birthday, Athena.'

CHAPTER SEVEN

ATHENA GOT INTO the car, rested her head back, crossed her legs and clasped her hands together. She could feel every staccato beat of her heart, a thud that pounded in her throat and rang in her ears. The shyness she'd felt entering Draco's dining room that morning had nothing on what she was feeling now. The tension she'd felt within her own body on the drive to the restaurant had nothing on the tension she was feeling now. She was close to nausea with nerves, and she didn't even have anything to be nervous about!

She'd blown the candle out and had wanted to cry.

She'd blown the candle out and had wanted to crawl across the table and fling her arms around him.

The last person Athena had flung her arms around had been Draco's mother.

The car set off.

'Music?' Draco asked.

'Some grime would be lovely.'

She felt him give her that stare of his, and giggled.

'You don't really like that shit, do you?'

'Only when I want to annoy people,' she admitted with another giggle. She chanced a glance and saw him shake his head with amusement. She also saw that he'd subtly angled his body away from her, just as she'd angled hers from his.

He named a singer she adored enough to have flown to London, New York and Buenos Aires to watch perform live.

'He'll do,' she agreed nonchalantly, biting her tongue from excitedly sharing her adoration. It shouldn't make her heart race even harder that Draco liked one of the singers she liked. There were so many musicians in the world that the odds of them not mutually enjoying at least one was infinitely tiny. It didn't mean anything. She wasn't an adolescent desperately striving to find something in common with her crush to prove they were meant to be together. Athena had never had a crush but she'd witnessed plenty of her peers have them, had always felt condescension at their stupidity.

The first track of her favourite album by the singer came through the speakers. It was an upbeat, funky song. Her throat tightened in anticipation of the second track, a low-beat song about unrequited love. By the time it piped through, their efforts at conversation had fizzled out. Her heart was thrumming so hard she could no longer feel its staccato. The collar of her jumpsuit felt tight around her neck and she grabbed it to loosen it so she could breathe, but it didn't help. It wasn't the jumpsuit stopping her breathing properly.

Four more torturously tense tracks passed before the driver pulled up in his usual spot outside her apartment.

Pulses rocketing, she swallowed before summoning a bright smile and turning her face to Draco. 'Thank you for a lovely evening, boss, and, well, for everything. As far as bosses go, you're actually an okay guy, and, well...'

Brain scrambled and her tongue tying itself in knots,

she unthinkingly leaned into him to plant a goodbye kiss on his cheek at the same moment he turned his face to her. The corners of their mouths met. Beard stubble, softer than she'd imagined, brushed against her cheek.

She sucked in a shallow breath at the shock of it.

The world hung suspended.

Cheek to cheek, neither of them moved. Athena *couldn't* move. It was as if the heat of Draco's skin and the divine scent she so adored had fused to overdose her senses in one big hit of Draco, paralysing her. The only sound was the roar of blood in her ears, and though she knew on a hazy but fundamental level that she needed to move away, she couldn't. Draco's cheek against hers, so warm and rough and so *Draco*...

Warm fingers... Draco's fingers...pressed into her cheek. Eyes she didn't even realise she'd closed flew open and her lungs opened enough to suck in the tiniest breath of Draco-saturated air. Every vein in her body expanded and rose to douse her in a flush of heat.

Slowly, the fingers gently skimmed her jawline, trailing sensation. Slowly, he drew his face back, the bristles of his beard dragging exquisitely across her skin before his face tilted and a whispery tingle danced over her lips. Mouths barely touching, time slowed to nothing, the only movement the heady spinning of Athena's head and the racing of her pulses before his lips slowly parted and drew hers apart with them.

Breath like dark liquid gold filled her. She swayed into him.

Fingers holding her firmly, he languidly increased the pressure of the kiss until the whole of their mouths fused into one and Athena was coaxed into her first taste of heaven.

The first stroke of his tongue against hers was electrifying, dizzying, a wave of sensation that fizzed through her skin and burned through her veins. She met his unhurried demands tentatively at first and then with increasing boldness, and when his arm slipped around her waist to draw her closer to him and her breasts pressed against his chest, the shock of desire that ripped through her blew what little lucidity she had left. Wrapping her arms around him, Athena closed her eyes even tighter and sank into the intoxicating taste and sensation of Draco.

Draco had kissed his share of women over the years, but never had he tasted such sweet hedonism. Athena tasted of creamy dark chocolate, an addictively moreish taste that drove out the last of his sanity.

There was relief in this newfound insanity. He was done with fighting. He wanted this. He wanted Athena. He wanted this infuriating, viperous, vulnerable, sexy, funny vixen and to hell with the consequences. He'd spent weeks living with Athena infuriating and enchanting him by day and hanging like a spectre in the periphery of his consciousness by night, and that day he'd suffered the imprint of her body as a compression on and beneath his skin, a thrum that had grown stronger with each passing hour, a complete takeover of his body and mind. The longer their meal had gone on, the stronger his awareness of her had grown until he'd been unable to look at her mouth without imagining what it tasted like... It tasted incredible. Her soft, pliant lips felt incredible, and when she splayed her fingers through the hairs on his nape the sensation was so powerful that he shuddered.

No more suffering. He wanted her, badly. And she wanted him. It was there in every passionate stroke of her tongue against his and every soft moan from her delectable throat.

'God, Athena,' he murmured, brushing kisses over her cheek and down the arch of the slender neck he'd stopped himself imagining kissing a thousand times. 'You taste like nectar.' Clasping her cheeks tightly, he kissed her again, his tongue plunging into the sweet depths, kissing her so hard and so thoroughly that by the time they came up for air he felt drugged.

One look in Athena's mesmerising eyes was all the proof he needed to know the drugged feeling was mutual. 'Are you going to invite me in?' he whispered.

Her gaze locked on his, she blinked and then blinked again.

'Or shall we go back to mine?'

Her lips parted, and he saw the faint apprehension clouding her stare. 'I can't.'

Breathing raggedly, he studied her, half-expecting her to crack a joke.

'I'm sorry.' Her words were so quiet he barely heard them above the roar of his heart. 'I just...' She shook her head, the apprehension now unmistakable. No, he recognised, not apprehension. Fear. And with this recognition came the remembrance of all she'd been through the night before, and he swore under his breath at his crass insensitivity.

She must have heard his curse because she shrank back, slipping away from him, which only made him curse himself in even stronger terms.

'I'm the one who should be sorry,' he said heavily. Painfully.

Chest heaving, her eyebrows drew in with confusion.

He took her hand and brought it to his lips. 'The last

thing you need after last night is for me to think I can help myself to you.'

She shook her head with more vigour. 'No. It's...' Suddenly she smiled that bewitching smile that made his chest tighten so, and then sighed. 'Thank you.'

Now he was the one to be confused.

'For backing off.' Before he could respond, she leaned over, cupped his cheeks and gazed intently into his eyes. 'If it could be anyone, it would be you.'

And with those enigmatic words she kissed his mouth, a sweet lingering kiss, before pulling away and tapping on the door for his driver to open it.

Athena slumped against her closed front door and pressed a trembling hand to her pounding heart. The other hand she pressed to lips still tingling from the glorious kisses she'd shared with Draco.

She'd never known kissing could be like that. Feel like that. Never known she could feel like she did. Like she was drugged, and, contrary to popular belief, she didn't take drugs.

In the living area, she hesitated before pulling back the curtains. Her hands were still shaking.

Draco's car had gone.

She pressed her hand to her heart again and closed her eyes as a swell of dejection rose within her.

She'd wanted to. For one dizzying, lust-induced moment she'd wanted to lead him into her apartment. Into her bedroom.

But how could she? This was everything she'd never wanted and just because her body was telling her she did now want it... Oh, he would *never* understand. How could he? It was impossible.

Her phone buzzed.

Her heart skipped to see his name.

She opened his message.

Have changed flight time to earlier slot. Will collect you at 3. If you're not ready on time, you'll be put in the cargo hold. D.

PS: Sleep well.

Wiping away a tear, a smile as wide as the pulse of light his message had injected into her heart broke free. She fired a message back.

Yes, boss. A.

PS: Sleep well too.

Athena wasn't sure if she was relieved or disappointed that Grace was already in the car, seated beside Draco, when she climbed in. She was still trying to work out if she was relieved or disappointed that Draco hadn't got out of the car for her.

She'd woken at seven with a buzz in her veins and a weight in her stomach. To distract herself from thoughts of Draco and thoughts of her family celebrating her nephew's christening that very day without her, and especially to distract herself from emotions she couldn't begin to dissect, she'd spent the intervening hours doing her laundry, a task she'd hated when she'd first had to do it—alas, her salary did not stretch to dry-cleaning bills—but now found quite soothing. As a result, she'd been waiting outside her apartment block with her luggage when Draco's car pulled up. She'd thought someone would be impressed at this exemplary show of effort and timekeeping, but no. It was almost as if her being ready on time was the bare minimum expected!

'Sure you packed enough stuff?' Draco's PA asked archly, referring to the four large suitcases the driver was wrestling into the boot.

Athena plonked herself opposite the woman who seemed to hate her more than anyone outside of the Tsaliki family and gave her best Athena-everyone-loved-to-hate smile. 'I can always go shopping if I run out.'

'This isn't a holiday. There will be no time for shopping or hairdressing appointments or beauty treatments or any of the other frivolous things you like to waste money on.'

Athena pouted. 'That's such a shame—I was going to surprise you with a girly day out.'

If Grace hadn't then given her a look that quite clearly said she'd rather spend the day in a car filled with hornets, there was a slim chance Athena wouldn't have then said, 'I had it all planned. I was going to take you shopping and then find a decent beautician to sort your moustache out.'

'Ladies, that's enough,' Draco interjected before Grace could launch herself off her seat and rip out Athena's hair. 'Athena, apologise.'

Scowling, she folded her arms. 'Why?'

'Because that was rude and because I said so.'

She puffed out a breath. So what if she'd been rude? Grace despised her and never missed an opportunity to put her down. If the lunch Grace gracelessly threw on her desk every lunchtime wasn't prewrapped, Athena would assume she'd laced it with arsenic. But this was Draco asking and she could deny him nothing...even if she couldn't currently look him in the eye. Lifting her chin, she flashed her teeth in her latest nemesis's direction. 'Sorry for being rude, Grace.'

Grace just stared at her mutinously.

'Grace, you need to apologise too.'

Grace looked as startled at that directive as Athena felt. 'For what?'

'I saw the look you gave Athena and all the other looks you've given her these last few weeks, and I'm not going to spend the next week with you two at each other's throats. Athena doesn't know any better but you do, so lead by example.'

'I do know better!' Athena said indignantly.

The piercing blue eyes she'd been avoiding locked onto hers, the left eyebrow raised. 'Are you really admitting that?'

The warmth that filled her... It stained her skin and expanded her chest, flying out of her throat as a short laugh. 'No.'

His lips twitched. The lips that had kissed her senseless. But his eyes...they danced with meaning and for that one tiny beat of a moment it could have been just the two of them in the car's cabin.

Her chest swelled so hard and so fast that the stain on her skin deepened. Feeling her tongue starting to tie itself, she swallowed and turned to Grace, leaning across to take her hand. 'I really am sorry. I'm a defensive, prickly pear and I say mean things, not always without thinking, but you didn't deserve that and I promise to make more of an effort not to be a bitch to you this week.'

Not for Grace's sake but for Draco's. Because he'd asked.

But then Grace's eyes softened, only a tiny amount, but it was a definite softening, and she gave a tiny squeeze of Athena's hand, and a different kind of warmth filled Athena's chest that made her want to cry and laugh all at the same time.

They were met at the airport by Theodore and Stav, the remainder of Draco's core entourage who, with Grace, worked across all of Draco's businesses. One day, Athena thought, she might get around to finding out what they actually did. But not today. Today, her stomach was too knotted to do much more than arrange her face and stop herself from continually seeking out Draco's gaze. She had nothing to distract her. Nothing physical. Not on a fourteen-hour flight where even Draco didn't pretend to have any work for her to do and she'd packed her drawing stuff in one of her suitcases.

Every time their eyes locked it felt like an explosion in her heart.

Although there was nothing physical to distract her, she still sought a means to occupy herself. Draco's plane was as big as the family jet her father used to pile the Tsaliki brood into whenever they travelled, Athena and her siblings all having their own private space with a bed. While there wasn't much real private space on Draco's plane, the interior designed around business rather than pleasure, the ten seats in the main section all reclined into beds and all had their own privacy screens.

With Draco and his entourage busy discussing business in the conference area and none of them bothering with the charade that her presence was required, Athena swiped a notepad and pen from the stack on the table and settled on the reclining seat she'd taken for her own. Draco had taken the space across the aisle from hers. He'd placed his overnight case on the seat that reclined into a bed closest to hers before his gaze had glanced across hers, a blink-and-you'll-miss-it moment that had sent her pulses haywire.

Drawing with a pen was good practice, she decided after she'd been scribbling away for an hour. Being unable to erase and refine made her decisive about each stroke. And being decisive meant concentrating harder than ever, which meant no time for seeking out eyes of blue so bright they made the summer sky seem dull. It meant, too, that she didn't have to think about the significance of Draco placing his overnight case on the seat that reclined into a bed closest to hers.

Dinner was shared with the others at the oval dining table, a five-course feast she struggled to finish.

'Are you not going to eat your baklava?' Grace asked when Athena pushed her dessert plate to one side.

It was right on the tip of Athena's tongue to say, *And you shouldn't either, not with your acne*, but there was only hungry interest in Grace's voice and no snideness, and so she bit the rudeness back and pushed the plate Grace's way. 'It's all yours.'

Grace smiled. 'Thank you.'

She had a pretty smile, Athena realised, having never been on the receiving end of one before. 'You're welcome.'

She only just resisted seeking Draco's gaze. He was seated opposite her, a huge contributory factor in her lack of appetite. One kiss, the first kiss of her whole life she'd felt in the whole of her body and not just in her lips. She'd wanted it to go on for ever. And now she was all knotted and coiled, half in fear of it happening again and half in fear of it never happening again.

Draco had never struggled to concentrate before. Not like this. Although Athena had disappeared to her seat, leaving them to finish their work, he was as aware of her presence as he'd been when they'd been eating, and when he sensed movement he was unable to stop his head from turning. He caught a sweep of her blonde hair before she slipped into one of the bathrooms.

Stav said something to him. Draco asked him to repeat it.

The discussion continued, Draco present but not there, his antennae on alert for the bathroom door opening.

After what felt like an eternity, she reappeared.

Her eyes found his.

His chest expanded.

God, she was beautiful. He could still taste her kisses. Still feel the compression of her mouth against his. And now here she was, dressed in another pair of those disgustingly awful grandmother pyjamas, her face scrubbed of make-up, and he allowed himself to see what he'd never allowed all those early mornings—that even in those disgustingly awful grandmother pyjamas he wanted her more than he'd ever wanted anyone.

He watched her raise her pretty heart-shaped face and fix the smile to her face he knew was the smile she wore as armour. 'I'm going to get some sleep,' she called over to them. 'Don't miss me too much and don't work too hard!'

'Goodnight, Athena,' Grace called back, and then Stav and Theodore followed suit.

Draco, his throat suddenly too tight for words, inclined his head.

Her gaze locked on his one last time before she returned to her seat and raised her privacy screen.

The reclined seat made such a comfortable bed that even people with back problems would wake up refreshed.

There was no reason Athena couldn't fall asleep. She was a master of sleeping on planes. Master of tuning out noise and falling into slumber at will. It was waking up she'd always struggled with!

The noise from Draco and the others was so low as to be hardly audible. She had to strain to hear them.

It was only when she heard footsteps coming towards her and her breath caught in her throat that she understood that this was why she'd not yet fallen asleep.

The footsteps passed her. More footsteps came and went.

Snuggling tighter under the duvet, she rolled over and squeezed her eyes shut.

There were ten reclining seats on the plane in pairs of two. Enough for them to have two beds each. Just because Draco had put his overnight case on the seat closest to hers didn't mean he'd settle in on it, and even if he did, the aisle would separate them. And besides, her privacy screen was up.

Movement close by had her eyes springing open and her heart jumping into her throat.

Sitting up, she heard the low buzz of the privacy screen closest to hers rising.

Nothing more. Once her heart rate had reduced from a Speedy Gonzales level to a mere canter, she lay back down.

Her eyes refused to close. However hard she willed them and however stern a talk she gave them, they stayed stubbornly open.

Another low burr, this time of a seat in recline, sent her heart from a gentle trot to Speedy Gonzales-on-steroids in a beat.

She tried to breathe, spent an age trying to concentrate

on feeding herself air and not thinking of Draco lying so close to her, but the growing ache inside her made that impossible, and she wished she could live that moment of waking in his arms again, a moment she looked back on with regret for not savouring it while she had it.

He'd saved her and protected her the whole night through. No one had ever done anything like that for her before, and though she'd been drugged, there had been such a sense of safety in his arms, and she longed to feel it again almost as much as she longed for the man who'd provided that safety.

But how could it be? she despaired. How could she take from him without giving anything of herself? She'd always worn her selfishness with pride, all part of the Athena everyone loved to hate persona, but she didn't want to be selfish with Draco. She just didn't know how to be any other way and didn't know how to give of herself either.

She'd thrown the duvet off, swung her feet to the floor and opened her privacy door before she could question what she was doing.

Draco's privacy door was only a step away. Heart pounding, she took the step and lightly tapped her fingers to it.

The roaring in her ears was so loud she only just heard the low, 'Come in.'

She pushed it open a fraction. Her heart stopped and then exploded before the rest of her senses took in the hulking bearded figure lying on the narrow bed.

She opened it some more. In the dim lighting, their eyes locked.

Without saying a word, he lifted the duvet in invitation.

Maybe if he hadn't been wearing grey pyjama bottoms and a white T-shirt, she would have frightened herself into backing away. She would never know because he *was* wearing them. And so she slipped into his private space and closed the thin door.

CHAPTER EIGHT

HAD HE WILLED her to come to him telepathically? Draco wondered dimly. He'd chosen the space closest to Athena consciously because positioning himself further up the aisle away from her would only add a layer to the torture of this insanity he'd fallen into. Here, he was as close to her as he could be with only the thin walls of their respective privacy screens separating them. And she knew it too.

He wouldn't go to her, not after the way she'd backed away when he'd thoughtlessly asked her to invite him into her apartment, before she'd kissed him, that sweet, sweet kiss, and delivered those enigmatic words. But he'd hoped she'd come to him. Hoped without any expectation. The spiking of her drink had made Athena vulnerable, and for him to knock on her privacy door without explicit invitation would put her in an invidious position. The first move had to come from her.

The bed was so narrow there was barely space for him on it, but, as silent as a ghost, she laid on her side and snuggled into him. His chest swelling, he covered her with the duvet and wrapped his arms around her, holding her close in a tangle of limbs.

It didn't need saying that nothing could happen. It didn't matter that the plane's engine made an ambient background noise; the three closest members of his work-force were only feet away from them.

But knowing something intellectually and feeling it were two very different things, and as much as he willed his body to behave itself, he was only human and this was Athena in his arms, pressed so tightly against him, her breasts crushed against his chest, her thigh slipped between his. Her soft fragrance he was breathing in with each inhalation.

She shifted slightly and his arousal pressed into her abdomen. She sucked in a breath.

'Ignore it,' he commanded softly, kissing the top of her head.

Athena wrapped her arms tighter around him and sighed shakily into his throat. Though she was half-draped on top of him, it felt as if she was cocooned in Draco. So many feelings and emotions were careering through her, feelings and emotions she'd spent her life avoiding and hiding from, but here, cocooned in Draco, the fear that had always driven her had fallen silent.

The beep of his watch woke Draco from the light sleep he'd fallen into. He hadn't expected even that, not when sharing such a tight, intimate space with the woman who'd taken over his mind and for whom desire coiled in the very essence of his being.

With a deep sigh, he stroked Athena's back, knowing he should wake her. There was a routine to the long flights to California, sleep kept to a few hours due to the ten-hour time difference. Soon, the cabin crew would serve the human fuel needed to power them through the last three hours of the flight. When they landed it would be six in the morning in Athens but evening in California.

Knowing he should wake her and wanting to wake her were two very different things. The only thing that could improve this awakening would be if they were both naked and he could roll her over and…

He cut his thoughts off sharply. He needed the brain in his head functioning, not the brain between his legs.

Just as he was telling himself he *had* to wake her, she lifted her head from his chest and smiled sleepily. 'I should go.'

His chest tightened then swelled. Spearing his fingers through her hair, he nodded. God, she was so beautiful it hurt to look at her.

Her smile widening, she carefully levered herself up and pressed the softest of kisses to his mouth.

At the privacy wall door, she turned for one more look before slipping out with the same silent grace she'd slipped in.

As they were heading straight to the hotel from the airport, Athena donned a pair of ripped skinny jeans and a heavy bright pink poncho. She'd been to California in January before and had not liked the coolness of the weather. Greece was sunny all year round, and yes, temperatures in the winter months dipped, especially at night, but California felt much colder on her sun-loving skin. For extra weather protection, she donned a pink woolly hat and pink leather gloves before disembarking, matching it all with funky high-heeled, multi-coloured ankle boots and ignoring the amused glances exchanged between the others. If they wanted to be cold, that was their problem.

There were two cars waiting for them. One was for Draco, who had his own home near Silicon Valley, the other for his entourage. Athena, as part of this entourage, would have headed off with the others if Draco hadn't caught her eye and beckoned her to his car.

'I thought I was staying at the hotel,' she said, confused. There had been a lot of talk over breakfast about the hotel, which was a five-minute walk from Manolis Technology HQ. From the general gist of things, it was the hotel Draco's entourage always stayed at when they visited California.

Though his eyebrow was raised and his tone playful, his eyes were intent with meaning. 'Do you really think I'm going to let you loose in a hotel? You're staying under my watchful eye until the end of your contract, which means you're staying at my place with me.'

The thrill that raced through her at this was beyond anything.

While it hadn't actually been stated that she'd be staying at the hotel with the others, there had been no indication that she wouldn't. She'd assumed. Sure, her employment was massively different to the others, namely they were employed in proper roles and performed vital tasks, whereas she was there under everyone's sufferance for a limited time. But still, she'd assumed, and since leaving Draco's bed had been mentally preparing herself for their separation, cheering herself up with the long days in the office she had to look forward to with him. Who'd have thought she'd look forward to long days of working?

But then, who'd have thought she'd feel despondent at the thought of being parted from anyone, let alone a man? Which provoked a whole different kind of emotion: fear. Not of Draco, but his expectations and how she could never meet them.

Athena had allowed her craving for his company over-ride everything else. She'd wanted to experience that feeling of safety in his arms again, and she had, and though she'd slept through most of it, they had been the most magical few hours of her life.

She'd climbed into Draco's bed knowing nothing physical would happen between them. That it couldn't. And so she'd been able to switch off her brain and her fears and sink into the safety of her Draco cocoon.

Now it would be just her and Draco. The safety net Grace, Theodore and Stav had provided would be located in a hotel miles away, and Draco would have expectations because she'd fed them by climbing into his bed, and she kept feeding them with every look they exchanged because she was helpless not to. For the first time in her life, Athena was in lust and it was terrifying for so many reasons she couldn't begin to count them.

Draco thought he knew her.

He was going to be left bitterly disappointed.

For now, though, all she could do was what she always did and Athena her way through the fears. Tilting her head, she sweetly said, 'You're very brave.'

The piercing blue eyes glimmered. 'I know.'

'Do you provide an all-you-can-eat buffet for breakfast and room service, and do you have a swimming pool and gym? Because that's what the others are getting and it strikes me as a bit discriminatory if I'm not going to be provided with those same basic amenities and services.'

Amusement and desire swirled.

'Athena?' he said pointedly.

'Yes, boss?'

'Get in the car.'

'Yes, boss.'

* * *

Considering she'd only had two hours sleep in the last twenty-four hours, Athena was as alert as she'd ever been when they travelled the sweeping drive leading them to Draco's Californian home in the small but ultra-exclusive town of Crespi Valley. Through the thick woods surrounding and encircling them, artfully positioned solar lights revealed lushly manicured grounds, the house itself a distantly lit blob that gradually took shape as they drove closer, revealing itself to be a sprawling one-storey sandstone villa with a graceful loggia at the front and arched doors to the wings at its side.

They circled a dazzling fountain of naked cherubs at play before the car came to a stop. That was when her stomach plummeted and her heart really went into overdrive.

Throughout the short drive to Draco's home, she'd kept up her perky front by peppering him with questions about his Californian home and the area it was located, terrified that if she stopped talking her tongue would tie itself and she'd be sick from the nerves coiling so tightly inside her. She knew what she needed to tell him, knew she needed to do it sooner rather than later, but had no idea how to say it. A giant elephant was sitting between them but only she could see it.

'Is this where we go in and you start hosting international video calls to prove what a dedicated workaholic you are?' she said in the same bright voice she'd asked all her questions during their time in the car. 'I've got a nail file with me so I won't be bored. I might even look at painting my nails myself—it can't be that hard, can it? Although it might be a little tricky doing my right hand as I'm right-handed and not in the least ambidextrous, and...'

'Athena?'

She closed her eyes, barely able to comprehend how much she was coming to adore the way he said her name in that stern, pointed tone. Except this time his gruff voice was more soft than stern, and there was a catch in her own voice when she gave her standard, 'Yes, boss?'

'Look at me.'

'Yes, boss.'

Draco recognised immediately that the smile Athena wore when she turned to him was her armour smile, and inhaled slowly through his nose. His instinct throughout the short drive that she was carrying tension had been right. She was still Athena but with the slight brittleness that suggested something was going on beneath the surface, and he had a good idea what that something was.

He gazed intently at the green eyes that were shining just a little *too* brightly, as if she was forcing the shine.

'While we're sharing my home you will have your own room,' he said quietly. 'It will be for you alone. If you want to share my room and my bed, then there's plenty of room for two even if you're not ready for this thing between us to go anywhere. We go at your pace and if your pace doesn't take us past the starting line then that's how it will be.' If his immediate future entailed frequent cold showers then so be it.

Athena's heart had raced into her throat. She knew why Draco was saying all this. He thought her fears—and that he could see them when no one else ever had would be blowing her mind if her mind wasn't filled with so much else—came from her being traumatised at the spiking of her drink, when the truth was she'd been too wrapped up in Draco since to give it more than a few thoughts. The men had been arrested and charged; they couldn't hurt her.

They hadn't hurt her because Draco had saved her, and she wished she could find the words to tell him all this, and wished he could read her mind so she didn't have to find the words to explain the truth, because she wished as hard as she'd ever wished for anything that things could be different and that she could repay him in the way they both longed for without being the crushing disappointment it was inevitable she would be to him.

'I'm...' She closed her eyes. Draco had provided an open goal for her to shoot the truth into but the words wouldn't form.

'You're what?' he asked into her silence.

She looked back at his gorgeous, rugged face and thought if she was capable of falling in love with anyone it would be with him. But love didn't exist. Not the love of books and songs. Not for her. Athena had known since she was a little girl that she was inherently unlovable and that the only way to protect herself was to coat herself in a wall of prickly steel. Push them away before they pushed her because all loving someone did was give them the power to hurt you.

But Draco was different. It wasn't just that he'd saved her or that she'd been helpless to stop herself from desiring him and wanting...craving...to be with him, it was his patience and thoughtfulness. The five weeks he'd put up with her as a constant presence in his life were the longest anyone outside her family had endured before, and even her family could only endure her in small doses. Whether it was pride at not wanting to admit defeat or not wanting to pay the hefty bill that came from admitting defeat with her didn't matter. He hadn't given up on her, and she adored him for this as much as she adored him for anything. Maybe she was too far gone in her prickly wall of steel to ever love, but all that she was still capable of feeling she felt for him.

Reaching for his hand, she covered it with her much smaller one and squeezed. 'I'm ready to take a tour of your home.'

His eyes narrowed as if he knew she was holding something back, but then he shook his head with a smile and turned his hand to thread his fingers through hers. 'Then let's do it.'

Draco's Californian home was every bit as spacious and opulent as its exterior promised. It had a warmth to it, too, something Athena, thinking back, realised his home in Athens also had. She hadn't noticed much about his Athens home at the time, but as he led her through the rooms of this one she recognised the similarities. Draco had an aesthetic he preferred, one of high ceilings, light walls and an abundance of lead-lined windows that contrasted with dark woods and dark furniture. It was just as well they weren't destined to marry, she joked with herself; her preference for pink did not fit his aesthetic *at all*. It was a joke she kept to herself, one of many jokes she made in her head to distract her from the swell in her chest holding hands with Draco was inducing.

It had been over twenty years since she'd held anybody's hand. She'd tugged at a few people's hands a few times over the years when she'd wanted to get their attention, but the actual holding of a hand, the actual sensation of having her hand clasped in the hand of another...

She was shown the bedrooms with the same matter-of-factness that she was shown the entertainment room that would make an excellent nightclub, and for this she was grateful. There were a number of guest houses in the grounds but she'd been given the one guest room in the sleeping quarters of the main house, a suite with a door that faced Draco's. The only time he released her hand was so she could explore her room alone, and she adored him for that consideration even when she eyed the emperor bed and her pulses raced to imagine being naked with him on it...

It was a thought she shut off, just as she shut off the same thought when he let her nose around his bedroom. Once she told him the truth—and she would, she would find the words, she must—there was every chance he would decide she wasn't worth the bother and lock himself away in his spacious, ultra-masculine private space.

She had to find the words, and soon, because it was already getting late and both of them were shattered after the long flight. Soon, she would be expected to decide whose bed she wanted to sleep in. Once he knew the truth, it would be Draco making that choice.

Although Draco's home had two dining rooms and a kitchen island that could seat eight people, they settled down to eat on one of the abundant sofas in the main reception room.

'How long have you owned this place?' Athena asked as they dug into their moussaka, a dish Draco's Italian chef had spent years trying to perfect so it tasted as good as the one his mother made.

'Eight years.'

'I thought it had to be a while. It's got a permanent feel to it rather than that hotel vibe you get from homes that are only used a few weeks a year.'

'I still consider this to be my main home,' he admitted.

'Do you consider California itself to be home?' Until a few years ago, Draco had mostly lived in California.

He thought about this and shook his head. 'Greece is where my heart lives, but this home is more mine than my home in Athens feels.'

'Once you've got Tsaliki Shipping working how you want it, will you step back from it and spend more time here?'

He nodded. 'Since the buyout, the majority of my time has been spent in Athens—you know that yourself—but the long-term plan is to appoint someone to run the shipping business for me so I can concentrate on my technology businesses. That's where my real passion lies.' There was no point in lying. Athena knew why he'd bought her family's business.

Wanda, his head of housekeeping, appeared from the sleeping quarters, where she'd been unpacking Athena's luggage.

'Everything is done,' she said to Draco in English. 'Can you please tell Miss Tsaliki that if she's not happy with how anything has been put away, to let me know and I will rectify it immediately, and ask if there is anything else she needs to make her feel at home?'

'If you've unpacked as well as you keep the house then I know it will be perfect, thank you,' Athena interjected. 'Everything here is perfect. And please, call me Athena.'

Wanda's face fell. 'I'm so sorry, Miss… Athena. I didn't think you spoke English.'

'You had no reason to know,' she assured her with a smile.

Wanda's relief was apparent. His housekeeper, Draco guessed, had done an internet search on their houseguest and expected the worst. Everyone expected the worst of Athena, a state of mind she perpetuated as, he heavily suspected, a means of self-preservation. But that wasn't the real Athena. The real Athena behind the Mean Girl façade was vivacious and funny and highly intelligent, the sweet, loving girl his mother had described appearing in flickers that grew longer and more stable with each flash.

Something was troubling her though. She was conversing and eating normally, but the slight brittleness in her demeanour that was only detectable if you knew her well enough had returned, and he noticed when Wanda said she was retiring for the night that her jaw briefly clenched so hard the tendons in her neck elongated.

He waited until Wanda had disappeared before shaking his head. 'How the hell did you keep the fact you speak fluent English under the radar?'

Her cheeks colouring, she shrugged. 'It's not the kind of thing you drop into conversation, is it.'

He gave her the stern look she usually responded to with sassiness. 'You were asked when you started working at Tsaliki Shipping to list anything that could be useful to the company. Your list was blank.'

She pulled one of her many amusing faces but he could see it was an effort for her, that she was going through the motions and her mind was elsewhere. 'Draco, we both know that I am as useful in business as a chocolate coffee pot. When my contracted time with you is done it will be a competition between us over whether I run out of the door first or you push me out.'

'Trust me, I'll win that one,' he jested lightly, even as a weight pushed down on his stomach to imagine a time when Athena wouldn't be a part of his daily life.

But there was no answering riposte or laughter or even a smile. The little sparkle still left in her eyes extinguished like a candle being pinched out, and she broke the lock of their stares to put her plate on the coffee table. 'I'm sorry, I can't finish it.'

She'd eaten barely a quarter of her portion.

'What's wrong?' he asked, no longer willing to pretend that there wasn't a tension running through her. Athena wasn't the biggest of eaters, but she normally ate a healthy amount. 'Talk to me. I can tell something is troubling you.'

She drew her legs up and hugged her knees, her pretty top teeth biting into her bottom lip.

Her voice, when she finally spoke again, was low. 'I'm a virgin.'

CHAPTER NINE

DRACO'S FIRST INSTINCT was to laugh. Athens'… *Greece's…* premier party girl, a woman infamous for her wide and varied sex life, had just declared herself a virgin. 'Say that again.'

'I'm a virgin.'

The men Athena had been pictured with over the years flashed through his head, a collage of Athena and her myriad lovers pictured together falling out of nightclubs, on her family's yacht, at parties, out shopping…

She wasn't the only one of the Tsaliki offspring to shamelessly embrace her carnal nature—before he'd settled down, Alexis had been one of the biggest playboys in Europe. Naturally, Alexis had been celebrated for his sex drive and conquests, while the whiff of old-fashioned double standards had seen Athena's embrace of her sexuality spoken of and written about in unflattering and disapproving terms. That she'd been so blatantly unashamed about it had only added to the opprobrium.

'I didn't know you were that desperate,' Tobias had said in The Playroom when Draco had been looking for her. He'd wanted to hit him for that, but Tobias had only been vocalising what so many people in Greek society thought.

His brain was starting to burn.

So much of the Athena the world thought it knew was a constructed façade, but a virgin? It wasn't possible.

'If you don't want to sleep with me then just say so,' he said roughly. 'There's no need to lie.'

Her leg flew forward, the sole of her bare foot slamming into his thigh before she twisted off the sofa and jumped to her feet. 'Fuck you,' she spat, her beautiful face contorted with pain.

She'd reached the end of the living area before he absorbed what had just happened.

'Athena, wait!' he called as he strode to catch up with her.

She ignored him and charged down the corridor towards the bedrooms at a run.

He reached her just as she was slamming her bedroom door shut, would have successfully locked him out if he hadn't wedged himself into the gap and forced his way in.

One look at her stricken face was all he needed to know how badly he'd got it wrong, and he kicked the door shut and closed the gap between them to haul her into his arms.

'I'm sorry,' he said, holding her rigid body tightly to him. 'I should never have said that. I know you're not a liar.'

She didn't say anything, didn't make any response at all, not an arm around his waist or a hand to his chest to push him away.

It was only when he felt his shirt dampen against his skin that he realised she was crying.

He held her even tighter and pressed his mouth to her head. 'God, Athena, don't cry.'

Her whole body shuddered before she sagged against him and buried her face into his chest with huge, gulping sobs.

His chest twisting painfully at her desolation, he scooped her into his arms and carried her to the bed. There, he sat with her on his lap and propped himself against the headboard so she could curl into him, and just held her close as she sobbed her heart out.

It felt as if she was sobbing his heart out too.

Athena didn't know why she was crying. She'd expected incredulity, but Draco's accusation of lying had cut something open in her, and now it was as if the floodgates of all the pain she'd spent a lifetime smothering had opened and she didn't know how to close them, could only cling to him as if he was the life raft stopping her from drowning.

It took a long time for the heaving sobs to subside. When she was finally spent, her throat was raw and her heart wrung. Her whole body felt wrung.

But there was comfort there, too, in the tenderness of the hand stroking her back and the fingers gently combing through her hair, and she came close to crying again when the fingers stopped working their magic.

'Here,' he said quietly, having reached for the box of tissues on the bedside table for her.

Disentangling her arms, she took a handful and blew her nose noisily. 'Thank you,' she whispered.

He pulled her back to him and kissed the top of her head. 'I'm sorry.'

It was a long time before she could bring herself to speak again. 'It wasn't you,' she said hoarsely. 'I knew you would struggle to believe me—it's why I found it so hard to tell you. I wouldn't have believed me if I was in your shoes.'

His fingers burrowed back into her hair. 'Then what was it?'

She shrugged helplessly. 'Everything. All the things I want to keep in the past coming back to haunt me.' She tilted her head to give him an accusatory look. 'Which, now I think about it, is your fault. I was having a lovely time forgetting everything and living for the moment but then you came along and brought with you all the old memories and all the old feelings. So yes, on reflection it was you who made me cry.'

The sad smile his firm lips pulled showed he understood she was trying to lighten the heaviness of all that had just happened. 'Were you really having a lovely time forgetting?'

She helped herself to another tissue and wiped her nose. 'Sometimes. But I never did forget. Not really.' Wrapping her arm back around him, she pressed her cheek against his chest. 'It was always there, festering away in my soul. My mother chose a house and money over me. That's what it all came down to. I loved her more than anyone. She was my whole world and she let my father pay her off in exchange for leaving me with him. She let me be sidelined from her life without a fight, and I will never, never forget how she walked away without looking back at me while I was screaming at her and begging her not to leave me.' She swallowed. 'I assume your mother's told you all this?'

'Yes.'

Draco had imagined the emotional impact it must have had on her, but hearing it in Athena's own words and hearing the raw pain in her voice told him he'd hugely underestimated how much it still affected her.

'Did she tell you how I transferred all my love to her?'

'She said you became her little shadow.'

A smile came into her voice. 'I loved her very much. She'd always been a fixture in my life and I'd always adored her. When she was there, I felt safe and loved. My father was all wrapped up in Rebecca and her daughter, but Cora always made time for me. She would never have chosen money over you, would she.'

'No,' he agreed, even though it hadn't been a question.

'I was so lost and unhappy, and Cora just seemed to know what I needed, and she gave it to me, all the love and affection that had been taken from me, and it destroyed me all over again when she was fired. I missed her desperately and was still missing my mother desperately, too, and it all hurt so much that I just shut down emotionally. The world I knew and trusted was gone. My mother was gone, Cora was gone, my father had a new wife and another baby on the way, and on top of all that Lucie, Rebecca's daughter, came to live with us for a while, too, and my father doted on her. I'd gone from being the baby of the family and being loved and coddled by everyone to nothing. The only time I ever got attention was when I acted out…and so I acted out and over time the Athena everyone loves to hate was born.'

'It was deliberate?'

'In part.' She lapsed into silence before whispering, 'I didn't care if people hated me.'

'It was better than letting them get close to you?'

She lifted her puffy, tear-stained face to stare at him. 'Yes. Please don't think I'm trying to play the poor little rich girl victim card. I've had a charmed, privileged life and I'm starting to understand why Alexis wanted to pull me out of it and give me a reality check—I took it all for granted. And my family does love me in their own way, and I do love them, but as a family we're one big screwup and I can't say I wouldn't have become the same person if that stuff with my mother and your mother hadn't happened.'

'I can.'

She gave a tremulous smile. 'That's sweet of you to say.'

'It's not lip service, Athena. I keep seeing glimpses of the woman you were meant to be. She's in there, but it's up to you to let her out.' He took a deep breath before admitting, 'I've seen your drawings.'

She flinched.

'They're exquisite. That charcoal portrait you did of your nephew... I assume it was your nephew?'

She gave a jerky nod.

'It's beautiful and full of love. No one whose heart is made of stone could produce something like that.'

Fresh tears filled her eyes and she blinked vigorously to hold them back. 'Stop making me cry! I don't do tears!'

He smiled ruefully. 'If you need to cry then cry.'

'You told me to stop crying earlier!'

'That's because I don't do tears either.'

She gave a burst of laughter and flung her arms around his neck, burying her face in the arch of his throat. For the longest time they just held each other until she said in a small voice, 'Where do you want me to sleep tonight?'

'As I said earlier, that's a choice for you to make.'

'Oh. It's just that I thought...'

'That I'd run a mile when you told me you were a virgin?'

She nodded. 'I'm not who you thought I was.'

'Would you call me an arsehole if I told you I was glad?'

'Yes. Arsehole.'

Laughing, he held her even tighter and buried his mouth and chin in her hair. 'All those men you were pictured with...weren't you ever tempted?'

'Never. Those men really were arseholes and I felt nothing for them. They were like my father and my brothers in their attitude to women—they didn't care about me, they cared about who I was and what was between my legs, so no, I wasn't in the slightest bit tempted. I was having fun…or so I liked to tell myself.'

'But you weren't?'

'I think you already know the answer to that. I chose them as deliberately as they chose me.'

'But how come the truth never came out?'

'I never told any of them I was a virgin. I just told them to keep their hands to themselves and strung them along and then dumped them when they got fed up waiting for me to say yes. I went everywhere with two humungous bodyguards so they weren't going to argue with me and they weren't going to tell anyone either. Who wants to admit that party girl Athena didn't put out for you? Their egos would have been destroyed.'

'You've been playing with fire.'

'I know.' Her voice caught. 'Friday night made me realise what a dangerous game it's been. I had a few lucky escapes over the years where my bodyguards had to step in.'

'Your bodyguards slept in your room?'

'What are you talking about?'

'You've taken men on family cruises before.'

'Yes, but I always insisted they sleep in the adjoining cabin and then locked it so they couldn't come in. You're the first man I've ever shared a bed with.' She swallowed. 'You're the first person I've trusted since your mother left my life.'

It was the starkness in her tone that pierced Draco, more so than her words. 'I'm not a saint, Athena. Never

think that. I like sex as much as the next man. When I was
a teenager, my sole purpose in life was to have as much
sex as I could.'

'And did you?'

'Not as much as I would have liked, but that changed
when I started earning money and making a name for
myself.'

'Power and money is an aphrodisiac,' she stated.
'Women flock to you.'

'Yes. I would love to tell you I've never taken advantage
of it, but believe me when I tell you I'm not a saint and
I've never pretended to be. But I don't cheat and I don't
lie, and I never make promises I'm not going to keep.' He
sighed. 'This thing between us…'

'It can't go anywhere. I know.' Her voice was sad.

'I don't want to hurt you.'

'Which is why it's got to be you.'

'Athena…'

She drew back to cup his cheeks and gaze into his eyes.
'I know it can't go anywhere. I know I'm all wrong for
you even without my reputation. But I also know you're
the best man I've ever met and that for the first time in my
life…' She smiled and pressed a kiss to his mouth. 'When
you kiss me, I feel it all the way to my toes. Just being here
with you like this…' She kissed him again. 'It makes my
veins fizz. *You* make my veins fizz. All these feelings…
I want to explore them, but only with you because it can
only be you. I know you'll take care of me. You can't hurt
me more than I've already been hurt or more than I've
been hurting myself. I don't want to hurt any more, Draco.
I want to feel. I want to feel *you*. Just you.'

A pulse was throbbing in Draco's head. An hour ago,
he'd have taken what Athena was offering without a sec-

ond thought but her virginity put a whole different complexion on things. In truth, he was still reeling from the shock of it, and now there was a weight of responsibility sitting on his chest that if he went along with this and didn't get it right, he could hurt her, in more ways than one.

She was putting her trust in him but she had no idea what she was asking of him. Did she not understand how damned sexy she was? She felt his kisses to her toes? Her kisses connected directly to his loins. It was all well and good talking in hypotheticals but right now they had their clothes on. Finding the restraint needed to make love to her without hurting her...

He didn't know if he possessed it.

He would have to find it because he couldn't walk away. Not now.

Drawing in a long breath, he combed his fingers through her hair. Eyes red and puffy from crying and exhaustion, she'd never looked more vulnerable or adorable.

He kissed the tip of her nose. 'Let me draw you a bath. You'll feel better for it.'

She smiled that soft smile he knew was only for him.

The bath in the pretty guest bathroom was a deep oval cocoon that looked out over the vast grounds. Athena, her hair piled on top of her head to keep it dry, lay back in its steamy warmth, closed her eyes and expelled the longest breath of her life.

There was a strange lightness in her heart. There had been something cathartic in bawling her eyes out the way she'd done with Draco, and now it felt as if she'd exorcised something demonic that had always lived inside her.

Maybe the people who said it was bad to bottle up your emotions were onto something.

She yawned widely. The heat of the bath was soaking through to her bones while the long, long day was now accelerating to catch up with her. She'd had no more than two hours' sleep in thirty hours and suddenly it felt like the easiest thing in the world would be to let the heaviness pressing on her brain win and take her off into slumber. And probable drowning.

Yawning again, she forced herself upright and gave her face and body a cursory clean before forcing her legs upright and climbing out of the bath. After wrapping herself in a lovely warm, large fluffy towel, she used the last of her energy to brush her teeth.

The room was empty. Draco had gone off to shower in his own room. After only the slightest of hesitations, she dropped the towel on the floor and climbed into the bed naked to wait for him.

Draco knew the moment he stepped back into the room that Athena had fallen asleep. Curled on her side, she'd burrowed into the thick duvet, only the top of her face and hair visible.

He padded silently to the other side of the bed, removed his robe, slid beneath the duvet and turned out the light.

His heart so full he could feel it in his throat, he lay unmoving for a full three minutes before moving closer to draw her into his arms.

It was only when she curled into him with a deep sigh that he realised she was naked.

Pressing his mouth into her hair, he drew a ragged breath and closed his eyes.

CHAPTER TEN

ATHENA WOKE TO the heavenly sensation of being co-cooned in Draco's arms. For the longest time she stayed exactly where she was, savouring the feel of her face nuzzled in his naked chest and their limbs being entwined.

Sighing, she stretched a leg and pressed a gentle kiss to the warm skin beneath her mouth. The fine hair covering his chest tickled her nose.

The arm hooked around her waist tightened. Her heart thumped, and her eyes fluttered open. Dusky early morning light cast his bronze chest in a sepia hue.

The thumping of her heart increased as she felt movement against her abdomen. For a long moment she forgot how to breathe, suddenly attuned to his heart beating strongly beneath her ear and the weight of his growing arousal pressing low in her belly. Draco was as naked as she was…

Suddenly needing air, she lifted her face from its snug confines…and found herself locked in Draco's piercing stare.

His strong throat moved but he didn't speak. Neither of them spoke. Athena couldn't. Her throat was too full of her swollen, pumping heart. Without any thought, she extended her neck and brought her face to his. His eyes closed and then opened, jaw tightening, breaths deepening.

Breathing him in, she crept her hand from the warmth of his back and slid it up his chest, so lost in the piercing blue she could only dimly marvel at the smoothness of his skin and how similar and yet so very different the texture was to hers. Higher her hand slid, over broad shoulders powerful even in stillness, cupping the base of his neck and pressing her palm where a pulse was violently beating. Feeling as if she'd fallen into a dream, she closed her eyes and stretched her neck the last fraction needed to bring their mouths together.

Their kiss was featherlight, a barely-there whisper. The hand splayed on her back, so big it covered almost the whole width, drew upward, fingers making an unhurried trail up her spine that sent a trail of electricity zinging through her veins.

Fingers now splaying in her hair, his lips, so firm and so in control, moved in an undemanding invitation for her to move with them. She met his invitation by sliding her fingers into his hair and tentatively sliding her tongue between his lips.

She felt rather than heard his distant groan before he deepened the fusion of their mouths and his tongue met hers in an unhurried erotic dance she felt like fire in every atom of her body.

With a tenderness that broke her thumping heart, he rolled her onto her back so their legs were still entwined... the rough hairs on his bristled deliciously against the smoothness of hers...and his chest covered hers, crushing her aching breasts, and lifted his face to gaze into her eyes. 'Any time you want me to stop, you must promise to tell me,' he said huskily.

Dragging her fingers through his hair, she gave a shaky smile and whispered, 'I promise.' But she wouldn't. Sick excitement was growing, her heart racing so hard and fast it had blurred to a distant roar, but beneath the nervous fear of the unknown lay a deep certainty that if she were to walk away she would regret it for the rest of her life. 'I want this,' she said hoarsely. 'I want *you*, Draco. All of you.'

His throat moved, hooded eyes closing before fixing back onto hers. 'I have protection in my robe, but...' He breathed deeply. 'Are you protected?'

'I'm on the pill.' Her stepmother, assuming she was sexually active, had put her on it when she was sixteen. She'd stayed on it only because she liked the way it regulated her periods.

He pressed his nose to hers without breaking the lock of their stares. 'You must never trust any man who says this but I have never had unprotected sex before.'

She smiled, both at his seriousness and his contradiction. 'I trust you, Draco. I wouldn't be here if I didn't.'

He matched the smile, his whole gorgeous, rugged face lighting with it. 'And I must trust you, too, to even suggest this.'

If she'd thought her heart was swollen before...

And then the smile faded. 'I'm afraid of hurting you.'

'You won't.' She pressed her mouth to his and gently coaxed his lips apart before breathing into him, 'Make love to me, Draco.'

His next kiss was tender and lingering. Closing her eyes, she sank into it...sank into him. Sank into her trust of him.

She tasted divine, Draco thought dimly as he slid his mouth down the arch of her graceful neck. A taste and scent made entirely for him. So soft, too, her skin like butter, and his fingers glided down her sides with the sensation that she was the first woman they'd ever touched,

and in his head the dawning, almost overwhelming comprehension that her virginity wasn't just an abstract entity
but something very real, that this was her first time, that
his were the first fingers to glide down her buttery skin.
When he took one of her breasts, so much fuller than he'd
imagined, into his mouth, the knowledge he was the first
man to have done this to her, the first man to hear her soft
moan of pleasure...

The sound of that moan didn't just dive into his loins
but into his chest.

He lifted his head to look at her...he could look at
her for ever. 'You're perfect, Athena. Never let anyone
tell you differently.' And then he took her other breast
in his mouth, encircling her nipple with long strokes of
his tongue, bringing it to a peak, slowly laving and sucking and licking, alert to all her responses, her moans, the
hitches of her breath, the elongation of her neck.

As if time were an infinite resource, he gently explored
the rest of her exquisiteness, making love to her with his
hands and his mouth, all the way down to her pretty toes.

Foreplay had always been an enjoyable transaction, but
ultimately just a transaction, the payment of the starter
for the enjoyment of the main course. Nothing felt trans-
actional about this.

Transcendent...

The word floated into his mind as he tenderly kissed
his way up her succulent inner thighs before gently parting them. For the first time, he sensed a tension in her
and looked up.

She met his stare. Her beautiful face was flushed, her
jaw tight.

'Do you want me to stop?'

She expelled a ragged breath and shook her head.

He gazed at her a beat longer before softly smiling. 'Close your eyes, my sweet, and just feel.'

Swallowing, she rested her head back on the pillow and reached a hand for him. Threading his fingers through hers, he breathed in the musky scent of her desire before putting his mouth to the most intimate part of her.

If Draco hadn't been holding her hand Athena thought she might have bolted out of pure fear at the intimacy of what he was doing to her. But he *was* holding her hand, and having his fingers laced through hers grounded her, reminded her it was Draco doing all these wonderful things to her, and so she closed her eyes and let him carry her away to a brand-new realm.

He opened her like a flower in bloom, touching and kissing her in a place she'd never even touched herself, fear wrapping her desire so tightly that until Draco had come into her life she'd thought it missing, had been *glad* of it.

But it had been in her all along, waiting for Draco to unwrap it, and now heat was pulsing deep in her pelvis, the strokes of his tongue building sensation upon sensation, pulling her towards a shimmering precipice that...

Sensing she was on the brink of orgasm, Draco pulled away, denying them both the rapture of her climaxing in his mouth. *Next time*, he silently promised her as he kissed his way back up her belly and between her breasts and grazed his mouth up her neck. For this, her first time, he needed her to be as ready for him as she could be.

He positioned himself between her legs and kissed her gently.

Her eyes were a darker, deeper shade of green than he'd ever seen before, almost liquid in her desire, her breathing ragged.

'You are so beautiful,' he murmured as he gently parted her thighs. 'Raise your bottom for me.'

Wordlessly, her eyes not leaving his, she did as he asked while he took hold of his arousal and positioned it at the entrance of her slick, swollen heat.

Her eyes widened and her breath hitched.

'Trust me, my sweet,' he whispered, covering her mouth with his. 'I'll take care of you, I promise.'

Propped on an elbow to keep himself steady and in control, he kissed her sweet mouth as slowly, slowly, he fed his way inside her. Draco knew he was bigger than most men, knew for this to work and to become an experience Athena would treasure for the rest of her life that he had to take his time, but, God, the sensation of being bare for the first time in his life intensified everything. He could *feel* everything, every stretch of her tight muscles as they adjusted to his slow filling of her, and all the while he kissed her with the same sensuality that he was taking her, slow burn kisses that deepened with every deceptively lazy stroke of their tongues. So deeply concentrated was he on making it as comfortable and good for her as it could be that he knew the exact moment he pushed through the final barrier a semi-beat before he heard the short suck of her breath.

He stilled a moment, giving her time to adjust, only continuing his slow inch inside her when her lips parted against his and her arms wrapped around him in silent encouragement.

Other than the fleeting moment of discomfort, the pleasure consuming Athena was beyond anything she could have dreamed, and she opened herself up to him, heart, body and soul, until their groins were fused as tightly as their mouths and he was fully in her and on her, as close as two people could ever be, and her body was throbbing and it was all so breathtakingly wonderful that she could cry from the heady beauty of it.

With the same control that he'd filled her, he began to move, slow, measured thrusts that carried her higher and higher until the pleasure became almost more than she could endure and she slipped over the shimmering precipice, sobbing Draco's name, her heart on fire and her body convulsed in rapture, and when he joined her there, shuddering as he spilt his seed deep inside her, the only words to echo in her head were that she loved him. Loved him. Loved him. Loved him.

Loved him.

Draco's heart was thumping violently, trying to escape the confines of his ribs.

He could feel the thrash of her heart, too, right below where his beat. He could almost fool himself into believing their hearts were trying to find each other.

He blew out a quiet, ragged breath. He knew he should ask if she was okay, but couldn't find the words, not just to ask but to speak at all. From her uncharacteristic silence, Athena was struggling to speak too.

He hadn't just felt her climax, he'd lived it. It had pulled him over the edge when he hadn't even known he'd reached it.

He'd never experienced anything like that before. Nothing came close.

There was no telling how long they lay there, Athena curled into him, the fingers of her hand not threaded through his making soft circles on his chest, the fingers of his hand not threaded through hers combing through her silky hair. He knew they needed to get up but his body was in no rush to move.

Maybe they would have spent the whole day like that, but the real world intruded with the sound of a ringing phone.

He felt the breath of her sigh against his skin. 'That's mine,' she said with another sigh and lifted her head.

Their stares locked together.

His heart clenched.

With her hair all mussed and her beautiful face all sleepy and content, she'd never been more beautiful.

She smiled that beautiful soft smile and kissed him with the same softness.

His heart clenched again to watch her pick the towel up from the floor and wrap it around herself, a reminder that only a short while ago she'd never been with a man, that for all her risqué clothing, she was shy about her body. Shy because no one had seen it before. No one but him.

Only when the towel was secure did she pad to the dressing table where she'd left her bag and pull her phone out.

She cleared her throat and brightly said, 'Hi, Grace.' She listened a moment. 'Oh, really?' Another listening pause. 'No, I've only just woken up. Do you want me to check?' Another pause. 'Okay, hold on a minute, I'll see if I can find him… Yes, I know, not like him at all. Bit of a cheek if you ask me, seeing as you lot made it in on time.' She turned to Draco, winked and put her finger to her lips before speaking again into the phone. 'Hold on, just reaching his bedroom.' Then she put the phone by her side, banged loudly on her own bedroom door and yelled, 'Are you up yet? If not, get up—the board meeting starts in thirty minutes and you're going to make us late. You, not me, so don't blame me for your tardiness.'

Phone back to her ear, she said, 'I can hear movement.

I'll let you know when we're on our way.' She listened again, nodding wisely. 'Definitely. See you soon. 'Bye.'

The call ended, she looked again at Draco. Her cheeks coloured. 'Was that okay?' Hints of uncertainty and shyness crept into her voice. 'I didn't think you'd want me to tell her you were in my bed.'

Although they both knew this was undoubtedly true, he couldn't bring himself to agree with her. 'What time is it?'

'Eight-thirty.'

He pinched the bridge of his nose. He hadn't realised it was that late. His fault for leaving his phone, which he used as an alarm clock, in his bedroom.

He was never late. Ever.

Still standing by the dressing table, her top teeth were biting into her bottom lip.

'Are you okay?'

She shook her head and confessed, 'I don't know what I'm supposed to do.'

He could think of a few things...

But no, he needed to pull his head out of the sex and Athena stupor it had fallen into and put it back in the game. That didn't stop him swinging his feet to the floor and opening his arms to her. 'You can start by coming here.'

Obeying, she stood between his feet and rested her hands lightly on his shoulders.

Squeezing her hips, he gazed into her eyes. 'What happens now is that you and I take a shower and go to work. When we're done for the day, we come back home and do whatever you want to do.'

'So you think you might want to share a bed with me again?'

If she hadn't been still so shy and uncertain he would think she was joking.

He pulled her closer and trapped her between his thighs. 'If you thought you were tethered to me before, you have no idea what it's going to be like now. I'm not letting you out of my sight for a second, and if you weren't likely sore from what we just shared, I'd make love to you again right now...' He gripped the top of her towel and pulled it down, exposing her succulent breasts. Taking one into his mouth, he sucked the rosy-pink nipple, bringing it to arousal.

Gazing back into her eyes, he slipped his hand between her thighs and lightly cupped her sex.

She swayed, her fingers tightening their grip on his shoulders.

Gently massaging her nub, already lubricated from their earlier lovemaking, he closed his lips over her other nipple. Her moan of pleasure landed straight in his groin, but he ignored it. Between licks and sucks of her breasts and with a steadily increasing pressure of his thumb, he whispered, 'What you and I did earlier is only the beginning. A taster.' He turned his hand so the top of his palm was doing the massaging, and slipped a finger inside her sticky heat. 'There is a whole world of pleasure out there, my sweet...' her hips were rocking against his hand '... and I'm going to teach you all of it. Now, let yourself go...' Her breaths shortening, she cradled his head and pressed her cheek to his. 'That's it, my princess,' he encouraged hoarsely, maintaining the pressure but letting her find the rhythm she needed, entranced at how damned responsive she was to him. 'All the way. Let yourself go.'

When she came, it was with a long cry before her lips found his cheek and sucked, and her whole body spasmed until, finally, she went limp.

Moving his hand, he held her tightly, stroking her back, thinking he might have to consider having her moved to a different office because he didn't know how the hell he was going to concentrate on a damned bit of work with his beautiful, sexually receptive Athena sharing the same walls as him.

'Draco?' she whispered a long while later.

'Yes, my sweet.'

'Can I ask you something?'

'As if you need my permission.'

She finally pulled her face away from his cheek and gently replaced it with her hand, kissing him with a reverence that made his heart sing. And then she grinned. 'Now that I'm sleeping with the boss, does that mean I get a pay rise?'

Laughing, he wrapped her back into his arms and kissed her hard. 'Only if you do some bloody work.'

He was still laughing to himself when he stepped under the showerhead in his bathroom, having thought it best to shower separately to Athena, seeing as he'd just proved he was already incapable of keeping his hands to himself when he was with her.

For the first time in his working life, he didn't care that he was going to be late for work. The only thing he cared about was how the hell he was supposed to keep his hands off her in the office and keep things professional enough that no one suspected what was going on between them.

Athena replaced her mascara with her lip gloss and smeared it over her lips, then stepped back to check her appearance from all angles. She'd chosen a grey scoop-necked dress that fell to mid-thigh and would fit in any office environment but, so Draco didn't think she was going soft, paired it with a three-inch thick hot-pink leather belt with diamonds studded into it and purple tights. For her feet, she chose a pair of six-inch red heels that even she had to concentrate to walk in. She had a feeling she was going to have to do a lot of concentrating that day, mostly in an effort to stop her face showing her feelings.

Reminding herself that she was a professional at hiding her feelings didn't bring any solace. For the first time since she was a little girl, she didn't want to hide them.

It was imperative that she did, for Draco's sake.

Just to think his name was to make her heart skip.

Just to spend forty minutes getting ready for work in a different room was to miss him.

Had she fallen in love with him?

When she'd climaxed the first time, her heart had spoken it to her, but now her brain was engaged and she had to remind herself that falling in love with him was the worst thing she could do. Draco wasn't hers to love and he never would be.

But he was hers to love for now, she decided, cheering herself up, and she would love him until her contract ended and she returned to her old life. That was if she even went back to her old life. For the first time since her brother had laid down the law, the thought of returning to her old life with all its riches and splendour and backbiting and bitching—and she was well aware that she was the cause of much of that backbiting and bitching—made her feel queasy.

Her family brought out the worst in her. Draco brought out the best, and if she only had him for these few short weeks then she would make the most of those short weeks, and she would love him with everything she had. But never tell him. That would be the worst thing she could do.

She had a feeling that seeing his pity for her love might just kill her.

CHAPTER ELEVEN

WAS HE IMAGINING things or was Athena doing the unthinkable and actually working?

Curiosity...and the compulsion to be close enough to breathe her perfume in...had Draco crossing the office floor to her desk. Though she kept her head down, he knew from the slight shift in her body language that she was aware of his every step towards her.

She lifted her gaze and fixed him with an imperious stare that was even more effective with the gold horn-rimmed glasses she was wearing and which she absolutely did not need. 'Can I help you?'

Arousal twinged strongly, a state of affairs that seemed to be getting worse rather than better. He'd assumed that after another night of marathon lovemaking he might be a little less like a horny dog, but no. That Athena was wearing a pink frilly blouse, grey waistcoat and tie, and a grey skirt that, whilst perfectly respectable in length—for Athena—still showed off the glorious length of her legs didn't help. For some unfathomable reason, it was easier to concentrate when he could see the colour of her underwear than when it was left to his imagination, and this was despite him knowing perfectly well that she was wearing purple lace. It was also easier to concentrate when she wore her hair loose than tied in a severe bun with a pink ribbon, as she wore it today. All he could imagine was pulling that ribbon out and watching her hair tumble down.

Propping himself on the edge of her desk next to the ream of paper she was working through, he murmured, 'Nothing that wouldn't get me arrested for indecency.'

She gave an extremely prim blink. 'Excuse me?'

'I said I'm just checking in to see what you're doing.'

'I thought that's what you said. As you can see, I'm still going through all the email addresses on this printout and cross-matching them with the unsubscribed names on the database. It's very riveting and, I'm sure, extremely necessary and worthwhile.'

He wanted to yank at that tie and pull her to him. 'If you're bored, I can think of something to pass the time.'

Her expression was as severe as her bun. 'And what would that be?'

She was driving him insane. This was their fourth full day in California, their fourth day as lovers, and his desire for her was accelerating rather than settling.

Their first day in the office had been unsettling. He'd never had an affair with any of his staff before, let alone with someone as unpredictable as Athena, but that first day she'd clearly made a concerted effort to behave entirely normally around him. Only when they were alone and their eyes met across the office floor did she allow any of her inner feelings to show. Just a look but it was enough to fill his chest and shoot his concentration. Their second day...those looks had increased. Whenever she'd put a cup of coffee on his desk, she'd skimmed her fingers over his hand before sashaying back to her desk. He'd come within an inch of pulling her onto his lap.

The third day had been worse.

Today, their fourth day, he'd made the mistake of watching her dress before they'd left for the office. It had been a reverse striptease that had turned him on so much he was still suffering the effects of the arousal she'd induced. Athena had proven herself a very willing, enthusiastic student in the art of sex. Very willing. Very enthusiastic.

And now he, the man who'd spent every day of his working life with one hundred per cent focus, was struggling to find even ten per cent focus on anything but Athena.

He leaned forward and breathed in her perfume, fisting his hands to stop himself from reaching for her tie. 'Nothing that wouldn't get me slapped with a sexual harassment lawsuit.'

Her eyes darkened, but even as colour stained her cheeks, she lifted her chin. 'Then I suggest you return to your desk before you do or say something that forces me to sue you for more money than I could spend in a lifetime.'

He gave a low growl. 'I'm starting to think the financial hit would be worth it.'

There was a knock on the door, immediately followed by Grace walking into the office...and stopping short when she saw Draco sitting on Athena's desk. 'Am I interrupting something?'

'Not at all,' he denied smoothly, ignoring Athena's flaming cheeks. 'Athena was just complaining about boredom so I've decided it's time to give my ears a rest and give her something she can get her teeth into. The agenda for next month's AGM—print off the English translation and give it to her to proofread.'

He didn't know which woman looked the most gobsmacked.

'It turns out our airhead is fluent in English,' he explained as he strode back to his desk, 'so let's make use of her talents while we've still got her.' He took his seat. 'What did you want me for?'

If Grace was suspicious, she hid it well. 'Diego's flight's been delayed so I've rearranged your lunch for dinner.' Diego Guardiola was the Spanish owner of a social media site fighting to join the ranks of the big American-led behemoths in the social media world and wanted to use the system Draco's company had been developing that made age verification over ninety-nine per cent foolproof.

He cursed inwardly but kept his features even. 'You've booked Delevingnes?'

'Provisionally, yes. He's brought his PA with him and wants her to join you. Do you want me to come, too, to even the numbers?'

'Probably best. Include a place for Athena too,' he added casually. 'It will do her good to see something of the area, other than my villa and this office.'

'I've been to California loads of times,' she piped up from the other side of the room.

Not only was she bilingual, a superb artist and had a better memory than an elephant, but she also had better hearing than a bat.

'You've been to Miami,' he stated.

'Exactly.' She gave that beatific smile. 'You should look at moving your American headquarters there—the shopping is amazing.'

Biting his cheek to stop himself from laughing, he turned his attention back to Grace. 'Anything else?'

'No. I'll confirm the reservation with Delevingnes and print the agenda off.'

As soon as Grace closed the door, Athena's stare landed on him like a laser. 'An *airhead*?'

He shrugged and mimicked one of the many faces she

liked to pull. 'Isn't that the impression you always like to give people?'

She harumphed.

He laughed. 'I know you're not an airhead. You're much cleverer and shrewder than you let people think... I think you might be the smartest person I know.'

For a moment Athena's tongue tied itself in a way it hadn't done in days, and when she felt heat crawl over her cheeks, for once it wasn't embarrassment or desire but pleasure.

Draco thought she was the smartest person he knew!

He wouldn't think she was so smart if he knew she'd fallen in love with him, but seeing as she'd vowed to keep that to herself, there was no need for his estimation to dip again.

She hugged her love for him tight in her heart and there it stayed, happy just to be with him. Not only was Athena a pro at hiding emotions she didn't want to reveal, but she was also excellent at not thinking about things that hurt, and as the day her contract with Draco ended meant the end of them, and very likely hurt, she didn't let herself think about it. Better to take each day as it came and enjoy the ride while it lasted because it would be the only ride she'd ever go on.

Draco was a one-off. She didn't know if him being Cora's son had made her more receptive to loving him, but he was and she did. She loved him for being Cora's son and she loved him for being Draco. For opening her heart and for seeing through the façade she'd constructed all those years ago and bringing her out of the shell she'd locked herself into for self-protection.

'If I'm so smart then how come I didn't think to pack something suitable for a business dinner?' she said.

She smiled at the narrowing of his eyes and his, 'You brought four suitcases of clothes with you.'

'I know! Aren't I an airhead!'

'You want to go shopping?'

'For business purposes, which means you should let me go on my lunch break and if I'm not back within my allocated time not go all Draco on me.'

He gave her the stern look she so adored.

'Of course, I can go straight from work if you'd prefer, but I was really hoping my sexy boss lover would take me straight home and spend a couple of hours screwing my airheaded brains out before heading out to dinner...' Holding his stare, she shrugged nonchalantly and was rewarded with a pained stare.

'Are you trying to kill me?'

Loving the sensual power she had over him, she fingered her tie...she'd seen the way he'd looked at it...and was about to answer with something that probably *would* kill him when Grace came back into the office.

'The AGM,' she said, placing the papers on Athena's desk. 'If you could highlight any translation errors and place Xs on the right-hand side of the sentences you find them on, that would be perfect.'

'No worries.' Pulling her head back into Office Land, she took a moment to look at the sheets of paper and compose her features. She had a feeling Grace knew something was going on between her and Draco and didn't want to prove it. She also knew perfectly well this translation was another pointless exercise, but she had the feeling, too, that if she did it well, she might be given less pointless translation work going forward. She wasn't sure how she felt about that.

'Grace,' she called as the PA made to leave the office. 'Do you know where the best shopping districts locally are?'

Grace named a couple of shopping malls and a boulevard.

Athena beamed. 'Great. I'm taking an extended lunch to buy something reasonably suitable for tonight's business dinner and you're coming with me.'

'That's out of the question. I have far too much work to do.'

'But I need supervision, and also, you need to buy something, too, because this is a business dinner, and we both need to dress the part. Draco said we can use the company credit card.' She deliberately did not look at him as she said this. 'Come on, Grace—you never take a break. I bet he owes you a million hours' overtime.'

'Just go with her,' Draco cut in, a mingling of amusement and resignation in his gruff tone. 'At least this way we can be reasonably certain she'll be back in time for the meal.'

Draco had been played. Outwitted. Outsmarted. And all by the woman he'd once believed to be a vacuous airhead.

On the plus side, without Athena's distracting presence, he got through more work in three hours than he had in the last three and a half days...but then his attention wandered back to her and he reached for the AGM agenda she'd proofread and set on his desk for him to look through before sashaying off to go shopping on work time.

One glance told him she could add eagle-eyed to her list of attributes. She didn't miss anything. And then he reached the third page and his stomach lurched. She'd encircled the name Cora and placed a sticky note above it with an arrow pointing to it. On the sticky note, she'd written in elegant writing:

I guessed you'd planned something like this. Cora Shipping is perfect. Your mother will love it and Rebecca and my father will hate it. I promise to do my best to keep my mouth shut until the big reveal x

He rubbed his eyes before reading the note a third time, searching for any hidden meaning in her words.

Had he ordered she proofread this document subconsciously knowing she would see it and so could be prepared for the fallout that was bound to happen because of it? And there would be a fallout. The change of name was going to be revealed at the party he was throwing to celebrate his purchase of the company. The whole Tsaliki family, the entire shipping world, international business media and most of Greek society would be there, Georgios Tsaliki's friends and peers, all there to witness the great Tsaliki name vanish into the annals of history, replaced by the name of the woman they'd left destitute out of spite. They would be forced to smile and act as if they didn't care when Draco knew they would be spitting with fury and injured pride.

He only realised how quiet the place had become when Athena bounded back in half an hour before they were due to leave the office. 'Sorry we took so long,' she said brightly, 'but I managed to get us into a salon for a cut and dry.'

Her hair did indeed look a bit bouncier than normal but nothing particularly noticeable, but then he caught sight of Grace hovering behind her, red-faced with embarrassment, and he understood in an instant what Athena had done.

The Grace who'd left the office with Athena was a thirty-five-year-old woman who looked a good decade older. She'd returned looking a decade younger.

'You put it on the card?' he said, not missing a beat.

'Of course!'

'And you both found an outfit for the evening?'

'Yes, and you'll be delighted to know Grace only let me buy one outfit and only gave it her stamp of approval when she was satisfied my knickers weren't showing.'

As if the moment couldn't get more surreal, Grace giggled. Grace, who barely ever raised a smile, giggled like a schoolgirl.

Shaking his head, he looked at his watch. 'Right, ladies, let's call it a day.'

As they left the building and Draco and Athena were heading to their car, he turned back to his right-hand woman. 'Your hair looks great, by the way.'

Grace went pink with happiness.

Alone in the car, he reached for Athena's hand. 'That was all for Grace, wasn't it.'

He loved that she didn't pretend not to understand. 'Not entirely. I haven't been shopping since you sent me off to buy *appropriate work attire.*'

He flashed a grin. 'You're learning the art of subtlety.'

'Only with people who deserve it. Grace is friendly to me now.'

'Only because you're being friendly to her.'

'But that's only because you basically ordered me to.'

'I didn't order you to take her shopping and give her a makeover.'

'She needed it. You work her too hard—she never has the time to pamper herself or just generally look after herself. She lives on caffeine, junk food and nervous exhaustion.'

'She's my best employee and I pay her an excellent salary.'

'Which is great but she doesn't have the time to spend it. She's always in the office before us and is still there when you take me home, and yes, I know you continue working when you go home but it's your company. Grace is an employee and at the rate she's going, she's going to burn out.'

He didn't point out that he'd done minimal work in the evenings while they'd been in California. 'You've given this a lot of thought.'

'Not really. It just seems obvious.'

'Like it seemed obvious that I was going to change Tsaliki Shipping's name?' he dropped in casually.

'Obvious to me,' she agreed. 'What else was there if you weren't prepared to dismantle the whole organisation?'

'Doesn't it bother you at all? When it's gone, your family name will diminish into nothing.' Her brother Alexis had a multi-billion empire of his own but none of the businesses under its umbrella bore his name.

'A little bit, but that's more for my father's sake than mine. He's a lousy father, but he's still my father and he built the business from the ground up. And I'm sorry but the Tsaliki name isn't going to diminish into nothing, not for generations. I can imagine being in my nineties and people still associating my name with wildness and debauchery.'

He couldn't disagree with that. Of all the Tsaliki offspring, Athena's name was the one everyone knew. It didn't matter what the truth behind the façade was—her reputation preceded her and she would carry it for the rest of her life.

Delevingnes was an upscale French restaurant in the heart of San Jose with a no-phones policy that meant patrons had to talk to each other rather than bury their faces in their screens. For a semi-formal business dinner, it was perfect, and Athena spent an age poring over the menu, mostly to avoid Diego Guardiola's stare.

She'd seen the recognition in his eyes even before the introductions were made, seen the cynical smile that had played on his lips as he weighed her up. She knew his sort, and a few months ago she would have made eyes back and flirted outrageously with him, would have let him believe she wanted him and then taken great pleasure in stringing him along, followed in short order with dumping him.

It wasn't just that she didn't want to be that woman any more—and she didn't—it was that she didn't think she could *be* that woman now. The thought of even brushing cheeks with another man made her stomach turn.

The only person she wanted to flirt with was Draco. The only person she would ever want to flirt with was Draco. Unfortunately, the way they'd been placed around the cosy round table, with Draco two to her left, meant direct eye contact was difficult unless specifically looking at each other. It was Diego, sitting to Draco's left, who was directly in front of her and, though the bulk of his conversation was with Draco, his stare rarely left her. It made her skin crawl.

Sandwiched between Grace and Diego's PA Josefina, she felt like a spare wheel. Josefina spoke excellent English and spent the meal talking over Athena to pepper half-English Grace with questions about American working practices and customs in comparison to European ones and whether her boss should take the plunge as she was encouraging him to do and move his business to California.

Having zero interest in working time directives and corporate sustainability, Athena tuned them out, only perking up and zoning back in when she detected flirtation between the two women. Who knew a decent haircut and an eyebrow and moustache threading—Athena had pretended her non-existent one needed doing so Grace would feel more comfortable and natural doing hers—could give someone such instant confidence? Grace looked amazing and she knew it, and it had lifted her, making her glow from the inside out.

Maybe she could start her own makeover business, Athena mused. Take a dowdy, unconfident woman and coax her into being the best version of herself. She could work on Evangeline in the finance department next. She was quite sure Evangeline walked with her head bowed because she knew her clothes were all wrong for her and not because she was worried about tripping over her own feet. Next payday, she'd badger Evangeline into going shopping with her and steer her into the stores that catered for the fuller figure with more than racks of unflattering colour-clashing tents for their customers to choose from.

Yes, a makeover business could be feasible. She loved her art, but it was also a stress release and a way of expressing her bottled-up emotions. She didn't want to make a career of it because then it would become work and all the things that made it special to her would be lost.

She had a very strong feeling that when the time came to say goodbye to Draco she'd need her charcoal more than ever.

The deal Draco was chatting through with Diego Guardiola could, if the stars aligned, be an incredibly lucrative one. However, if Diego didn't stop looking at Athena as if he wanted to eat her, Draco might just give in to the urge to break his wrist, and then the only lucrative thing would be the lawyers' fees when Diego sued him for assault.

He could understand why the Spaniard was taking such a blatant interest in her—Athena was beautiful, and that evening the V-necked purple wrap dress she wore showcased her spectacular figure while managing to be reasonably demure. She looked incredible. But just because he understood Diego's interest did not mean he had to like it and he especially did not like the predatory nature of it.

It was when Athena had disappeared to the ladies' and the coffee was being poured that Diego casually said in an undertone, 'Is the Tsaliki girl staying at the Hemsworth?'

Draco's hackles, already on alert, rose to red flag, but he didn't let his amiable expression change, smoothly replying, 'Athena is staying in my home as my guest.'

Diego looked him up and down. 'Is that what you call it?'

'Athena is my employee,' he said through teeth he only just stopped himself from gritting.

Diego dropped his voice and leaned into him. 'If she was my employee I'd move her into my house too. I hear she goes all night and then demands more for breakfast.'

Now his teeth did clench, and it took all his control not to clench his fists with them. 'I can assure you, the stories you have heard about her are wide of the mark.'

'I doubt it. That one has no morals. She seduced her brother-in-law.'

'She doesn't have a brother-in-law.'

'Thanasis Antoniadis,' Diego answered with a knowing smile. 'He's married to her stepsister. She was seen leaving his office weeks before the wedding. Rumour has it, he had lipstick on his collar.'

'And where did this rumour originate, other than in the gutter?' he asked icily.

'Don't shoot the messenger. I'm just relaying what I've

heard and, from what I've heard, the rumours originate from within Antoniadis Shipping.' He laughed. 'You can't be surprised by it—that slut will sleep with anyone.'

The anger that had been rising morphed into a scalding rage that pumped every muscle in his body and contorted his face into a snarl. Bringing his face right up to Diego's, he spoke in a quiet, venomous tone. 'You should know better than to repeat rumour as fact and if I hear you repeat it I'll break your wrist, and if I ever hear you speak about Athena again in such a degrading way...if I even hear her name from your mouth... I'll break your fucking neck.'

As he rose to his feet, ready to draw the waiter's attention and tell him to give the bill to the Spanish bastard, he turned his head and saw Athena stock-still, barely two feet behind him. From the tightness of her features, her bat hearing meant she'd heard every word.

CHAPTER TWELVE

ATHENA CLIMBED INTO the back of the car with Grace and Draco. She felt sick. The evening had gone to hell, and now Draco sat in brooding silence, Grace in less brooding silence but clearly thinking about Josefina and wondering if the poison that had erupted between their respective bosses meant the first shoots of romance between them had been trodden on. Athena's silence came because she didn't know what to say. An evening that had started with high expectations of a lucrative deal had ended terribly, and it was all her fault.

The goodnights exchanged with Grace when they dropped her at the hotel were muted.

The knots of guilt making Athena nauseous tightened, and she side-eyed Draco and wished she could read what he was thinking. He must be deeply regretting inviting her to the dinner.

After a long beat of silence he stiffly said, 'I apologise for what you heard. You can rest assured I will not be doing business with that man.'

The guilt knotted even tighter. 'But I thought it was a good deal that had the potential to make you a lot of money?'

'I cannot do business with a man like that.'

She could hear the anger still underlying his rough tone.

That he'd stood up for her, had been so furious on her behalf…

For that, she could only love him more.

'Draco,' she said quietly, 'don't throw the deal away because of me. What Diego told you was true. I did try to seduce Thanasis.'

She felt him tense beside her.

'That's why I was banned from their wedding and banned from my nephew's christening. I tried to steal Thanasis for myself, and now Lucie and Thanasis won't let me set foot on Sephone or be at any family event they're attending.'

There was a long exhalation of shocked breath. 'When did this all happen?'

'Last summer.' She rested her head back and closed her eyes. She owed him the full story and if he hated her for it then she had no one to blame but herself. 'Do you remember all the negative headlines last year when the war between my father and Thanasis's father hit the press?'

The Antoniadis and Tsaliki patriarchs had been at war for decades but a year or so earlier their escalating methods of retaliatory fire had made headline news, causing both of their shipping companies serious reputational and financial difficulties.

'I remember.'

'The wedding was a sham to calm the investors.'

'I had my suspicions,' Draco said slowly, remembering how the engagement between Thanasis Antoniadis and Georgios Tsaliki's beloved stepdaughter Lucie had caused many suspicious raised eyebrows, 'but if it's all a sham then they're damn good actors.'

Along with the rest of Greek society, Draco had attended the eventual wedding—a car accident involving the bride meant the initial date had been postponed—and it was at the reception that Draco had first approached Alexis, who'd taken control of Tsaliki Shipping and was steering it back to robust health, about buying the company. It was also at the wedding that Draco's intuition that none of the Tsalikis associated his name with his mother had been confirmed…all except one Tsaliki, who had not only associated it but known exactly who he was.

But that one Tsaliki hadn't been at the wedding. This absence had been explained by the family telling everyone Athena had Covid, and now she was telling him she'd been barred from attending.

His guts roiled heavily.

'They fell in love for real,' she said.

He had to fight to keep his voice steady. 'Did you know that when you tried to break them up?'

Her voice fell to barely a whisper. 'They were still at the stage of hating each other but I knew Lucie had fallen for him.'

He pinched the bridge of his nose. It had been too easy to fool himself into believing the Athena he'd got to know was the 'real' Athena and forget who she'd always been. 'Is that why you did it?'

She was silent for a long time. 'I would love to tell you that had nothing to do with it, but it played its part. I've loved and hated Lucie since she came into my life. I suppose I loved her because I couldn't help but love her—I want to say she's a horrible bitch like Rebecca but she isn't—but I hated her for stealing my life, and when I learned Thanasis had wanted to marry me, I blamed her for stealing my future too.'

A pulse of nausea cramped his guts.

'Alexis brokered the deal. Thanasis wanted to marry me

but my father refused and so it was Lucie who was pushed forward to marry him instead, and I hated her for it.'

'You *wanted* to marry him?'

'Yes, and when I learned I'd been his first choice I decided to make it happen.'

'Even though you knew she was in love with him?'

'Even though I knew she was in love with him,' she echoed.

He felt Athena's stare fall on him through the darkness. 'I went to his offices and tried to seduce him. He rejected me, and so I went to Lucie and told her the truth, that the only reason she'd been pushed forward for the role of marrying Thanasis was because my father wouldn't let his real daughter marry the devil's spawn.'

Just when he'd thought there was nothing about Athena that could shock him... 'Why would you act so cruelly?'

Her voice caught. 'Because I'm an evil bitch and hurting people is my default, and you shouldn't throw away a deal with Diego out of a misplaced sense of honour for me. He didn't say anything the rest of Europe doesn't think, and if he's heard that I tried to seduce Thanasis into dumping Lucie and marrying me instead then that means it's leaked and probably everyone's heard it.'

He swore under his breath. His head was pounding, guts as cramped as they'd ever been. 'So everything you've told me has been bullshit and all along you wanted Thanasis.'

'No,' she refuted, swallowing. 'I leapt at the chance of marrying him out of spite for Lucie and because I knew he would never push for the marriage to be consummated. I could have the big white wedding I'd always dreamed of without a proper groom and be the centre of attention.'

'You tried to seduce him,' he stated through gritted

teeth. Even to think of Athena putting her lips to another man's collar sharpened the cramping in his guts and pushed blood roaring into his head.

'At his office, where there was no danger of it being taken further than I could bear. Thanasis is a gentleman. He was safe. I knew if I told him no for the whole two years the marriage was agreed to last that he would respect that and never try to force himself on me.' There was another catch in her voice. 'So not only am I a bitch but I'm a selfish, vindictive bitch. I spent over twenty years waiting for an opportunity to hurt Lucie and when it came, I took it. I felt that she took my place in my own life, and I was so jealous that both her parents wanted her so much that she spent half her time with her father in England, whereas my mother left without looking back at me and even when she moved into a house on the same street as us never seemed to want me there. I never let myself see that Lucie was a child, too, and she'd had no more say in where she lived than I did, and I hurt her deliberately when she never did *anything* to deserve it.'

The words flowed without any conscious thought, but the more they flowed, the more Athena knew they were right and the deeper the gnaw of self-loathing. Memories filled her, the two of them sneaking onto the top deck of the Tsaliki yacht in the middle of the night, gazing at the stars and talking about everything and nothing until the sun came up, making each other laugh so hard their ribs hurt.

Lucie had been the only person in the world she'd ever laughed with. Until Draco.

The silence this time was so profound that she heard Draco's hand move through the air before it covered hers and he gently squeezed.

She swallowed hard and pulled her hand away. 'Don't be nice to me, Draco, please. I don't deserve it. I hurt people. I hurt everyone. I've even hurt you and you're the best person I know.'

His voice was heavy. 'But only because of the hurt done to you.'

'That's no excuse. I'm an adult. My actions belong to me and me alone, and the consequences of them should belong to me alone too. I can't bear to think of you being tainted by your association with me.'

'If you're thinking of Diego, then don't. You're worth a million of him.'

'I'm really not. I'm a horrible person.'

The car had stopped but, instead of getting out, Draco took her hand and clasped it between both of his so she couldn't pull it away again. 'Athena, you've developed a self-awareness most people never find. You've done some awful things but that's not who you are now and it doesn't need to define you for ever.'

'How can you say that?'

'Because I can hear the pain and guilt in your voice... I can *feel* your guilt.'

She could barely choke the words out. 'Right now, I think I'm feeling a lifetime of guilt.'

How could she have done that to Lucie? She'd done so many cruel things to her over the years, their relationship a push and pull, love and hate, but to do *that*?

He brought her fingers to his mouth and gently kissed the tips. 'Then make it right. Apologise to Lucie. If she won't speak to you, write her a letter. I don't know if she'll accept it or if she'll forgive you, but I do know that the guilt will stay lodged in you until you purge it.'

'You've dealt with guilt?'

'Everyone deals with it in some form or other. The difference is your conscience has been repressed almost your whole life, but it's found you now.'

'What have you ever done to feel guilty about?'

'I wasn't there for my mother as I should have been when she lost her job and then our home. I was too wrapped up in my own life to help her or take any of the burden off her shoulders. I didn't see how much she was suffering until she had a nervous breakdown.'

Draco caught the shocked widening of her eyes and stroked her cheek. 'I've spent my adult life making it up to her but there are times when the guilt at how badly I let her down still catches me.' He'd been powerless to help her, as powerless as he'd been when she'd lost her job and they'd lost their home.

'I bet she doesn't want you to feel guilty.'

He smiled. 'You're right, she doesn't.'

She gazed into his eyes. 'It would have been very easy for you to destroy my entire family in vengeance for what my father and Rebecca did.'

'Very easy,' he agreed. 'But then I'd have had to deal with the guilt of all the innocent victims on my conscience.'

'How can you stand to employ any of us or even be in a room with us?'

'I didn't think I could, but you're not your father or Rebecca and neither are your brothers, and I've come to see in our time together that you and your brothers have suffered at their hands more than anyone.'

'My brothers would disagree with that assessment.'

'I don't care about your brothers. Only you.' He pressed a kiss to her mouth then pulled away to tap at the door for his driver to open it.

* * *

Athena lay in Draco's bed, waiting for him to finish a conference call with his senior staff in Athens. Her thoughts were racing at a million kilometres an hour. She'd searched for her name and Thanasis Antoniadis but there was nothing online linking them, other than through his marriage to her stepsister. The guilt that was racking her allowed only a morsel of relief. She didn't care for her own sake if the news leaked to the wider world, but she cared deeply for Lucie's sake. Of all her family, Lucie was the one she loved the most. She was also the one she'd hated the most. That love and hate had lived side by side for over two decades, but now it was as if the hate had never existed and all that was left was the love, and a deep guilt and sorrow for the terrible way she'd treated her, not just with regard to Thanasis but all her horrible behaviour to her over the years. Of everyone she needed to make amends with, Lucie was at the top of the list.

She cared deeply, too, about the news not leaking for Draco's sake, because another search, this time of her name alongside his, had brought up rumours of them 'enjoying an affair'.

Enjoying an affair. Words that used to make her cackle with glee now sounded seedy and demeaning.

But it *was* just an affair. That had been established before it had started. There could be no future for them. That had been established too. Except…

Except she'd fallen in love with him and Draco had told her only an hour ago that he cared about her and, as foolish as she tried to tell herself that it was to hope, those words had opened her heart into hoping that maybe, just maybe, his feelings ran as deep as hers did.

Whether they did or they didn't, he had feelings for her.

He cared about her. He'd turned his back on a potential multi-million—even billion—deal out of anger over the way she'd been spoken of. And he'd listened to her darkest confession. He'd listened. And he'd understood. Understood her. Understood who she'd been then and who she was now...well, who she was trying to be. Who she wanted to be. He seemed to have more faith than she did that the woman she was morphing into was the woman she was supposed to be.

The bedroom door opened.

A drumming set off in her chest.

He gave a weary smile. The lines on his rugged face seemed deeper than usual, exhaustion settling into the grooves.

His tie and jacket already discarded, he stripped off his shirt and headed into the bathroom. A few moments later, the shower started up.

It felt like for ever before he came back in the room, time enough for Athena's thoughts to go into overdrive as to why he hadn't invited her to join him in the shower or even kissed her before going into the bathroom.

Naked and smelling divine, he crossed the floor towards her. With no playful smile on his lips or gleam in his eye, anxiety gnawed at her, only ebbing when he slipped under the duvet, turned out the light and drew her to him.

Locked in his arms and cradled into his strength, she tried not to think that their time in California was speeding by. Soon, they would go home to Greece and all they were sharing here would be gone. She couldn't bring herself to ask if he wanted her to stay with him in his Athens home until her contract ended. Couldn't bring herself to ask anything about their future.

All the certainties she'd had, that the end of her contract meant the end of them, that the end of her contract meant her return to her old world... Neither had to be true. Draco had thrown away a multi-million deal *for her*. Was it possible that his feelings for her had developed enough that he might want her to stay in *his* world?

His arms tightened around her, a deep sigh coming from his throat. Her heart swelled so large that it threatened to lodge in *her* throat.

She didn't know how she was going to bear saying goodbye to him.

Wriggling to loosen his hold around her, she lifted her head and gazed down at him. With only silvery moonlight to see by, the rugged features she loved appeared even stronger, and she pressed a kiss to his mouth before gently kissing every line and plane of his face, nuzzling her nose into the bristles of his beard and filling her lungs with as much of his scent as she could manage, as if breathing him in so deeply meant a physical part of him would lodge into a physical part of her, and as she trailed kisses down the throat she so loved, her heart caught to imagine Draco's child growing inside her. Caught and then tightened with unbearable sharpness to admit to herself that she would never be the one to carry his child, that all her foolish hopes for the future could never come true.

When his fingers speared her hair the way that always made her stomach feel squishy, all she could think was how much she wanted...needed...to show him everything that he meant to her.

Bringing her face back to his, she kissed his mouth in a languid, sensual fusion and, as it slowly deepened and their tongues meshed, she trailed her fingers over and across his muscular chest and down the hard abdomen before trailing her tongue down his throat.

Touching and tasting him as if for the very first time, she used her body to pour out her heart to the man who'd poured sunshine into her life and taken away the pain and loneliness she'd spent a lifetime hiding from.

She couldn't tell him that she loved him but she could show him, and she drove her fingers through the dark wiry mesh of his pubic hair and took his velvet hardness into her hand. It throbbed at her grip and somehow grew even harder and bigger, and when she put it into her mouth his groan drove straight into the hot spot between her legs.

Draco would go to his grave with the memory of the first time Athena had taken him into her mouth, would never forget the shyness in her eyes when she'd asked him what he liked.

That early, untouched tentativeness had gone but there was something about the way she was making love to him now that felt like that first time. Where that first time he'd been too concerned with her enjoying it to allow his brain to fully switch off, this time she was so fully engrossed in pleasuring him, her movements so tender and passionate, that all he could do was close his eyes and savour the sensations she was evoking, let them drive out the poison that had lodged in his veins, not at Athena's confession of deliberately hurting her stepsister but her confession that she'd wanted to marry Thanasis.

That had been jealousy he'd felt. There was no other explanation for the red-hot rush of blood to his head and the vice-like grip in his guts. That it came hot on the heels of the red-hot rush of blood to his head at Diego's inflammatory words about her had left Draco feeling as far from himself as he'd ever felt, as if there was something alien burrowed beneath his skin.

Let that feeling be purged by Athena's passion. Let it all be driven out of him.

Kneeling between his legs, she took him deep into her mouth, using her hands as well as her mouth to pleasure him, her hair falling like a blonde cloud over his stomach and thighs. Groaning his pleasure, he submitted himself entirely to the bliss of Athena. The sensations were incredible...*incredible*.

She was incredible, and when she laved her tongue back up his chest and gently bit a nipple with her teeth before straddling him and sinking onto his length, euphoria flooded him and he lifted his head and caught her face in his hands, kissing her hard enough to bruise both their mouths.

Lying back down, he gazed at her with glazed eyes as she began to ride him. Hands on his chest, her own glazed stare focused entirely on him, she rode his length with breathless moans that lengthened until her nails dug into his chest and she cried out and he experienced the glorious sensation of Athena's orgasm tightening and spasming around his hardness and pulling him deeper into her. But it wasn't enough for him to let go, too, not yet, not this time.

Like a drug to him, he needed more of her, much more, needed *everything*, and he flipped her onto her back and roughly pushed her thighs up and apart before driving his full length inside her with one thrust.

Pinning her hands, he soaked in her flushed beauty and thrust in and out of her slick tightness, driving himself as deep as he could go with deep groans he had no control of, the sensations absorbing into every crevice of his being. All abandon gone, he pounded into her, the scratching of her nails down his back and her thickening moans of pleasure and encouragement spurring him to thrust even harder, even faster, harder and faster, until he lost all control and bucked into her with a strangled cry that came from another realm, and he was taken to another realm, barely conscious that Athena was gripping his buttocks and grinding herself into him as she climaxed again, only aware that when their mouths and tongues found each other as they drew out the last ounces of the pleasure, the only thought in his head was that this was how he wanted to die.

CHAPTER THIRTEEN

THE LOOK FROM every employee Draco passed the next morning as he made his way up to his office made it clear that the incident with Diego Guardiola had already got out.

His gut instinct proved right when he entered the boardroom and found he didn't have to tell his directors that the deal with Diego was a non-starter. It took everything he had not to look at Athena, sitting where she always sat in meetings, in the corner of the room with a bottle of water in one hand and a notepad and pen she wouldn't use in the other.

Growth had always been his business mantra. He actively encouraged innovation and lateral thinking amongst his staff and welcomed debate because only by debate could bad ideas be discarded and good ones develop and flourish. He allowed no political bias or personal preferences sway decisions on what was developed or who they collaborated with. It was a rare occasion that he walked from a deal that could make him money, the last time being four years earlier when he'd caught the figurehead of the company he was looking to go into business with snorting cocaine off a keyring at eleven in the morning. His gut had already been telling him there was something off about the man and that incident had solidified his instinct.

And so walking away from a business deal that, if it had reached its full potential, could have added billions to Manolis Technology was as shocking to his staff as if he'd announced that everyone was being made redundant. His obvious bad mood meant no one spoke up to question this or ask what had gone wrong, but they filed out of the boardroom at the end of the meeting muttering between themselves.

'You look like you need coffee.'

He closed his eyes before bringing a tight smile to his face and turning to Athena, who'd moved next to him. 'A coffee would be great, thanks.'

With the utmost discretion, she stroked his hand with her little finger before darting towards Grace, who was reading something on her phone, saying, 'I'm making coffee, Grace. Want one?'

His PA looked up with a tired smile. 'Please.'

To his puzzlement, Athena then put an arm around her recent enemy for a quick hug and squeezed her hand as if in sympathy before disappearing from the boardroom.

About to ask Grace if she was okay, he stopped himself. He had enough going on in his head without adding Grace's potential problems to it. That enough was Athena.

She hadn't just infected his life but his mind. Everything he was feeling for her...it was all wrong.

He'd never lied to himself that what they were sharing wasn't serious, had never lied to himself that what he felt for her wasn't more than he'd felt for another before, but what they'd shared in his bed had blown more than his mind.

He'd lost control with her.

She'd slipped into his veins and if he didn't get her out, soon he would bleed only Athena and then he risked the potential of losing everything.

He'd walked away from a deal for her. Thrown potential billions away for her.

It was as if some kind of madness was swallowing him and if he didn't act fast it would consume him.

The tiny heat of sensation on his hand where her little finger had touched it... He rubbed his thumb over it as if it could erase the sensation and said, 'Grace, call the flight crew and tell them we're flying back to Athens this afternoon.'

'But we're not due to leave until—'

'It's not up for discussion,' he snapped. 'Just do it. I want to be in the air no later than six—make sure Theodore and Stav are packed and ready to leave on time, and call Wanda and tell her to pack Athena's stuff and arrange for it to be couriered to the airfield.'

'Whose room shall I tell her to take it from?'

It took a beat for him to understand what his PA had just said. 'If you repeat anything like that to anyone else, you're fired.'

'Do it,' she snapped back, her bottom lip trembling. 'It will save me quitting.'

'You even think of quitting on me then I really will fire you.'

She spun on her heel and stomped out of the boardroom, throwing, 'You're an arsehole,' over her shoulder.

Clenching his teeth, he grabbed his hair and pulled air in through his nose and swore under his breath. Not only did he have Athena to deal with, but he now had a moody PA to deal with too.

When the cat's away, the mice will play, and with Draco holing himself up in meetings he didn't feel the need to force her to sit through, Athena decided to play. For five minutes. That was how long it took for guilt to kick in, especially as Draco must now deem her responsible enough to be left unsupervised, and so she got her head down and did the translation work Grace had given her. It was boring but it made her feel useful and that she was playing her part, and it helped time speed along a little quicker until Draco got out of his boring meetings.

Her translation work done, she left the office to give it to Grace and found her putting her coat on. 'Where are you going?'

'To the hotel to pack. Are you done with those documents?'

'Yes. Why are you packing? Are you moving to a new hotel?'

'No, we're flying back to Greece in a few hours. That was quick work, thank you—I was going to get one of the team to scan it for me, but I can take it with me.'

'You're welcome, and since when are we flying back to Greece?'

'Since His Highness decreed it.'

'Why?'

'He didn't see fit to tell me—hasn't he mentioned it to you either?'

'No…do I need to go…' she stopped herself saying *home* by the skin of her teeth '…and pack too?'

'Wanda's getting your luggage together.' Grace planted a kiss on Athena's cheek. 'I need to go. See you on the plane.'

Athena watched Grace bustle to the elevator with a mixture of warmth fizzing through her veins at the affectionate kiss—no one ever gave her affectionate kisses—and a sense of trepidation swirling in her belly.

She'd woken to Draco's sleepy kisses, shared a shower

with him and some rather more energetic kisses…and other things…had dressed in front of him, dried her hair and made-up her face in front of him, had shared her first coffee of the day and a light breakfast with him, had travelled to work with his hand holding hers and not once had he even hinted that he was planning to cut their stay in California short.

By the time they landed in Athens, Athena's trepidation had turned into full-blown fear.

The flight home had been much like the flight out, with long meetings at the conference table and plenty of food served at regular intervals. Everyone had retired to their sleep pods earlier in the journey, and though Draco welcomed her silent presence into his narrow bed and cupped her breast as he'd spooned himself into her and his erection had rested against her pyjama-clad buttocks, she'd sensed a distance that had never been there before. She'd been unable to sleep, fully aware that he was awake, too, and that something was on his mind.

She had the awful feeling that something was her.

The journey from the airport was a reverse of the journey out, too, and it was at Athena's apartment that the driver made his first stop. With Grace sharing the ride with them, she could do nothing but wish them both a goodnight.

'Enjoy the rest of your weekend,' Grace said.

'You too,' she whispered before pulling herself together and brightly adding, 'I'm looking forward to a lot of sleep!'

As soon as she was safe inside her apartment, she sent Draco a message:

Do you want to come back to mine once you've dropped Grace off? x

His reply took too long to come.

I'll be with you in twenty minutes.

There was no kiss.

Draco took a deep breath before ringing the doorbell. One short ring.

The door opened so quickly she must have been standing on the other side, waiting for him.

One look at Athena's face and the way she was holding herself told him she'd guessed what he was going to say.

Her chin lifted and then she stood aside to let him through.

'Coffee?' she asked when they stepped into her open-plan living area that somehow seemed to have shrunk since he'd last stood in it.

'No. But thank you.' He attempted some brevity. 'I can feel jetlag coming on so caffeine probably isn't the best thing to feed it.'

She didn't smile. 'You're ending it, aren't you.'

He sighed heavily and closed his eyes. There was no beating about the bush with Athena. He would not allow himself to think that her directness was one of the many things he adored about her. He was firm in his mind that they had to end their affair now, and would not allow himself to be diverted by rogue thoughts and feelings.

He'd already succumbed to weakness on the plane when he'd held her in his arms that one last time.

'We both knew it wouldn't be for ever.'

'Can you at least look at me while you're dumping me?'

'I'm not…' He shook his head and locked his stare back

onto hers. 'We both knew before we started that it wouldn't be for ever.'

'I know. You don't have to repeat yourself. You've had your fun with me and now we're back on home soil you want to walk away.'

Her brittleness struck him like a slap. A brittle Athena meant she was hurting, and it hurt his heart to see the flicker of pain in her eyes, but it was a pain that reinforced that he was doing the right thing by ending it now. The way she'd made love to him that last night…

He wasn't the only one who'd got in over his head with their affair.

'You know it isn't like that.'

Athena just stared at him. The beats of her heart, strangely calm since he'd given the short, sharp ring of her doorbell that had confirmed her deepest fears, were getting quicker and weightier.

The broad chest she'd kissed every last millimetre of rose slowly. 'This thing between us…it's become heavier than I think either of us anticipated, but what we have isn't sustainable, we both know that. We could drag it out for the last few weeks of your contract but—'

'Drag it out? My, you do have a way with words.'

His lips tightened. 'You know what I mean.'

'I know that you made your mind up about us yesterday morning. That's why we came home early, isn't it—you didn't want to share your bed with me again. You've had your fun.'

'Stop saying that. I think you're great, Athena. You're beautiful and sexy and smart and funny—'

'Don't forget to add bilingual to your checklist of my attributes. I can create a CV with them.'

Ramming his hands into his trousers pockets, he rested

his head back against the wall. 'What do you want me to say? We both knew when—'

'If you say *we both knew* one more time I'm going to punch you in the face.'

A pained smile flickered on his face. 'You'd break a nail.'

'It would be worth it.' The weightiness in her heart was increasing, panic and agitation spreading through her like a tsunami. 'I assume you were listing my attributes for a reason—what was it? It better be something good.'

'Only that as great as you are, we've gone as far as we can go.'

'Not as good as I was hoping, but something I completely agree with.'

He eyed her warily. 'You do?'

'Of course.' Fixing the Athena-everyone-loved-to-hate smile on her face, she crossed her arms over her painfully thrashing heart. 'Did you seriously think that giving you my virginity meant anything more than sex? I'm Athena Tsaliki, remember? The slutty socialite who can be relied on to behave disgracefully in any given situation. You're a sexy man, Draco, but ultimately, that's all you are—a man, and like all men you think with the appendage between your legs.'

His flinch should have made her smile. Instead, it slashed a burn through her chest and unleashed even more of the heavy sickness destroying her through her tongue. 'What, do you think you're something special? That you're somehow more than other men? Because, I hate to tell you, you're exactly the same as the rest of them, and I include my father in that...' She laughed at the flash of anger he fired at her even as the walls surrounding her closed in tightly, compressing her into a fight or flight mode where the only option was to fight. 'You don't like to hear *that*, do you, Mr Morally Superior. Well, ask yourself this—if you're so much better than him, what the hell were you doing sleeping with his daughter? You were thinking with your dick and letting yourself be guided by it, that's what you were doing, just like my father's always done. I was a bit of fun while we were far away from those who know what a slutty socialite I am, until Diego Guardiola came along, and now that we're back on home ground...' She shook her head in mock understanding. 'Can you imagine what people will say if it's confirmed that the rumours about us are true?' She widened her eyes and clutched at her throat. 'The scandal! People you respect will question your judgement! Your fellow billionaires, the ones you do business with who are all perfect paragons of virtue, might think a little less of you!'

'That's enough,' Draco dragged out through a throat that felt as if it had a jagged boulder lodged in it. Athena was right about Diego Guardiola, not for the reasons she thought but because his feelings for her had led him to throw away a business deal potentially worth billions. He was in too deep and needed to get out, now, before he lost the last of his control and drowned. 'I know we're ending things sooner than you thought we would and I'm sorry if that hurts you, but what you're saying...this isn't you.' Not the Athena she'd become.

He'd known this would be a difficult conversation. He'd known it would hurt her.

He hadn't anticipated how much it would hurt him too.

Her green eyes were wild. 'Oh, yes, I forgot! I take it all back! You've changed me! Give yourself a pat on the back.'

'Athena, stop, please.'

She smiled manically. 'Okay. I'll stop. See? The Athena

reprogramming has worked wonders! Before you see yourself out, I have those clothes you kindly let me wear when you charged to my rescue and saved me from those bastard men. Hold on a moment.' Not giving him time to argue, she sashayed off to her bedroom, quickly reappearing with his clothes folded in her arms.

Thrusting them at him, she said, 'I did debate packing them for California but then I worried about giving them to you as I knew you wouldn't want me handing them over in front of anyone—can you imagine the raised eyebrows?' She raised her pretty eyebrows in imitation and folded her arms. 'Obviously, that was before I knew I would be spending my time in California in your bed and not a hotel bed. Not going to lie, I did hope something might happen between us while we were away but that was a masterstroke of planning on your part. Still, as I've already said, you've had your fun, and so have I, and now you can see yourself out.'

When he didn't move, she flapped a hand in the direction of the door. 'Go on. Off you go. Chop-chop.'

His heart tight in his throat, he reached the narrow hallway before turning back to her.

She was still staring at him with that bright, brittle smile and with her arms still folded across her chest.

'Don't demean yourself or what we've shared,' he said quietly. 'You mean far more to me than a bit of fun.'

A host of emotions danced across her face. 'You mean you really expect me to believe you're calling it quits now because it's become too heavy and I've turned into a distraction? Because that sounds like a platitude, and...and...' Her voice caught, eyes suddenly brimming with unshed tears. Her voice now a choked whisper, she said, 'It sounds like a platitude because if you feel a fraction for me of what I feel for you, you…you…you wouldn't be walking away from me like everyone else I've ever loved.' And then her face crumpled and she burst into tears.

Horrorstruck, he watched her sink to the floor and bury her face in her knees with gut-wrenching sobs.

He felt every sob as if it came from his own chest.

Chucking the clothes on top of the nearest armchair, he sank beside her and gathered her into his arms, holding her as he'd done what felt like a lifetime ago.

She clung to him as she'd done what felt like a lifetime ago, and it destroyed him to know he was the cause of her agony.

He should never have let it get this far.

He should never have let it start at all.

'I'm sorry,' she wept into his chest, her tremors vibrating through him. 'I didn't mean those cruel things I said, I swear.'

'I know you didn't,' he whispered into her hair, squeezing his eyes tightly closed to fight the burn behind them.

Rubbing her back, wishing there was something to soothe his own pain and guilt, he continued to hold her until her tears had been purged and she swallowed and said, 'I really am sorry.'

'Don't be. You were in pain.' Was in pain. He'd inflicted new wounds on a woman who'd spent her life hiding away from pain.

She shook her head, her hair tickling his nose and chin. 'No. You didn't deserve that.' She swallowed another sob and tightened her hold around him with a sigh. 'You're the best person I know, Draco Manolis.'

He exhaled raggedly and fought off another burn of tears. 'And you're the smartest and bravest person I know, and I wish…'

'Don't,' she cut in, her voice suddenly low with tiredness. 'It will only make it hurt more. This is how it has to be. We both knew it from the start.' She gave a weak laugh. 'I might have to punch myself in the face for that.'

He kissed her head, holding his mouth there and breathing in her scent for what he knew would be the last time.

'You should go,' she whispered, finally disentangling herself from his hold.

Draco got to his feet and held a hand out to her. She slipped her fingers into it and let him help her up.

They faced each other, drinking each other in for the last time with the intimacy that would be over when he walked out of her apartment.

Lifting her chin, her chest and shoulders rose as she smiled, the smile that was for him alone. 'I'm going to miss you. Now, please go before I start crying again.'

With nothing left to say to each other, Draco picked his clothes up from the armchair and walked out of her apartment for the last time.

Only when he was cocooned in the back of his car did he sniff the clothing. It smelt freshly laundered.

The thought of Athena working out how to use a washing machine shouldn't make him feel even worse, but it did.

CHAPTER FOURTEEN

MONDAY MORNING ROLLED AROUND. Jetlag and heartbreak had combined to weigh so heavily on her that Athena had slept for the best part of twenty hours straight, waking only to force food down and write a letter, then slept again until her alarm clock woke her.

Draco wouldn't be waking her today, not with the long drill of her doorbell or with a kiss.

It was over.

That didn't stop her heart from jumping when her doorbell rang at eight a.m.

Fully armoured in her favourite work outfit of shirt, tie, waistcoat and shorts, and with her face fully made-up, she greeted Draco's driver with her best smile, maintaining it even when she climbed into the back of the empty car.

Grace was, as expected, already at her desk. Her smile was tired. 'How are you feeling?'

Athena shrugged. 'A bit thick-headed from the jetlag. You?'

'Same.' Grace's smile faltered. 'He's waiting for you.'

She nodded, not out of agreement but just because.

Grace hesitated before darting her stare around the office to make sure no one was listening and lowered her voice. 'There's something you should know.'

'He's transferring me?' Athena guessed. At Grace's

widening eyes, she smiled sadly. 'Don't worry—I already knew.'

Her heart had known.

It wasn't tenable for them to continue working so closely together. It was a conclusion she'd already reached.

Her self-possession almost came undone when she wrapped her fingers around the door handle of Draco's office and blood rushed like a torrent through her, burning her veins and her brain with a force that threatened to double her over. She fought it, forcing air into her lungs, then lifted her head high and opened the door.

Even as her eyes connected with Draco's, she noticed the absence of her desk.

She'd been excised.

She'd expected it. It still felt like a knife to her heart.

She closed the door.

For the longest time, neither of them spoke.

Sitting at his desk, Draco broke the silence, softly saying, 'Please, take a seat.'

She looked at the sofa she'd first sat on when he'd told her he was tethering her to him and folded her arms across her stomach. The rush of blood had drained away and now her head felt light. The whole of her being felt light, as if she could float to the ceiling.

'Thank you, but I won't be staying. I just wanted to give this to you.' She pulled the envelope out of her handbag and crossed the floor to drop it on his desk, holding her breath so she didn't have to breathe him in.

'What's this?'

'My resignation.'

The silence that followed pulsed like a beat.

'I would ask if you know what you're doing,' he said slowly.

'Thank you for not insulting me.'

His smile was faint. 'How do you plan to support yourself?'

'I'm going to sell off most of my wardrobe and jewellery collection, and use the money I make to keep me going while I set up my own business.' How she could speak at all, never mind brightly and fluently, was something she didn't think she would ever understand.

'Can I ask…?'

'Of course. I'm going to set myself up as a personal stylist—one thing no one has ever said about me is that I don't have style!'

A grin broke over his rugged face. 'That sounds perfect for you.'

She nearly came unstuck at this, and it took a long beat for her to say, 'I'm glad you think so. That means a lot.'

He pulled in a long breath through his nose. 'If you get stuck for money while you're making it all happen, there's always a freelance translation job here for you.'

'Thank you. Hopefully, I won't have to take you up on it!'

'Anything you need…just call me, okay?'

She laughed sadly. 'I think we both know that's not going to happen. Anyway, I should go. I just wanted to hand my resignation to you personally—it wouldn't have felt right going through HR.'

The lightness of his features slowly fell, the finality of her words piercing them both.

It felt like for ever passed between them before he broke the silence shrouding them. 'Are you still coming to the launch party? It will be a good opportunity for you to network for your new business.'

'I'll think about it,' she lied. She didn't know how she could cope with spending hours maintaining a smile and trying to pretend that sharing the same air as him wasn't the worst pain in the world, not when being in an office for a few minutes, unable to touch him, felt like she was bleeding from the inside out.

There was no hiding from it. All her old coping mechanisms had gone, and now she needed to get out of this office and move far away from him before she gave in to the desperate need to throw herself at him and beg him to please love her.

He nodded, understanding etched in his rugged features.

She bit into her lip and stepped to the door. 'Will your mother be there?' she asked impulsively.

'Yes.' His stare was meditative. 'But you don't have to wait until the party if you want to see her. She's never stopped loving you, Athena.'

They held each other's stares for one long, last time and then Athena slipped out of his office for the last time.

After a moment spent fighting to hold onto a composure that was unravelling, she embraced Grace tightly. 'Call Josefina,' she whispered. 'And that's an order.'

Then, after a firm kiss to Grace's cheek, Athena walked out of Tsaliki Shipping with tears rolling down her cheeks but with a whole new future in front of her that was entirely hers for the making.

That this whole new future didn't include Draco was something she would just have to learn to live with.

Draco's office had never felt so quiet. Or so empty.

Shaking the feeling off, he called Grace in and got to work.

* * *

Athena pressed the intercom on the high wall to the side of the gate.

It was a long time before it was answered. She knew whoever was viewing the security camera had recognised her.

A disembodied voice said, 'Can I help you?'

'Can you please tell Lucie that Athena is here to see her?'

'She is unavailable. May I take a message?'

She didn't point out that this was her third attempt and that she'd already left two unanswered messages with the disembodied voice. Athena knew Lucie was home because she'd been spying on the house and had watched her get out of the car and go inside only five minutes ago.

Weary and close to defeat, she quietly said, 'I just want to talk to her. I swear I'm not here to cause trouble but there are things I need to say to her. Please, I promise I won't take up too much of her time.' Feeling tears forming—she couldn't seem to stop crying—she blinked hard to clear them and whispered, 'Please. I wouldn't be here if it wasn't important. Please.'

There was a long passage of time followed by a beep and then the iron gates began to open.

Lucie and Thanasis's house could have been built in Ancient Greece, Athena thought as she walked the long driveway to the main entrance, being all marble columns and pillars and surrounded by lavish grounds filled with marble statues and waterfalls, but all put together in a non-classical way. There was a bohemian classiness to it all that perfectly suited its female owner.

Before she reached it, the door opened and a tiny figure with a mass of black corkscrew curls appeared. Lucie. Behind her, the much taller figure of Thanasis, who wrapped his arms protectively around his wife's waist.

They both stared at her, stony-faced.

Athena cleared her throat. 'Thank you for seeing me.'

'What do you want?' Lucie asked coldly.

It was a coldness she thoroughly deserved but it still hurt. However prickly and bitchy Athena had been to her, Lucie had always forgiven her, had always snatched at the scraps of friendship Athena had thrown at her.

But Lucie had wanted to be more than her friend. She'd wanted to be Athena's sister. And, as repayment, Athena had treated her like dirt.

She met Lucie's cold stare. 'I'm here to apologise. I can't say sorry for every mean thing I've done to you over the years because there are just too many of them, but I am sorry, for every mean word and deed, and I'm sorry most of all for trying to steal Thanasis from you. It was unforgivable. I blamed you for your mother usurping my mother and blamed you for stealing my place in my own life when none of it was your fault. You were the only good one amongst us and if I could do it all again I would treat you as the sister you always wanted me to be because the truth is, you are my sister, and I will never forgive myself for always throwing your love and friendship back in your face.' She wiped away tears that had leaked out unbidden and sniffed back more. 'I am so happy you two made it back to each other. You're made for each other.'

The stony faces had slowly unfrozen into stunned amazement.

Lucie took a hesitant step towards her. 'Athena…are you okay?'

Athena shook her head and rubbed more tears away.

'I'm not suffering from anything I haven't brought on myself.'

'Why don't you come in?' Lucie asked gently.

She gave another shake of her head. 'If you ever make the offer again I will say yes, but you need to think things through before you decide if you want us to try and form a relationship again. Also, now I've spoken to you, I've got a lot of other people I need to make apologies to— you had to be the first because you're the one I caused the most damage to.'

All the wind was knocked out of her when Lucie hurled herself at her and flung her arms around her. 'I love you, Athena,' she whispered, hugging her fiercely.

She hugged her back with equal ferocity. 'I love you too.'

It was as Athena was walking back towards the gate that Lucie called out, 'That list of people you're planning to apologise to? Please tell me my mother's not on it.'

Athena turned around and walked backwards as she replied, 'Hell will freeze over before I apologise to that bitch.'

Lucie smiled and blew her a kiss.

Athena plucked up all her courage and pressed the intercom belonging to the last name on her list.

All her apologies had been made. She'd even received a few in return.

Her favourite reception—after Lucie's hug, of course— had come from her brother Alexis and his wife Lydia. She'd framed the charcoal portrait she'd drawn of their baby son and gift-wrapped it.

Their response had made her cry and reinforced why she couldn't make a career from her art. It was too intensely personal for her to share with anyone she didn't love, and now she was about to make contact with the woman she'd missed as profoundly as she'd once missed her mother.

Her mother was not someone Athena had sought out. She would always be a part of her life, but the damage her leaving and subsequent distance had caused was the one thing that could not be healed. She was okay with that. Not everything could be fixed.

'Hello?'

She swallowed. 'Cora?'

There was a long pause. 'Athena?'

Minutes later, the decades melted away as she was enfolded in the gentlest, most loving embrace of her life.

It had been exactly ten days since Athena had given Draco her resignation letter. To the minute. Ten days since he'd seen her. Ten days since he'd spoken to her. And it was as he was making his way up the stairs, late—for him—having overslept due to an insomnia he'd never suffered with before, thinking about her...he always seemed to be thinking about her...that he reached the eleventh floor, glanced through the glass door that led into the finance department, and found his foot hovering on the next step to the top floor.

He could have sworn he'd just seen her.

Turning, he looked again.

Unless he was hallucinating, Athena, dressed in her favourite pink, was in his finance department, talking animatedly with Evangeline, who was holding a large boutique box in her arms.

Athena leaned into her and lifted one of her flat locks of mousy hair, then whipped a notebook and pen from her handbag—it was the notebook she'd always carried to the meetings he'd forced her to sit through—and scribbled something on it before ripping the page out and handing it to his finance director, who was…and he was quite sure he wasn't imagining this…blushing.

As if in a trance, he watched them a while longer, only pulling himself out of it when Athena gave Evangeline an affectionate kiss on the cheek and secured the shoulder strap of her bag.

She was preparing to leave.

Adrenaline driving him, he took the stairs three at a time and closed himself into his office.

His heart was pumping harder than it did after an hour-long workout.

Instinct had him stand out on the balcony of the window that overlooked the main entrance, looking down at the figures bustling about their business that busy working day.

A swish of blonde hair caught his eye. His heart tried to break free.

She darted across the road, dodging vehicles as if she were impervious to the danger they posed to her fragile body, and took a left, heading, he guessed, to the Metro.

And then she stopped and stood still, as impervious to her fellow pedestrians having to walk around her as she'd been to the cars on the road.

Slowly, she turned her head and lifted her stare to him.

His heart made another desperate effort to break free.

He thought he saw her smile that special smile that was only for him before she faced forward and set off again.

Soon, she was lost in the crowd.

An hour later and Draco was still on the balcony, his gaze fixed on the last point he'd seen her before she'd disappeared.

The adrenaline that had carried him up the last flight of stairs still pumped hard, but no one looking at him would have seen it. It was all contained in his head.

He'd let her go. He'd let the brightest star in the sky, the woman who'd breezed through the staid corporate world he inhabited, daubing its walls with colour—usually pink—and attitude, slip through his fingers.

And why? Because she didn't fit the image he'd had in his mind of the ideal wife? Because she was Georgios Tsaliki's daughter? Because of her reputation? Because of *his* reputation? Because the brightness she shone with dazzled his eyes and distracted him from his life's work?

What the hell had he been building everything for if he was prepared to throw away the only person he could ever enjoy the spoils with?

She was too distracting? Well, he couldn't concentrate a second without her. Couldn't eat. Couldn't sleep.

He'd never known such loneliness existed.

He'd been every bit the selfish bastard her father was. All those things she'd thrown at him before breaking down in tears had been true, except for one thing—Draco hadn't ended it because he'd had his fun with her. He'd ended it because the depth of his feelings had terrified him, threatening the control he'd ruthlessly exerted and bound himself in since those powerless days when his mother had lost her job and their home; the smooth, orderly life he'd created for himself on the cusp of falling into chaos.

Let chaos reign.

He hadn't changed Athena, she'd changed him. Her love had changed him, brought out the man he should have been.

And in return he'd broken her heart.

He didn't know if he could ever repair the damage he'd

inflicted on her, but there was one thing he could do to show her and the world that his heart was entirely hers, and he strode back into his office and yanked the door open.

'Grace!' he barked. 'Tell the senior members of the launch party team I want them in my office.'

'When?'

'Now.'

Athena cast a final critical eye over Evangeline and beamed. 'Perfect. Cinderella is now ready to go to the ball.'

Evangeline blushed with pleasure. The green and gold dress Athena had sourced for her was the perfect fit for her fuller figure, flatteringly showcasing her curves without drowning them. Her mousy hair had been highlighted and cut into a chic bob that added volume, and the touch of make-up she'd trusted Athena to apply highlighted her pretty grey eyes. She was the best version of herself she could be and Athena had no doubt that when she walked into the hotel ballroom she would walk tall.

Her phone buzzed. She answered the video call with a bright smile.

'Are you sure this lipstick works?' Grace immediately asked.

'Stand further under the light,' Athena ordered, then nodded once Grace had done as asked. 'Yes. That dress needs a bold colour. Now, put your phone on a shelf so I can see the whole of you... Perfect! You look gorgeous! Josefina won't be able to keep her hands off you.'

Grace blushed as hard as Evangeline had done. 'Shouldn't you be getting ready?'

Athena shrugged, suddenly finding it a struggle to maintain her happy demeanour. 'I guess so.' The last thing she wanted was to attend the launch party. The only thing making her go was that this would be the perfect opportunity to network for her new business. Oh, and seeing Rebecca's face when the new name for Tsaliki Shipping was revealed.

The biggest reason she was going, though, was for Cora. She'd promised her, and tonight, in front of hundreds of Athens' wealthiest and most powerful people, she would make her allegiance known. It wouldn't be the mother who'd left her that she'd stand with or Rebecca, who made the Queen in *Snow White* seem like a loving stepmother, but Cora Manolis, the mother she'd chosen for herself.

If she could only stop herself from missing Cora's son, she might consider herself happy.

Inside, she felt dead. She didn't even cry any more. She'd shut down emotionally, just as she'd done as a little girl, but this time with a determination not to let the awful, bitchy Athena who'd taken her over get a foothold once more.

She would never be that Athena again. If she couldn't be happy then she would fake happiness until real happiness found its way back to her, however long it took.

With Evangeline's help, she climbed into the red cocktail dress she'd found in a high-end charity shop. Strapless, it skimmed her cleavage like a heart and fell to her ankles, a modest slash at the side displaying flashes of leg, but not so much that everyone would be able to see the colour of her knickers.

As a thank you for styling her, Evangeline had insisted on paying for Athena to have her hair cut and dried for the party, and her blonde hair had been styled into soft waves. She applied her make-up with care and subtlety and then put on a pair of gold earrings shaped like dreamcatchers in the forlorn hope they would protect her from the nightmare of seeing Draco again.

With her feet in a pair of gold stilettoes, she was physically ready.

Emotionally, she was as far from ready as she'd ever been.

The ballroom of the Dionysus Hotel glittered both from the multiple chandeliers and the jewellery gleaming on the guests filing in.

Draco's team had pulled out all the stops to make the party work, and as a string quartet played jaunty music, high society mixed with select employees and scions of the shipping industry, sipping champagne and nibbling on the canapés that would sustain them until the meal was served. Holding court, Georgios Tsaliki, the man who'd spent decades at the forefront of Greek shipping, a maverick and innovator who, from his body language, was expecting to be eulogised that evening.

Draco couldn't even bring himself to care about how the bastard who'd destroyed his mother would react when the new name was revealed. He was too busy scanning the growing crowd for Georgios's daughter.

His heart thumped a beat before his eyes locked onto the vision in red walking through the door with a woman who looked much like his finance director.

From across the crowded room, her gaze lifted to his, eyes locking together for a beat long enough to make his thumping heart ache to fly to her.

She'd never looked more beautiful.

She broke the lock first, turning to another guest.

He took a deep breath. He needed to play this right. He couldn't go charging to her and throw himself at her feet. Not yet.

Draco and his guests circulated and greeted each other a while longer until everyone was invited to take their seats.

It was nearly time.

Whoever had done the seating plan deserved to be shot, Athena thought miserably. The way the round tables had been set out meant she could have been placed anywhere and facing any direction. Instead, she'd been placed directly below the top table where Draco, Cora, her father and stepmother, and the seven other most honoured guests were seated, her view a direct line to Draco. Not even seeing the expressions on her father and stepmother's faces at their recognition of Cora could lessen the sting.

She picked at her food, made small talk with the rest of the table, and willed time to speed up. As soon as the speeches were over, she'd be gone.

Time, however, refused to play ball, crawling torturously.

Every time she glanced Draco's way, which was roughly every three seconds as she was helpless to stop herself looking at him, her eyes would catch his.

She didn't feel dead inside any more. Now she felt only despair.

Finally, the desserts were finished. Merciful escape was only a speech away.

Soon, the scent of coffee filled the air and Draco took to the stage. Chairs scraped as everyone angled themselves for a face-on view.

'Good evening, ladies and gentlemen,' he said, tall and heartbreakingly handsome in his hand-stitched tuxedo. 'Thank you for joining me this evening as we celebrate my acquisition of Tsaliki Shipping. As you will all know, it's been three months since I bought the company and, so far, it's been one hell of a learning curve.'

There was a small outbreak of laughter.

'When a new owner takes control of a company, change is always inevitable,' he continued. 'And it's no different for me. Effective immediately, Tsaliki Shipping as an entity no longer exists.'

There was no laughter this time. Only hushed silence.

A projector light shone on the heavy stage curtains behind him, and without warning a white screen filled with the image of a female goddess wearing an ancient Greek chiton. She was standing in front of a cherry blossom tree and had a spear in her hand and a warrior helmet on her head.

It was the goddess Athena.

The words beneath her read *Corathena Shipping*.

The room was spinning around her so hard Athena didn't even think to look at her father or Rebecca. Even if she had thought to look, she wouldn't have been able to see them, not through the tears streaming down her face.

'I chose Corathena to celebrate the two people who I love more than anyone—my mother Cora and the woman I hope will agree to be my wife, Athena Tsaliki.'

There were audible gasps. She barely heard them over her thrashing heart.

Corathena...

She wiped her tears and clutched her burning cheeks as the magnitude of what Draco had done sank in.

The magnitude of what it meant.

His stare landed on her.

His chest rose. 'I love you, Athena. Now and always. Please marry me.'

Five hundred pairs of eyes were fixed on her but Athena felt none of them. The only face she saw was Draco's.

She rose unsteadily to her feet.

'What do you say?' he whispered, dropping the microphone that was no longer needed because the silence in the ballroom was absolute. 'Will you do me the biggest honour of my life and be my wife?'

Feeling like she'd fallen into a dream, she glided to him.

He stepped off the stage and stood before her.

Not speaking, she placed a trembling hand on his cheek…he was trembling too…and rubbed her palm into the soft stubble of his beard, her heart swelling as if all the helium in the world had been funnelled into it.

His piercing eyes glistening with unshed tears, he rested his forehead to hers and drove his fingers through her hair. 'You are everything to me, Athena. *Everything.* You are my sun and my moon and all the stars in the sky, and worth more to me than all the gold in the universe. I'm sorry for being such a fool…'

The tenderness of his touch spread through her, flooding her with a warmth she'd never believed she would feel again, and she covered his mouth with her fingers. 'No apologies. You never wanted to hurt me.'

He gently moved her hand. 'But…'

Closing her eyes, she wound her arms around his neck and silenced him with a kiss, holding her mouth to his and filling herself with the scent and taste and everything that was Draco. 'Draco, you didn't just save me from those men, you saved me from myself. Your love set me free from the chains I'd put around myself, and my heart and my life belong to you. I would marry you this minute if it was possible. You're my heart and I love you.'

There was a groan from his throat before his lips parted

against hers and he was kissing her with the same desperate need for her that she'd carried all those long weeks for him.

'I love you, Athena,' he murmured passionately. 'I will be yours for ever.'

When they finally came up for air, it was to a roar of cheers and applause, and when Draco produced an oval diamond engagement ring from his pocket and slid it onto her finger—it was *perfect!*—five hundred camera phones caught the moment.

They were pictures neither of them ever grew tired of looking at.

Later, cheek to chest and fingers threaded tightly, Athena and Draco moved as one slowly on the packed dancefloor. Her engagement ring gleamed as brightly as the gleam in her heart.

Dancing close to them, Lucie and Thanasis, and Alexis and Lydia. Her other siblings, who she hoped with all her heart would one day find love, too, were hidden in the crowd, but they were there, and that made her happy. It made her even happier that they'd all chosen to continue working for Draco under the Corathena Shipping banner. Even her father and Rebecca had stayed to party. As selfish and vile as her father could be, Athena still loved him, and his tight embrace and whispered congratulations had meant more than she'd thought it would.

A fresh start for all of them.

In the periphery of her vision was Cora, in deep, animated conversation with a suave German shipping magnate. As if she felt Athena's stare, she turned her head and caught her eye. And then she smiled and raised her champagne flute, and Athena was thrown back in time to when she'd seen a photo of Cora's adolescent son and determined to marry him so she could have Cora as her mother.

Some wishes did come true.

Draco had made all her secret wishes come true.

She would love him for ever. And he would love her for ever too.

* * * * *

Did Greek Boss to Hate *sweep you off your feet? Then you're sure to enjoy its linked stories in the Greek Rivals duet,* Forgotten Greek Proposal *and* His Pregnant Enemy Bride*! And why not explore these other stories by Michelle Smart?*

Cinderella's One-Night Baby
The Forbidden Greek
Heir Ultimatum
Resisting the Bossy Billionaire
Spaniard's Shock Heirs

Available now!

FORBIDDEN PRINCESS'S BILLIONAIRE BODYGUARD

ANNIE WEST

MILLS & BOON

This book is dedicated to the wonderful Mr West,
who listens to me ramble about plots and characters,
who is there through thick and thin,
who *always* cheers me on, and
who builds me bookcases!
Happy sighs.

CHAPTER ONE

ROSAMUND SCANNED THE STUDY, antique bookcases rising to a frescoed ceiling. Up there haughty gods stared down at her from puffy clouds. She didn't need to look up to know how disdainfully they frowned at her. This had been her father's study. She'd spent too many hours here being told the many ways she didn't measure up.

She'd reminded him too much of her mother, more interested in people than rules. But her father was gone. Now it was her half-brother sitting behind the royal desk.

She turned to meet eyes so like their father's that for a second she was flung back to the last time she'd seen the old king. Even on his deathbed there'd been no rapprochement, despite her attempts. Any faint hope that he had, at some level, loved her, had shrivelled.

She should have known better.

Rosamund blinked. Leon's eyes were the same colour but he didn't wear their father's habitual scowl.

She saw shadows beneath his eyes that spoke of tiredness, and reined in her impatience.

'Leon, I've already explained I can't have a security detail from the palace.'

'Can't or won't?' His frustration was clear. 'It would be a temporary measure only.'

That was what her father had said when she was seventeen,

yet the situation had lasted until she was twenty-one, legally an adult, and finally able to refuse it.

Four years of having not just a single discreet guard but a group of burly, hatchet-jawed men who were as unobtrusive as a diamond tiara in a dole queue. They'd shadowed her so closely she'd had no private space. No wonder they'd scared off even her friends.

Which had been the idea. After the scandal her father hadn't focused on keeping her safe but ensuring she didn't embarrass him again. She'd naively fallen for a charming, handsome man only to learn he just wanted her as a stepping stone to power. When she ended things he'd retaliated, leaking salacious stories to the press with damning photos, some not even of her but carefully doctored.

That didn't matter to the king. She'd damaged the royal family's reputation. He'd never forgiven her.

Her skin prickled at the humiliating memories. Of being continually surrounded by men who treated her like a prisoner rather than someone needing protection. It had been a very public, very deliberate punishment.

'It's not feasible. I have an aversion to oversized thugs being privy to my personal life.'

'If you're averse to thugs, you shouldn't have got mixed up with Brad Ricardo.'

Rosamund rolled her eyes. She'd tried to explain she wasn't mixed up with the man, but no one wanted to listen. She should have known better than to try. The palace never listened.

'I have no intention of seeing him again.'

'He might have other plans. You don't think a man like that might view you as unfinished business?'

Not in the way everyone thinks!

She remembered Ricardo's eyes when he realised what she'd done. That dark stare had been like a honed blade, threatening to eviscerate her.

That night she'd acted on impulse but she couldn't regret

her actions. She'd met people like him before, so engrossed in their own needs they'd take advantage of anyone who got in their way.

'He and I aren't even on the same continent. I've got no plans to return to the States soon.'

This time the silence held a different quality. Not mere frustration but something that made her nape prickle.

'Leon, what aren't you telling me?'

'He's threatened you, and a man like him has a long reach. He has contacts in Europe.'

Her stomach curdled. She'd told herself his threat had been bluster but never quite believed it. That was why she'd abruptly ended her American stay.

'You're saying he's dangerous? Physically dangerous?'

There was a pause as if he decided how much to tell her. 'Talk to me, Leon. I have a right to know.'

'The authorities in America are investigating him.'

Rosamund sank back in her chair, a shiver working its way down her backbone. She'd known the man was poison, but a criminal? 'For what crimes?'

'Embezzlement and assault.'

Her shiver became a shudder and she wrapped her arms around her middle. Embezzlement didn't surprise her. She'd seen how plausible and charming he could be in pursuit of money. As for assault...she'd told herself that malevolent stare he'd given her didn't matter. Now she wondered.

'How bad was the assault?'

Leon looked grim. 'Bad.'

Rosamund opened her mouth to ask for details then decided she didn't want to know. 'If the police are investigating, Ricardo will have more on his mind than me.'

Her half-brother wasn't convinced. 'The assault charge won't proceed. The victim refuses to testify for fear of reprisal.'

A lead weight dropped in her stomach. She'd known Ricardo was bad news, but this…

Leon pressed on, his expression stern. 'Ricardo doesn't yet know about the big embezzlement investigation. If they prove the case he'll be imprisoned for years. Your protection would be for a short time while the police investigate. After that, hopefully he won't be a problem to anyone.'

It seemed far-fetched that the man could harm her in Europe. But she couldn't forget that venomous look, the blood-chilling words he'd spat at her.

'How short a time?'

'A week or two.'

Rosamund shook her head. 'I've got important public engagements coming up.'

Engagements she couldn't attend with a mob of the palace's anything-but-discreet minders surrounding her. It would make a mockery of the events and detract from their purpose.

Her chest squeezed. Being guest of honour at the festival to honour her mother's remarkable career would be a double-edged sword, a proud moment and an emotional trial. But she *had* to attend.

The world had known Juliette Bernard as a gifted actor before she married a king. To Rosamund she was the one person who'd loved her unconditionally. She'd been her role model, a beacon of warmth against the king's cold, judgemental presence.

'I know you have engagements, Rosa.' Leon's use of the rare diminutive surprised her. As did the unfamiliar note almost of apology in his voice.

She tried to recall when he'd last called her that. When she was a little girl, she supposed.

She didn't loathe Leon as she had their father. They simply led separate lives. In fact they didn't really know each other. Leon was so much older, the son of the king's first wife, so that when Rosamund was born he'd been away at boarding school.

Now he lived in Cardona's royal palace while she had an apartment on the far side of the city. But for the last several years, while their father was alive, she'd spent more time out of the country than in it and Leon was always busy with royal duties which usually didn't involve her.

'I know how important the festival is to you. That's why I'm not suggesting you cancel, though you'd be safer here.'

She stiffened, gripping the arms of her chair. Her father had been dictatorial enough to prevent her leaving the kingdom on at least one occasion. 'Go on.'

'I'm offering a compromise. Instead of a close protection team from the palace, you'll have one companion. Not an official bodyguard but someone I trust and know can keep you safe.'

She stared suspiciously. '*Not* a bodyguard?'

'Definitely not. He's a businessman these days, but he has the necessary skills to keep danger at bay.'

Rosamund's eyebrows rose. 'Some businessman. What does he do, run a karate school?'

Leon's lips twitched. 'He's more of a policy advisor.'

She knew the type. She'd seen them with their briefcases and frowns, buzzing around the royal offices. Yet he must be more than that for Leon to suggest him. She was about to ask for more detail when something clicked.

'You've already arranged this, haven't you? Without asking me.'

Leon shrugged and spread his hands. 'You refused a security team when my secretary contacted you. But I can't let you go without *any* protection.'

She frowned. Her father had washed his hands of her. It felt odd to have someone watch out for her. 'That's a lot of trouble to go to, locating someone able to blend in *and* intervene if there's trouble.'

Serious eyes met hers and she felt a dart of shock as she read Leon's concern. 'I don't want you hurt, Rosa. You're my sister.'

A lump lodged in her throat. He wasn't worried about the outcry if something happened to a member of the royal family. He was concerned for *her*. *His sister*, not merely his obligation. It wasn't what she'd expected when she'd been summoned to the palace.

She'd barely ever spent time alone with Leon. She wasn't used to tenderness from her family, not since her mother died years before.

'I...' She cleared her throat. 'What arrangements have you made?'

Seeing relief spread across his features, Rosamund knew she'd accept his plan. He'd taken the trouble to find a compromise she could live with. That was unprecedented. The palace never compromised. And he'd done it because he cared.

She silently vowed that when she returned to Cardona, she'd spend some time with the brother she barely knew.

'He'll meet you off the plane in Paris. There's just one condition.'

'Go on, I'm game. What is it?'

'The only way he can reasonably be by your side all the time without appearing like the bodyguards you detest. As far as the public's concerned, you're a couple. That will explain why he's at your side at every event. Just don't say anything to dispel the idea and there'll be no questions raised.'

A pretend lover? 'But—'

'That's the deal, Rosa. You've got no idea how difficult this was to organise. But he's agreed, on condition he calls the shots. Any hint of danger and he's in charge.' The warmth she'd seen in Leon's expression vanished, leaving him looking almost as stern as their father. 'So, Rosamund, will you take it or leave it?'

You should have left it. You should have said no and walked straight out the door. He wouldn't have barred you from leaving the country. Probably.

But regrets were pointless. She was almost there. Far below, she saw the sprawl that was Paris. Leon had loaned her the king's private jet. The main thing was that she'd be at the event as promised.

That was what she had to concentrate on.

Not the way all her plans had been disrupted.

She'd been on her way to the airport when she learned her Paris hotel booking had been cancelled. Ditto the car she'd rented to drive south when the Paris events were over.

Then, after rushing to be at the airport by the revised deadline, she'd discovered the earlier departure time wasn't because Leon needed the plane but because his bodyguard-who-wasn't-a-bodyguard had decided she needed to arrive in Paris early.

Without consulting her. About anything! He'd just decreed and somehow everything had changed.

Rosamund chewed her lip, banking down fury at the man's high-handedness. If this was how he operated, they were going to clash. Despite her father's view of her, she wasn't flighty or stupid, and she appreciated common decency. Like a request and an explanation. Not finding out after the fact that everything had been altered.

Fotis Mavridis clearly didn't believe in consultation.

It irked her that in the little time she'd spent researching him she'd found virtually nothing. He was Greek. He ran a company called Mystikos, which she learned was Greek for secret or hidden. The word was annoyingly apt because though she'd found a few sparse references to it providing advice to various governments, she couldn't find the company website or details of its business.

As for Fotis Mavridis, he could almost be a figment of her brother's imagination. There were no photos, few biographical details, almost nothing to indicate what sort of man she was about to meet.

Apart from bossy, rude and, by definition, unlikable.

She thought of the policy advisors she'd met. They led sedentary, office-bound lives. It was hard to imagine one of them protecting her should Ricardo try to get even with her for disrupting his plans.

Her mouth twisted wryly as she tried to imagine a balding bureaucrat standing between her and danger, his agitated breaths straining his shirt across a podgy stomach.

There must be more to this man than Leon's description suggested.

The jet landed and taxied to the edge of the private airfield. There was a bustle at the door as steps were put in position.

Rosamund was reaching for the shoes she'd slipped off when her skin prickled. The atmosphere changed, becoming charged, like at the onset of an electrical storm.

She looked up, and up further. Dimly she was aware of her pulse thudding a quickened beat. Of a spasm low in her body and her nipples peaking, abrading her bra.

All that in a millisecond as she took in the stranger before her.

His shoulders were straight and wide under his black leather jacket. There were black jeans too and a dark T-shirt that hinted at a steel-toned body. Black-as-night hair, winged ebony eyebrows and a dusting of midnight stubble on his hard-hewn jaw. But shockingly his eyes were light. They reminded her of the sea, a mix of blue and green and maybe even gold, as if the sun glittered over liquid depths.

With his strong features—she couldn't call him handsome but arresting—Rosamund could imagine him cast as a fallen angel. Not just any fallen angel. With his incredible presence he had to be Lucifer, their leader.

Maybe those eyes were a reminder of those glory days before he was kicked out of heaven. Rosamund had never seen anything like that colour which, even as she watched, seemed to glow more golden.

Something shuddered inside her. Something shockingly like recognition. Awareness.

Nonsense! The artist in her simply wondered how to capture that precise shade.

'Princess Rosamund.'

It wasn't a question but a flat statement of certainty. Yet it was more too. In just five syllables his softly modulated baritone conveyed disdain. Scorn, even.

Suddenly, shockingly, she knew who this man must be and discovered she'd walked into a nightmare.

This was the man sent to protect her? Who'd act as her partner for the duration of the trip?

Disbelief and dismay filled her. Despite his arrogance and his contempt, it would be easy for a woman to find him attractive. To want to put her hands on him, test that tensile strength and try to learn the secrets of his body.

No wonder every instinct screamed a warning.

It was impossible to sit under that scorching scrutiny.

Ignoring her shoes she rose, standing tall and cloaking herself in the illusion of confidence as her mother had taught her. She'd never been more grateful for those early lessons.

'*Kyrie Mavridis. Kalimera.*' She inclined her head as if graciously accepting a compliment and felt a flicker of satisfaction at his momentary surprise.

'You speak Greek?'

Clearly he hadn't expected that and she dearly wished she could claim that advantage. She suspected she'd need every advantage she could muster to deal with this man who was *not* like any policy advisor she'd seen. So much for a balding, paunchy bureaucrat. She'd have words with Leon when she returned. He should have warned her.

'Alas, no. Just a few pleasantries.'

She paused, far too aware of their height difference now they stood toe-to-toe. She rarely wore high heels and wished she'd worn some on the plane. As it was, barefoot she had to tilt her head to meet his eyes.

He inclined his head, his unsmiling mouth betraying no pleasure in her company.

What was the man's problem? Couldn't he even pretend to the usual social niceties?

It intrigued her that Leon had managed to persuade this man who looked as persuadable as a block of basalt, into looking out for her.

Did he owe Leon some debt?

'You're ready to go?' His tone was brusque.

'In a moment.' His eagerness to be gone and his refusal to play nice spurred her to take her time, letting down her hair then gathering it up, winding it around her hand and fixing it more securely. Only when she was satisfied it would pass muster for any paparazzi did she turn to accept her jacket, held out to her by the steward. She gave a man a warm smile. 'Thank you very much, Philippe.'

Then her shoes. She slipped them on, wishing the heels were three times the height.

She was reaching for her shoulder bag when her Greek minder said, 'I came on-board to discuss the ground rules before this goes any further.'

Rosamund's eyebrows lifted. She'd promised Leon she'd be discreet about this arrangement. It seemed Fotis Mavridis hadn't got that memo. Or, she realised as she met that challenging stare, he had his own priorities. Any thought that he was dependent on her half-brother vanished.

'Thank you, Philippe.' She nodded at the steward. 'We'll follow you out in a moment.'

When the cabin was empty she gestured to the empty seats. 'Shall we sit while we talk?'

'That won't be necessary. This won't take long.'

His voice was uninflected, his stare blank, but she knew it hid disapproval if not dislike. She had enough experience to know.

Once, long ago, that would have hurt, to be judged and

found wanting for no good reason. But she wasn't naïve anymore. She was a woman who got on with her life, forging her own path. If she allowed herself to be upset by negative opinions, she'd be a hermit.

Even so, she was tempted to sink back into her seat and let him stand there, alone. Except she'd get a crick in her neck and he'd probably enjoy looming over her.

'So. Ground rules.' She smiled encouragingly as if unaware of the negative energy thrumming off him. 'Please continue.'

For a heartbeat she sensed curiosity behind the mask. 'Actually, there's only one. I'm in charge. What I say goes, otherwise the deal's off.'

'In charge of what, precisely? Countering any physical threat? Believe me, I'm happy to leave that to you.'

Any thought that he mightn't be up to the task had disintegrated. He radiated competence and though his stance was easy, there was a restrained power about him that made her think he could handle any threat.

'In charge of you.' He paused to let that sink in. '*I* decide where you go. When and how you go and where you stay. Any problem with that and I'm out.'

He talked to her as if she were a six-year-old, not a twenty-eight-year-old who'd made her own way in the world for a long time. Not like a client. Or a royal, for that matter.

Indignation rose and a burning desire to tell this man where he could get off.

But Leon would immediately replace the man with a team of bodyguards, despite her wishes. Besides, she was curious. She was used to people who didn't know her judging her, but this felt different.

Why? They hadn't met before. There was no way she'd have forgotten this man. Maybe he didn't like royals. Or women. She shook off the notion this was personal. That wasn't possible.

'So,' he said with a telling curl of his lips, 'if you're going to opt out, now's the time.'

That's what he wants. For you to end the deal and walk away. Why?

The temptation to agree was strong. She didn't like her instant and all-consuming awareness of him. She didn't like *him*. She'd prefer not to see him again. But that was what he wanted. Why else stomp in here and bark out his ultimatum?

Okay, okay. So he doesn't bark. He doesn't raise his voice. In fact the sound of that deep baritone voice, so soft it whispers across your skin, is ridiculously appealing.

Rosamund drew a slow breath, ignoring the regrettable things that voice did to her hormones. She could play into his hands but all that would achieve was her lumbered with the team of security guards she'd already rejected.

'Opt out?' She looked up with wide eyes that belied the welter of anger and indignation churning in her stomach. 'I was told you'd protect me from threat. If you're able to do that I'm grateful.'

What she was *actually* grateful for was that her mother had been an esteemed actress. She'd learnt from the best how to conceal her thoughts, how to project the emotions she chose, no matter what she felt.

She saw the flicker of something cross his features. Surprise? Disappointment?

'I understand you're the expert on my safety.' No matter how galling that was. 'I note you've already come up with alternative plans for my accommodation and transport. Perhaps that was because it's better not to signal in advance where I'm staying and how I'm travelling?'

For the longest time he said nothing but finally he nodded curtly. 'Yes.'

See, that wasn't so hard was it?

She stifled the temptation to say it aloud. No point prodding the bear.

Except, while she might have learnt to put pragmatism before pride, she had her limits. It didn't take a genius to know this man would test those limits to the full.

Besides, if the bear deserved prodding...

'As long as you can get me to the events I'm scheduled to attend, and the people I need to see, that's fine.'

She smiled benignly. *That's what your job is after all.* But she kept her lips closed.

His scrutiny intensified, those uniquely coloured eyes regarding her with a laser focus that scraped her skin.

Annoying man, but clever. He knows there's something going on behind the smile.

That made two of them. She could almost hear the wheels turning in that arrogant head of his.

'So, are we done here, Mr Mavridis?'

He nodded. 'As long as you'll obey me, we're done.' He turned away without waiting for an answer.

Obey! 'There's just one thing,' she murmured. 'You didn't ask if *I* had any ground rules.'

Satisfaction was a pleasing glow as those broad shoulders stiffened. She wondered if he'd pretend he hadn't heard and simply walk away. But slowly he turned.

'And you have ground rules, of course.'

He didn't grimace but his tone spoke of barely contained patience. What was he expecting? A request that they detour so she could shop for designer handbags? A demand for vintage champagne in the limo? A coy request that they not get too close when they pretended to be a couple in public?

As if she had any fears on that score! Whatever this man's weakness was, it wasn't her. He looked like he could barely stand her presence.

What a relief.

'Just one.' Rosamond waited long enough for him to raise his eyebrows at the delay. Good. She had his full attention. 'Courtesy, Mr Mavridis. It's non-negotiable. You might be in charge, as you so succinctly put it, but I expect to be consulted, not ordered. You might not think much of life's little courtesies. Greetings, please and thank you. But most people prefer to be treated with respect. I'm one of them.

'Besides, if we want the public to believe you're my companion rather than my bodyguard, you'll need to practise politeness, with me and the people we meet.'

'And you'll reciprocate?'

Rosamund picked up her bag and straightened her jacket. 'Of course. Haven't you noticed?' She moved past him towards the door. 'If I weren't polite I'd have already mentioned you're the most arrogant, objectionable man I've met in a long time.' She paused to look over her shoulder into his narrowed stare. 'Shall we go?'

CHAPTER TWO

FOTIS FROWNED, REPLAYING her parting words at the plane.

Not that he wanted to be amused, or impressed. But Princess Rosamund of Cardona had surprised him.

That was unusual. He made it his business to be prepared. Yet from the moment he'd boarded the royal jet everything had been out of kilter.

It wasn't a sensation he liked. He'd spent a lifetime ensuring he was in control of his world, not the other way around. His mouth flattened as he watched the Parisian streets go by.

In his peripheral vision he saw her, busy on her phone. She hadn't looked at him since they'd climbed into the back of the limo. Such complete disregard was deliberate.

Like the way she'd sashayed down the plane's steps. She hadn't wriggled her hips or tossed her head. Oh no, she was too regal for that, but the proud set of her shoulders and her absolute composure proclaimed nothing he'd done or said fazed her. He was beneath her notice.

For a millisecond he considered doing something that would *really* ruffle her feathers.

On the plane she'd casually let down her hair then redone it, just to make the point that *she* set the timetable. What would she do if he reached out now and tugged it undone, threading his fingers through the shining tresses, dragging her head back so her throat and mouth were vulnerable to him?

The idea was tempting even for a man who didn't allow himself to be provoked. Who did *not* manhandle women.

Admittedly she'd had a point. He'd ditched social niceties. How that must have shocked a woman used to smarm and charm and getting her own way.

It was a timely reminder of who and what she was.

This was the last place he'd be if he hadn't been virtually blackmailed into it. He despised her, with good reason. He knew her sort intimately. Usually he ignored them, but when others suffered it was different.

Inevitably pain resonated as he thought of Nico.

His little brother had died because Fotis had failed to protect him. And because their mother had been too absorbed in seducing a rich new lover to care for her children. She was another shallow, self-absorbed woman, used to getting what she wanted.

Yet despite his hatred of vain socialites, he lingered on the memory of Princess Rosamund's hair settling over the upper slopes of her peaked breasts. She'd worn a silky camisole the colour of mountain violets that clung enough to reveal as much as it concealed.

To his chagrin he'd imagined cupping those breasts and feeling her pebbled nipples against his palms.

Cursing under his breath, he dragged out his phone. He might have been corralled into looking after a spoilt madam but that didn't mean he'd neglect his own business.

The car slowed and Rosamund looked up from her email as it swung off the quiet street and into a private garage. The street wasn't familiar and she didn't even know which *arrondissement* of Paris they'd entered. She'd been too busy trying to ignore her dour companion to keep track of the city.

She turned to ask their location but he'd already exited the vehicle. So had the driver. She put her phone away and gathered her bag, by which time the driver was holding her open door.

'Thank you.' She smiled and received the tiniest nod in

response. Had his boss ordered him not to get friendly? Or for some reason did he, like Fotis Mavridis, view her as the enemy?

She told herself her imagination was running away with her, something her father had often complained about. Yet she didn't need to be clairvoyant to know Mavridis really didn't want anything to do with her. What *was* his problem?

She moved away from the car, noting the garage door had shut behind them with a soft thud. It was sensible, bringing her somewhere she wouldn't be seen alighting from the vehicle in the street.

Mavridis knew what he was doing. With the limo's tinted windows no one had seen her in the traffic. No one knew her location unless they'd followed from the airport.

For a shockingly claustrophobic moment, standing in the dimly lit garage at an unknown location, brought by men she didn't know, fear spidered across her skin, drawing it tight. Her pulse thudded in her throat. Even Leon didn't know where she was.

Tension roiled in her stomach and she felt a sickeningly abrupt rush of adrenaline. She made herself exhale slowly, short breath in and a longer one out. She loosened her jaw, dropped her shoulders and felt her heartbeat slow.

Then she noticed her unwilling bodyguard in an open doorway, light spilling from behind him. With his face in shadow it was impossible to read his expression. Had he noticed the way her hand had crept into her shoulder bag to clutch her phone?

She made herself walk towards him across the bare cement floor. She'd almost reached him when he turned and walked away.

His lack of manners was a slap in the face. That intrigued her for, though she was a princess, in daily life she didn't live as one. She did her share of royal events but instead of living in the palace, had her own apartment. She didn't get the red carpet treatment except at official events. Friends and work associates called her by her first name, never her title.

But he'd been employed to look after a princess. For all he knew, her royal position was her full-time job. Turning his back wasn't polite for anyone, but with royalty it was a damning insult. Was that why he'd done it?

Rosamund mulled that over as she followed him down a hall. He wasn't to know that far from revelling in her royal birthright, she'd always craved a normal life. Aristocratic privilege wasn't all it was cracked up to be.

It was tempting to tell him he'd have to try harder with his insults. But why bother? He was a necessary encumbrance for a short period. The less time she wasted thinking about him the better.

Yeah, right. After you spent the whole car ride reading the same page in the new contract. Just because Mr Macho Grumpy was beside you, taking up all the oxygen.

He hadn't spoken. Hadn't looked her way. But his presence had overwhelmed her.

Rosamund didn't do overwhelmed. She didn't give any man power over her. It had been a hard-won lesson but one she'd committed to heart.

'Where are we?' she said as she followed him into a big, sunny kitchen that looked onto a surprisingly large and inviting garden.

'The house where we'll stay while you're in Paris.'

'You rented a whole house?'

She'd only seen the massive garage, a marble-floored hallway and this state-of-the-art kitchen. But that was enough to know this was no ordinary house.

'You think your brother can't afford it?'

She plonked her bag on the island bench that looked bigger than the average kitchen, then planted her palms on the cool stone. 'I pay my own way. I'm not here at the state's expense. Usually I stay in a hotel.'

Did she imagine a flicker of surprise in his eyes? 'This is more secure.' After a moment he added, 'Don't worry, I don't expect you to pay. It's not a rental.'

Slowly she nodded. The man had connections. Sourcing a luxury home like this for a short period was near impossible.

She waited. He had something to say, presumably details of how this arrangement would work. She watched him watching her and refused to ask. Instead she paced the big room, hands brushing custom-made cabinetry and slick stainless steel.

But eventually his silence was too much. 'About this arrangement, pretending to be partners—'

'Lovers.'

That baritone voice remained soft yet that single word made her pulse skitter. She paused, fingers clenching around the handle of the biggest fridge she'd ever seen.

She resumed walking towards the end of the room where sunlight streamed through French doors onto an impressive glass-and-wrought-iron table and cushion-covered chairs.

Rosamund turned to find his eyes on her. Even for a woman used to public scrutiny, his intense regard made her almost self-conscious. 'As you say, a couple.'

When this man was involved she much preferred 'couple' to 'lovers'.

'So.' She focused on essentials. 'We'll be seen in public together. Are you coming to every event? I can give you the schedule.' Now she'd broken her silence she couldn't seem to stop.

'I have it and yes, wherever you go I'll be there.'

That should have reassured, considering what she'd heard about Ricardo and his nasty ways. Yet it sounded more like a challenge, even a threat, than a promise.

She was about to ask if he had appropriate clothes for the formal events but stopped the urge to babble. A man who conjured a multi-million-dollar luxury home in Paris could manage formal clothes.

She folded her arms, waiting for him to speak. Had he brought her here to discuss how to go about convincing people they were a couple?

Heat detonated low inside as she recalled her body's instantaneous, disturbing response to his.

To counter it she reminded herself they simply needed to be seen together. Public speculation and the voracious paparazzi would see to the rest.

They wouldn't attend events where public displays of affection were required. The most she'd have to do would be stand close and smile at him.

That could be a problem. She doubted if he knew how to smile back.

But Rosamund didn't really care if people believed the fiction. She refused even to note the stories the press ran about her and her apparent multitude of partners. Her lip curled and a tiny snort of disgust escaped.

His stare sharpened, his nostrils flaring as if in distaste. 'You have something to say? Something you want to get off your chest?'

As if she needed to explain herself to him!

'Nothing at all.' Suddenly fatigue swamped her. It had been a long day after a series of long days and the emotional strain of anticipating the next few days took its toll. She was both eager for this event and dreading it. 'Can you show me to my room?'

'Of course. I just thought you should know where the kitchen was. Security staff will monitor the premises but you won't see them. Otherwise there's no staff. You need to know where the food is so you can prepare your meals.'

Alone in this lovely house, free to keep her own hours when she wasn't attending an event? Despite the headache she'd fought since landing, Rosamund smiled. She could imagine herself breakfasting on the sun-drenched patio. 'Excellent. I'll enjoy that. Thank you.'

* * *

Rosamund surveyed the place she was to sleep for the next several nights. Tall-ceilinged and elegantly furnished, it managed to be welcoming despite the grandeur of both the sitting area and bedroom. A luxurious, modern bathroom was visible through an open door.

'It's a beautiful suite.'

She didn't care about the antiques or the grandeur. With pain now humming in her temples and growing by the minute, all she cared about was that bed. She imagined lying down and finally closing her eyes.

When she was alone.

She turned, and noticed another door. 'What's through there?'

She'd already turned the handle when Fotis Mavridis said, 'My room.'

Rosamund spun around, grateful for her hold on the doorknob when the world kept spinning and pain notched higher.

'You said I'd be here alone!'

He stood just inside her doorway, feet apart, hands folded across his broad chest, watching. She refused to admit it but she was beginning to find that too-steady gaze getting on her nerves.

Stupid when she'd spent her life under scrutiny. But this felt different.

You're tired, that's all.

'I said there'd be no staff. I'm your minder, remember?' His tone held a thread that might have been censure or sarcasm. It was hard to be sure over the painful thud of her pulse in her temples. 'I need to be close in case there's a threat.'

She looked down at the door then opened it and looked at the other side. 'There's no key.'

'If there's a problem I need to be able to get to you quickly.'

Oh, there's a problem all right. You're the problem.

As for him getting to her, he was already doing that.

No one since her father had got under her skin but this man

excelled at it. Unlike her father, he even managed it with a few laconic phrases or raised eyebrow instead of a full-scale rant.

She turned to find him surveying her. His expression hadn't changed but abruptly she *felt* his self-satisfaction. He liked the fact this wasn't what she wanted.

Tomorrow she'd wonder why. For now she had other priorities.

Pushing weary shoulders back and drawing herself up to her full height, she inclined her head. She'd learned to choose her battles.

Much as she hated the idea of him able to invade her privacy, it was obvious he had no intention of coming to her room. He might be smirking beneath that rigid stare, but he didn't want to get close to her any more than she wanted him to.

'How very sensible.' The pain now was so bad she didn't even attempt a smile. 'Now, if you'll excuse me, I'd like privacy.'

Without waiting for a reply she turned, picked up her bag and made for the bathroom.

By the time she'd taken some painkillers he was gone. She glanced at the connecting door and pursed her lips. Pulling out the chair at the writing desk near the window, she carried it across and propped it under the doorknob.

There was no key in the door to the hall and nothing she could use to bar it. She'd think about that later.

And about her compulsion to keep Fotis Mavridis at a distance. She didn't know why he unsettled her so much. It wasn't just his disapproval. She'd had years of that from her father. There was something else, gnawing at her, making her aware of him, making it impossible to ignore him.

Shucking her shoes and slipping off her jacket, she undid her hair with a sigh of relief and crawled onto the bed, letting herself relax fully as her body met the mattress. It seemed like forever since she'd been able to stop and switch off.

But her last thought was of eyes the colour of the sea, changeable and full of censure.

* * *

Fotis spent some time confirming arrangements with the security staff, checking the perimeter cameras and alarms and refamiliarising himself with her schedule.

So many days out of his own schedule to do this favour for the king of Cardona! But it would pay dividends in the end. Leon had promised his unwavering support for the initiative Fotis had finally got off the ground. *That* was all that mattered. For that he'd look after a bevy of beautiful, spoiled, narcissistic princesses!

As day turned to evening Fotis focused on his own work, checking in with staff, catching up on messages, and delving into a draft report on a particularly complex issue prepared by a new but promising staffer. It would need finessing before being presented to the client but the bones were good.

Rolling his shoulders, he realised he'd been sitting too long and glanced at the time.

He frowned. After making coffee and a sandwich hours ago, he'd retreated to his room. No matter his personal views on the woman on the other side of the door, he'd promised to protect her. It was unlikely any threat would reach her here, but he'd given his word. Fotis always kept his word.

Yet there'd been no sound from her room in hours. She hadn't gone to the kitchen for food or rung out for a delivery. Subconsciously he'd been listening for the sound of her moving around but there'd been nothing.

Why hadn't he realised before? He'd let the intriguing issues in his report distract him.

His mouth flattened as he acknowledged how determined he'd been to put her from his mind. Because thinking about her destroyed his concentration.

He'd let his response to her interfere with what had to be done. It was inexcusable.

Grimacing, Fotis moved to the connecting door and listened. Nothing. She had no light on but looking through the keyhole he saw something move. It took a heart-stopping second to realise it was a long, sheer curtain billowing at an open window, its movement caught by silvery moonlight.

She probably just liked fresh air. But the instinct that had kept him safe during his military career kicked in. He had to be sure. He turned the door handle, only to discover the door wouldn't budge.

Seconds later he was out of his room and in the corridor. Hand on her doorknob he paused, listening, but heard nothing. Silently he turned the knob, relief singing in his blood as the door opened without obstruction.

There was no sign of disturbance and he could see a form on the bed.

Keeping away from the light spilling through the windows, he moved soft-footed and silent along the wall, senses alert as he approached the bed.

It was definitely her. He recognised the pale trousers and dark camisole. He also recognised the sumptuous waves of reddish-blond hair loose around her shoulders, the arch of those definite eyebrows and the natural downturn at the corners of a mouth that in repose hinted at sultry sensuality.

His heart beat a quick tattoo as his lungs emptied then refilled.

Good to know she wasn't abducted on your watch, Mavridis.

The sarcastic voice sounded like his old special ops commander.

He dragged his attention from the way one breast looked about to slip free of her top. His hands flexed as he recalled her pebbled nipples hard against the silk as she gave him sass laced with contempt.

Not a woman he should hanker after.

Okay, she was here, but was she all right? Why was she still dressed? She lay so still that she was either an incredibly deep sleeper or…

Fotis leaned over the bed until a drift of cinnamon and vanilla scent, laced with warm female, assaulted his nostrils. He drew it in, barely noticing his surprise that she should smell so sweetly wholesome. Wholesome but addictive.

Frowning, he moved closer and finally had the confirmation he needed. The softest waft of breath caressed his chin. He looked down and at last discerned the gentle rise and fall of her breasts which a moment before had seemed so still.

Abruptly he straightened and stepped back. She seemed safe enough. But she hadn't bothered to bathe or change, much less eat. What was her problem?

He hadn't wasted much time on a detailed background check. He'd already known more than enough about Princess Rosamund before her brother contacted him. He knew her character and her predilection for scandalous assignations. Was there also a drug habit? Was that why she hadn't changed or eaten and why she seemed so deeply asleep?

A quick sweep of the bathroom revealed nothing. But returning to her room he noticed something on her bedside table. Scooping it up and turning away, he inspected it with a penlight torch. Painkillers. Not heavy dose prescription medications but over-the-counter tablets in common use against headaches.

He switched off the torch and surveyed the sleeping woman, replaying their last encounter.

She'd looked pale, standing in the garage staring with wide eyes, and she'd blinked against the afternoon light coming into the kitchen. Then there was the way she'd hunched her shoulders, like someone in pain, though she'd been quick to straighten. The tiny lines puckering the centre of her forehead. He'd thought that due to temper. Could it have been pain?

It must have been bad for her to fall, fully clothed, onto the bed.

Fotis prided himself on his ability to notice things others didn't. To collect clues and transform them into a complete picture before other people had an inkling there was anything wrong. Hell, it was a core component of his business!

But he'd missed this. He'd let personal feelings hinder his ability to observe, collate facts and analyse.

No security system was inviolable. If there *had* been an intruder, Fotis might have been too late.

He put the tablets back and moved away so that light, sweet fragrance didn't tease him anymore.

His chest rose on a deep inhalation. Ignoring her wasn't good enough. He'd given his word to protect her. Despite his inclinations, he vowed that from now on he'd pay close attention to every move she made. He couldn't afford to miss any threat.

What had been a deeply annoying job had suddenly become almost impossible. He'd do it because he had no choice. But some primal self-knowledge was already screaming a warning.

He despised everything she stood for. Particularly her overweening sense of entitlement and selfish belief that she should get whatever and whoever she wanted with no thought to anyone else. But it wasn't just contempt he felt.

Brutal honesty forced him to admit to a thread, a powerful thread, of lust.

It had been there from the first and only strengthened each time she challenged him with those knowing grey-blue eyes and pert rejoinders. Her attitude as much as her body underpinned her sex appeal.

He'd thought, given his history, feeling such attraction would be impossible. Surely he had better taste.

Scowling, he stalked out of the room.

CHAPTER THREE

THE LIMOUSINE CRUISED down a street that housed some of Paris's most famous fashion showrooms. 'There's no need to come in,' she said. 'I'll text when I'm ready to leave.'

She didn't even look at him. Because she thought the person keeping her safe didn't deserve courtesy?

You weren't exactly courteous yesterday, were you? For once you didn't bother to hide your feelings.

Fotis ignored his double standard. He wasn't paid to be friendly. He wasn't even being paid!

Yet her curt dismissal rankled. He didn't want this woman's attention but he was stuck with her. He loathed people who took what they wanted without gratitude for those who made their lives easy.

But last night he'd promised himself not to take his eye off the ball. He couldn't let personal dislike interfere with that duty.

'I'll come in with you, no need to text.'

That earned him a sharp stare. Cool grey eyes surveyed him as if suspecting an ulterior motive. 'It's unnecessary.'

The car stopped and he glanced past her to the gold-and-cream awning leading into the showroom. The window display was artfully minimal and a couple of tourists took selfies.

'Don't worry, Princess. I won't follow you into the changing room.'

He watched her eyes widen fractionally and her mouth

tighten. To his surprise he felt a tug of satisfaction in his belly, knowing he could pierce her complacency.

'Besides,' he murmured, 'it's the perfect chance to be seen together as a couple. It would be wise to give our fake relationship a trial in public before tonight's event. We need to look believable together.'

Her eyebrows lifted. 'Frankly I don't care if people believe we're a couple.'

'Do you really want to draw attention to the fact you need a bodyguard glued to your side rather than observing at a distance? That's guaranteed to attract public speculation. It would draw attention away from the event and fix it squarely on you.'

Maybe that was what she wanted.

But when she blinked he was surprised to read uncertainty in her expression.

Since they'd met she'd been supremely confident. For a bare second she looked almost vulnerable.

'Very well.' Her voice was clipped. 'You can come in. There's a lounge area where you can wait. As for our relationship...' Her head snapped around, eyes stormy. 'Don't say *anything*, even if asked.'

'Yes, ma'am,' he drawled. 'Whatever you say, ma'am.'

Did her lips twitch? He couldn't tell if it was amusement, annoyance, or a trick of the light. Before he could be sure she turned towards the door.

'Wait! Don't get out until I'm there.'

Did this woman have no idea of basic safety precautions? She *must* have had close personal protection before. It was an intrinsic part of being royal.

He filed that away to ponder later.

Fotis got out and walked around the rear of the limo. As arranged, the driver stayed behind the wheel, ready to accelerate to safety if need be. After surveying the street, Fotis opened the back door, keeping his focus more on their surroundings than her. A professional guard, a man he'd known in the military, strolled towards them down the pavement as if merely passing. Everything was under control as planned.

Yet Fotis' concentration splintered as he put his hand to her elbow to usher her towards the building.

The sudden, visceral response to his flesh touching hers stunned him. There was rocketing heat and a blast of awareness that made his fingers tighten on her cool, bare arm while everything inside him tensed. With *need*.

Forcing out the air trapped in his lungs, he withdrew his hand, holding it behind her back as they walked through the door that opened for them.

Repressing a scowl, Fotis nodded to the doorman and forced himself to take in their surroundings. The likelihood of a threat inside here was slim but even so…

Looking for threats took his mind off that powerful stab of awareness when he touched her. *Sexual awareness.*

Grim amusement eddied. It was laughable, of course. He wasn't masochistic enough to hanker after a woman like her. She had too much in common with his hedonistic, social butterfly mother, a type he'd always avoided. His reaction now was his body's way of reminding him he hadn't been with a desirable woman for…how long?

Fotis jerked his attention to his charge, now surrounded by fawning female attendants. He took his place beside her, preternaturally aware of her as if he'd entered a force field. His skin tingled and his hands flexed as a phantom drift of cinnamon teased his nostrils.

'This way please, Your Highness.' The older of the pair turned to him with a gracious smile. 'Monsieur.'

But her attention was clearly on her client as she led them to another room fitted with comfortable sofas, plush carpet and a raised podium surrounded by mirrors.

A third staff member arrived bearing a bottle of vintage champagne and a pair of tulip glasses.

The princess said, 'Thank you, but not for me.'

Fotis also declined a drink, and the offered canapés. He strolled the perimeter of the room, taking in the large, adjoining dressing room, entering just far enough to be sure there was no separate access to the space.

'No.' The single word sliced through the low murmur of voices like a blade through butter. 'Absolutely not.'

He swung around, senses on alert because, while his charge hadn't raised her voice, her implacable tone jarred. He stalked closer, curious.

'But, ma'am,' the older woman said, 'it's been arranged. The work has been done.'

'I'm sorry there's been confusion, but I intend to wear the dress I ordered last month. I wasn't consulted about a change.'

'Ah, in that case, let me show you.' The saleswoman's expression eased into a smile as she clicked her fingers and a minion hurried off. 'I'm sure, when you see it, you'll approve.'

The underling returned with a red dress draped over her arm. She cradled it as gently as a mother with a newborn child and the other attendants smiled enthusiastically.

'*Voilà!* With Your Highness's colouring and figure it will look spectacular.'

But Her Highness's expression wasn't enthusiastic. Fotis saw a ripple of emotion across her face, a frown on her brow and something stark in her eyes. A second later she smoothed her features. But there was tension in the set of her jaw and stiff shoulders. Anger?

Two attendants held the dress up between them. Even he could see it was stunning. On the right body it would stop traffic.

'As you see, that shade with your colouring—'

'No.' This time the princess's voice was the merest whisper, but it stopped the woman in mid flow. 'I won't wear it.'

'But Monsieur Gaudreau specifically requested it. It's been an honour to work on such an iconic piece. It will be the centrepiece of the whole...'

The princess turned her back on the mannequin and Fotis saw the other woman's smile disintegrate. 'I'll wear the dress I ordered. I assume it was completed?'

The other woman licked her lips, frowning. 'Of course, Your Highness. But this would mean so much, not just to Monsieur Gaudreau but to everyone who—'

'I'm sorry, madame. But it won't do.' She didn't sound sorry and Fotis saw the other attendants frown at each other, eyes wide with horror. 'I'll try on the dress I ordered.' When no one responded she added, 'Or I could wear an outfit I brought from Cardona.'

That caused a stir. Within seconds the red dress had disappeared, replaced by one in blue. The jubilant mood of minutes ago was replaced with awkward wariness.

Without glancing his way Princess Rosamund disappeared into the dressing room with several attendants.

What had just happened? Fotis was no expert on women's fashion. The red dress was stunning and it was clear from the reaction of the staff that her rejection of it was deeply shocking. He knew the significance of tonight's opening gala to the retrospective of Juliette Bernard's films. Especially for Antoine Gaudreau, an old man who'd worked with Bernard and was revered by many as something approaching a national icon.

Fotis' mouth twisted. Clearly her high and mightiness didn't take kindly to having their plans altered by anyone but her.

She'd reacted to the new dress as if they'd tried to foist a canvas sack on her, instead of a beautiful creation that would make her look a million dollars. Her refusal had to be sheer pique at having her plans thwarted. What other explanation could there be?

He'd known Princess Rosamund was selfish. Now he added callous to his list.

She'd ignored the staff's eagerness and the fact they'd clearly worked hard to produce the red dress. The fact it meant a lot to an old man at the very end of his career, and by the sound of it, many others, meant nothing to her.

She didn't care about others' feelings. Clearly she didn't subscribe to the idea that privilege came with responsibility to others.

Distaste soured his mouth and he reached for one of the canapés.

He'd been in her company less than twenty-four hours and couldn't wait to be rid of her.

Fotis spent the rest of the day in his own company. After the debacle at the couturier, and a stop at a famous store to buy a beribboned gift box of macarons, they'd returned to the house. He'd been with the princess only long enough to see her make a salad before she disappeared to eat in her room and spend the afternoon there.

He'd been startled by her easy competence in the kitchen, whipping up a dressing and deftly chopping ingredients as if it were second nature.

What surprised him even more was that she'd left half the salad for him to save him getting his own lunch. Even now he found it hard to credit. She'd barely looked at him as she moved around the big kitchen, absorbed in her own thoughts.

Or determined to ignore the staff.

Yet the unexpected gesture was surprisingly generous. How did that fit with the spoiled persona?

Curious, he'd dug into the salad and found it surprisingly tasty.

There was that word again. *Surprising.* Fotis didn't like surprises. He preferred answers.

He'd spent much of the afternoon searching for more information on the woman he'd been blackmailed into minding. But there'd been nothing new, no startling revelations.

There were inevitable photos of her as a cute child, looking docile at grand events. A touching photo of her as a slender young girl at her mother's funeral. Then, when she was seventeen, a slew of behind-the-scenes snaps. Draped in the arms of a good-looking boy a few years older. Being helped out of a sports car, laughing in a barely-there dress, long legs on full display, wearing a smile that hinted at inebriation. Some that were more scandalous. Persistent stories of wild parties and decadent behaviour.

After that she'd been more circumspect. But always in the background were reports of her busy love life, her penchant for sophisticated parties and refusal to settle down. She had no job other than as a royal presence at various events and she lived off the royal purse.

Princess Rosamund seemed to have no aspirations to do anything to further herself.

She was another addicted to the privileges of wealth.

Memory conjured a woman with flashing dark eyes. His mother had a siren's ability to make you feel special. For as long as you had something she wanted. But behind the beauty was a corroded soul, interested only in her own pleasure.

With brutal efficiency Fotis shoved aside thoughts of his mother. He shrugged his shoulders into his dinner jacket and knocked on his charge's door. 'It's time.'

The sound of footsteps and the door opening startled him. He hadn't expected her to be punctual. Yet she was clearly ready, carrying a beaded purse and a transparent wrap of silver blue that matched her long dress.

He stepped back, giving her space, and himself time to acclimatise.

She was stunning.

Delectable, growled a husky inner voice. Not just husky but hungry. *Ravenous.*

Every male hormone hummed and Fotis registered a heavy awareness pooling in his groin.

Her reddish-blond hair was caught up with a few wisps artfully loose around her neck, drawing attention to its slim length and her bare shoulders. Miniscule straps held up a simple dress that skimmed her from breasts to toes. It wasn't tight, yet the way the light played across shimmering, shifting material revealed a body that made his mouth dry.

Want rose with a sharpness that left him short of air.

She turned to close the door and his gaze fastened on the smooth, golden flesh of her upper back.

Fotis felt the hard punch of response reverberate from his ribs to his belly, and lower.

He'd felt something similar last night, seeing her asleep. And before that, on the plane, when she'd looked so supercilious that he'd wanted to silence her sass with his mouth on hers.

Not. Going. To. Happen.

She was a client, even if an unwanted one.

He had too much self-respect to fall for the wiles of a woman so like his self-absorbed mother. *She* used men to get what she wanted. To her they were disposable. Even her innocent sons.

His voice grated over the bones of ancient hurt. 'We need to leave now if you want to arrive on time.'

Blue-grey eyes lifted and he caught Rosamund's curiosity. Unblinking, he met her stare, wishing she'd object to his brusqueness and break their deal in a fit of pique.

Disappointingly, she simply nodded and moved to the stairs.

Which meant he had to spend the evening at her side, smiling and pretending to enjoy himself. But not touching. Not even skimming his knuckle down her bare arm or testing the softness of those teasing strawberry-blond tendrils.

Fotis glowered as he accompanied her downstairs and into the waiting limousine. Bad enough to waste his time looking after a spoiled princess but to have his body quicken whenever she was around... It was the ultimate betrayal.

Fortunately keeping his mind on potential threats would give him no time to think about his sudden unaccountably bad taste in women.

* * *

Rosamund reminded herself she was used to discomfort. Royal duty was often tedious if not downright trying. But tonight she wished she could run away.

Impossible! She *wanted* to attend. This was important to her. She'd known it would be tough, but today's events at the couturier had thrown her more than she wanted to admit.

The idea of wearing that dress… It brought memories of the secret pain her mother had hidden behind optimism and a determination to look forward, not back. She wouldn't betray her mother's memory by wearing it.

She shuddered and bit her lip, turning to look at the passing view of Paris in the street lights, not wanting the man beside her to see—

'Are you cold? Do you want the air-conditioning changed?'

Silently she cursed his perspicacity. Fotis Mavridis saw too much. Whereas most men looked at her and saw what they wanted to see, she had the uncomfortable notion he was different.

Keeping her real self private had been the key to her survival. The thought of anyone breaching that barrier unnerved her. Usually she was confident about hiding her feelings and vulnerabilities. But today, anticipating tonight's event, she felt too raw, as if someone had scrubbed her skin with a steel brush until it bled.

Stop being a drama queen. You can do this! Think of all those years when your mother hid her feelings so successfully that the public had no inkling of her hurt.

But thinking of her mother only made everything worse. She'd been her rock. Rosamund missed her love, her guidance, her company. Sometimes she felt so terribly alone.

She dreaded tonight as much as she longed for it.

Rosamund sensed the big man beside her on the back seat shift his weight. 'Princess?'

'No, thank you. The temperature is fine.'

Schooling her features, she turned to look at him, but avoided his eyes. He'd make a stir tonight. Not handsome yet brutally attractive with severe features that had their own stark beauty. A superb body that looked just as good in a tuxedo as it did in a leather jacket and jeans.

What would he look like, naked?

She felt her eyes widen at the wayward thought and almost welcomed the distraction.

The press would have a field day when she arrived with him. It would fuel a whole new round of rumours and speculation. By tomorrow there'd be stories that she'd torn him away from his long-term love. Or that they were part of a scandalous love triangle. The options were endless.

After the press shredded her reputation, there'd been a stage when she'd frequented parties that veered towards the scandalous. No amount of effort had convinced her father or anyone else that she'd been an innocent, wronged by a vengeful lover. So in a fit of indignation she'd decided to live up to her party girl reputation.

That phase had been short. It wasn't the life she wanted. But though that was years ago, the press still typecast her as a shallow fun-seeker. No doubt tomorrow's stories about her and Mavridis would be salacious or full of innuendo.

At least Mavridis wouldn't look out of place at the formal event, or as her supposed lover.

Imagine the reaction if she'd turned up with the podgy, balding bureaucrat she'd first imagined him.

'Something amuses you?'

His low voice was a deep purr, brushing her skin and making her nipples bud. Instinctively she folded her arms across her body.

'I was just imagining how popular you'll be tonight. You could well have talent scouts approaching you. The place will be full of casting agents, among others.'

He didn't look impressed. She doubted much impressed this man. Certainly not her. 'I already have a job.'

'Just what does your business do, *Kyrie* Mavridis?'

'Fotis. We'll need to use first names in public.'

Silently, she formed the word in her head, wondering how it would taste on her tongue. Inexplicably she wished she could keep calling him by his surname. It felt safer.

'Of course. And your company?'

Unreadable eyes held hers. 'We provide confidential advice on complex matters to a range of clients.'

She raised her eyebrows. He made it sound like a state secret. Or did he think she was too dim-witted to understand whatever technicalities were involved?

Before she could ask anything else, the car halted and she became aware of the crowd thronging the pavement. At least he'd distracted her for a short time from the ordeal to come.

And, because of him, she wouldn't be walking into the gala with a full complement of security agents hemming her in and making her into even more of a spectacle.

Without thinking, she gave him a quick smile as he opened his door. 'Thank you for doing this for Leon.'

Minutes later they stood together on the red carpet, surrounded by camera flashes and demanding voices.

Her arm was through his, her hand resting on his forearm, the fine weave of his jacket soft beneath her fingertips. He was so solid, so steady that for the first time she wondered what it would be like to attend such events with a real partner. Not a stranger protecting her for commercial benefit, but someone who cared about *her*.

She thrust the idea aside and smiled for their audience.

It was an exclusive event, full of VIPs, but there were others here, hoping to catch a glimpse of the attendees. Many waved photos and some called her name.

They were about to climb the stairs into the imposing building when Rosamund halted. 'I'll be back soon.'

She moved to slip her arm free but he stopped her. 'Where you go, I go.'

It was a statement of fact. He was being paid to keep her safe, yet his words resonated powerfully.

She jerked her head up to meet that ocean-bright stare and felt a longing so powerful, so unexpected that for a second she forgot all about the crowd and the photographers.

Something had changed. It had started with that smile in the car. The one that transformed her face from haughty composure to something…genuine.

If you can believe that.

But despite his ingrained doubt, Fotis had seen a different woman in that smile. Someone impulsive and generous rather than arrogant and selfish. Princess Rosamund didn't want him around but it seemed she appreciated him for her brother's sake. As if the favour he did benefited the king rather than her. And she wanted her brother to be happy.

The shock of it had eddied through Fotis as he took his place at her door, standing between her and the crowd. He'd just regained his equilibrium when she'd slipped her arm through his, creating a quake of longing deep in his belly.

He'd been a paratrooper operating in difficult situations, then spent years carving out his business. Yet in that moment it felt as if nothing had tested his control as much as remaining aloof and alert while Rosamund of Cardona snuggled up to him.

Despite his hormonal rush, he could tell she wasn't trying to tease him. Her touch was light and impersonal.

A pity his body didn't think so. He'd never been so close to full, unwanted arousal in public since his teens. It should be impossible. But this woman turned everything upside down, even his instincts.

He made himself focus on the crowd, assessing body language, alert to sudden movements. But it was Rosamund's abrupt move that surprised him as she tried to slip away. 'I'll be back soon.'

His reaction was instantaneous, his grip tightening. 'Where you go, I go.'

She turned, bright eyes locking on his, and something behind his ribs tightened. Then she nodded and drew him towards the crowd on the side of the carpet away from the cameras.

It was only then that he realised some of the people calling her name weren't press, but members of the public. Instead of waving and making her way indoors, she approached with a smile on her face.

Instinct kicking in, he held her close and pulled her to a stop as he scanned the crowd. 'No. This isn't a good idea.'

She sent him a sideways look under her lashes that did ridiculous things to his hormones, especially when she leaned closer and he caught that delicious spice and warm woman scent that made him forget all the reasons she was poison. 'A few minutes. That's all.'

He was weaker than he'd thought, nodding even as he cursed his weakness.

He released her, keeping both hands free in case something went wrong. Anyone watching would guess he was hired muscle, but it didn't matter. He mightn't like her but he was damned if he'd let anyone get to her on his watch.

There were smiles all around and lots of excitement as she chatted with fans. She was good with the crowd. She made total strangers feel they were seen and appreciated.

But people-pleasing was a useful tool, not evidence of a good heart.

'If you want to get inside in time for the opening...' he murmured.

Finally she nodded and let herself be led away.

They followed the red carpet and he recognised several famous faces. They were about to enter the grand building when a man standing to one side caught his eye, but just as Fotis paused, senses alert, the stranger disappeared into the crowd.

Then they were inside the soaring space, resplendent with brilliant chandeliers and glittering guests. The crowd parted as they entered.

Training kicked in, making him focus on individuals, movements, anything out of place. When he heard the sharp hitch of his companion's breath, he was surprised, for he'd seen nothing to make him wary.

Her uptilted gaze was fixed on the far wall.

High up an image was projected. A stunning young woman with blue eyes and flame-red hair smiled as if the world were her playground. She wore red, a provocative dress that revealed lots of toned, honeyed flesh and clung lovingly to her sinuous body.

Of course he knew the photo. He suspected that image had featured in the wet dreams of men all around the world.

Juliette Bernard in the year she burst onto the cinema scene, causing a sensation. Tonight's opening party was an homage to a woman who'd won resounding critical acclaim for her craft.

Juliette Bernard, the English-French actress who'd later cemented her place in public mythology with her fairy-tale marriage to the King of Cardona.

He felt a quiver rack the woman beside him and turned to see her eyes, now more grey than blue and overbright.

Without allowing himself time to think, he stepped in front of her, blocking her from curious stares, and took both her hands. They were cold, but even as he registered that, she blinked and firmed her lips.

Fotis bent his head, surprised at his surge of concern. 'Are you all right?'

She blinked again and for a long moment emotion shimmered in that bright gaze. Grief so stark it sucked his breath away.

Then it disappeared. There was a flicker of a moment when

something else softened her expression as she met his gaze. Gratitude? His hands involuntarily tightened.

But seconds later she was again the soignee socialite he'd met yesterday. A woman without a care and with the world at her feet.

'Your Highness.'

The princess looked past him and moved to greet the man who'd approached. She was gracious and charming, as if those moments of earthquaking emotion hadn't happened.

Fotis felt the world shift beneath his feet. It was unnerving to realise the woman he despised had hidden depths. That, despite her unforgivable actions in New York a month ago, she wasn't simply a shallow, selfish woman who trampled anyone to get what she wanted. That she *felt*, and felt deeply.

Who was the real Princess Rosamund?

And why did he want, badly, to uncover her secrets?

CHAPTER FOUR

ROSAMUND CHEWED HER PENCIL, trying to concentrate. But her thoughts jumped all over the place.

Exhausted, she'd slept deeply last night and should feel refreshed. Instead she jangled with nervous energy. Partly it was from reliving last night's events and the emotional upheaval of being thrust into that star-strewn world about which her mother had been so ambivalent. The world which had been both fulfilling and destructive.

Yet it wasn't the evening spent as her mother's proxy that unsettled her. It was Fotis Mavridis.

She glanced across the patio to the open doors into the kitchen. He'd looked in again an hour ago, grabbed a drink and left, with barely a nod to acknowledge her presence.

His expression had been as dour as ever. No hint of a smile, not that she'd ever seen him smile. He'd looked as cold and blank, as judgemental, as ever.

Yet last night at the reception she could have sworn there'd been a change in him. When she'd held his arm heat had arced between them and despite his poker face she'd *felt* the spark of shared awareness.

More than that, he'd stunned her with that unexpected moment of understanding.

Despite all her preparation, Rosamund had been overwhelmed at the sight of her mother's image, while standing in the place where her mother should have been, accepting her accolades. For a second all she could think of was how much her mother had missed out on. And how much Rosamund still missed *her*.

The sight of Fotis blocking out the photo, and the crowd, leaning towards her with concern in his voice and sympathy in his eyes, had stunned her.

She'd known an all-consuming impulse to lean her head against his broad shoulder, breathe in his strength, and step off the merry-go-round of public expectation and royal duty.

For the tiniest instant it had felt like he *saw* her as no one else did. Saw deep inside to the turmoil, doubt and isolation. And understood.

There was something about that flash of solicitousness that told her he knew grief too. Knew the toll it took to keep pretending everything was okay.

Of course it wasn't true. Fotis Mavridis knew nothing about her, except, she guessed, the lurid headlines. He didn't know *her*, any more than she knew him. It had been wishful thinking. And, she admitted as she sipped her cold coffee, loneliness.

She put the cup down with a clunk and turned to the paragraph she was writing. She hadn't felt inspired all morning. But she was a professional and knew she couldn't wait for inspiration. Sometimes she had to coax it into appearing. Her editor, not to mention her readers, were waiting for the next book.

Frowning at the scrawl on the page she knew she'd be better spending her time doing something else. She slapped shut the notebook, secured the elastic band around it to stop any loose pages slipping out, and shoved back her chair.

She'd been here since dawn, trying to get ahead with her story but all she had to show for it were ramblings she knew she couldn't use and a page full of doodles, cartoonish images of a severe-featured man whose eyes she couldn't capture. As if she could use *those* to illustrate the book!

Rosamund was at the coffee machine when a change in

the atmosphere made her still. She looked towards the open French doors, expecting to see the daylight darkened by storm clouds, but it was still bright and sunny.

Yet the fine hairs at her nape and along her arms stood up. Slowly she turned.

Fotis Mavridis stood in the doorway, feet wide, arms folded, wearing faded jeans and an olive-green shirt with sleeves rolled up to reveal strong, sinewy forearms.

A weight plummeted from her chest to her abdomen, sending ripples of awareness radiating to every part of her body. Suddenly the peaceful room felt unnervingly different and out of kilter.

She lifted her gaze and met eyes that today glowed more green than blue. Heat fired her blood, warming her skin.

She turned back to the machine, grateful for something to do. 'Coffee?'

'I've had mine.'

His tone was brusque, telling her they were back to being enemies. That suited her. Disapproval and dislike she could deal with. That strange...yearning she'd felt around him was an aberration.

Her lips twisted as she frothed hot milk. 'Is there a car I can use, apart from the limousine?'

'Why?'

Rosamund bit her lip rather than blurt out an angry answer. For some reason he was trying to provoke her. She was tempted to wonder why he disliked her so much, but refused to waste mental effort on it. 'I have an appointment.'

When the silence extended she picked up her cup and turned. Only then did he say, 'There's no appointment in your diary until this evening.'

She refrained from rolling her eyes. 'I'm visiting a friend and I'd rather not take the limo. Is there a car I can use or shall I get a taxi?'

'I'll take you.'

'I'll be quite safe there. As I said, I'm visiting a friend.'

Yet her assurance only provoked a frown. 'How well do you know this *friend*?'

Rosamund blinked. If she didn't know better she'd think that sounded like pique or even... No, impossible to think it was jealousy.

'Well enough to know I'll be safe.' She refused to explain. She was entitled to privacy.

Strolling across the kitchen, she scooped up her notebook and stopped only because he blocked her exit. When he didn't move she sipped her coffee and let the familiar taste soothe her ruffled edges.

'If you'll excuse me, I'll get ready to leave.'

For a second she thought he'd refuse to move. Her pulse quickened and something like excitement jagged through her.

Finally he stepped aside with a mock bow, just far enough for her to exit. But he stood close enough for her to feel his body heat and detect the scent of soap and virile man.

Her nostrils quivered and that weight in her abdomen became a hollow ache as female hormones blasted into awareness.

Rosamund breathed out quickly, fighting the tug of attraction. It was horribly unfair that this provoking man aroused her. Silently she cursed her biological clock or whatever it was that made her susceptible.

He was waiting when she came downstairs carrying the enormous gift box of macarons.

'What's the address?'

Of course a greeting was too much to expect. But even surly, he commanded her attention. Damn the man!

She walked towards the garage. 'You can drive but you're not going in with me.'

'I don't care about your secrets, Princess. Whether your lover's married or why you want to keep your assignation quiet.

I promised your brother I'd keep you safe and I intend to do just that. I need to check the place.'

Her lover!

Indignation rose, but it was quickly swamped by weariness. Her father had always judged her harshly, their characters too different for her to fit his expectations. The press had cast her into a convenient role years ago and now invented stories about her. It should be no surprise this stranger did the same.

Yet it infuriated her that he, like so many others, felt he had the right to jump to conclusions and condemn her.

Let him. She wouldn't waste her time on explanations.

As he took the box and secured it on the back seat of a gleaming grey four-wheel-drive, she slid into the front passenger seat and gave him the address, catching his frown at their destination.

'Well, well, well. Your macho man isn't such a prig after all.'

Rosamund looked up from the kitchen table where she was putting delicate, pastel-coloured macarons in a battered biscuit tin. 'Sorry?'

Lucie was peering outside. 'Your man, Fontis.'

'Fotis, and he's not my man.'

Which Lucie knew full well. The old lady's brain was as sharp as ever. Rosamund caught her speculative glance and shook her head. 'Truly, Lucie. We barely speak and certainly don't like each other. It will be a relief to go our separate ways in a week.'

When they'd arrived, Fotis had insisted on coming to check out the flat. If he'd been surprised to meet a grey-haired woman in a wheelchair instead of a lover, he hadn't shown it. Rosamund had explained he was her temporary bodyguard— she had no intention of lying to her old friend—and shut the door on him as soon as he'd finished his security inspection.

But annoyingly, over the next two hours her thoughts kept straying to him. Was he standing guard outside the ground floor flat, or minding the luxury vehicle, since this area of social housing was known for its crime rate? She'd suggested he leave and return when she texted, but the set of his jaw and glitter in his eyes had told her what he thought of that.

'You take me for a fool, *cherie*?'

Rosamund looked up to see Lucie watching her, head tilted as if fascinated. 'Of course not. I'm telling you the truth. We can hardly stand to be in the same space as each other.'

'Get on each other's nerves, do you?'

Rosamund met Lucie's bright eyes and realisation dawned. 'You can't possibly think—'

'I don't *think*, I *know*. I may be old but there are some things you don't forget. The way you pretend not to look at each other, yet you're both completely attuned to each other. The air sizzled between you.' Lucie waved her hand as if fanning herself. 'And the intense stares when the other one isn't watching. Tss! I remember that heat.'

'Pure dislike,' Rosamund said quickly.

'You're not that naïve. And your mother would never raise a fool. There's more than dislike going on between you two.'

Rosamund caught her lip with her teeth. It wasn't true. Fotis had made his distaste obvious. He avoided her when he could. She'd never known anyone so eager to get away from her.

As for *her* feelings… Yes, there was a powerful physical attraction, but no one knew better than she not to trust that. Once, she'd naively let attraction lead her astray and years later she still paid for that mistake. She'd learnt her lesson. She found it hard to trust any man now.

'He tracks you with his eyes, did you know that?'

Rosamund's heart jerked hard against her ribs and she felt a betraying flutter low inside, but frowned and said, 'He's my bodyguard! He supposed to keep an eye on me.'

Lucie's voice softened. 'You're not as good an actor as your mother, *cherie*. But if you don't want to talk about it…'

She didn't. For some reason Fotis Mavridis loathed her. It

was shaming to admit, even to herself, but she could neither fully reciprocate that feeling, nor conjure total disinterest.

'What are you looking at out there?'

She knew the view beyond the net curtain was of cracked concrete and overgrown wasteland.

'Come and see for yourself.'

Reluctantly, she crossed the small room to look through the opaque curtains.

Fotis wasn't waiting in an attitude of boredom or intent alertness. He was dribbling a basketball, weaving between a gang of teenagers before passing it to a huge youth with dreadlocks who shot it into a lopsided basketball hoop.

A ragged cheer went up and a smaller kid dashed in and grabbed the ball. Fotis cut a glance towards the flat then away, joining the ragtag group as it chased up the makeshift court.

Rosamund and Lucie watched for several minutes. The game was quick and the rules flexible and she was fascinated to see that while the locals gave no quarter, nor did they deliberately jostle the outsider. They accepted him.

Every couple of minutes he turned to look at the flat, clearly checking she didn't need him. Then he'd immerse himself in the game. Watching him move was a treat. He was agile and fast. She noticed he also shared the ball, including with the slower, less talented kids.

'You're right,' she murmured. 'Not such a prig after all.' Just with her. What had she done to warrant the judgemental attitude?

'Don't you have another event to prepare for?'

Rosamund dragged her attention from the action outside. 'Are you attending? I could collect you—'

'Not my scene. It never was. I was happy behind the cameras but not in the limelight. Now...' Lucie's suddenly stern voice brooked no opposition. 'It's time you left. I can see you haven't been sleeping. You'll need extra time with the concealer before tonight.'

Rosamund rolled her eyes, torn between a smile and chagrin that it was so obvious. But then Lucie was an expert. 'Yes,
ma'am. Any other tips?'

'Only one.' The older woman reached up for a hug and
squeezed tight. Rosamund returned it fervently. 'Stop torment-
ing yourself and sleep with the man. He mightn't be perfect,
no man is, but I'd like to see you with a real sparkle in your
eyes again.'

'You're very quiet.' His deep voice broke the silence.

Rosamund lifted one shoulder and watched the pedestrians
strolling down the now tree-lined streets, so different from
Lucie's neighbourhood. More than once she'd offered to help
her find a new place but she'd refused, insisting the flat was
home and she didn't want to leave.

'I could say the same to you.'

Tired of her circling thoughts, she turned to watch him
drive. His dark hair was rumpled and there was a faint sheen
to his olive skin, making her wonder if it would taste salty on
the tongue.

Biting down a snatched sigh, she squeezed her thighs together, trying to ignore the thoughts Lucie's frank advice had
unleashed. And the melting sensation between her legs.

For the last fifteen minutes she hadn't been able to eradicate
thoughts of what it would be like to sleep with Fotis Mavridis.

Sleep! That's the last thing you want to do with him.

Lucie was right about one thing. Rosamund was attuned
to him. He'd insisted on holding the car door open for her,
which meant she'd passed close by him. The faintest tang of
fresh male sweat and hot man lingered even now in her nostrils, teasing her. He smelled better than any cologne, better
even than sunshine on mown grass or freshly baked bread.

She swallowed hard, again pushing away thoughts of licking his skin, tasting his mouth.

Maybe she should take Lucie's advice. But *not* with Fotis

Mavridis. She wasn't masochistic enough to make herself vulnerable to a man who held her in contempt.

Though, now she thought about it, the look in his eyes as she'd moved past him into the four-wheel-drive hadn't been contempt. Nor had it been boredom. She'd felt the weight of his regard in every feminine corner of her body. Felt it again now as he cast her a sidelong look from narrowed eyes.

Heat shimmered in the air between them.

You're imagining things just because Lucie thought—

'Tell me about your friend. How do you know her?'

'Why? She's not a security threat.'

Did he grit his teeth? It would be some recompense to know she tested his patience as much he did hers.

'I'm just curious. You live in separate countries. You're a princess and she lives in social housing. How did you meet?'

'She was a friend of my mother's,' Rosamund said after a moment. It wasn't a secret, after all. 'She was a make-up artist and often worked with my mother. They did a lot of films together.'

'And you still keep in contact.'

Rosamund stared at his profile, trying to read his expression, but couldn't. She shrugged. 'She's a friend. I've known her all my life.'

She's the closest thing I have now to a mother.

Not that Lucie was particularly maternal, and she always brushed off Rosamund's offers of assistance, as she had Rosamund's mother's. But Lucie was genuine. She cared and was frank with her opinions and advice.

'She worked with your mother yet didn't attend the reception last night?'

'She doesn't have much patience for showbiz glitz and there were people there she didn't want to see.'

Lucie's outspokenness had won her many friends but powerful enemies too.

Seeing he was about to question her again, Rosamund asked one of her own. 'Why did you slip that kid your card?'

For a second deep-set eyes met hers from under winged black brows. 'You saw that?'

'Was it meant to be secret?'

'No.' But he lingered over the word as if wishing she hadn't noticed. Finally he said, 'I thought he had promise.'

'At basketball?'

To her astonishment the corner of his mouth quirked up, creating a tiny curling groove in his lean cheek. 'Hardly. But we got talking about maths. One of his friends was ribbing him about being a nerd.'

'Maths?'

That groove deepened and she stared, fascinated at what could almost be a hint of a shadow of a smile. Who'd have thought it of the iceman?

'You know, numbers. Algebra.'

'I do indeed.' She'd been a competent maths pupil but competent hadn't been enough for her father. He'd wanted excellence in all things. He'd engaged a university lecturer to give her extra tuition. How she'd hated those sessions. 'Why give him your card?'

'Because if I'm right about his promise, it would be a waste for him not to fulfil it. He's in his last year of school. I told him if he made it through the year with good marks, to contact me.'

Rosamund sat back in her seat, astounded. 'You offered him a job?'

'Of course not. I don't know enough about him. But, if he has the determination to finish, with decent grades, he could have potential.'

'To work for you? You need mathematicians?'

After a pause he nodded. 'It's one of the skill sets we use. But there's a big gap between raw talent and fulfilling it. I don't believe in holding out false promise. But if I'm right, we could find a university scholarship for him. If he grabs the opportunity and proves himself hard-working, it would help him build a career, even if not with my company.'

Flabbergasted, Rosamund stared as he focused on the road, apparently unaware of how astonishing his actions were. She'd thought him many things but not philanthropic.

The fact it was a teenager he aimed to help impressed her too. That was the age, as she knew, when many fell through the cracks. 'You seemed to get on well with those teens.'

'You thought I wouldn't?'

She shrugged. 'People often respond well to cute children but can be less generous with older kids.'

'They all need support and encouragement, whatever their age. Too often kids are vulnerable.'

His tone made her instincts twitch. This mattered to him. 'Were you?'

He shot her a look designed to shut her down. Instead it heightened her suspicion that this was personal. His early days had been tough. 'Few of us have picture-perfect childhoods.'

A sharp laugh escaped before she could prevent it. 'You think *I* did? Don't believe everything you read.'

Her father had been a tartar, continually belittling his wife and daughter for being too friendly or informal. The vivacity and charisma he'd first admired in his wife had later enraged him, when he saw how small he looked in comparison. Rosamund took after her mother so had spent most of her life being berated and punished.

She looked away as they continued in silence.

But surreptitiously she watched his easy competence, driving through the congested streets. He had an alert confidence, an air of control, and she wondered what his story was. Her attempt to discover more about him online had revealed little.

He annoyed her and seemed to delight in showing how little he liked her. Yet she felt an uncanny certainty that he knew what he was doing, not just in protecting her, but in seeing promise in a Parisian schoolkid. He'd even won Lucie's approval, though she'd pretended not to be impressed.

But if his judgement were so good, why treat Rosamund as a pariah? She was on the verge of ignoring pride and asking when he said, 'You did an impressive job last night, playing to the cameras. Everyone bought your story.'

'Sorry?' She'd smiled and mingled but the edge to his voice told her he meant something else. 'What do you mean?'

'The photos of you gazing up at me with those big blue eyes. No one will question my presence at your side now. They won't think I'm a minder. They're all sure I'm your latest conquest.'

There it was again, the taint of scorn in his voice tightening around her like a whip, scoring her skin. Just as she'd begun to think he could act reasonably around her.

Silently she turned to stare at the busy street, surprised how much that hurt.

Much later, in the privacy of her room, she finally broke her self-imposed rule and searched for stories about last night's gala. Sure enough there were photos of her and Fotis Mavridis on the red carpet and more of them inside the splendid event.

For once the stories weren't focused solely on her. The reports were full of speculation about the 'reclusive businessman' who was rumoured to be a formidable force among international power brokers but rarely attended public events. Questions were posed about what they had in common and where they'd met. The avid conjecture meant public interest would only ramp up from here.

The vague hints about his power intrigued her but she, like the reporters, was distracted by the photo that got most coverage. It showed them looking into each other's eyes, him leaning so close that just seeing the image, she felt the phantom touch of his breath on her face.

Rosamund swallowed, discomfited. It looked like the most intimate of moments. His hands held hers and her face was upturned to his, eyes wide and lips parted. She looked like a woman yearning to be kissed. And he looked like a man about to claim his lover.

She dropped the phone as if burnt.

She remembered that moment, when the noise faded and the world eclipsed to a pair of sea-bright eyes and a man who, for a second, seemed to promise all she needed. But it had been an illusion.

Photos lied all the time. The child of an actor knew that better than most.

She'd been in shock last night, that was all. She'd expected there to be photos of her mother, but not that one and not so large. Though she should have known after Gaudreau's interference with the dress.

It had taken her a second to get a grip on her emotions, and she'd been thankful to him for giving her momentary respite from prying eyes.

But not, it seemed, from the cameras.

As for *his* expression, it was a trick of the light and the angle of the lens.

She snatched up the phone, stuffed it in her bag then left her room. Tonight surely wouldn't be as much of a trial as last night. After all, she'd spend much of it sitting in the dark watching a film.

At least if she felt emotional, she'd be safe from the cameras.

She was heading for the stairs when a voice drawled, 'So you *do* wear red.'

She swung around to see her minder emerging from his room. Again he looked spectacular in evening dress, his bespoke jacket moulding broad shoulders. The combination of silky black bow-tie and white shirt against his olive skin was lethally attractive. The midnight shadow across his jaw and the coiled energy she sensed in him made her think of a marauder, masquerading as a civilised man.

Rosamund ignored the jiggle of excitement deep inside. 'Is there some reason I shouldn't?'

The dress was one of her favourites, with a demure but flattering boat neckline that left the top of her shoulders bare and a full skirt that swished around her knees as she walked. It even had concealed pockets, though royal etiquette meant she wouldn't use them in public.

'After your temperamental performance at the couturier yesterday, I thought you had an aversion to the colour.'

Astonishment slammed into her and her bodice tightened as she fought for air. 'Temperamental performance?'

He sauntered towards her and she hated that even with that derisory expression he looked so good. That she noticed.

'A talented team of people worked hard to make it in a short period of time. Not just any dress but one that had great significance to the gala's guest of honour, Antoine Gaudreau. But none of that mattered to you, did it? You couldn't even unbend enough to accept a change to please other people.'

For a second she stood, stunned by his vitriol. Strangely— since she'd spent years telling herself the opinions of people who didn't know her couldn't affect her—she felt hurt. Until that was swamped by fury.

'You're misinformed, Kyrie Mavridis. Gaudreau directed several of my mother's films, including her first, but this week is a retrospective dedicated to *her* work, not his.' She paused and focused on keeping her voice steady, horrified to feel herself tremble at the sudden storm of emotions. 'As for the dress, you can keep your arrogant opinions to yourself. You have no idea of its significance.'

She turned and stalked down the stairs. It was too late to make other arrangements for tonight. But tomorrow she'd ditch her unwanted bodyguard, no matter what Leon said.

CHAPTER FIVE

SILENTLY FOTIS CURSED as the limo took them to tonight's event.

Princess Rosamund of Cardona didn't matter to him, except for the need to keep her safe. Her flawed character was none of his business. He should have left well enough alone.

But she had the unique knack of getting under his skin with her mixed messages, one minute haughty and selfish, the next apparently a considerate friend or happy to find time to chat with strangers for no apparent personal gain.

She'd hinted her past wasn't what it seemed.

In a bid for sympathy? Yet the starkness in that single huff of laughter had been real, he was sure of it.

She drove him crazy. And it wasn't just her mixed messages. For there was one message his body received loud and clear, and had from the moment he'd met her.

Attraction. Desire. Need.

Every time that visceral, unmistakable hunger raked its talons through his gut and clamped his groin, self-disgust stirred. Because that hunger made him a traitor to poor Dimi, who'd suffered because of this woman's casual cruelty. The princess hadn't cared about collateral damage when she'd decided to romp with someone else's man.

These feelings made him into a fool. Everything he knew about himself, everything he'd learned about treacherous, selfish women, should have made it impossible for him to desire her. She shared the same remorseless selfishness as his mother.

Fotis had been a victim to that, but not the only one. He knew the damage she'd inflicted, still felt the trauma of it. Still carried the guilt of failing to save his brother.

His response to Rosamund of Cardona should be pure disgust, untrammelled by anything else.

And yet...

When she'd stepped out of her room in a dress that clasped her tight from breasts to narrow waist, that shimmered and rustled with every sashaying step...

He'd wanted her with a primal need that shattered logic. His body had surged in instant arousal. He'd seen the sheen of lustrous red-blond hair and all but felt its phantom slide against his greedy palms. He'd imagined anchoring his fists in it, tugging her head back to meet his mouth.

That was why he'd lashed out with that crack about the dress she'd refused. To remind himself, and her, that she wasn't worth his attention.

The ploy had backfired when she turned, her lush red lips an O of surprise. His imaginings had turned X-rated, his arousal threatening to become obvious at the idea of those lips on his naked body, pleasing him in all the ways he'd dreamed through the last two nights.

As well as surprise he'd seen a fleeting glimpse of hurt in her eyes that made him feel like a sadistic brute.

She was doing his head in and he was letting her, turning into someone he didn't like. Someone without the control he'd relied on all his life. Without that, what was he?

They approached tonight's venue. Another grand building, another red carpet, and lots more paparazzi, no doubt fed by last night's photos.

Fotis told himself it was her fault, looking up at him with those big, needy eyes, putting on a show for the crowd.

The difficulty was, he couldn't convince himself. He knew

what he'd seen. She'd been genuinely distressed and he'd responded to her pain, wanting, despite everything, to ease it…

'Aren't we getting out?'

She didn't turn towards him, but then she'd ignored him the whole trip. Fotis knew an urgent desire to make her meet his eyes. He disliked the woman but having her ignore him was unbearable, though he deserved it.

'Wait,' he growled, pushing his door open.

He needed to get a grip, fast. Striding around the car he catalogued the crowd, thicker than last night and more excited, but nothing to raise an alert.

He opened the door and held his arm out to steady her. Last night she'd worn high heels but tonight she'd chosen spindly red stilettos. He didn't want to be catching her if she wrenched her ankle and fell on her face.

For a second she hesitated, looking at him under veiling lashes. Then she took his arm lightly, rising from the vehicle with an easy grace that sent his thoughts tumbling into the bedroom and the joys of a fit, limber lover.

As she stepped onto the pavement, an unexpected surge of movement from the crowd made him wrap his arm around her, jerking her close so abruptly she lost her balance and leaned against him.

'My purse,' she hissed under her breath.

Fotis bent to retrieve it. As he did so, a volley of voices called their names. Rising, he turned swiftly just as Rosamund turned in the opposite direction.

It would have been better if they'd knocked heads. Instead their noses met, and their mouths. It was so swift it took a moment for his brain to catch up. That was what he told himself later.

For now he simply responded instinctively, forgetting the crowd and his tumultuous emotions, tilting his head to one side and brushing his lips across hers. He felt her mouth tremble, felt the quiver run down her spine as he held her close. Then her lips parted under his and he tasted sweetness.

Bolts of lightning soldered his feet to the ground. He pulled her in, flush against him, drawing bewitching softness against a body turned to stone.

Her hand pressed to his chest, slipped under his jacket's lapel to settle over his thundering heart. He liked her touch, almost as much as he liked her delectable lips opening beneath his.

It took everything he had to drag himself free of the erotic fog clouding his brain. With a muffled groan that sounded disturbingly like surrender, he pulled back, straightening to his full height.

But the distance didn't obliterate his hunger. For a second longer her head was upturned, crimson lips parted and half-lidded eyes tempting him to kiss her, properly this time.

A wolf whistle pierced the hubbub and her eyes widened, body stiffening. She thrust against his chest as if to make him move. Of course she couldn't, but Fotis eased his hold around her waist and she took a step back. He felt her wobble but only for a second. When he knew she was steady he released her, hiding a grimace that felt like disappointment.

The noise of the crowd had become a roar. Cameras flashed as photographers fought for better positions.

Beneath the cacophony he heard a husky, cultured voice swear in an undertone. Even her voice turned him on, making him wonder how she'd sound in the throes of ecstasy. How his name would sound if she cried it out in rapture.

Not helping, Mavridis.

His burgeoning erection would be visible soon if he couldn't stop it. Playing for time, he'd curved his lips into a smile, lowering his head so he could murmur in her ear. 'Any suggestions on how to play this, Princess?'

She shifted away, far enough that he could see her eyes

blazed more blue than grey. 'We carry on as if nothing happened. Never excuse. Never explain.'

With those words she changed. It was like a cloak falling around her. He couldn't put his finger on it but she seemed taller, more aloof. She smiled directly up at him but there was no heat in her eyes, nor softness, nothing to indicate she'd quivered on the brink of capitulation just seconds ago.

She held out her hand and he placed her clutch purse in it. Then he held out his arm and she looped her other hand around it before they took their time going inside.

The evening was more of a trial than the previous night. Then he'd stood beside her as she charmed guests, scrupulously introducing him and including him in the conversation, though he played little part. He'd observed and kept watch as they moved through the throng.

Tonight was different. It was a screening of one of her mother's films. Which meant sitting beside her in the dark, close enough that he *felt* each move she made, heard too the occasional hitch of her breath.

It was Juliette Bernard's last film, made not long before she married and gave up acting. Instead of an ingenue or a sexy starlet, the woman on the screen was mature and riveting, eliciting emotion and engagement even from him. The story was poignant but ruthlessly realistic. No wonder both critics and the public raved about it.

What must it be like for her daughter, seeing her mother on the big screen, so long after she'd died? Beside him, his charge stirred. He glanced across and froze.

She wasn't aware of his scrutiny. She was utterly absorbed in the movie and in its shifting light he saw a solitary tear slide down her cheek.

His throat closed over useless words of sympathy. She wouldn't want him seeing her sadness.

But for the rest of the film, his focus wasn't on the movie. It was on the puzzle of Princess Rosamund.

He'd assumed she was a carbon copy of his mother, narcissistic and grasping. His mother had cared for no one but herself despite her ability to convince people to the contrary, at least for a while. He'd seen that again and again as she hunted for newer, richer husbands, ignoring her children except when it suited her to use them as decoys.

Rosamund on the other hand, was moved to tears, though her mother had died over a decade ago.

He reminded himself he wasn't here to analyse her, just stop Ricardo from hurting her. But Fotis felt disquiet, as if he'd made a fatal error. He hated uncertainty. His business was unravelling mysteries and protecting truth.

He needed to understand her. Maybe then she'd stop messing with his head.

It was late when they arrived at the house. Rosamund was weary yet wired. Too tired to sleep or work, too emotional.

'Fancy a drink?'

The click of her heels on parquetry faltered and she stopped, amazed. He wanted to share a drink? 'Why?'

They'd reached the bottom of the staircase that swept up to the bedrooms. Wall sconces and a large pendant light lit the foyer, casting shadows across his steely features, somehow concealing more of his thoughts than they revealed.

'To clear the air.' His mouth firmed, eyebrows burrowing down into a V over that decisive nose. 'I need to apologise.'

It was the last thing she'd expected. Shock ran under her skin as she considered telling him what he could do with his apology. Tomorrow they'd go their separate ways. Whatever arrangement he had with Leon couldn't continue after his behaviour.

But she was intrigued.

By the fact he'd decided to apologise.

Plus there was the memory of that moment on the edge of the red carpet. She'd turned at the sound of her name just as he rose and turned his head, and their lips had met and clung. It could only have lasted seconds. But it had felt far longer.

She recalled the weighty beat of her pulse, her breathless anticipation. The faintest taste of him—unfamiliar and delicious. The hunger for more. And the look in his hooded eyes, a glow that turned her insides molten.

Facing public scrutiny after *that* would have been impossible if it hadn't been for a lifetime's training in appearing calm under stress.

'Okay.' She'd hear his apology, at least.

Soon she was ensconced in an armchair, sipping triple sec on ice while her nemesis sat opposite, frowning down at the fine brandy he swirled in his glass. The lights were low, casting shadows across his face that reminded her of her initial impression of him as a fallen angel. He looked powerful, brooding and starkly attractive.

His eyes met hers and energy crackled along her bones. It was a mistake, spending time with him. She moved to put her glass on a side table when he spoke.

'I'm sorry. I was out of order, judging you over what happened at the couturier's. I shouldn't have spoken. It's not my business and you're right, I don't know the circumstances.'

Rosamund held his gaze then lifted her glass, letting the intense orange liqueur send a fiery trail from her tongue to her chilled middle. She welcomed the blast of heat.

'You made assumptions about me.'

Slowly he nodded. That frown and the almost sulky set of his sculpted mouth should repel, not entice.

Lucifer, whispered that voice in her head.

'I did.'

'Why?' She leaned forward. 'What made you think you have the right to judge me?'

It was something she'd wanted to ask so many times when people she didn't know criticised her unfairly. She'd believed she was reconciled to it as a necessary evil, given her family's position. But this time her accuser was here before her.

More, something about him had burrowed under her defences. His accusation had hurt.

'Because of what you did in New York.'

Her glass slammed onto the side table and she scooted to the edge of her seat, heart pounding so fast she felt nauseous.

It should be impossible. Leon would have double-and-triple-checked this man but... 'You're a friend of Brad Ricardo?' Was he here to hurt her?

'No! I don't know the man, and I don't want to.'

The fingers she'd dug into the upholstered arms of the chair eased a little, yet she couldn't relax. 'If you're not a friend of his, then what's your problem?'

'The way you treated Dimi.'

'Dimi?' The man spoke in riddles.

If she thought him Lucifer-like earlier, the curling snarl of his lips made him positively demonic. 'Dimitria Politis. Or wasn't she important enough for you to remember her name?'

Understanding began to dawn. Rosamund sank back. 'You know her?'

'Yes, and I care when someone hurts her.'

For a split-second Rosamund felt envy for the young woman she'd met so briefly. She pushed it aside.

'So you *do* remember her,' he said softly. 'You just didn't care that you hurt her to get what you wanted.'

'You've got it wrong. I *saved* her.'

Now his knotted brow showed confusion rather than anger. 'That doesn't make sense. You'd never met before that night. She told me.'

Rosamund remembered the young Greek woman, gentle and a little timid but excited to be at the glamorous party. She'd liked her. And seen something in the twenty-one-year-old that reminded her of herself, long ago.

'No, I'd never seen her before, never heard of her. But...'

How did she explain her sudden, emotional reaction to what she'd discovered that night? Her visceral response and her impulsive decision to deal with it. 'She was vulnerable. I wanted to protect her.'

Fotis regarded her with a stiletto-sharp scrutiny and definite disbelief. Rosamund held his stare.

Finally he said, 'You're implying you created a scandal to protect her? Why?' He leaned forward and she felt the air thicken. 'Why harm your reputation for a stranger?'

Rosamund reached for her glass and took a fortifying sip. It was tempting to explain. She *wanted* to clear the air. Wanted him to think well of her. Wasn't *that* worrying?

But in revealing her reasons, she'd have to skirt hurts and mistakes she'd put behind her years before.

'It's personal.' She paused, resisting the impulse to lick her suddenly dry lips. 'I'd need to know you wouldn't share what I have to say.'

'I don't betray confidences.'

If only it were that easy. 'I'd feel more inclined to trust you if I knew something about you.'

'What are you after?' His eyes narrowed. 'Commercial secrets?'

Despite the thrumming tension, Rosamund couldn't stifle her huff of laughter. 'Hardly. But you're an enigma. I don't know anything about you. Just that Leon believes you can protect me. And that you're judgemental, grumpy and rude.' And powerfully, shockingly male. 'I'm offering a quid pro quo. I'll tell you if you satisfy my curiosity.'

His expression was unreadable. 'What do you want to know?'

Even now he couldn't just agree. He had to probe and assess before committing himself. She recognised the tactic. She did it too.

In her case it was a self-protective habit she learned over time. Was he the same?

* * *

Fotis watched her eyes turn bleak. Was anything about this woman simple? He'd thought he had her measure when they met, but with every hour he had more questions and less certainty.

Maybe there was a scintilla of truth in her story. Maybe the photos in New York that caused a sensation meant nothing to a woman with her reputation. From her teens she'd been a wild child, teetering just on the right side of respectability but ever ready to party to excess. She lived off the royal purse yet her only repayment was attending a few official functions when she occasionally deigned to live in Cardona.

'How do you speak English so well? You sound like a native speaker, yet you're Greek. You live in Greece, don't you?'

Of all the things he'd imagined her asking, this wasn't one. 'I do. But I went to boarding school early. Most of my schooling was outside Greece.'

He waited, wondering what came next.

'Why did you agree to look after me when you have a business to run? What does my half-brother hold over you?'

Interesting that she didn't call him her brother. What was the story there?

Fotis swirled his brandy, inhaling its rich scent. 'He doesn't hold anything over me. But there's an initiative I want to see implemented. Something he supports too. He promised if I did this, he'd actively promote it at intergovernmental levels.'

He watched her think that over and decided to forestall her next obvious question by interrupting. She already regarded him as judgemental, grumpy and rude. Strange how that irked when it was completely deserved.

'Is that all?'

She shook her head. 'Tell me more about yourself.'

Fotis frowned. He had no intention of spilling private details.

But then her laugh, surprisingly rich and full, cleaved

through his distrust to dance over his body, shimmering like summer heat just under his skin.

'If you could see your face! Don't worry, *Kyrie* Mavridis,' she said in that mocking tone he disliked but found himself increasingly enjoying. 'I'm not asking you to confess your dark secrets. Just let me in enough to know who I'm dealing with. What does your company do? How did you come to start it? That sort of thing. I want to know who you are so I can decide whether to trust you.'

That he could understand. 'I was in the military—'

'Doing what?'

'I was a paratrooper.'

'*That* explains why Leon thought you could keep me safe.' She leaned back. 'How did you go from that to running your own business?'

'I spent time in special operations and one aspect of that is intelligence. It was a good fit.'

At her enquiring look he continued. 'I was always good at maths. Once that's what I wanted to do, devote myself to pure mathematics.' Until Nico's death. 'I'm good with numbers, patterns, analysis and codes.'

'Ah. I begin to see the link.'

'The military was good to me but it didn't suit me long-term. I'd inherited some money and started a company providing cryptography and other services to government and industry. We protect information. We also analyse complex data and provide insights, sometimes about things other entities want kept secret. We provide a very specialised service.'

Her head tilted. 'Specialised and successful, since you don't have to advertise for work.' At his questioning stare she lifted one shoulder. 'I did an internet search and was surprised at how little I found.'

'There's no need for publicity, either for the company or myself. I prefer privacy.'

'Lucky you. I prefer privacy too but it's hard to come by.'

'Which brings us to New York and the scandal you created.'

She breathed out what sounded like a sigh. 'One last question. Your company's services. They are available to anyone who pays?'

He held her gaze. 'Not to criminals, dictators or regimes that repress their people.'

'There'd be money to be made there.'

'We have our standards.'

'And so do I,' she said after the tiniest pause.

It was a direct challenge. She was taking him at his word. Would he do the same for her? Two days ago he wouldn't have believed anything she claimed. That had changed. 'Go on.'

She picked up her glass and took a slow sip.

'I'd never met your friend, or Ricardo. I saw them together at the party and was introduced but didn't spend much time with them. Later, I was on the roof terrace getting some air and overheard Ricardo and another man.'

Rosamund stared at the ornate marble fireplace. 'They thought they were alone. He was boasting about his little Greek innocent. How she was in love and he had her where he wanted her. She'd do anything for him.' Her lip curled. 'I'm paraphrasing. He was discussing money and sex and he was much cruder. He wanted her fortune. He didn't care about her.'

Fury streaked through Fotis. Ricardo was a lowlife, living beyond his means. Of course he was interested in a pretty innocent who also happened to be an heiress.

Fotis hadn't known about the romance then and would have put an end to it once he discovered what Ricardo was like. But given Dimi's fragile sense of self-worth and her history of depression, he'd have found a way to do it without breaking both her heart and her ego.

'Go on.'

Eyes that looked more silver than blue met his and Fotis caught the hint of a flush on her cheekbones. 'He was pushing her to announce their engagement, but she wanted to tell her grandfather first. He was sure he could persuade her in the next day or so without the old man's knowledge. Once it was announced he knew she wouldn't back out.'

Fotis knew the old man, a friend of his dead father's, was unwell. It was one of the reasons he felt so protective of Dimi. His hands fisted on his thighs. 'Go on.'

Rosamund shrugged. 'I saw red. I'd only spoken to the girl for five minutes but she clearly had no idea what her lover was really like. *I* knew, so I acted.'

'You deliberately let yourself be caught in a compromising situation with him?' Fotis shook his head. 'You might be a princess but why would he give up an almost-fiancée for someone he'd never met? Marriage to an heiress would be better than a fling with you.'

A smile that wasn't a smile curved Rosamund's lips and her eyes glittered. 'Of course he didn't expect to marry me. But he likes sex and I *do* have a certain reputation.'

There'd been no particularly damning photos of her for years but her name was constantly linked with a passing parade of men, none of whom lasted long.

'I waited until the men were rejoining the party and accidentally bumped into him. I may have appeared a bit wobbly when I spilled my drink.' Her lips curled in a savage smile that made Fotis like her more. He had no doubt that despite the impression she'd given Ricardo, she'd been perfectly in control of her actions. 'He got me another drink and while he was gone I moved closer to the lights.

'When he returned we got better acquainted. It didn't take long. I knew people would be coming out to see the fireworks. All I had to do was make sure we were found in a clinch when they arrived with their phones.' Her voice held a razor-sharp edge. 'You know how people enjoy a scandal.'

Fotis remembered the photos. Her dress strap had hung down her arm and her gleaming hair was loose around her shoulders while Ricardo cupped her breast. He had her jammed up against a wall as they kissed and her bare leg was up near his hip. They were obviously moments away from sex.

Was her story true?

'Why not just tell Dimi?' The images had shattered her.

One shapely eyebrow arched. 'You think she'd have believed me, a stranger? Of course she wouldn't. She was besotted. She needed to see him for what he really was.'

'But why put yourself out for a stranger? You took the flak for those photos. Why not let her make her own mistakes?'

In his experience people rarely looked out for others, especially people they didn't know. In this case the gossip hadn't just been about the pair being caught in a compromising position, but about the princess being a man-eater, stealing a pretty innocent's partner from under her nose.

Rosamund's eyes met his and strong emotion arced between them. She wasn't amused now.

'I know what it's like to be in her position. I was even younger than her when I was seduced by a man who didn't care for me. I was just a means to an end. I wish I'd had someone to stand up for me then.'

CHAPTER SIX

THE NIGHT WAS BALMY, the company convivial and the vintage champagne excellent. There was even a huge, full moon hanging over the Mediterranean, creating a silvery path right up to where the sea lapped the shore below the spectacular villa. As if even nature were determined to add its lustre to the A-list event.

Rosamund had had a busy time in Paris and then in Cannes for the film festival, where there'd been a special screening of her mother's most famous film.

Tonight's party, along the coast from the festival, signalled the end. Tomorrow she'd go home.

And Fotis would return to Greece.

She sipped her champagne but suddenly it tasted stale.

She tried to focus on the conversation in the group surrounding her, and satisfaction that the events dedicated to her mother's memory had gone so well.

But her mind was elsewhere.

On the man standing proprietorially close beside her, so close she felt his body heat down her side. She should be used to it by now. They'd spent a week playing the role of lovers in public, attracting a huge amount of media attention. But after the night when she'd explained what happened in New York and they'd settled into a truce, the role had seemed insidiously more real.

It had become second nature to expect that ripple of awareness under her skin when he stood near. The tug in her belly when he bent his head, holding her gaze, as if unable to look away. And when he touched her, as he did so frequently now, the shimmering heat in her pelvis was utterly familiar.

It was all for show but her responses were real.

It was as if that night, when she'd shared what happened with Ricardo and Fotis had believed her, a vital part of her had been torn away. A part that had protected her from responding too much to any man.

There'd been men in her life since that catastrophe in her teens, but only a few. Nowhere near the number the voracious press implied. She'd learned to be discriminating and cautious.

What she felt now, with Fotis, wasn't cautious. It felt almost too big to hold inside. The thought of parting from him tomorrow created a poignant ache behind her ribs that was hard to bear.

It had become harder *not* to react to his touch, or more correctly not to reveal her reaction. Dislike had disintegrated. Now she discovered that had been her only effective barrier against his brand of brooding charisma.

She hadn't given him details of her experience, and he hadn't pressed, only reiterating his apology for judging her. But after that there'd been no disdain, no judgement. She often caught him looking at her in a totally new way. She couldn't read his thoughts but the weight of his gaze *felt* different.

She'd discovered a man unlike the frigid enemy she'd thought him.

He cared deeply for his friends and sought to protect them. He was reserved rather than overtly charming, but that reserve hid a quick mind and a thoughtfulness that surprised her, particularly when dealing with people who seemingly had little in common with a hugely successful entrepreneur.

She'd begun to understand just how successful. He might keep a low public profile but after a week in his presence she'd been impressed by the number of powerful men and women who wanted to spend time with him. Clearly his opinions and his company's services were valuable to governments and industry leaders.

A warm hand pressed against the small of her back, urging her forward as a waiter manoeuvred past with a tray. But when he'd passed, the large hand remained where it was, distracting her.

She shot Fotis a sideways look yet he didn't remove his hand. Gleaming eyes locked with hers and lightning speared her. She felt effervescence in her bloodstream and a tingle in suddenly heavy breasts that strained at the black velvet of her bodice.

Her breathing shallowed and she sucked air through parted lips, moving restlessly under his touch.

His attention dropped to her rising breasts in her low-cut bodice. Rosamund shifted her weight, aware of dampness blooming at the apex of her thighs.

All week this smouldering awareness had been brewing. All week she'd fought it, nervous of the neediness he inspired in her. Now that neediness blossomed into raw hunger.

He bent his head, murmuring in her ear. 'This is our last night in France. Do you want to spend the rest of it here?'

That velvet-over-gravel voice did appalling things to her self-control. Did he know?

But as he pulled back enough to meet her eyes she read his tension. It was in the broad frame of his shoulders and the tic of his pulse. His hand stroked a tiny circle low, low on her back and her buttocks tightened. She had to work not to flex her pelvis in response to that drugging touch.

You don't want an affair. You barely know him.

But how long since any man made you feel this way?

Rosamund sucked in more air, shoring up her resolve because *no* man had ever made her feel like this. Not even in her teens when she'd imagined herself head over heels in love with a suitor who turned out to be a scumbag.

Whatever this was, it was phenomenally powerful. *That* was what made it dangerous. Pursuing a relationship with him, however short, would be perilous to her peace of mind, no matter what her clamouring body said.

Did she really want a one-night stand with a man who'd awakened her in this way, knowing they'd separate tomorrow? He had business elsewhere and she was expected in Cardona, where hopefully she'd be safe until Ricardo was behind bars.

She stepped forward, forcing Fotis to drop his hand. It was the hardest thing she'd done in a long time. But it was for the best. Any entanglement with him threatened the placid, safe life she'd built.

'I'm afraid it's time we left,' she said to their host. 'It's an early start tomorrow.'

Through the murmurs of protest and regret she was supremely aware of Fotis, frowning, beside her.

When they left the group she caught Fotis' eye. 'If you want to stay at the party feel free. A driver can take me to the hotel. I need to pack. I have a busy schedule from tomorrow.'

She didn't explain that the schedule focused on her writing and she only had one royal engagement in the next few weeks. She could work almost anywhere. Including the Riviera, if she chose to accept the offer she'd heard in his voice and seen in those stunning eyes moments before.

'Where you go, I go, Princess.'

Once again those words affected her more than they should. She wondered what it would be like if they signified more than a bodyguard's determination to keep her safe.

Her neediness was only partly sexual. A week with Fotis Mavridis had scraped her bare of pretence, uncovering a powerful desire for affection. Partnership. Love. None of which she'd get from him.

That hadn't mattered in the past, because she'd learned to be pragmatic in her expectations of relationships. Yet, despite the almost overpowering need to lose herself in the pleasure they could share, she baulked.

Rosamund pressed her hand to her middle, trying to stop the useless yearning, then dropped it when he watched the movement as if fascinated.

'Thank you, Fotis. For everything.' She faced him, tilting her chin to hold his gaze, letting him hear finality in her voice. 'I appreciate everything you've done.'

She still marvelled that Leon had persuaded such a man to watch over her for a whole week. Whatever the favour he'd promised, it was obviously vital to her companion.

'No need for thanks.' He paused. 'You're sure, Rosamund?'

Anyone listening would have noted his gruff voice but only she understood what he didn't say. That if she said the word, they'd be lovers tonight.

Her throat constricted. It was ridiculous to want a man so much. Downright dangerous to want a man who, she sensed, might take a part of her with him when he left.

She nodded before she could change her mind as regret grew to an ache. 'Completely sure.'

He inclined his head then led her through the villa to the vast porte-cochère.

'Wait here while I get the car.'

Prestigious as the residence was, parking in the grounds was limited. Fotis had dropped her at the front door, then parked down the road.

'Couldn't we go together, just this once?' Having decided to be sensible, Rosamund found herself wanting to eke out her time with him, even just the few minutes it would take to walk to the vehicle. 'It's a beautiful night.'

She had the unnerving feeling he understood her internal battle. His scrutiny was thorough. Finally he said, 'Just this once,' in a voice so husky it abraded her senses and made her wish she dared change her mind.

He folded his hand around hers. They fitted together perfectly. Did he feel the tremor coursing through her?

'Come on, Princess. It's time we got you safely back.'

They followed a guard through the scented garden to a secret exit well away from the estate's grand entrance. The exit was around a curve in the road, out of sight of the coterie of waiting photographers. The guard paused, viewed the image of the street on his device, then unlocked the door.

Fotis paused, frowning. 'Actually, it's better that you wait in the grounds. I'll come back with the car.'

Rosamund shook her head. They had so little time left together. She didn't want to miss a moment. She'd decided to do the sensible, responsible thing and walk away from this man. Surely she deserved a few minutes more, walking beside him, feeling his hand on hers and the heat of his body close to hers.

'Please, Fotis.'

It was the first time she'd asked him for anything. Did he realise how out of character that was?

Gleaming eyes locked on hers and her breath caught. Finally he tugged her closer, and it felt…wonderful. Almost as wonderful as that moment in Paris when their lips had touched and she'd longed for it not to end.

'Come on, let's get you in the car.'

They passed several luxury vehicles parked up against the pavement, and were just about to pass a small van, when his stride changed. His hand tightened on hers as they slowed.

'What is it?' she whispered.

'The street light's out.' Belatedly she noticed the gloom. 'We'll go back to the villa and you can wait there.'

Rosamund was about to protest that there was enough light when there was a burst of movement ahead. A figure emerged from behind the van, lunging towards them.

Fotis shoved her behind him then leapt forward. She reeled, heart pounding. Between the shadows and his form blocking her view, she couldn't see what was happening. But it didn't sound pretty. There were grunts and a thud, then a loud crack that she told herself sickly couldn't be bone breaking.

Frantically she scanned the pavement for a weapon she could use to help Fotis.

A second later came the sound of splashing. There was a hiss of indrawn breath followed by a high-pitched shriek of pain that made all the fine hairs on her body stand on end.

The figures broke apart and she was relieved to see Fotis standing tall, broad shoulders heaving, whereas the other person—a man she saw now—writhed on the ground.

She started forward. 'Fotis—'

'Stay back!' His head whipped around to check she was okay. The other man wasn't. She heard incoherent sobbing from where he huddled on the ground against the van. 'Don't come closer but call an ambulance and the police.'

With shaking hands she pulled out her phone. She was aware of Fotis bending over the man and was happy to keep back. There was a strange smell in the air and that terrible, unnerving keening that sounded more animal than human.

The police must have been cruising the neighbourhood because soon cars appeared, washing the scene in lurid light.

People in uniforms crowded around, medics as well as police and over their heads Fotis watched her even as he spoke to them. She stood metres away, hands twisting together, heart still racing.

Someone had tried to attack them, attack her, and Fotis had saved her. Was he hurt? He didn't look it but she couldn't be sure. She started forward but he moved faster, murmuring something to the uniformed officer beside him then striding across to her. In the distance she saw other officers holding back a straggle of onlookers, some with phones raised.

'Come on, I'm taking you to the hotel. The police have agreed we can give a statement later.'

His jacket was gone, his shirt pale in the gloom as he put his arm around her shoulders and drew her against him. His warmth seeped into her and she burrowed close, so weak with relief that she trembled. Because he was okay. She kept reliving the moments of the struggle and her fear he'd be hurt.

A few vehicles away he bundled her into the car then took the driver's seat.

The interior light revealed his grim expression. She'd thought she'd seen him angry in the past but nothing before compared to this. Nostrils flared, mouth hard, the angle of his jaw screamed danger. He looked like some ancient god of war, indestructible and lethal.

But it wasn't his fury that stopped her breath. 'Don't shut the door!' She needed to see.

'What's wrong?' His gaze fixed on her.

Rosamund pointed at his shirtsleeve. The pristine white was marred by marks. Red marks. She stared, trying to make sense of what she saw. It took long seconds to realise they weren't stains smattered across the sleeve but holes. And through the holes, bloody flesh was visible.

'Fotis?' Her voice wasn't her own. 'What's that? You need to get it treated.'

He pulled the door closed and the light went off. 'Once I've seen you safely back to the room.'

He reached forward to start the ignition but she stopped him, her hand on his shoulder. 'Tell me what that is.' Her stomach churned, imagining the pain he must be in. The wounds were small but looked painfully raw.

'Tomorrow. I—'

'*Now*, or I march back there and get an answer from the police.'

A rough sigh broke the silence. When he spoke his voice was preternaturally calm. 'Some sort of acid. He had a canister of it.'

Bile rose in Rosamund's throat and she wondered if she might vomit. Her heart thundered in her ears and all her organs seemed to writhe in protest.

Someone, presumably sent by Brad Ricardo, had lain in wait for her with a canister of acid. Wanting to maim or maybe kill her.

Because of that Fotis was injured and undoubtedly in pain, despite his macho effort not to show it.

Her eyes squeezed shut. He was lucky he hadn't taken the full brunt of the acid. She assumed that in the melee it had spilled over their attacker.

'It's all right, Rosamund.' His voice was a rich, soothing velvet caress. 'Everything's okay.'

She shook her head, reeling. How could he think that? Why had she insisted on walking with him to the car? Because of her...

Her eyes snapped open to see him leaning in. She wanted to haul him close and not let him go. Instead she swallowed over the aching constriction in her throat and tried to find her voice.

'I'm sorry, Fotis. I wouldn't have had this happen to you for the world.'

'It's okay—'

'I can't thank you enough for protecting me.' She dragged in an unsteady breath. 'But don't patronise me.' She heard her voice wobble and sat straighter. 'It's not okay. Nothing like it. Now...' She reached to unbuckle her seat belt. 'We're going back. I'm not leaving until a medic checks you out.'

CHAPTER SEVEN

THE DAY DAWNED bright and clear, sunlight shimmering on the ocean from a sky of perfect cerulean blue. As if bad things couldn't happen here.

Fotis grimaced as he glanced at his bandaged arm with its low-grade hum of pain.

After his disturbed night, what he needed was a workout, a few hours in the gym or a swim to re-establish his equilibrium. But the medic had insisted he not get his injuries wet and though the exclusive coastal resort was well protected, Fotis refused to leave Rosamund alone in their separate suite, even to go to the hotel gym.

Being cooped up with her only increased his frustration. For the last ten minutes he'd watched her swim laps of their private pool, screened from the rest of the resort by high walls on two sides and a sheer drop to the sea on a third.

He'd spent the night reliving those moments when someone had tried to hurt her, but in his troubled dreams the man had succeeded. The screams he'd heard had been Rosamund's and it had jolted him awake, heart pounding and nausea bubbling.

But melded with his concern for her safety was something else. The fascination that had begun the moment he'd met her had morphed from disdain into rampant curiosity, through unwilling respect then admiration. And ever-present lust.

She wasn't the smug, selfish woman he'd imagined. He regularly saw her concern for others. Her wheelchair-bound friend in Paris. The people who gathered outside events just to catch a glimpse of her, and who'd been rewarded when she inevitably talked with them. Last night despite her shock at being targeted, it had been *him* she'd worried about.

Then there was the mind-boggling news that she'd acted to *help* Dimi, at huge cost to herself. That she herself had been a victim. Fotis had discovered a whole new level of feelings as he learned more about Rosamund. He was furious she'd put herself in danger, yet proud and protective. He wanted to find the man who'd hurt her and make him pay.

His hunger for her knew no bounds. Even last night when she turned him down, her actions had made him want her more.

For once her expression hadn't been guarded, so he'd witnessed the struggle, the decision to say no, because of course they had no future. They lived different lives. He'd seen what the refusal cost her. He too had felt that yearning for more as they walked in the soft darkness, hands clasped because that was the only touch they could permit.

He turned and reached for his phone.

Fifteen minutes later, Fotis stood at the end of the pool, watching her steady progress.

So much for the idea she expended her energy on partying. With her morning yoga, regular gym sessions and chamomile tea, she didn't fit the party girl mould. She liked champagne but didn't drink to excess. She'd relaxed and laughed, the sound of her husky amusement running through his body like fingertips on aroused flesh. But she'd turned down every offer to party except last night and they'd left that early.

She didn't fit *any* mould he knew. Whenever he thought he understood her, something happened to make him reassess.

She neared the end of the pool and he crouched, touching her outstretched arm. He felt a shiver ripple up her arm and pulled his hand away, rising to his full height.

She flicked bright hair off her face, her gaze making his blood quicken and the morning sun sharpen on his skin.

He gestured to the table positioned to make the most of the sea view. 'Breakfast.'

She hauled herself out, sunlight glistening on wet skin. On strong, supple legs. On her toned torso with that intriguing dip to her waist and flare of her hips. On the upper slopes of her heaving breasts.

Fotis' fingers tightened on the towel he held. He offered it to her and turned towards the breakfast he'd organised.

But as he crossed the terrace it wasn't the sea or the breakfast he saw but Rosamund. Her bikini was rainforest green, all lush foliage, with tiny dots of colour here and there. A red butterfly. A half-hidden blue Macaw. A pair of yellow eyes from a dark feline face. All designed to catch the eye, but none intrigued like the woman wearing it, her golden skin glowing with vitality.

His hands clenched and so did his lower body.

He sat and reached for the coffeepot. 'The police want us to stay longer.'

She settled opposite him, the towel wrapped around her body. He didn't know whether to be relieved or disappointed.

'For how long? We've told them everything we know. We're supposed to leave today.'

He read her tension. He knew the feeling. The sooner they left the better. Staying with her in his Paris townhouse had been both surprisingly easy yet increasingly claustrophobic. Because he was aware of her in ways no bodyguard should be.

'You really want to pull the privilege card? What did you have in mind? Storming out of here as if the police don't have a job to do?'

He paused, knowing his anger was with himself, not her. Because he'd weakened last night and let her walk with him. Because he'd *wanted* her and that selfish decision had left her open to attack.

Because everything felt wrong this morning.

'Their investigation can only help you. If they can make a link between the man last night and Ricardo...'

'I know, I know.' She reached for her coffee but instead of drinking, held the mug in both hands as if needing its warmth. 'I'm overreacting. It's just that every time I think of last night—'

'You're safe, Rosamund.' He wanted to reach for her but forced his hands into immobility. 'Between me, the hotel security staff and the police...'

'I was thinking about *you*. You could have been badly injured.' Something in his chest pulled tight as her voice turned husky with fear for him. Her gaze dropped to his arm, making him wish he'd worn a long-sleeved shirt. 'How bad is the pain?'

'It's fine.' Though he was glad for the painkillers he'd taken. '*I'm* fine. We got off lightly.'

Unlike their attacker who was in critical care.

'Look at me, Rosamund.' When she did, that familiar spark of connection ignited again, worrying yet welcome. 'There's no point going over and over what happened last night and imagining a different outcome. We're both *fine*. You need to accept that, not fret about it.'

Her chin tilted and he welcomed that familiar hint of spirit. 'How do you know that's what I've been doing?'

Because I've been doing exactly that, imagining you hurt or worse.

'It's what people do after a traumatic event. But it won't help. It will just distress you more.'

She nodded. 'That's why I was swimming, trying to clear my head.' She gestured to his arm. 'You need to get it checked out properly today. We'll go to the hospital after breakfast.'

'Not the hospital.' It was unlikely Ricardo had another minion here ready to attack her, but Fotis wouldn't take that chance. 'I'll arrange a house call to the suite.'

'Why? What aren't you telling me?'

He repressed a sigh. 'The press got hold of the story. You saw how much attention we got in Paris.'

It had increased every day, with rampant speculation about their whirlwind romance. Their agreement not to comment on their relationship had only sent the press into a frenzy. The reclusive billionaire and the party-girl princess was too intriguing a proposition to ignore.

'There's a gang of photographers camped on the other side of the hotel. So unless you particularly want to run the gauntlet of the press, I vote we stay at the hotel until it's time to leave.'

He watched her face shutter. She'd never spoken of how press attention affected her and she always faced the cameras with apparent serenity. But a week at her side, often with his arm around her, meant he'd felt her muscles tighten each time they navigated the cameras. He had some idea what that show of calm cost her.

He respected her courage and determination not to let them see weakness.

'It doesn't bother you? What they're saying about us?'

He found himself hoping she hadn't read some of the more lurid headlines. Over the last week most reports had focused on the glamour of the events and of the photogenic royal, not to mention the fact she'd apparently enticed 'the world's most reclusive billionaire from his lair'. But others had twisted innocent situations with all sorts of negative speculation.

'Which bit do you mean?'

She gave a lopsided smile. 'I don't *read* them. I gave that up years ago.' Her voice was firm yet he discerned a note almost of vulnerability that made him feel something deep inside. Protectiveness? 'I mean generally, you and me being linked. It doesn't cause…complications for you?'

'Is this your way of asking if I'm in a relationship?'

'No! I just meant as a CEO, don't you have to be careful about your image?'

He regarded her closely, trying to read the truth behind

those hazy blue eyes. Because he liked the idea she wanted him to be unattached? Because he wanted her to want him?

'I don't think being seen with a charming princess will harm my business. As for my image, I prefer to keep out of the limelight. But that's personal preference, not a necessity. Frankly, I don't pay attention to public speculation or what the media says about me.'

This week he'd made an exception. Since he'd agreed to undertake protection duties, his staff provided regular updates on media reports, as well as on Ricardo's whereabouts.

'I don't have a lover at the moment, if that's what you're worried about.' Something shifted in Rosamund's gaze. Interest? Relief? Was *that* why she'd turned him down last night? 'Do you?'

He hadn't intended to ask, but his tongue had a mind of its own.

Her shake of the head created a buzz of approval so strong it distracted him until she spoke again.

'What about your family? They don't take an interest in who you date?'

Dating seemed a curiously old-fashioned, almost innocent word. Fotis didn't date, he took women to bed.

He didn't have emotional relationships with them. Not after watching his mother use sham affection for the males in her life, solely to get the lifestyle she craved. Besides, after losing his father and brother, he'd found it easier not to engage emotionally. His affairs were short-term, exclusive while they lasted, and with no expectation on either side that they'd lead to anything more than physical gratification.

'There's no one worrying about who I spend my time with.'

'No one? You don't have family?'

He hesitated on the brink of a terse response. Something sharp that would deter more questions. Except he knew now that Rosamund wasn't a spoilt socialite probing for fun. She'd been genuinely distressed and concerned for him last night, not leaving his side until he'd received treatment.

He couldn't remember the last time anyone had worried about him like that. It made him feel…raw. Yet part of him hankered for more.

His voice roughened. 'Only my mother and she doesn't take an interest in things like that.'

Blue eyes surveyed him, unblinking, making him wonder what was going on in Rosamund's quick brain. 'But if the press knows there was an incident last night—'

'She won't worry.' He saw Rosamund wasn't convinced. 'We're not in contact. I don't even know where she is. She could be incommunicado at some Pacific beach resort, or shopping in New York.'

It was a lie. Of course he knew where she was, on a luxurious, privately-owned Caribbean island. Even after all these years he kept discreet tabs on the woman. If he knew where she was he could ensure their paths never crossed.

Time to change the subject.

'I talked with your brother.'

'Leon? He rang?' Fotis heard pleased surprise in her voice. As if a call from the king was an unexpected pleasure. What were *her* family relationships like? He doubted they could be worse than his.

'I called to update him.' He paused. 'The US investigators are closing in on Ricardo. They're hopeful it won't take much longer to finish building the case and arrest him. But you'll need continued close personal protection for a while longer.'

If he'd expected her to be pleased, he was mistaken.

'He's already tried an attack on me and failed. The police have the attacker in custody.'

'They've yet to prove the link and that doesn't mean you're out of danger. What's to stop Ricardo trying again?'

Rosamund paled. 'Is that likely? Surely he has other priorities if he's running out of money.'

Fotis' mouth flattened. He knew how reckless a thwarted narcissist could be, his mother was a perfect example. Ricardo might not expect money from Rosamund, but Fotis guessed he felt she owed him for what he'd lost.

He leaned across the table, willing her to understand. 'You made a fool of him in public. You denied him the fortune he desperately needed. And he *is* desperate. That makes him angry and dangerous. The scandal you created means even if he did have another woman in his sights, they wouldn't trust him after reading those press reports. If he's going down, he'll want to take you with him.'

Fotis saw the brutal words sink in, hating their necessity.

Rosamund gave a shuddering sigh then put her untouched coffee down. 'So Leon wants me to have the full complement of royal bodyguards when I get back to Cardona.'

'That's one option.' Fotis measured his words carefully. 'Or you could come with me to Greece. I can protect you there more easily. After all, the world believes we're lovers.' He ignored the blast of pleasure his words elicited. 'No one will think it suspicious if we spend time together.'

'To Greece? With you?'

Her astonishment was such that he might have suggested they fly to the moon instead of across the Mediterranean.

'You don't trust me to look after you?'

Her gaze went to his bandaged arm then to his face. 'Of course I trust you.'

There it was again, that peculiar feeling of loosening and warmth, deep inside, as if she'd tugged free a too-tight knot in his gut. He didn't let himself wonder why her trust mattered.

'Why would you do that? You fulfilled your end of the bargain. Leon will deliver on his promise.'

Fotis was the first to look away, fixing his attention on the navy blue sea. 'There are benefits to having a king in your debt.'

'You negotiated another deal with him?'

He shrugged. Let her think that. It was easier to let her believe his interest was in fulfilling his own agenda than a simple determination to keep her safe.

He cared about her well-being.

That was rare. For years he'd cut himself off from relationships. There were few exceptions, like Dimi Politis and her grandfather. Life was easier when you were totally self-sufficient. And far less painful.

'He should have spoken to me before making any arrangements.'

She folded her arms, inadvertently tugging the towel down to reveal her breasts, plumped up by the gesture. Fotis made himself look away, wrestling his unruly thoughts under control. He couldn't be distracted by that lush body and what he'd like to do with her.

'I have a busy schedule. I can't just hare off to Greece.'

'Leon had someone check your royal diary. He said there's nothing that can't be rescheduled.'

The look she gave him ignited, as if he'd poured petrol onto hot embers. Her eyes blazed and perversely he wanted to draw closer and bask in that heat.

'I haven't been living in Cardona full-time lately. Leon has no idea of my schedule.' She bit the words out, all clipped indignation. 'Not all my commitments are in the royal diary.'

Fotis crossed his arms. 'Is there somewhere else you need to be in the next week or so? Something else you need to do?'

A suspicion had formed over their time in Paris. They'd attended a lot of events together. Some expected, like formal galas and film screenings. Some surprising, like a community college awards night where Rosamund had presented scholarships to teenagers studying acting and related disciplines. Scholarships in her mother's name.

Rosamund wasn't the woman he'd first imagined. But as time passed he'd seen the hours she'd spent frowning over her laptop, or engrossed, writing in a tattered notebook. Both of which she'd snap shut whenever he approached.

He supposed he could confirm his suspicion easily enough, but he didn't want to investigate her any more than he already had. She'd had enough people pry into her life.

He'd rather she told him herself.

'Rosamund?'

She firmed her lips and looked away. Her schedule for the next month consisted of solid days working on the draft of her new book, and ideas for illustrations. But she was *not* going to explain that. The idea of spending more time with him made her feel vulnerable. She'd had enough trouble trying to get work done this last week, always hyper-alert to his presence in the Paris house.

Her life wasn't perfect but it suited her. She was heart whole and set her own priorities. That had always been enough for her, hadn't it?

Yet having him at her side, looking out for her, had made her wonder what it would be like to be with someone. *Really* be with someone. To *matter to them.*

As if you'd ever matter to Fotis. He's only here because he's done a deal with Leon.

Rosamund remembered his contempt when they'd met. She understood his anger at what he thought she'd done to Dimitria Politis. After a lifetime of being judged and found wanting, Rosamund resented that he'd done exactly that.

She deserved better. Far better.

And maybe you're scrounging for reasons to keep your distance. When you explained what happened in New York, he believed you. He stopped being so judgemental.

Maybe you're jealous of the Greek girl who arouses him to such protectiveness. Last night it was all you could do to resist tumbling into his bed.

Her problem was that this man made her feel unfamiliar

emotions. As if it weren't enough that she was targeted by an unbalanced criminal.

Her mouth tugged down in a rueful half-smile. Life was never simple, was it?

'I don't like people talking about me behind my back.' Which was hilarious, when she thought about it. That was the story of her life. 'Organising things on my behalf, I mean.'

She'd hoped, after that recent meeting with Leon, that perhaps she was more to her half-brother than an unwanted responsibility. It was stupid to feel hurt that he'd discussed the situation with Fotis, not her. After all, Fotis had called him. Rosamund had been too shell-shocked last night to call Leon. For most of her early years he hadn't been around. She'd certainly never got in the habit of confiding in him.

She was simply out of sorts today. She didn't know what she wanted. That exasperated her. She never dithered.

Rosamund turned to meet Fotis' intense stare. It felt like diving into the ocean, letting the currents drag her deep. As if she could float there safely.

The intensity of the illusion pushed her into speech. 'I don't want a bodyguard, even for another week.'

She didn't want to feel beholden, knowing he saw her as an obligation. The physical pull between them might be strong but one glance at that proud face reminded her Fotis' priorities would always be business.

'But,' she said as he opened his mouth, 'I'll consider going with you to Greece.'

No! This is a mistake.

She silenced the warning voice in her head. Just as she ignored her illicit thrill at the idea of going to Greece with him. Last night she'd told herself parting from him was necessary. Today her willpower had seriously fractured. The thought of leaving him filled her with dread.

Those winged, black eyebrows lifted. 'You'll consider it?'

'On one condition. First, we go to the hospital and get your arm checked properly, not by the house doctor here, but by an expert. Then—'

'That's two conditions.'

'Live with it, Fotis. This is non-negotiable.' She waited until he inclined his head. 'Secondly, we lunch today at a venue of my choice. Not here in the hotel but somewhere public.'

He frowned. 'Didn't you hear what I said about possible danger?'

'I heard it and I have no intention of putting either of us at risk. At the same time, I hate that Brad Ricardo is affecting what I can and can't do. That he's hurt you—'

'I'll recover. As for what you can do, it's not for much longer. The police will find the connection between last night's attacker and Ricardo. He'll pay, I promise you.'

Warmth spread as his words sank deep. She heard his sincerity, read it in the determined angle of his jaw and the promise in his eyes.

'I believe you. But this isn't just about Ricardo. It's about having my actions dictated by others. I refuse to let that man, or the press, force me to cower in a hotel suite, no matter how luxurious. I want to show them, and myself, that I make my own choices. I'm not running scared.'

It was how she operated. In her teens she'd struggled to cope with the outpouring of negativity from her father and the press. The stories they'd printed, most pure fiction, had made her cringe and retreat into herself.

Until she realised she was building a prison for herself. That was when she'd decided to live up to her father's expectations, for a few months seeking out scandalous parties just to annoy him. But it wasn't what she wanted, just bravado in the face of deep hurt and loneliness.

That was a long time ago. Since then she'd carved her own life, undertaking royal duties but mainly concentrating on her own work. It was a matter of pride to put on a public face and ignore the negative comments, especially when she attended high-profile events. She mightn't read the gossip but she heard enough to know she was still fair game for the press. She wouldn't, *couldn't* stop now. Because hiding equated to weakness and she'd vowed always to be strong when it came to the press.

She drew a deep breath. 'Those are my conditions. A hospital check, a session with the police, then lunch out.'

From his grim expression she expected an argument, if not downright refusal. So it felt ridiculously like a victory when he inclined his head.

Several hours later they were seated at the premier table in the Riviera's most exclusive restaurant. Of course they'd had no trouble getting a table. Set apart from the other diners, they were on an expansive terrace with a phenomenal view of the Côte d'Azur. Below the terrace an unscalable wall dropped to the road below. They were safe from intruders.

A crowd of photographers had followed them from their hotel to the hospital, then a growing number from the hospital to the restaurant. Plain-clothed security guards had held the crowd back as she and Fotis entered the building.

Rosamund had kept her chin up as she stepped from the car, confident in a stunning blue dress that brought out the colour in her eyes.

It was only when Fotis leaned close and whispered, 'Don't look so fierce,' that she'd remembered to smile.

After that, it was easy to play her part, for he'd looped his arm around her hip and drawn her close. It had been the most natural thing in the world to snuggle up to him, the shouts of photographers blurring into white noise.

Now he sat relaxed, watching her over the remains of his dessert. He was resplendent in a tailored jacket and trousers with an open shirt of pale aquamarine that made his skin look like bronze, his eyes like the sea.

'Was it worth it? Coming here?'

She shrugged. Perhaps it seemed petty to him, her need to

show herself uncowed. But the attack on him last night had left her feeling close to undone. Today's outing might be symbolic but it was important to her. In her experience, appearing strong was the first step to being strong.

'Absolutely. Not just because of the press. I've enjoyed our meal. Thanks for coming with me.'

The food had been superb but the company had made it special. It was the first time they'd shared a meal and it had been remarkably easy. The conversation had been engaging, never awkward, and she felt more relaxed than she had in days. In fact, the meal she'd planned as a defiant gesture had turned into a delight.

'My pleasure.' His half-smile warmed her as they left the table, detouring across the terrace and pausing to admire the view. 'So, Greece?'

Rosamund turned to find him a breath away. Her pulse galloped.

He didn't look like a man who saw her as a responsibility. The hot glint in his eyes didn't signal detached professionalism. It matched the hunger that roared through her blood, a suddenly unstoppable force.

She'd spent her life learning *not* to be impulsive, overcoming her natural spontaneity and thinking before she acted. But he was so close, and she'd resisted so long.

And she'd been so worried about him since last night.

Suddenly she couldn't find the willpower to hold back any longer.

She lifted her hand, feeling the scrape of his close-shaved beard, the heat of his flesh and the strength of his powerful jaw. Her breath hitched as pleasure spread from her sensitive palm. Her nipples budded against her dress, more sensitive without a bra, and her breath escaped on a rush of reckless excitement.

Rosamund raised her head and brushed her lips against his, and the world disappeared.

CHAPTER EIGHT

THERE IT WAS, the jolt of connection, the instant hunger. Heat and fire and a whole maelstrom of feelings rushing inside him as her mouth touched his.

He'd seen the kiss coming. He'd had plenty of time to stop it and hadn't. It was like last time, when an accidental meeting of mouths had undone him.

This time he'd had a choice. But how could there be a choice when his craving for her grew so great it kept him from sleep? From concentrating on work, from everything but thoughts of her?

Fotis looped his arms around her, hauling her in, slicking the open seam of her lips and pushing in to taste her.

She tasted like chocolate, courtesy of the handmade truffle she'd had instead of dessert. And of warm, luscious woman. He angled his head, delving deep, drawing her closer, repressing a sigh of satisfaction at the feel of her breasts crushed against his body and her hands slipping around his neck, pulling his head down to hers.

She smelt of cinnamon, vanilla and needy female.

Her low hum of pleasure tickled his tongue. It pulled his skin tight and weighted his hands as they slid around to grasp her hips and hold her close.

He drew her tongue into his mouth, sucking hard as blood pooled in his groin. He wanted…

Sounds intruded. For a second he couldn't even identify it

as a sound, just in awareness of something else, something beyond the pair of them. Then, finally he heard a voice calling their names.

The world crashed back. Even then, knowing they weren't alone, it took everything he had to lift his mouth from hers. And more again to withstand temptation when he saw her, eyes closed and lips parted, rising on her toes to follow his retreat as if she *needed* his kisses.

Another shout destroyed the illusion of intimacy.

From the corner of his eye he saw, on the road below them, a photographer with a massive telephoto lens trained on them. Instinctively, Fotis swung around, shielding Rosamund from view.

Was that why she'd wandered over here? To give the press fodder for their stories?

At least they were screened from the other diners in the restaurant by a collection of large, potted oleanders.

His fingers tightened on her hips. Had she used him to make her point that she was unfazed by last night's threat? To feed the story they were lovers? His lips twisted as a sour tang filled his mouth. But then she opened her eyes, looking dazed and undone. Unguarded. And the beginnings of anger clenching his belly dissipated.

Anyway, what did any photos matter? He didn't care what the press printed about him. A photo of them kissing was hardly a disaster. It only rankled momentarily because of his inveterate disgust at being used.

But looking down into those slumbrous eyes, he couldn't believe she was anything like the woman who'd used him as a convenient puppet time and again. Rosamund was complex and not easy to read but she wasn't like his mother who'd brought out her sons only when she needed them, then shunted them off and forgotten them as soon as she had what she wanted.

He remembered Rosamund in Paris with those eager teens. Her interest in them had been genuine. She'd stayed late at the awards ceremony, alight with enthusiasm as they talked about their aspirations.

'Fotis?'

'Did you know about the photographer?'

Rosamund frowned. 'Photographer?' She swung around towards the restaurant, dislodging his hold, and he had his answer. She looked baffled as she surveyed the thick foliage between them and the other diners. 'They'll be at the entrance, waiting for us to come out. Is that what you mean?'

He shook his head. 'It doesn't matter.'

It was a lie. It *did* matter. Not the photographer, but Fotis' reaction to that kiss. The mere touch of her lips and he'd dropped all pretence of staying alert to protect her from danger. What had happened to his laser-sharp focus? The instincts he'd always relied on? His need for caution while responsible for her safety?

The barrier separating him from others that had become innate over the years.

A frisson of warning skimmed his spine. Even with lovers, sharing the most intimate passion, Fotis never gave up his whole self. Yet with Rosamund a simple kiss made him lose himself.

He forced himself into speech. 'There's a photographer down on the road. He must have grown tired of waiting for us to leave.'

Rosamund's face flushed and her mouth set in a straight line. But her lips were still full from their kiss and he knew a crazy urge to forget where they were and resume what they'd just started.

'He saw us?'

'Saw and photographed. But it doesn't matter. You wanted to prove to Ricardo you're not hiding in a corner. We definitely succeeded.'

She frowned and looked like she was about to protest.

'It's done, Rosamund. No point fretting about it.'

After a second or two she nodded and his admiration grew. He had some inkling how hard she found the intrusive press attention. He'd only been subjected to it occasionally but she'd faced it all her life. Instead of ranting about it she moved on, choosing to put it aside.

That took courage. And incredible determination.

As he watched, her posture and expression changed, tiny alterations he could barely catalogue. But within moments she transformed from the unguarded, sensual woman he'd just kissed into a princess, serene and aloof. He felt a pang of loss.

Yet her lips were plumper than before and her eyes held a hazy shimmer that, this close, spoke of arousal.

Heat shafted through his lower body and his hands flexed against the need to reach out and ruffle her newfound poise. To pull her hard against him and make them both forget photographs and headlines and duty.

But he had to keep her safe. Not ravish her in public. So he took her arm and they walked through the restaurant, nodding to a couple of acquaintances and thanking the staff.

No one else knew he still tasted her on his tongue. That her sweet and spice scent teased his nostrils. That his body was tense with the memory of her lithe waist in his hands and the delicious curve of her body, straining against him.

His task was a thousand times more difficult than before. How could he ignore the way she made him feel, so he could keep her safe?

The sun was low as they flew across a scattering of islands so tiny they looked like pearls against the deep blue sea.

Now they reached a larger island and the helicopter began to descend. The land rose steeply from the shoreline to a razorback ridge topped by a row of ruined windmills. They were roofless stone shells. Only the last one was whole, whitewashed and with sails neatly furled.

Rosamund craned to take in the iconic building, striving to

concentrate on the view, not the man beside her. Or the fact they were going to be alone together for the foreseeable future.

Excitement warred with worry. When they'd first met it had been much easier, because she'd told herself she hated him.

That didn't last, did it?

Now she felt like she teetered on the brink of something momentous. Because of Fotis.

It didn't make sense because she never let thoughts of any man cloud her judgement. Been there, done that, learnt her lesson. She'd been duped so easily, she didn't trust her thinking around a man who made her feel too much. Even her mother, the person she'd most looked up to, had been taken in by the man she'd married.

Yet it was hard to think of that with Fotis.

Why did you kiss him in a public place, in front of a paparazzo?

Rosamund firmed her mouth and peered again at the scenery.

Past the steep ridge, the other side of the island was more fertile. Gentle slopes interspersed with ancient stone terraces sprawled down towards a semicircular bay. A village sat on the shore. She saw orchards and a breeze ruffled the grey-green foliage in olive groves.

But what held her attention was a jumble of rocks on a steep hill between the razorback ridge and the village. Late sunlight turned the rubble into blocks of bronze.

The chopper banked and she found herself looking down on a roofless building. And another, a cobblestoned street wending between them. Then the terracotta tiles of a domed Byzantine-style church. Sprawling stone steps that led nowhere. Large trees shivered and swayed as they dropped closer.

'*This* is where you live?'

Fotis nodded, his attention on the instrument panel and the scene before them. 'One of the places. I have a home in Athens but this is my retreat. Easier to keep you safe here than in the city. There's excellent electronic security and any outsiders would be noticed immediately.'

The island was too small to be on the tourist map and any stranger would be obvious. But a deserted town?

They swung around a curve and there, seeming to grow straight up from a sheer cliff, was a long two-storey building, old but clearly renovated. Rows of windows looked towards the sea and the terracotta roof was a blend of old and new tiles.

Fotis flew low over it to land on a crisply painted helipad.

Of course he didn't live anywhere as ordinary as a modern apartment or conventional house. The man cloaked himself in mystery. Even his business was about keeping and decoding secrets. Why not live in a deserted mediaeval town?

'What's the joke?' he asked as she took off her headphones and the sound of the rotors faded.

'You thought I was elitist because I was born in a palace. Yet you live in a...' She surveyed the large building. 'Castle?'

'Abandoned monastery.'

Rosamund couldn't help it, laughter bubbled up.

His winged eyebrows rose but there was a gleam in his eyes that might have been wry amusement. The sight made her stomach do a curious sweep and shimmy motion that had nothing to do with their chopper flight. 'And that's funny because...?'

'You really are reclusive. Like those monks who cut themselves off from the outside world, looking for peace and tranquility. Does anyone else live here?'

'Just me. A couple from the village look after the place.'

So you're going to be alone with him there.

They'd been alone in the Paris house and she'd enjoyed the relative peace, even managed to do a little work. But things had changed. *She'd* changed, become so attuned to him that it was hard to think of anything else.

'I bring some of my team here when we're working on something that requires close collaboration.'

Rosamund didn't know whether to be impressed, jealous, or disturbed that he lived in an eyrie, perched on a rock in the middle of an isolated island.

There were times when she wished she had a bolt-hole where she could truly escape when she needed to concentrate. 'You don't get lonely?' she asked as she undid her seat belt.

'I'm happy with my own company. Anyway, I find company when I want it.'

His voice dropped to a deep note that made her lift her head to meet his stare. His eyes seemed brighter, his expression intense and she realised what he meant by company.

Women. Sex.

It was as if he'd flicked a switch inside her. Far from being weary from the journey to Greece or distracted by her churning thoughts, she was suddenly hyper-aware. That hooded stare made her breasts grow heavy, heat brewing in that secret feminine place between her legs.

Suddenly all the things she'd been trying *not* to think filled her brain.

Rosamund imagined his gaze holding hers as he drove himself deep inside her, filling her to the brim. Those callused palms stroking her breasts, skimming her thighs and then the place where need throbbed hard and fast. She remembered the taste of his mouth and imagined having the freedom to taste him all over.

She jerked her head around to stare out the side window, nostrils flaring as she dragged air into constrained lungs.

All day they'd skirted around the sexual awareness clotting the air between them.

Her stupid impulse to kiss him at the restaurant had been a mistake. She'd known it but hadn't been able to resist. Had barely been able to resist the temptation of him last night when his murmured invitation to retire early had sent her into a tail-spin of longing.

She couldn't understand this man's power.

Like her mother, she had a strong impulsive streak. Like her mother, it had got her into trouble when she was young. But circumstances and the strictures of her royal role meant Rosamund had finally curbed what her father had curtly labelled her waywardness.

At twenty-eight, Rosamund had learnt to think before acting. Yes, setting Ricardo up had been impetuous, but based on sound reasoning. She couldn't stand by and allow him to destroy an innocent's life. Dimitria Politis wouldn't have believed her, if she'd told her about Ricardo's sickening bragging. The girl was besotted and would trust her lover over a woman she didn't know.

But kissing Fotis Mavridis? That had been utterly foolhardy. Because now he was in her mind, in her blood, in a way she'd never experienced before.

The door opened and there he was, well over six feet of impressive masculinity. Her heart gave a silly flutter which she chose to ignore, just as she ignored his outstretched hand and stepped down without help.

It felt like a victory, given how badly she wanted his touch. But she couldn't allow herself to be swept along thoughtlessly.

Control. That was what she'd worked hard to achieve and it had kept her safe for years.

He closed the chopper door behind her. 'This way.'

He led her around the corner of the building, past a huge, spreading tree. On the far side of the space were other buildings in various stages of disrepair, some with empty windows that allowed her to see right through to the stunning views beyond.

'It's not just a monastery is it? It's a whole town.'

'It was. It was abandoned when most islanders left for the city or migrated abroad. A century ago all those terraces and fields were cultivated, supporting a larger population.'

'And there are windmills,' she murmured. 'They're very striking.'

Rosamund was amazed that her voice emerged evenly when

there was a riot going on in her body. Tiny detonations of awareness ignited in her blood because he walked so close, shortening his stride to match hers.

Was it any wonder she tried to fill the silence? If they weren't talking, there'd be nothing to keep her from her circling, needy thoughts.

'We've restored one of them.'

The hint of pride in his voice made her want to survey him but she kept her attention on the large door on the far side of the courtyard.

Control, remember?

'We?'

'The residents. We get supplies in from the mainland but it's sensible to be as self-sufficient as possible, besides, it's good to maintain some of the place's heritage.'

She was about to say something about the importance of preserving heritage but they'd reached the door and she'd reached the end of her small talk. It was too much effort.

The door was ornate and imposing but instead of a key, Fotis pressed his palm to a sensor and the door swung wide. 'Welcome to my home, Rosamund.'

The way he said her name, flawlessly yet with just the tiniest hint of an Aegean accent, made her skin tighten. It always did, ever since he'd stopped calling her Princess in a scathing tone. She'd become addicted to the sound of it in that soft, deep rumble. It was one of the things she'd miss when they eventually went their separate ways.

Rosamund swallowed hard and stepped over the threshold.

She wasn't sure what she'd expected of his home but it wasn't this, she realised, as she looked around the spacious foyer and the glimpses into other spaces.

The building was old, its gracious bones clearly visible in the high arched ceilings and thick walls. It might have been tempting to leave the place bare and spartan, or turn it into a showpiece of ultra-modern design.

Instead she was surprised to find it…warm. The proportions were enormous, designed to accommodate large numbers, but the use of soft ochres and cream on the walls softened that. As did the eclectic mix of furniture, reclaimed as well as meticulously craftsman-built.

On one huge wall was a monumental painting. Ochre earth, grey stones, the deep blue of the sea and, bathed in the golden hues of sunset, a row of dilapidated windmills, like battered but still-fierce guardians. The artist had imbued them somehow with a quality that was more human than inanimate.

Drawn, she moved closer, searching for a signature.

As if reading her mind, Fotis said, 'He doesn't sign his work.'

'He doesn't? That's…' She shook her head. 'Unusual. Why?'

'You'll have to ask him that.'

The voice came from right beside her and she made herself focus on the bold brushstrokes rather than the heat dabbling her skin from where he stood so close. Finally his words sank in. 'The artist lives here? On the island?'

She turned, only to be ensnared by those crystalline eyes. Her ribs squeezed around her lungs and her lips parted, eager for air.

Or eager for something else. Another taste of forbidden fruit? It took everything she had to keep her gaze locked on Fotis' eyes, rather than drop to his mouth.

'He does. Tassos is very private about his art. He prefers to keep it to himself. I believe that's not uncommon with some creative people.'

Did Fotis' voice turn challenging, or was that imagination? He couldn't possibly know about her writing. Yet his direct stare made her wonder how much he'd seen.

Rosamund looked again at the painting. 'Is that why he lives here? He sees it as a haven?' Maybe that explained her impression that the rough mountain and the windmills weren't simply starkly beautiful but represented a protective bulwark.

The silence drew out. 'You do see a lot, don't you?' Fotis said in a voice that defied definition. 'This place has always been a haven. Generations upon generations lived here. They even moved their town up onto this hill centuries ago, to protect themselves from marauding pirates.'

'Pirates? Really?' It was easier to focus on colourful history than the awareness zinging through her blood, because of a man who was only beside her because he'd promised Leon he'd keep her safe.

'Really. They were dire times, but the cliffs and high walls kept the people safe most of the time.' He paused. 'Now there are no pirates, but it's still a haven.'

For him too? Rosamund desperately wanted to know. She wanted to understand him. What had made him a recluse? What had given him the drive to build a multibillion-dollar business? Why, in repose, was his expression often so stern?

But if she quizzed him, the quid pro quo meant he'd have every right to question her.

She turned, and just as she'd known, he was scrutinising her, not the artwork. His brow furrowed as if she intrigued him. It was arousing and terrifying, having that fiercely insightful mind turned on her.

Almost as arousing as the idea of them together, naked, the way she'd been imagining.

Without a word, he beckoned for her to follow him, leading her up the wide staircase. At the end of an upstairs corridor he opened a door. 'This is yours. I'm next door if you need anything.'

The room was simple but pure luxury. Windows down one wall gave spectacular views towards the sea and through an open door she glimpsed a well-appointed bathroom.

Another luxurious, empty suite.

Another lonely, empty night.

Rosamund paused in the doorway. It struck her suddenly,

how much time she spent alone. How she ached for...more. Ached for *him*.

She liked solitude, needed it for her work, but still there was a yearning inside her, a yearning so powerful it bubbled up, an unstoppable force. She wondered if he could read it in her face.

'Rosamund? What is it?'

Her pulse quickened. Was she really going to do this? After all the effort she'd put into being sensible?

Part of her couldn't believe it. Another part screamed at her to hurry up. Once that inner voice, the impulsive one, had dominated. But years learning caution had stifled it so now she didn't know whether to trust it.

'I do need something.' How glorious it was, how freeing, to admit it.

He stepped before her. 'What is it you need?'

'You, Fotis.' She put her hand to his darkly stubbled jaw, tracing its strong lines, feeling his solid heat under her hand with something like relief. 'I need you.'

CHAPTER NINE

HE WAS SILENT so long, she wondered if he hadn't heard her.

Oh, he heard. Those eyes blazed so hot they scorched her.

'What, exactly, are you suggesting?'

What part of *I need you*, didn't he understand? She hadn't imagined his implicit invitation to share his bed last night, had she? No, his meaning had been potently clear.

She angled her chin up. 'You and me together. Naked.' She watched a pulse throb at his temple, felt his muscles move as he swallowed.

'Is this guilt talking?'

'What do you mean?'

He nodded towards his arm. 'Because I got hurt. Your way of making amends? Paying me back?'

Rosamund dropped her hand and stepped away, suddenly trembling. She *did* feel guilty that he'd been injured because of her. More than guilty. Thinking of him in pain was hard. But this was something else.

Suddenly what had felt so simple had become tainted.

'You think I use sex as a payment? A way of balancing the books?' Her stomach rolled so much she felt almost sick. Over the years people had tried to make her feel cheap but it was rare they succeeded. But now… 'Strangely enough, I've never propositioned one of my bodyguards before.'

'I didn't mean—'

'It's okay, Fotis. I know what you meant.' He imagined she used her body as a commodity.

'No! You don't.' His voice was strident, a far cry from his usual even tones. He ploughed his hand through his hair, leaving it ruffled and ridiculously appealing. She hated that she noticed. 'I'm not insulting you. I thought you were feeling sorry for me. You shouldn't feel guilty about what happened when it's not your fault. It was mine for letting down my guard.' He took a deep breath that lifted his powerful chest. 'I should never have let you leave the premises with me. You could have been hurt.'

To her amazement his voice was uneven.

'You thought I was offering pity sex?'

Those broad shoulders lifted. 'It's a possibility.'

Rosamund shook her head. 'It was my decision to leave the party with you. You gave your professional advice and I ignored it, so it was *my* fault. I regret what happened to you and I *do* feel guilty. But that's got nothing to do with this.'

'No?' He folded his arms, making her wish he'd move away from her doorway so she could go inside and shut the door behind her.

'No!'

'Good.'

'Good? What do you mean?' Somehow she'd lost track of the conversation. Why had she thought telling Fotis she wanted him would make things easy? Nothing had been easy between them.

'Two adults acting on pure sexual attraction sounds perfect to me.'

Her mind must have slowed because it took a second for his meaning to sink in. When it did it was like a bomb exploding inside, reigniting the desire his earlier words had doused. 'Perfect?'

She didn't think she'd ever had perfect in her life. But the thrill she got just from being close to this man and the confidence he exuded, made her suspect being with him could come close. His eyes glittered with an unholy heat that made her knees loosen.

'There's just one thing,' he added. 'I don't do long-term relationships.' His gaze dropped to her mouth and it was as if he'd drawn a line of heat along her lips then down to her breasts and further, deep into her womb. 'I'm not after emotional attachment. I don't want that. If there's any danger of you getting emotionally involved—'

'No. There's not.' She almost wished there was. But her experiences had soured that possibility. Romantic dreams were for innocents. Rosamund was a pragmatist now. 'All I'm hoping for is mind-blowing sex.'

'That,' he said with a slow-growing smile that twisted her insides in knots, 'I can deliver.'

He moved so swiftly, he took her by surprise, hoisting her into his arms and up against his chest. She was surrounded by hard male and heat so intense it seemed almost feverish. She planted one hand on his chest, pleased to feel his heart thudding as fast as her own.

He turned his back on her room. 'Fotis?'

'What is it?' He stopped, looking down with a frown. 'You want to wait?'

Held securely in that iron-hard embrace, she *felt* his urgency and saw it reflected in his features. She almost smiled her relief. 'No! I just wondered why you're walking away from a perfectly good bed.'

He moved swiftly along the hallway, shouldering his way through another door, and she marvelled at the intriguing feeling of weightlessness as he carried her so easily. 'Mine has a stock of condoms in the bedside table.'

Her breath snagged at the febrile glaze of desire in his eyes. She'd only seen him fully clothed but she had an excellent imagination. He was a tall man and well-built. She suspected that naked he'd be imposing. He certainly was in her taunting, erotic dreams. She wanted to watch him roll on a condom while he watched her with that naked hunger in his eyes.

'Then what are we waiting for?'

A smile hooked up the corner of his mouth and something inside her dissolved. Serious or disapproving he was stunning. But amused and approachable he was downright dangerous.

Deliciously, temptingly dangerous. She wanted to lose herself in that smile. In his arms, his body, and not surface for a long, long time.

With an ease that spoke of impressive strength, he lowered her slowly to her feet. Their bodies brushed together, centimetre by centimetre, the friction teasing and delighting. She swayed against him, hands going automatically to his shirt buttons. She started at the top while he reefed the shirt free of his trousers.

The top of his shirt gaped wide and her knuckles brushed hot flesh and crisp chest hair over tight muscles. She looked down, following the narrow trail of dark hair descending from his chest over glowing, golden skin.

She'd been so right about his body, she decided as she pushed his shirt off with a silent sigh of appreciation.

He had broad shoulders and the leanly honed muscles of an athlete. As she stroked down his body those tight muscles twitched under her touch. As if she had power over him.

As he did over her. Just the sight of Fotis, half-naked, had turned the needy place between her legs butter-soft. Her breasts swelled and low inside she ached.

Her fingers reached his trousers. His belt. She wanted…

'My turn.'

His voice was raw gravel and only added to her arousal. She looked up and there she saw the same desperation she felt. It slammed into her, an affirmation so powerful she couldn't remember ever feeling so good.

And they'd barely started.

His hands rose to her shoulder straps, then slowly down,

skimming the fabric that crossed above her décolletage, then lower, feathering the material that covered her breasts.

Her hum of approval sounded more like a growl as she pressed into his hands, squeezing her thighs tight together against a tide of liquid pleasure as he cupped and squeezed her breasts. She'd never been more grateful that a bra was impossible in this dress.

'Do you have any idea how hard it's been, keeping my hands off you? Especially in that dress. Did you wear it to torment me?'

'Of course not,' she groaned as he weighed her breasts in his palms then followed the fabric lower, to where the two wide bands of fabric parted, leaving an upside-down V of flesh bare at her midriff. His fingertips stroked her skin and even that felt like erotic overload.

'The dress is perfectly respectable,' she croaked. The skirt was knee-length, and while the straps revealed more than usual of her back, the bodice was modest but for that small triangle of bare flesh above her waist.

But appearances lied. The wide crossed straps covered her breasts fully but once over her shoulders they narrowed, crossing over her back before circling her waist to tie at the front. Everything essential was covered but undo that tie and yank the straps...

She'd worn it because it made her feel bold and attractive. Defiant.

'So you were making a point for the cameras, not me, with all that sultry sexiness.'

She put her hands on his, intending to drag them back to her aching breasts. But then he spanned her waist in what felt deliciously like possessiveness and she confessed, 'Maybe I dressed for you too.'

Not to tease, but because she'd wanted, badly, to have him look at her like an attractive woman one more time, not like someone he'd simply sworn to protect.

'I'm glad. I approve.'

His teeth flashed in a feral smile as he grasped her hips and yanked her to him.

Rosamund's mind went blank as she registered the thick length of his erection pressing against her abdomen. Then she rose on her toes, grabbing the hard muscles at his shoulders, and ground her pelvis against him.

So good. So very, very good.

Eyelids at half-mast, she saw him grit his teeth, a man on the edge. Excitement spiked.

'You have three seconds to undo that dress before I damage it when I rip it off you.'

For a shocking second she toyed with the idea of calling his bluff. But she loved seeing Fotis teetering on the brink of control. She intended to wear this dress again, often.

Before this, sex had been enjoyable but never thrilling. She discovered she liked thrilling.

Leaning back, she swiftly undid the discreet bow at her waist then dragged down the wide straps covering her chest. The bodice dropped, leaving her naked from the waist up.

Rosamund didn't understand Greek but she didn't need to. His whispered words were heartfelt and made her stand taller so her breasts jutted towards him. His husky voice and the avid gleam in his eyes made her feel like a goddess.

But when he stroked his hands, feather-light, over her bare breasts, she was all woman, surging forward into his hold, grabbing at his shoulders for balance as he wrought the most incredible sensations in her needy body.

'Fotis.'

It sounded shockingly like a plea and she didn't care. Nothing mattered but the promise of carnal pleasure. This, between them, was more profound, more intense than anything she'd experienced.

He bent to suck at her breast and her head arched back in rapture, fiery trails of sensation coursing through her.

Clamping his head to her breast she reached down between them, fumbling with his belt. As magnificent as this was, she needed more. She needed everything.

More Greek words, this time a growl, and suddenly she was at arm's length from him, gasping at the interruption.

'Take your dress off.'

She blinked up at him, trying to decipher his words. His accent was suddenly so pronounced it took a second to realise he spoke in English. Or maybe it was the rush of blood in her head, affecting her hearing.

He was already stripping off his shoes and socks as she kicked off her sandals, undid the zip and pushed the dress to the floor.

The sight of Fotis in that moment was something she'd never forget, even if she lived to be a hundred.

Hair tousled, bare feet planted wide, hands frozen in the act of yanking his belt undone, his chest heaved mightily as if he struggled to drag air into that spectacular body. But it was his eyes above all that entranced her. Eyes that glittered with a sharp possessive hunger mixed with something like awe.

She knew the feeling. She'd never seen a man so stunningly beautiful. Never wanted the way she wanted him. Never felt desire so untamed it felt primal.

For a second Rosamund shivered as something like fear coursed through her.

But she'd spent her adult life being cautious. She wanted, needed just this once, to follow her instinct. To forget responsibility and expectations and just *be*.

Holding his gaze, she hooked her fingers into her underwear, dragging the lace and damp silk down to drop onto the floor.

Fotis swallowed, the movement jerky as his eyes ate her up. Then with a few quick movements, the last of his clothes hit the floor and he stepped free of them.

She'd been so right. The man was stunning. Every line and

dip, every muscled curve and hard plane impressive. So impressive she felt a quiver of nerves at the thought of accommodating his rampant erection.

Nerves and anticipation. Her fingers flexed. She wanted to explore, touch and taste and discover all his secrets.

He leaned across and yanked open a drawer in the bedside cabinet, withdrawing a box of condoms. She took a half-step forward, about to offer to help, when he shook his head. 'On the bed,' he said, his voice rough. 'Please.'

He looked as strung out as she felt, and she wondered if he too felt on the edge of climax.

Just from watching him undress, and the feel of his mouth at her breast!

She wobbled her way to the bed then climbed up to lie on her back, watching as he stroked on the condom. Each movement of his hand felt like a phantom caress between her thighs. She twitched, shifting her weight and opening her legs, needing his body against hers, *in* hers as she'd never needed any man.

His gaze caressed her body and she felt it as surely as she'd felt his hands on her waist, hips and breasts. She licked her lips and willed herself not to beg.

A couple of strides and he was at the base of the bed, but instead of following her onto it, he reached for her ankles and tugged her sharply down its length. The move was so abrupt he was kneeling on the floor between her knees before she registered him moving. Another tug and her buttocks settled on the edge of the bed. She wriggled her hips to bring herself closer to all that glorious heat and hardness.

'Rosa.'

The diminutive startled her, but it sounded so right in that harsh sandpaper voice. Something behind her ribs loosened abruptly. As if a pinched nerve suddenly eased, leaving her limp and basking in unfamiliar approval.

Instinctively she reached for him and he captured her hands, pressing kisses to first one palm then the other, ratcheting up her eagerness. That loosening intensified as tenderness welled.

Fotis released her, but instead of easing his tall frame above hers, he sank low, pushing her thighs wide with his shoulders, his breath hot against her most private place.

She was already shaking her head. 'No, Fotis. I'm too close.'

'Good. I want to taste you as you come.'

The words sent her arousal skyrocketing and that was before he nuzzled her. Unerringly he found her pleasure point with a slow lick that made her arch off the bed.

'But I want—'

'I know you do, *asteri mou*, and I'll give you everything you want. Later. I promise.'

Shining eyes held hers as he kissed her and it was all she could do not to explode as excitement and carnal pleasure melded with something unexpected. Stunned, she just had time to register a wave of poignant emotion. Then what he did with his mouth scrambled all thought.

Needy hands speared his thick hair, holding him close. Then his fingers were on her, circling, exploring, insinuating into slick heat.

Her eyes must've closed because white light pulsed behind her eyelids in time with every thrust of his fingers and each caress of his mouth. Her hips rose, seeking, and he spread his other hand beneath her, angling her higher.

Rosamund scrabbled to regain control but was far too late. The splashes of white light were edged now with golden sparks, sparks igniting deep within.

Stunned at the intensity of sensation, she snapped her eyes open to find him watching her. 'That's it, Rosa,' he growled, his breath hot against tenderest flesh and his short beard scraping her inner thighs as she clamped her legs around him. 'Come for me. Now.'

As if on command, she convulsed, overwhelmed by a peak of pleasure that went on and on and on. Still he caressed her, as if needing to ensure she lost all control. She couldn't breathe, couldn't think, could only ride crest after crest of jubilation.

She was boneless, shaky with aftershocks and utterly euphoric. Never had a man taken her to such heights.

Another caress made her shudder, overloaded with bliss. But it took his withdrawal to lift her heavy eyelids.

'Thank you,' she croaked as he rose between her legs. 'That was amazing.'

He was amazing with his generosity and unstinting care for her pleasure.

'You're welcome.' His mouth hitched up in a smile that was positively devilish. 'But wait, there's more.'

'Good, because I need you.'

Despite the incredible orgasm, she felt a hollow ache inside. And despite clenching internal muscles, the need wasn't just physical. She wanted the intimacy of being heart to heart with this man. It might be an illusion but she craved more than physical satiation.

Callused fingertips ran down her thighs and along her calves then he lifted her legs up, draping her ankles over his shoulders as he leaned towards her.

It wasn't what she'd expected but when she felt the heavy nudge of his erection at her core it made sense. She felt open to him, completely dominated by his larger body, and it excited her.

'Okay?'

'Absolutely okay.'

He leaned closer, nudging her and pushing in a fraction. She felt her eyes widen as she stretched.

He planted his hands on the bed either side of her and bowed forward, lips skimming her breast. 'I thought this might be easier for you until you get accustomed...'

To the size of him. Rosamund nodded. She'd known he was big but...

Teeth closed around her nipple in the tiniest nip as he pressed further, the pressure so right. Still he slid deeper.

'Breathe, Rosa.' She opened her eyes to see him frowning down at her. 'Are you all right?'

She nodded, circling her hips, inviting him further. 'Fill me, Fotis. I want all of you.'

She wanted to possess him, experience his climax, feel him lose control, just for her. She was so hungry for him, it shocked her.

Holding her gaze, he thrust long and slow, impaling himself so deep it felt like he'd reached her heart.

For a breath neither moved. Then she squeezed him and was rewarded by a flicker of those long dark eyelashes.

It would be easy to feel overwhelmed by his sheer physical presence. Instead she was excited. She knew her own power, squeezing again as she gently raked her fingernails down his torso, feeling him shudder.

'Rosa!' His hoarse voice was somewhere between a warning and a plea.

'What's the matter, Fotis?' She gasped as he withdrew and surged back slowly, finding a deliciously sensitive spot that made her writhe. 'You can dish it out but you can't take it?'

For answer he withdrew then bucked hard, so hard she'd never felt anything so perfect. He did it again and again, his slow precision driving her wild. Even as her rough cries of pleasure filled the air she needed to bring him undone.

She reached down to where his thighs slapped against her buttocks with every hungry thrust. Questing fingers found his sac and slowly squeezed.

There was a rough gasp as he arched high before taking her again, his movements jagged.

'Don't.' He pulled her hand away, his gentleness at odds with the feral gleam in his eyes. 'I can't last like that.'

'Then don't.' Her voice was unsteady. 'I want you to lose

yourself.' Much as she'd rejoiced in her own climax, she wanted to be with Fotis when he reached that same point.

Their gazes held and she wondered what he saw in hers. Carefully he eased her legs down and she wrapped them around his hips. Now he lay over her, taking his weight on his elbows, his chest against hers, the friction of his hair-roughened chest against her nipples delicious torture.

Slowly he moved, retreating then surging. 'All right?'

'More than all right.'

She rose to meet the next thrust, matching his rhythm, drawn by instinct and the desire to give him the joy he'd given her. But somehow, the needs of her own body grew clamorous. She felt the wave rise, unstoppable. 'I can't—'

His mouth took hers, gently at first, then deeper, mimicking the sensual thrusts of their bodies.

Rosamund felt the ripples begin, then he came alive in an urgent explosion of movement, bucking frantically and pushing them both over the edge into ecstasy. The feel of him pulsing, losing himself deep inside her, was indescribably satisfying.

She swallowed his roar of completion, feeling her own blend of triumph, exquisite physical pleasure and, as she gradually came back to herself, tenderness for this man.

Her arms wrapped around him and her heart squeezed. He nuzzled the sensitive curve of her neck as he slumped over her, still trembling from his climax.

Even spent, his presence inside her took some getting used to.

Because he felt so good. Too good?

Rosamund felt such a profound connection. Her need for him to reach ecstasy had been more than a generous urge. It had been a necessity.

She'd wanted him to have everything he'd given her and more. Greedily, she'd wanted to be with him through it all.

She was discriminating about lovers and it was a very long time since she'd been with anyone. Yet, as she stroked the hot silky skin of his back, and felt a glow in her chest, she wondered if she'd just made a huge mistake.

Fotis lifted his head, heavy-lidded eyes meeting hers, then slid his arms around her and rolled onto his back so she was draped over him.

'Better,' he murmured, kissing her languidly.

Rosamund lost her train of thought.

CHAPTER TEN

FOTIS APPROACHED THE old windmill, a breeze riffling his shirt as he topped the ridgeline.

The door was propped open and Rosamund sat on the stone block that wedged it wide. She was writing, her attention on the notebook open on her lap. A broad-brimmed hat lay discarded on the ground. Even in the shade, her rose-gold hair seemed to catch the light.

Her legs were stretched out, casually crossed at the ankles. Fotis thought of how she'd locked those slim, strong limbs around him this morning as she urged him deeper, faster, harder.

He paused and drew a slow breath.

She wore a crimson cotton dress with narrow shoulder straps that left her arms and shoulders bare. He knew she wore nothing beneath it except a pair of skimpy, lace underpants. Lying on the rumpled bed, he'd watched her dress, only just restraining himself from reaching for her again, because she'd declared she needed fresh air after spending so long in bed.

He thought he'd done well, not mentioning that she'd been the one to disrupt his offer to prepare breakfast, her seeking, stroking hands revealing that it wasn't food she'd been hungry for. Inevitably she'd woken the beast in him and they'd stayed in bed for another hour.

Their affair had lasted for weeks and still they were voracious for each other. Just a look, a touch, a half-smile, and nothing mattered but satisfying that hunger. By mutual consent, and while Ricardo was still at large, there'd been no mention of her leaving.

Fotis had found himself working less than he usually did, only when she was busy on her laptop. His business ran well and he trusted his senior staff but soon, surely, he'd have to pull back from her and return to his well-ordered life.

Yet for hours the image of her, lifting the cherry-red dress over her head and letting it waft down over her almost-naked body, had made work impossible.

Besides, despite the safety of this isolated island with its state-of-the-art security monitoring, he couldn't rest easy if she wasn't near. Every day she explored, sometimes with him and sometimes ostensibly on her own. But Fotis always ensured either he or a trusted local was close enough to step in if danger threatened.

He wouldn't allow anything bad to happen to her.

Because you gave your word to her brother? Or because you can't stand the thought of her being hurt?

The answer was both. Yet his visceral reaction to the idea of her in danger had little to do with Leon or their deal.

Nor was his response based solely on sex. The carnal link between them was incredibly strong. But more than that Fotis *liked* Rosamund.

She wasn't afraid to challenge him and he enjoyed the give-and-take of their discussions, even their disagreements. Time and again she'd made him consider things in a new light. She was living proof that he wasn't always right and that first impressions could be wrong. A valuable reminder for a man in his field. In his work he'd never dream of jumping to conclusions, yet he'd done that with her.

'Are you hungry? I brought food.'

She lifted her head, expression brimming with a delight that made his heart thud. Her slow curling smile and the pleasure in her grey-blue eyes drew heat through his tightening chest, down past his belly and into his groin.

'Sounds wonderful. I'm famished.'

'So am I.' Not merely for food.

Fotis closed the space between them and dropped a kiss to her parted lips.

Immediately need rose. Her response was as instantaneous as it was generous. She palmed his jaw, leaning up towards him, and he felt her hunger. It matched his. For a deeper taste. For the feel of their bodies against each other. For the sweet bliss of communion.

But he pulled back, making himself straighten, his lungs working like bellows and every muscle protesting. Because he was determined for once not to tumble immediately into sex.

He'd known alluring women, enjoyed his time with enough of them. Yet none had had this effect on him. Weeks it had been since they'd become lovers, and in that time his desire for her, his *hunger*, had only intensified.

He needed... What? To understand this link between them. To identify the nebulous feelings she stirred. They were unsettling to a man who'd spent his life determinedly alone.

He swung the backpack off his shoulders and onto the ground. 'I've brought cheese and fresh bread—'

'*Yiayia* Irini's bread?'

He nodded, smiling as her face lit with greedy eagerness. 'Tassos brought some up especially for you.'

Because Rosamund had developed a weakness for the flavoursome bread and nothing, it seemed, was too much effort for the locals where she was concerned. She'd visited the village early during her stay and found the elderly woman removing a loaf of bread she'd baked from the old communal oven. The oven was only used by a few now, but some of the traditional ways hadn't died.

Naturally Irini had offered the visitor a taste of her loaf, using her smattering of English. A bond had sprung up between the princess and the tiny, sharp-eyed matriarch of the village. Not just with Irini. He'd lost count of the people who'd spent time with Rosamund and liked her.

He liked her. More than he'd thought possible.

He looked away from her shining eyes as he opened the pack. 'There are olives and tomatoes. Plus I've got a bottle of local wine and apricot tart for dessert.'

'It sounds like a feast,' she said as she closed her notebook and put it aside.

Fotis noted with pleasure that she hadn't snapped it shut the moment she saw him, like she used to do. She was relaxed, anticipation dancing her eyes.

He'd seen her at VIP functions that featured world-famous wines and exquisite gourmet delicacies. Yet here she was, licking her lips over rustic bread, tomatoes warm from the sun and a light wine that was tasty but would never feature on a list of must-have vintages.

Rosamund was anything but elitist.

He pulled out a rug and spread it out while she delved into the rucksack, busily setting out the food. She grabbed a knife. 'I'll cut the bread and the tomatoes if you'll open the wine.'

As Fotis uncorked the bottle and poured it, he tried to imagine any of his previous lovers enjoying such a simple picnic. He couldn't.

The women in his life hadn't been socialites, since he had an inbuilt hatred of the species. They were all intelligent, attractive women, not searching for a man to give them a life of luxury. Yet he couldn't picture any of them here on this superb but wild mountain, avidly eyeing his humble picnic.

He handed her some wine and she leaned in to brush her lips against his, lingering for a tantalising moment that tested his resolve, before withdrawing. She tasted of the sea breeze and cinnamon, and something deeply sensual that was unique to her. Something that made him want to lean in for more.

Blue eyes twinkled. She knew exactly how much he wanted

her. 'Thanks for hiking up with the food, Fotis.' She raised her glass. '*Yassou.*'

He lifted his own in salute. '*Yassou*, Rosa.'

He loved her reaction to the intimate nickname. The hint of a flush across her throat and the glow of pleasure in her beautiful eyes. It made him want...

Fotis swallowed a mouthful of crisp wine then reached for an olive, breaking their locked gazes.

'I have a question.' It had been on his mind for weeks, that incident in Paris that had set the seal on his initial negative opinion. An opinion that didn't fit the woman he knew.

She tilted her head. 'Go on.'

'Tell me about the dress in the Paris boutique. The red one you rejected.'

At first he'd imagined her reaction was simply selfishness. Now he knew better. Her manner at the boutique was at odds with the way she dealt with other people. Completely at odds with how she interacted with the villagers here.

Rosamund paused in the act of laying a tomato slice on a piece of bread. A tiny frown line appeared in the centre of her forehead as she took her time adding another slice. 'What do you want to know?'

He hated the wariness in her voice and how her lush mouth pinched at the corners. But he wanted more from her, more than sexual gratification. He hungered to *know* her. He told himself it was a form of self-protection to understand her, yet an inner voice warned he was in dangerous territory.

So be it. He'd crossed a line with this woman and he couldn't go back. He *needed* to understand her.

'It wasn't just any dress, was it? It upset you and you weren't yourself, the way you handled the situation.'

'In what way?'

'You were abrupt. Terse.' At the time he'd thought that was typical of her, that she was spoiled and angry when she didn't get exactly what she wanted. The way his mother had been when things didn't work out to her satisfaction, even the smallest things. 'That's unusual for you. You make such an effort to put people at ease, particularly those who aren't your social equals.'

Her eyebrows arched high. 'Don't be a snob, Fotis. Just because my father was a king doesn't mean I'm superior to someone who makes beautiful clothing, or who can ferry me safely through peak hour Paris traffic.'

As if to emphasise that she'd made her point, she took a big bite of bread and tomato.

He watched her chew vigorously then swallow, but without any sign of enjoyment, as if the conversation had tainted the taste of the food. Her eyes flashed with annoyance yet still he couldn't drag his eyes away. Her vibrant energy was captivating.

'I agree. And I know that's how you feel. Which is why I want to understand what distressed you.' For she *had* been distressed, he'd realised.

She looked away to where the indigo sea met the horizon. 'Maybe I was annoyed at being lumbered with an unwanted bodyguard.'

'I'm sure you were.' She hadn't held back with him. He'd been surprised at how much he'd enjoyed the cut and thrust of their battle of wills. 'But I know you'd never take that anger out on women who were just doing their job.'

Her head swung around abruptly. Was that dismay in her eyes? 'You think I was rude to them?'

'Not rude. Emphatic. They were clearly disappointed.'

Slowly she nodded, then looked down at the food in her hand as if wondering how it got there. She put it down and reached for her wine, sipping slowly. Her mouth curled wryly.

'You don't miss much, do you? You must be very good at your job, searching out secrets and hiding them.'

He said nothing, just reached for another olive and popped it into his mouth. Eventually she sighed and took another sip of wine. 'Okay, I'll tell you.' Her gaze snagged his. 'But it's private.'

'I won't tell anyone. Your secret will be safe with me.'

'It's not really my secret, but still...' She paused as if weighing something up. 'I feel like I'm the one who's always sharing with you. You already know I had an experience like your friend Dimi's. You know why I did what I did in New York.'

'And you want to know something private about me.' It was a statement, not a question.

She spread her hands wide. 'Fair's fair. You don't *need* to know about the dress to keep me safe, do you?'

Fotis expected an instinctive internal protest at the idea of sharing anything personal. Instead he found himself nodding. Whatever he told her, he knew it wouldn't go further. He trusted Rosamund and not just with his body, he realised.

Another first. He could count on the fingers of one hand the people he trusted completely.

'Okay.' He piled tomato and cheese onto a slice of bread and lifted it. 'Tell me about the dress and I'll tell you something private about myself.'

Her eyes rounded, as if surprised by his agreement, yet still she didn't leap at the chance to pry into his secrets. That set her apart from many he'd known.

The more time they spent together, the more he realised she was unique.

She leaned back against the doorjamb. The breeze lifted a few strands of richly coloured hair. His gaze traced the tender curve of her ear, the slim line of her throat and the tiny frown gathered across the bridge of her nose.

She looked...endearing. Sensual and alluring but without any hint of artifice. Affection stirred.

'You didn't recognise the dress?'

Her sharp tone punctured his thoughts. 'Should I have?'

Her mouth turned down, not in her naturally sexy pout but in definite distaste. 'The photo of my mother at the gala. The huge one projected on the massive wall as you entered.' Her eyes met his. 'The famous one with her wearing a dress that looked like it was about to slide off her at any moment.'

That dress. The one that revealed the maximum flesh while still being arguably decent. He pursed his lips in a silent whistle. 'They made a replica for you to wear to the gala?'

His larynx tightened, turning his voice into a growl at the thought of Rosa wearing such a dress where anyone other than he could see her.

Great. Possessive now as well as protective and curious. Where are you heading with this, Mavridis?

She inclined her head.

He scowled. Rosa was a princess, not a movie star or model. Surely that was—'Who arranged it?' But he had the answer. He'd heard her snap out the name. 'Antoine Gaudreau? He organised the event?'

'No!' The word shot out sharply and Rosamund paused to modulate her tone. 'He wasn't the event's organiser, but yes, he arranged the dress.'

'Without consulting you?'

'That's right.'

Fotis' eyes glowed with a martial light. 'I'm glad you didn't wear it.'

'You are?' She tilted her head, frowning. 'Others thought it was a good idea.'

'The women who'd made it? Of course they'd like you to parade it and advertise their work. You'd have looked stunning.'

The thought of wearing the outfit still made her flesh crawl, so she was astonished to discover how much she wanted to look stunning for this man.

It was unsettling. The last time she'd deliberately dressed to impress a guy she'd been seventeen and giddy with her first romantic infatuation.

'Yet you're glad I didn't wear it. Why?'

Was that discomfort in Fotis' expression? 'It's the sort of dress a woman wears for her lover. The thought of you wearing it in public, for everyone to slaver over...' He shook his head.

Pleasure buzzed low in her body. How could she not enjoy his protectiveness and that hint of possessiveness? For however long this affair lasted, she knew she'd revel in both. She refused to ponder why that was, when she'd spent so long carving out the right to make her own decisions.

With Fotis everything felt different. Another man's protectiveness, certainly another man's possessiveness, would irk her and feel constricting. With him she felt only a warm glow. Briefly she wondered if that was anything like how it felt to be cherished. Then she pushed the idea aside.

'That's exactly why I couldn't wear it.' She'd felt physically ill when they'd shown it to her. 'I'm not ashamed of my sexuality, but I'm not interested in being objectified.'

'Your mother—'

'My mother was barely seventeen when she wore that to the premiere of her first film, and it wasn't her choice.'

She saw Fotis' eyes widen.

'You didn't know? She was just sixteen when Gaudreau *discovered* her and gave her a small part in the film he was shooting. She and her parents were in a village near where the film was being made. By the time it was in post-production he'd decided to make her a star. Or at least a sexy starlet.' Her lip curled. 'He took her under his wing, had her live with him so he could *nurture her talent.*'

She watched Fotis' expression darken, instantly understanding the euphemism for what it was. The famous director had been a controlling predator.

'But her parents! If she told them—'

Rosamund shook her head. 'They traded their daughter for money. Everything she earned on the first films went straight to them. She was young and inexperienced and she *was* excited at the idea of acting. Until she found out the whole of what he wanted from her.'

Her throat closed as she remembered her mother telling her this. Not seeking sympathy, but as a warning about those who preyed on vulnerable young people, particularly women. 'She tried to leave several times, only to be told that if she did he'd sue her parents for breach of contract and ruin them.'

Yet, even knowing that terrible truth about her mother's early career, Rosamund had fallen for another sort of predator in her teens. She hadn't seen the parallels until it was too late. She could only guess how difficult it had been for her mother to be so frank about the abuse she'd endured. Every time she thought about it, Rosamund hated herself for being duped, as if it were a betrayal of her mother's trust.

She was only glad her mother hadn't been alive to witness her mistake. Though if she'd lived maybe things would have been different.

It was easier to think about the red dress. 'Gaudreau knew she'd upstage the star of the film wearing that dress. It made her a household name. Which boosted his career too, since he controlled hers. At least in the beginning.'

What was it with the women in her family and controlling men? First her mother, who'd taken years to find her feet and build a career separate from that loathsome old man. Then, when she was at the pinnacle of her career, she'd fallen for a handsome prince. Too late she'd discovered that while he lusted after the sexy screen siren, he was jealous of her easy charisma and popularity, continually finding fault with his vivacious, charming wife.

Then Rosamund. After her mother's death, her father had become ever more watchful and disapproving, decreeing what she could wear and whom she could meet. Was it any wonder she'd fallen for a handsome, laughing man who played on her need for love? Both men had used her for their own ends.

Was it any wonder she refused to be used anymore? Or that trust came hard?

'So, you see, I couldn't have worn it. That would have been a betrayal of my mother. Gaudreau was just trying to stir interest in those early films, the ones they made together. He wanted to make the event about himself.'

Warmth closed around her hand and she looked down to see Fotis' fingers curling around hers. As ever, she was struck by how well they fitted together, as if made for each other despite their disparity in size.

'I do see, and I'm sorry I misinterpreted the situation. Your mother would be proud of you.'

'I…' She shrugged, suddenly finding it hard to speak. Her mum had been her rock and Rosamund had felt adrift for so long after her early death. She still felt her loss.

Remarkably, it seemed Fotis guessed some of what she felt for he nodded. 'She raised a remarkable woman. Caring but no pushover. Fiery but clever and determined. I can't believe I ever thought you a spoiled socialite.'

His words stunned her. Their physical intimacy had changed their relationship into one of ease and respect. But there was still so much they didn't know about each other. Yet here he was, talking about her in terms that made her suddenly eager heart shudder open.

Inevitably, Rosamund thought of her mother, the only one who'd ever praised her like that.

Fotis might have read her mind. 'Here's to Juliette Bernard.'

'To my beautiful mum.'

The fruity wine trickled down her throat and spread with it a sense of peace. Maybe because, for the first time, she'd spoken unreservedly about the woman who meant so much to her.

Because Fotis understood. His anger when he heard what Gaudreau had done and his approval of her mum and herself felt like balm spread on unhealed wounds.

Over the years her father had twisted her mother's character into something negative. Enthusiasm was described as heedless passion. Generosity became recklessness. Warmth and charisma turned into undisciplined and unrefined behaviour. The very virtues that had attracted him, and won over his people, became character flaws he'd been determined to extinguish in his daughter.

Rosamund turned to the man beside her, who still held her hand clasped in his. His brow was furrowed in thought, his mouth flat as he stared over the vast Aegean.

If he'd wondered about her, it couldn't be nearly as much as she'd pondered him.

He fascinated her and with every day her curiosity rose. Fotis Mavridis wasn't the man she'd first thought, at least not all the way through. He could be harsh and forbidding. He was ruthless and capable, breathtakingly so. She remembered the efficiency with which he'd disabled her attacker in France, ignoring his own injuries as he kept her safe.

But he was thoughtful and generous. Their lovemaking was a revelation, his passion and tenderness unlocking something deep within her that made her want to know everything about him.

He'd happily connected with disadvantaged teenagers in a city slum, even offering one a remarkable opportunity for the future. Her visits to the village here had elicited stories about his generosity. Not just his ability to fund infrastructure, but his genuine involvement in the community.

Tassos, who'd been born on the island, had served in the military with Fotis and lost half his leg while on duty. According to *Yiayia* Irini, it was Fotis who'd dragged him out of his depression and funded extra therapy for him when he got his prosthetic leg. Later he'd offered him a job as an analyst. Now the man was rebuilding his life, working for Fotis and preparing to marry.

'What are you thinking about, Rosa? You look miles away. Is it your mother?'

She shook her head. 'A little. It's good to talk about her. There's no one else I can talk with about her, other than Lucie.' Her father had never wanted to reminisce and Leon had barely known her, for all they'd technically been one family.

She turned, gaze colliding with sea-bright eyes, and a quiver of sensation snaked through her. Desire mixed with a longing that wasn't merely physical. And something else too, delight at this open conversation, sharing in a way she couldn't remember doing before.

'Actually I was thinking what an enigma you are. I know some things about you.' She ticked off her fingers. 'You like your coffee black and strong. You have eclectic tastes in music. Everything from rembetiko,' a Greek style she'd never heard of until she came here, 'to classical. From jazz to hip-hop.'

She knew his dedication to keeping fit, running or using his indoor pool and huge gym, complete with climbing wall. She knew how his hands felt on her hips as she rode him to pleasure. How his deep voice turned deliciously rough when he gasped out her name as ecstasy took him.

Rosamund swallowed. 'I know when you give your word you keep it.' He'd promised to protect her and she knew how seriously he took that oath. 'But I know nothing about your past, only that you went to boarding school. Nothing about what made you who you are.'

'What do you want to know? I promised to share.'

Yet she saw the hint of reserve in his eyes. She guessed that a long time ago, he'd retreated into himself, throwing up a defensive wall far more impenetrable than hers. He'd even hinted his early life had been difficult.

She wanted to ask about that hurt, for hurt it clearly was. She wanted to know about his strained relationship with his mother, and whether he had other family. The way he'd spat the word *socialite* more than once as if it were a curse intrigued her.

But asking him to spill his deepest secrets might push him away. He was the most self-contained person she knew. So she'd begin small.

'How do you know Dimitria Politis?'

CHAPTER ELEVEN

SURPRISE MADE FOTIS jerk his chin up. *That* was what she most wanted to know? Rosa never ceased to surprise him. He'd expected something deeply probing, or painfully personal.

Like what she'd just revealed to him.

He was surprised and, he realised, honoured that she'd shared such intimate confidences.

True, they'd been mainly about her mother rather than herself, but he knew they affected her deeply. It didn't take a genius to realise her mother's experiences had impacted on Rosa. They'd affected him.

'Dimi's a friend, that's all.'

It hit him suddenly that perhaps Rosa thought he wanted to be more than a friend to Dimi. Could she be jealous?

The thought barely lasted a second. Dimi was too young and naïve for a man like him. She couldn't hold a candle to the woman beside him, whose self-contained façade concealed a vibrant passion and a generosity he couldn't get enough of.

'Come on, Fotis. Surely you can share just a little.'

Her tone was full of tongue-in-cheek challenge yet he saw disappointment in her expression. Did she think he was reneging on their bargain?

'I can and will. In the meantime you need to eat. You didn't have breakfast.'

Since when had he worried about what a lover ate?

Since Rosa. Only Rosa.

An electric frisson of warning crept across his skin but he dismissed it. He was being considerate, that's all. He'd interrupted her meal with his questions.

He plucked an olive from the container and leaned across to pop it into her mouth. Inevitably his fingertips brushed those plump, soft lips and he had to snatch his hand back. He'd promised her words, not seduction.

'I've known Dimi since she was a baby. We don't see each other much but we're family friends.' He paused then admitted, 'That's rare for me.' Because he had no family. None that he cared to acknowledge.

Rosa didn't speak, just nodded as she covered another piece of rich, nutty bread with slices of feta and tomato.

'Her grandfather was a good friend of my father's.'

That made Rosa catch his gaze but instead of commenting she took a bite of her food and this time he watched her eyes flicker, half closed in pleasure at the flavour. She was a woman who used all her senses.

He particularly liked her fondness for tasting and touching. A tremor of carnal pleasure scudded along his spine and he made himself look away.

'Both my parents were only children.' He knew it to be true in his father's case. For his mother he only had her word for it, which proved nothing. She reinvented herself regularly to suit whatever role she wanted to play. He forged on. 'So I didn't have aunts, uncles and cousins. But Costas Politis has always been like an uncle to me. My father died when I was young and—'

'How young?'

'Five.'

Her hand closed gently around his forearm. 'I'm sorry. It must have been terrible to lose your dad when you were so young.'

Her eyes were stormy grey, sincere with regret, and he felt a strange churning in his chest. Her sympathy dredged up ancient feelings of loss and pain that he hadn't let himself dwell on for decades.

With them came half-forgotten memories.

His father's voice, deep and kind. Riding those broad shoulders down to the sea where his *Baba* taught him to float and later to fish. Lying curled up on a chair in the dappled shade of a vine-covered courtyard, listening to the murmur of male voices and the quick click-click of tavli pieces moving around a playing board. His *Baba's* patience when Fotis scrambled up onto his lap, begging to play. That was how Fotis had learned his numbers, moving counters across the inlaid board, the soft rumble of his *Baba's* voice counting with him.

'It was a long time ago.' Yet strangely his throat felt tight.

'Anyway, Costas did what he could to be a mentor, though I didn't see him often.' He read Rosa's curiosity but she didn't ask, just waited for whatever he would share. Which made him decide to share just a little more. 'I lived with my mother for a while after my father died but I was sent away to school within a year.'

Rosa's fingers dug into his arm. 'That's *very* young, especially for a boy who's lost his father.'

'It was.' It was unspeakably hard, but no worse than facing his mother's neglect. He shrugged. 'Over the years Costas stayed in contact, tried to help where he could. He stood up for my right to inherit. I've always respected him for that.'

'Sorry, I don't understand. There was some doubt over your inheritance?'

It wasn't something he spoke about but he *had* been the one to mention it. Besides, it was a matter of public record, if one had the resources to dig deep enough. His mother had done her best to bury it.

'My father was wealthy. He left my mother an annuity, but the bulk of his estate was left in trust to me. It was managed independently and my mother had no access to it.' Fotis stared at the sea and the progress of a proud, white yacht, heading for the horizon. 'She challenged the will. She wanted control of everything. If she'd succeeded there would have been nothing left for me when I came of age.'

'She'd have spent it all?' No mistaking the shock in Rosa's tone.

'She'd have squandered it as quickly as she could. My father must have known that, to make his will that way.'

It pained him to know his *Baba* must by that stage have been disillusioned about the woman he'd married.

'Costas Politis is a respected and highly successful businessman,' he explained. 'His intervention helped ensure she didn't succeed. He guarded my father's fortune and later mentored me about business. He helped me make the most of the investments I'd inherited as well as building a new, highly successful enterprise. He was my last link to my father.'

Mouth dry, Fotis swallowed a mouthful of wine and turned to his companion. 'I like the man and I'm indebted to him. He's old now and ill, so when I can I keep a friendly eye on his orphaned granddaughter. Dimi had a difficult time after her parents died. She's impulsive and insecure and—'

'The perfect target for a greedy con man. Then I broke her heart by having a public fling with her boyfriend, even though I knew they were together. No wonder you hated me.'

'*Pretending* to have a fling,' he corrected.

She lifted her shoulders. 'The result was the same.'

'But your intentions weren't.' Their eyes locked and he felt that familiar pulse between them. Only this time the connection was far more emotional than physical. 'You saved her. Did I thank you for that?'

Rosa looked away, reaching for a slice of apricot tart. 'There's no need.'

'There's every need. You brought public speculation and censure on yourself for her sake. As random acts of kindness go, that's a big one.'

'My reputation can stand it. Besides, it was already less than pristine.'

'Because of those photos taken in your teens?'

For a second she held his gaze, then stared at the dessert in her hand as if wondering how it got there. She put it down. 'Yes.'

'Even though some of them were fake?'

Her head snapped up. 'You know about that?'

'Part of my job is sieving information for the truth.' He paused. 'I didn't pay much attention to them in the beginning but then after a while, when I knew you better, I wondered and took another look. You were the object of a concerted smear campaign.'

Rosa blinked, staring.

'You didn't know?'

Her mouth twisted. 'Oh, I knew. But no one believed me.'

'Who did you tell?' But the answer was obvious. 'Your father?'

'The first photos were real.' She shook her head. 'Why I thought it was a good idea to go to that nightclub in a mini-dress, when I had to climb out of a low-slung sports car...' She paused. 'The kiss was real, and yes, I'd had more alcohol than I should. But the photos made things appear far worse than what actually happened. The stories printed with them made them look like something completely different.'

Fotis remembered. The implication had been that she'd partied with her boyfriend and later had sex with him in the back of a car. It had been implied that she'd then had sexual encounters with some of his friends while drunk or high.

'The worst of the pictures were Photoshopped,' he added. 'I assume they hit the press after you broke up with your boyfriend?'

She nodded. 'He wasn't as clever as he thought. If he hadn't bragged about his influence in royal circles, I mightn't have discovered the truth until much later. A palace bureaucrat came to me, concerned about rumours that she and some others were going to lose their jobs to outsiders. She'd traced the stories to my boyfriend. When I confronted him, he blustered, but not well enough. He tried to explain with half-truths but his lies weren't good enough.

'He'd said he loved me but it was obvious he only saw me as a means to further his career and his friends'.' She drew a slow breath. 'I had him barred from the palace and never spoke to him again.'

'So he took revenge by blackening your reputation,' Fotis growled. He made a mental note to look into the guy's current situation and make life as difficult as possible for him. 'Why didn't your father help? He had the power to take some of the heat out of the stories.'

'He thought it was beneath the royal family to sue. Some of the worst photos, where they'd used my face and someone else's body, were taken down. Not that he believed they were fakes. He refused to listen. Insisted I learn the consequences of my actions and lumbered me with close personal protection for years. After that, even if I'd wanted to have a drink with friends in private, I'd never have managed it. I became a social pariah.'

Fotis' chest clamped painfully around his fast-beating heart. No wonder she'd vibrated with dislike at having another bodyguard.

Her story only made her courage in standing up for Dimi more remarkable. She'd put herself in the firing line of public censure for a stranger.

He groped for her hand and held it tight.

'You're a remarkable woman, Rosa.' Misty eyes turned to his and he wished things could have been different for her. 'I hope your father realised that eventually.'

She snorted. 'Hardly. According to him I was too like my mother. Emotional, reckless, more likely to act on the spur of the moment than follow royal protocol or common sense.'

'Your father sounds like a prig and a fool.'

She laughed, the sound snapping some of the tension that had grown as he heard her story. 'But a powerful prig.'

'And your mother... She was an incredibly popular queen.'

'Exactly. Far more popular than him. He liked everything done his way. He didn't like change or spontaneity.'

And Rosa, beneath her public veneer of calm elegance, was both spontaneous and passionate, bewitchingly so.

Fotis began to realise how tough her home life must have been, especially after her mother died.

'It seems like we were both cursed with one good parent and one we'd rather forget.'

She turned her hand to thread her fingers through his, chuckling. 'It's incredible we turned out so well adjusted, isn't it?'

Fotis' lips stretched in a rare grin. He was a recluse who specialised in keeping people at a distance. And for all Rosa's warmth, he suspected she had few true friends.

He found it hard to trust, women in particular, and he'd long ago decided not to have a family because caring deeply risked far too much pain. Nico's death still haunted him.

He suspected Rosa found it difficult to trust, men especially, and though she claimed to live her life exactly as she wanted, she felt the need to prove that to the press and the world at large. Which meant they still affected her decisions and she wasn't as free as she believed.

'You're right. We *are* incredible.'

He pressed his lips to her knuckles, hearing her indrawn breath. Her turned her hand over and tasted apricots.

His luscious woman.

She shuddered as he kissed her palm. 'Fotis.'

Her voice was a raw whisper that sent longing straight and hard to his groin.

'I want you, Rosa. Now.'

Her eyes darkened. 'Yes.'

Fotis tugged her closer, unbearably aroused by her answering desire. She never played coy games. He loved her ardour. It fed his own. Instead of dimming, their passion glowed hotter and more urgent with each day that passed. It was beyond anything he'd experienced.

But he refused to stop and analyse why.

'The food.' She was on her knees beside him, pushing aside platters.

But Fotis couldn't wait. Usually he could conjure at least a semblance of patience but something had changed as they shared their stories. Something deep and raw had opened inside him and he *needed* her *now*.

His heart ached for the pain she suffered. At the same time he was proud of her courage, her determination to stand strong despite others' judgement.

And her tenderness… There was something addictive about her tenderness.

Impatient, he swept aside the picnic. The wine bottle fell over, dousing his ankle through his sock. He didn't even look. He only had eyes for Rosa, pulling her closer.

'Lift your leg over me,' he commanded, voice harsh.

Instead of taking issue with his tone, she favoured him with a sultry smile that undid another of the complicated, emotion-proof knots he'd tied around his heart. He *felt* it come free, but didn't worry. He'd spent so long building barriers it would take more than a smile to destroy them all.

Rosa lifted her leg over his hips as he thrust a hand in his pocket and dragged out a condom.

Her eyebrows arched as she took it from him and tore it open with her teeth. 'Boy Scout?'

'Something like that,' he muttered as he fumbled to open his jeans. Now wasn't the time to explain that from the time of his father's death he'd learned to be hyper-alert, planning ahead. He'd had to anticipate his mother's mood swings and other dangers, like the one that had taken Nico from him.

But this time even the thought of his failure to protect his little brother couldn't dim Fotis' arousal.

Finally he pulled himself free of his jeans and underwear.

'Let me.' She shuffled back, her red dress teasing his erection until she brushed the cotton aside and leaned forward to smooth on the condom.

Fotis wanted to push her hands away. He gritted his teeth and summoned all his strength not to lose himself at her deliberate, slow strokes as she smoothed the rubber down his rigid length.

But nothing in this world could have made him look away.

No woman had ever been more seductive. Her pouting concentration as she worked and the press of peaked nipples against her dress were enough to make him wonder how long he'd last.

'Rosa!' It was a growl of warning but instead of retreating, she smiled and shuffled closer, kneeling high above him.

'Fotis?'

He heard the hint of laughter, the self-congratulatory tone of a woman who knew he was at her mercy. He adored it.

With Rosa he'd discovered sex could be fun. That spending the night with a lover could be a delight, rather than the potential burden he'd believed. For she'd made it clear all she expected was a short-term relationship.

Just as well, because that was all he could give.

'Rosa,' he purred, reaching under her dress, stroking up her satiny thigh to the narrow strip of lace between her legs. It was gratifyingly wet.

She tilted her pelvis, pushing against him as he rubbed the heel of his hand against her core. She bit her bottom lip, eyelids lowering as she ground against his touch.

Her hand tightened as she tested his length, almost sending him over the edge.

He lifted his other hand to her breast, cupping it through

the thin fabric. She moaned softly as he pinched her nipple and rubbed it between thumb and forefinger.

She scrabbled to lift her skirt, shifting forward until his erection nudged her underwear. Fotis dragged the lace barrier aside, felt her sink, just a centimetre till he was notched at her entrance.

'Ready?' Her wetness and the light tang of feminine arousal in the air told him she was. But he was far past the point of patient seduction and wanted her primed to accommodate him. He didn't want to hurt her.

'Ready?' She shook her head as she covered his hand with hers, pressing it hard against her breast as she circled her hips, tantalising him with the promise of what was to come. 'I've been ready since before you unzipped your jeans. What are you waiting for?'

'Well, if you're sure…' He slid his hand from beneath hers, her groan of regret turning to a sigh of anticipation as he shoved both hands under her skirt. He clamped her hips and, holding her stare, yanked her down as he thrust high off the ground.

Heaven had another name. Rosa.

Slick, tight muscles. Velvety heat that clutched at him as he pushed deep, impossibly deep, until he was embedded and there was no space between them.

Sharp pain sliced his chest as he forgot to breathe, but it was a small price to pay for the euphoria of their joining.

Her breasts rose on a jerky breath. 'Okay?' he croaked, unsure if pleasure or pain drew her features tight.

Until she nodded, gasping, 'You don't know how okay.'

She leaned forward, planting her hands on his shoulders. The changed angle slid him even further in, if that were possible. It felt so incredible, *she* felt so incredible, he couldn't trust his senses. Surely nothing had ever been this perfect?

Still gripping her hips, Fotis lifted her just a little, circling his hips, watching her expression change from taut to shocked pleasure. Again he pulled her down hard as he thrust, setting off detonations of piercing pleasure.

Their gasps mingled before being swept away in the sea breeze.

'More,' she demanded, lifting her hips.

Fotis revelled in his demanding lover, so eager for everything he could give her. Then thoughts spiralled away as he leaned up and drew her nipple into his mouth through the fine fabric and lust took over.

Jerking his hips higher, he slammed her down to meet him, senses overloading at the sheer perfection of them together. He sucked at her breast as she rotated her pelvis and threw them both off the pinnacle into bliss.

Fire engulfed him. Planets collided and splintered. Through it all he held Rosa tight, riding the shock waves, hearing her whimpers of pleasure.

Ages later when it was over, he lifted shaky hands to pull her down to collapse onto his chest. He felt her heart hammering, her breath steamy against his chest where his shirt had torn open. Her hair tickled his skin.

She was a dead weight, all that softness pressed against him. The air smelled of sex, the sea, and the cinnamon-vanilla scent of the only woman to undo him completely.

He'd never felt so…happy.

For the first time since adulthood he didn't question the rare sensation or try to analyse it. He just tightened his arms about her and let himself drift in a haze of well-being.

CHAPTER TWELVE

'WHAT WAS THE favour Leon agreed to do for you, Fotis?' Rosamund fixed her earring and looked at his reflection in the mirror of the vast en suite bathroom.

The man looked utterly scrumptious in a dark suit and crisp, white shirt. She was astounded she resisted the urge to drag him back to bed. But then, she acknowledged ruefully, her legs were still wobbly from his early afternoon lovemaking and her body felt warm and heavy from satiation. She probably didn't have the energy to tug him to bed.

Though the glint of approval in his eyes as he met her gaze made her wonder.

'He's backing a range of initiatives, including an updated international convention, to strengthen protection for children worldwide.'

'That sounds like something he'd do anyway.' She mightn't be close to Leon but he was a decent man. Anything to support vulnerable children would interest him.

Fotis nodded, his brow drawing down as he put on cufflinks. Because he was concentrating, or because of something else? He looked suddenly sombre.

'Yes, he'd always intended to sign the new convention on behalf of Cardona. But now he's also lobbying countries that are wavering about signing. Looking after children is one of those things everybody agrees on, but often their welfare ends up too low on the list of actual government priorities. It's time for that to change.'

She secured her second earring and said, 'Let me guess. They're afraid that if they sign the agreement they'll be held to account to do what they promise.'

His stern mouth rucked up at the corner and her heart gave a stupid little flutter. 'You've been around politicians too long. That's exactly it.'

'You've been working on this for some time?' She'd heard about the initiative but didn't know details. She'd look it up tonight, or perhaps tomorrow morning, since they were attending a party today.

'Years, but finally real progress is close.'

'That's wonderful.' She had some idea how long it took to finalise international initiatives. But her attention wasn't so much on the process as on Fotis and why this was important to him.

They'd spent a month on his island, an amazingly contented, wonderful month together with no sign of any threat, though the complicated fraud case against Ricardo was taking longer than expected to finalise.

Every day she woke with a feeling of well-being unlike anything she'd known. Not simply because she was safe, but because of Fotis and what they shared. Sex but friendship too, a bond she couldn't describe but which she'd miss terribly when she left.

Rosamund straightened her sapphire-blue dress. Fotis had given her glimpses into his past but she yearned to know more. She wanted to know everything about him, especially what made him determined to remain a recluse all his life.

'It's an important cause, Fotis. But I'm surprised at your level of involvement. Is there a particular reason you're so focused on this?'

He was knotting his tie but made a hash of it, jerking it too tight so he had to tug it undone and start again. 'Isn't it enough that it's worth doing?'

The angle of his jaw and his guarded eyes made her want

to step up and help him. Not because she was an expert on men's ties—she wasn't—but because some sixth sense warned he needed her.

Suddenly she sensed his disquiet. It rippled off him, an invisible force field designed to repel. She remembered it from the first days they'd known each other. Then he'd had an air of such self-containment she'd imagined nothing could breach it.

Or was she fooling herself? Fotis had always been self-possessed. Did he really *need* her?

She'd believed their intimacy was more than skin-deep but now she thought about it, *she'd* been the one to reveal so much about her past. Fotis had let her in but only a little way.

Mood dropping, she reached for her purse. For all their recent intimacy, there were still things he didn't want to share and she wasn't going to push.

'I'm ready. I'll wait in the bedroom.'

On her second step, warmth shackled her wrist. She looked down to see his hand loosely circling hers. Slowly she lifted her gaze. Blue-green eyes shimmered with a heat that scorched.

'Stay. Please.' His Adam's apple jerked as he swallowed. 'It's not something I talk about, ever.' His voice dropped to a rough-hewn, subterranean level that rumbled through her insides. 'But maybe it's time.'

Her hurt softened but she didn't want a forced confidence. 'It's okay, Fotis. I respect your need for privacy.'

The man was entitled to his secrets. Given his reaction to an innocent question, she was sure there *was* a secret behind his unwillingness to talk. Their relationship hadn't changed as much as she'd thought. Of course it hadn't.

'But I want to tell you.'

He didn't look like a man happy at the prospect, so she said nothing.

'It felt good the other day, telling you about my parents and my inheritance.' He must have noticed her eyes widen because he nodded, the lines of tension around his mouth disappearing. 'It's true. I haven't talked about that before, but it felt like a weight had lifted, sharing that.'

She stared. 'You haven't talked with *anyone*?'

He shook his head. 'Only with Costas Politis. He already knew the situation.'

Rosamund shook her head in disbelief.

But how many confidantes have you got? You've learnt to bottle up your problems too.

'I'll be ready in a second, once I get this tie right. We can talk on the way to the wedding.'

'If you like.'

'I do like.' He released her wrist, his fingers skimming up her forearm, making her shiver when they reached her inner elbow. Abruptly he dropped his hand but the expression in his eyes turned that shiver into a languid shudder of arousal. 'Have I told you you're beautiful?'

Pleased, she stroked her hand down the smooth fabric. 'Thank you. I wasn't sure what to wear to a village wedding.'

'What you're wearing is perfect. Dressy but not fussy. But I wasn't talking about the dress, I meant *you*.'

To Rosamund's surprise, she felt flustered as well as delighted. She was used to compliments, just as she was used to criticism about what she wore or how she carried herself. It came with the territory. People either flattered royals or found fault.

But this was different, not a careless compliment but meaningful.

'So are you.' There was beauty in the hard-hewn lines of his face and as for his body... Her breathing quickened.

Something flared in his eyes and he whipped around to face the mirror, concentrating on his tie. 'Maybe it's best if you wait in the bedroom. Otherwise we'll be late.'

Rosamund was still secretly smiling as they drove down the winding road in his four-wheel-drive.

'You asked why I'm interested in protecting children.' That

tore her attention from the stunning view and to the man beside her, easily handling the vehicle down the narrow road. 'They bear the brunt of social problems. They're vulnerable and too often we take it for granted that their families will look after them. That's not always the case.'

'I know. Sometimes families and children struggle.' That was a factor in her own work. As well as bringing joy, she hoped her stories encouraged resilience in the children and young people who read them.

'Plus…' He paused and she deliberately turned her attention from his strong profile to the road, giving him space. 'Things happened that make me want to make changes for the better.'

He's talking about his mother, trying to steal his inheritance. What else did she do?

Rosamund suppressed a shiver. She suspected this wasn't going to be pleasant, but for his sake, and her own, she needed to hear.

'I understand that.'

After a pause he said, 'My mother was beautiful and vivacious but not maternal. I assume she had me to please my father and after he died her focus was on finding another rich man to support her. I realised much later that I cramped her style so she sent me off to boarding school. But when she sent for me again, I thought she'd changed and wanted to be with me.'

Another pause. Longer this time. 'It turned out her lover wanted kids and she wanted to prove what a doting mother she was. It was confusing. She'd never played with me or read bedtime stories before. Only my *Baba* had done that. She got angry when I asked why she'd changed.'

Rosamund couldn't help it, she reached out and touched his sleeve. 'One loving parent and one cold and distant. It sounds like my parents but in reverse. But your situation—'

'It's okay. I was safe and well fed.'

Yet her heart squeezed for the little boy confused to find himself at the centre of his mother's affection for the first time.

'Did they marry?'

'They did and I was glad. I liked my stepfather and I wasn't sent back to boarding school because he liked having me at home. Then my half-brother was born. Little Nico used to follow me around.'

'And you were a protective big brother.'

His head swung around. 'How did you know?'

'It's there in your voice.' That made her terribly sad, because she guessed this didn't have a happy ending. She knew how loyal Fotis was to his father's friend, Costas, and the man's granddaughter. She couldn't imagine Fotis being so isolated now if his brother were around.

'He was a good kid.' Fotis steered them around a curve. 'But my mother didn't have luck with her husbands. Mine died in an accident and Nico's was diagnosed with aggressive leukaemia when he was still young. She was widowed again, but that time she had more money to enjoy herself. She packed us both off overseas to boarding school.'

Rosamund cleared her tight throat. Now she understood his coldness when speaking of his mother.

'Nico was a quiet kid and little. He got bullied. I was continually in trouble, fighting the bullies. It didn't help that Nico didn't speak English, plus I stood out because of my maths skills. Being called a prodigy didn't make me many friends. It didn't endear me to the maths master either. He seemed to take it as a personal affront, always looking at ways to take me down a peg or two.'

'What happened?'

Fotis' hands tightened on the wheel. 'The older boys waited until I was away from the school at a chess tournament, then locked Nico in an unused cupboard next to the maths classroom. He was there for hours. When the door was finally unlocked he was unconscious. He was asthmatic and would have been terrified.' Fotis' voice had a steely ring. 'He died.'

'I—' Words failed her. 'That's appalling.'

'Children need protecting, even ones in expensive schools.' He expelled a slow breath as if searching for control. 'It needn't have happened. One of the students overheard what the other boys had done and told the maths master since he was nearest. The master told him to mind his own business, that a little interaction with the older boys would toughen Nico's character.'

'Fotis!'

He pulled over to the side of the road and switched off the engine. 'The man was sacked. Eventually. At first they didn't want to believe the boy. Until others came forward with stories of bullying. There was quite a scandal though a lot was hushed up.'

She reached for his hand and held it in both of hers. 'And you? It must have been...' She shook her head. 'I can't imagine.'

One callused finger brushed her cheek with a gentleness that defied the harsh set of his jaw. 'I survived. I grew tough. I got into a lot of trouble as a teen but Costas Politis helped me, made sure I didn't go off the rails completely. Then I went into the army. The discipline changed my life, and then I found a chance to use my skills. Ah, Rosa, don't.'

She bit her trembling lip and nodded. She wasn't a teary person but his story, his and Nico's, broke her heart.

'Don't worry about me! I'm fine.'

She waved away his concern, embarrassed by it when *he* was the one who'd suffered. But that concern warmed her too. He *cared* about her. His tenderness made something inside her grow and blossom. A warmth she had no name for.

So much made sense now. His contempt for his mother. His dour determination to remain a loner. She knew he still felt his brother's loss deeply. Then there were his strong protective instincts. Even when he'd despised her he'd done everything necessary to keep her safe.

Despite his stern air and his determination to cut himself off, that protectiveness was intrinsic in him.

She'd never felt safer with anyone in her life. But she felt so much more too.

Maybe that explained the strange, fluttery feeling in her chest as he closed the space between them.

'It's okay, Rosa. It was long ago.' His gaze pinioned hers. 'The past makes us what we are but we keep going, don't we? We have that in common. The past has made us stronger.'

It was one of the most affirming things anyone had ever said to her. The most surprising.

She'd spent her adult life reminding herself she was strong, that she'd moved on past hurts and errors. That she could face anything. But no one had acknowledged that in her. Sometimes, on her down days, it was hard to feel so certain about herself.

Fotis' words made her feel strong, as if she could face anything, yet simultaneously left her craving more, craving things she'd told herself weren't for her. Emotional attachment. Belonging.

His warm hand cupped the back of her neck and he pulled her towards him, his mouth brushing hers as lightly as a morning breeze drifting across her skin.

Instantly she opened for him, breathing in his scent, his taste, her hands clinging to his straight shoulders. He was so solid, so imposing, yet his kiss was heartbreakingly gentle.

Did he know how that tenderness undid her? How precious it was?

No one had ever kissed like this.

As if he wanted to make her whole. As if she meant everything to him.

The shocking thought speared her consciousness. But then

he stroked her lips with his tongue, pausing as if seeking permission before delving deeper, and thoughts splintered.

She clung to him, trembling at the vast, burgeoning emotion that spread and spread until it filled her up.

'Fotis. Please, I...'

'*Asteri mou.*'

The words feathered her mouth and she knew what they meant now. My star. She'd looked them up.

She'd told herself it was a random endearment delivered in the throes of passion. But they weren't having sex now. Those two little words felt powerful. As if signifying something monumental.

Rosamund pulled back a little, needing to read his expression. But her withdrawal shattered the moment. She saw his unfocused gaze sharpen and he muttered something in Greek. 'The wedding. We're going to be late if we don't move now.'

Dazed, she nodded, hearing the words and knowing he was right, yet unable to move away.

Fotis caught her hand and pressed it to his mouth, his kiss to her palm a promise for later. She had to be content with that. She couldn't be utterly selfish and keep him from the wedding. These were his friends and she suspected he didn't have many true friends.

Scrounging up a semblance of determination, she sat back in her seat. 'Later,' she whispered.

His mouth unfurled in a slow smile that heated her to the core and spoke of pleasures to come. 'Absolutely.'

Then he turned and switched on the engine.

Rosamund couldn't remember the last time she'd enjoyed herself so much. The whole village had gathered under the plane trees in the square after the wedding ceremony.

The whitewashed church had been small and there'd been standing room only. Dark icons in polished metal frames decorated the walls. The scent of incense filled the space. So did the gravity of the couple's vows, even though Rosamund didn't understand a word, and the sheer joy of the occasion.

She still felt unsettled by the unexpectedly intense emotions she'd experienced, witnessing the wedding. It felt more real somehow, more meaningful, than any she'd attended.

Now, she was surrounded by people of all ages gathered around tables that had been brought out of houses and placed together so the community could celebrate as one. Snowy cloths covered the tables, some of them beautifully embroidered in what looked like traditional designs. Platters of food were emptying but the delicious scent of grilled food wafted from where a group of men manned a huge charcoal barbecue.

'More wine?' Fotis held the unlabelled bottle above her small glass tumbler.

No elegant stemware here, no silver service. Yet it was the most wonderful meal she'd ever eaten. Delicious and authentic in a way all those gourmet meals at exclusive events could never match. Perhaps because the people here were warm and genuine and she'd never felt so at home.

'*Ne, epharisto.*'

Irini, sitting across the table from her, grinned. 'Bravo!' She turned to the woman next to her, one of the bride's cousins. 'Our visitor speaks Greek.'

Immediately several people down the table clamoured for more information and the old lady switched to Greek, speaking emphatically and at far more length than Rosamund's couple of words warranted.

'I only said *yes, thanks*,' Rosamund whispered to Fotis as he poured her wine.

'Ah.' There was a twinkle in his eyes that she'd begun to see occasionally. She adored it. 'But your pronunciation was perfect and everyone has noticed how much you're improving. Now several people are claiming credit for your language skills.'

Rosamund leaned in, revelling in his closeness. 'Every time I come to the village someone teaches me a new phrase.'

He put the bottle down. 'You've impressed them. It's a compliment that you've begun using Greek phrases. Not every visitor bothers to learn any, and given most of the people here understand English it's not absolutely necessary.'

Before she could respond a hand reached for her. It was the bride, wearing a beaming smile. Around the square women were rising from their seats, joining hands to form a line as the musicians struck up a new tune.

Rosamund had done her share of dancing, from waltzing under chandeliers at royal balls to following the beat in the loud, thrumming heat at nightclubs. She'd never danced in the dappled shade of a cobblestoned square. Or with Fotis' eyes on her.

The dance was beautiful and deeply moving. Perhaps because of the group's bonhomie and their encouragement as she stumbled through the steps until eventually she learned the rhythm, as if she really were one of them. Or maybe it was because of the way the bride glowed with happiness. Or the expression on the face of her new husband, Fotis' friend and colleague, Tassos. He watched his bride as if he could never get his fill of her.

That only made Rosamund keenly aware of Fotis' gaze on her. She didn't meet his stare but *felt* it in every pore. Felt the thrum of awareness, the knowing, the anticipation, and something deeper too.

Then it was time for the men to dance. Tassos, shaking his head and pointing to his prosthetic leg, swooped his wife into his arms and onto his lap as he sat down at the table. Rosamund watched with interest as he said something to Fotis who, after what looked like initial refusal, stood, stripped off his jacket and rolled up his sleeves. He'd already discarded his tie.

The music was different this time, slow but with an energy that built and built. Again the dancers formed a line with first one then another taking the lead and adding embellishments to the regular steps. There were stately older men, surprisingly light on their feet, and young would-be acrobats who garnered whoops of approval.

Then Fotis took the lead, his expression grave and his steps measured, until suddenly he sprang high, his hand connecting with his outstretched leg, before dropping low in a manoeuvre that required incredible athleticism. His movements were precisely controlled, with sudden bursts of energy as he spun, rose and dropped only to rise again with an ease that astonished her.

Together the rhythm of the music, the steady clapping, and the raw emotion harnessed in his movements, stole her breath. She was on the edge of her seat, wondering at the pounding of her heart. Then someone else took the lead and Fotis moved back to give them space.

His gaze locked on hers, bright and searching, and the music faded, obliterated by the roar of white noise in her ears.

It felt like they were alone, despite the crowd, the claps and cheers. Fotis looked at her and it seemed the most natural thing in the world for her heart to rise against her ribs, its beat quickening at her instant, all-consuming awareness.

Awareness and acceptance. Acceptance at the joy she felt. At the knowledge this man and no other had forged such an intimate connection with her. That this was the man, would always be the man, she wanted by her side.

Her breath hitched as her brain caught up with her heart. It should be impossible, given her history with the opposite sex. Given the difficulty she had building trust in anyone.

Yet instead it was perfectly easy.

She was in love, utterly, wholeheartedly in love with Fotis Mavridis.

CHAPTER THIRTEEN

THE DAY AFTER the wedding, everything felt different.

They'd both enjoyed the wedding. Fotis had been surprised how much, since his natural inclination was to refuse group celebrations. But Tassos was his closest friend, one of a very few. In the end it had been easy and fun.

Rosa had made it fun, drawing him in so he forgot the reasons he usually avoided such events.

He didn't even mind that he'd opened up about his past. Remarkably, even knowing his secrets were no longer completely secret didn't bother him. He knew she'd respect his privacy.

Later, in bed… The sex only got better. Even the aftermath, lying with her in his arms, felt like nothing he'd known. Almost frighteningly good.

He frowned as he exited the house and made for the old orchard where she'd been for the last half hour.

Frighteningly good.

Why be frightened? Their time together was an unexpected gift. Spectacular sex. A sense of well-being more satisfying than any time he could recall. Engaging conversations that often challenged and stretched him. The best sleep he could remember.

Frightening because it's all about to end. Because you don't want it to be over. You like her too much.

He tried to dismiss the idea but a creeping feeling of dismay tightened his nape, confirming it.

The phone call he'd just received changed everything. But he realised, everything had already begun to change. Now the lingering glow inside conflicted with a new, jittery feeling in the pit of his stomach. Regret.

He wasn't ready for this liaison to end. But of course it must. They'd both known it from the start, and it had lasted longer than either had anticipated.

For the first time in many years however, logic was no match for his feelings.

That's what should frighten you. Feelings. For Rosa.

Fotis paused in the arched entrance to the orchard, his hand on the old stonework for support. He needed it as he grappled with his emotions.

Rosa sat on a chair in the dappled shade. Her head was bent over her journal, pencil racing across the page. Her strawberry-blond hair gleamed where the sun caught it, amber and gold. In cut-off shorts and a T-shirt, with a haphazard bun and her sandals kicked off, one foot tucked beneath her, she stole his breath.

There was no artifice about her. She was simply Rosa and he needed—

His hands clenched.

Not *needed. Desired. There's a difference.*

He'd designed his life around the absolute requirement that he be separate. Independent. Alone. He didn't *need* anyone.

The grief he felt over his brother's death, and the guilt—because he knew Nico wouldn't have been targeted if not for him—were permanently branded on his soul. He should have been there to protect his little brother. He'd failed him and nothing, ever, could change that.

The early loss of his father, then his stepfather, and his mother's narcissism, reinforced his compulsion to hold himself apart because loss was a terrible void that threatened to suck the heart from a man.

Trust was tough though not, he realised now, completely

impossible. He trusted Rosa. But grief and unending guilt were constant. He knew them well. He couldn't, wouldn't, make himself vulnerable again.

He'd let her under his guard and it had felt like the best thing he'd ever experienced. Now he saw how perilous it was, awaking yearnings for a life for which he simply wasn't cut out.

The phone call from America had come at an opportune time, before he fell heedlessly into a catastrophic error of judgement.

That didn't stop stark grief curdling his stomach. Because this was over and he didn't want it to be.

His avid gaze traced Rosa's profile. Lingered on the curve of her ear, the arch of her brow and the tiny hint of a dimple lurking at the corner of her mouth. Her resolute chin. Her nose with that tiny hint of a bump near the bridge.

The way her teeth sank into her bottom lip as she flipped to a new page and quickly started to sketch instead of write. He couldn't make out what she drew but her bold, sure strokes spoke of long practice. She was totally absorbed and he drank her in, knowing the news he brought would end this idyll.

There'd be no more moments like this.

That was good in the long term, but right now he battled an absurd, juvenile urge to forget the outside world and the harsh realities of life and pretend he hadn't taken the call. To continue, just a little longer, as they'd been doing for…five weeks! Was it really so long?

Hauling in a deep breath scented with sunshine and growing things, he moved closer. She was so absorbed she didn't notice his approach as he came up beside her.

Angling his head he saw the image she sketched.

Pride jabbed him at her obvious talent. That was swiftly followed by astonishment, first at the subject, then at some unexpectedly familiar details. The angled eyebrows he saw in the mirror every day. They were so distinctive he'd been teased about them as a kid. The severe expression in those narrowed eyes that he'd also seen in the mirror when something annoyed him.

'So that's how you see me, is it?'

She looked up, startled. After a moment those delectable grooves appeared in her cheek as she smiled. 'I think you make a fine dragon. Don't you?'

Fotis shifted closer, his hand settling on her shoulder, needing to touch her. Not merely because the news he brought meant the end of what they shared. But because, how could he not? It was as natural as breathing for them to touch. He held back a sigh of relief as his fingers covered her bare skin and the urgent thrum of his pulse slowed just a little.

Besides, he knew how significant this moment was. Rosa's smile and her invitation to look were unprecedented. She'd never mentioned what it was she wrote in her notebook and he hadn't asked. Nor had she explained the hours she spent on the computer, though he'd guessed it was some sort of work.

He knew it was important to her. She'd spend hours at a time utterly focused. In the first weeks she'd snap shut her notebook or laptop as soon as he appeared. Lately that had changed, and he'd hoped she'd let him into her secret.

How ironic that today, probably their last day together, was the day.

Heat closed around his throat, like a massive hand squeezing the air out. Panic scrabbled at him until, with a mighty effort, he swallowed and breathed again.

Fotis studied the image, noting how the angle of the beast's impressive, raised wings mirrored the set of its eyebrows. How the image seemed alive with energy.

'It's good. It looks like it could fly off the page. But do dragons have eyebrows?'

'This one does. He draws them down when he's grumpy. Or waggles them when he laughs.'

'He laughs, then?' Stupid to feel relieved.

'Oh, yes. But only with people he trusts. At first he's all

fire and brimstone. But when you get to know him he's unexpectedly charming.'

Her gaze was warm and he wanted to stay in this moment, having her look at him that way. He dragged the other ancient chair across and sat down so close their arms brushed.

The news from New York could wait. Selfishly, Fotis wanted to extend time before the real world intervened.

Coward.

He ignored the inner jibe. They couldn't have a future but he'd have this. He knew how much it meant for Rosa to open up about what she'd hidden so assiduously. It would take a worse man than he to rob her of this moment.

Besides, he wanted to know. And he was desperate to stave off what must come.

'Tell me,' he urged.

She did, slowly at first but with an enthusiasm that made her glow. How she'd always scribbled stories and drawn. Her mother had encouraged it and her father had declared it a waste of time and effort. Over time, after Rosa lost her mother and the world grew more censorious, she'd found increasing solace in writing fiction and drawing the worlds she created. It was her escape.

'It's a fantasy, part of a series for younger readers,' she explained. 'It's named after Princess Lily but my favourite is her friend, Daisy, the innkeeper's daughter. She lives in the village below the castle. She's practical and clever and competent. Lily always seems to find trouble but together they find their way out again.'

He was intrigued, not just by her words but by the images she showed him. 'And the dragon?'

'He's a newcomer and Lily's terrified of him, especially when she meets the handsome, golden-haired prince who's hunting him. He tells her terrible stories about the dragon. Until Daisy discovers the dragon's in pain, wounded by the prince's arrow. The handsome prince is a thief, trying to find the dragon's lair to search for dragon eggs and treasure. The dragon has led him away.'

Fotis huffed a laugh. 'So the grouchy dragon is a good guy, protecting his family?'

She shrugged. 'Partly. But he's not a villain. One of the themes is about not judging too quickly, not accepting at face value what someone says.'

Because handsome, plausible people weren't always who they seemed, and even grumpy beasts might prove to have hidden depths. Something swooped low from his chest to his gut.

'It's much more complicated than that and it's an adventure rather than a morality tale.' She shot him a sideways look. 'I hope you don't mind that I stole your eyebrows. And your death stare.'

That was what she called it? Was it any wonder he liked her so much?

'Fotis?' She looked suddenly unsure.

'Of course I don't mind. I feel honoured to help you visualise your dragon.' A wounded dragon. It wasn't far off the mark. For all his armour, he felt pain, knowing what was to come. 'I hope you're going to approach a publisher.'

It sounded like an intriguing story, plus it didn't hurt to learn young some of life's more painful truths. That good looks weren't always matched by a good heart. He thought of his beautiful mother and the handsome man who'd seduced and tried to use Rosa, then wrought his revenge when she rejected him.

'I already have a publisher. And readers. I have a deadline for this story.'

So his suspicions were true. Not that he'd known she wrote fiction, but he'd long since guessed Rosa did more than lead a life of leisure with a few royal engagements thrown in. 'Why haven't I heard of the books?' His search had found no mention of her writing.

She closed her notebook. 'I write under another name.'

Fotis thought it through. She'd been castigated by her father and the press for her actions and things she hadn't done. She still carried baggage from the experience.

Had she thought the critics would take their knives to her work because of who she was? Melancholy filled him at the idea of her hiding her talent.

'Why not reveal your identity to your readers? Take a bow for your own work.'

'I don't think that's a good idea.'

'Surely it's part of who you are. Even from that short description I can tell this means a lot to you. And I've seen you with young people in Paris. You connect with them and they listen to you. Not because you're royal but because you're interested and engaging.'

'I could say the same about you, playing basketball with those teens.'

They weren't talking about him. 'Don't you think your mother would have been proud, having another creative person in the family?'

Instead of answering she bent abruptly, reaching for her phone, frowning. 'I've got it on vibrate while I work, but this is the fourth time someone's tried to reach me.' She checked the number. 'It's Leon.'

'Rosa, leave it for now.'

He was too late. She'd already taken the call. He watched her hair ruffle in the breeze and couldn't help but stroke its gilded softness, astounded all over again at the instant well-being he felt with the physical connection.

Finally she hung up. 'Leon had news. But you already knew?'

He inclined his head. 'I came to tell you.'

She didn't say anything, probably wondering why he hadn't immediately told her that Ricardo was in prison and looked set to stay there a long time.

Her expression was inscrutable. 'So it's over. I don't need protection anymore.'

'Yes, it's over.'

She stared back as if waiting for more. But what could he say? Eventually she said, 'Thank you, Fotis, for looking after me. For everything.'

'It was my pleasure, you know that.'

How trite that sounded. As if protecting her had been anything other than a compulsion. He'd have done whatever it took to keep her safe.

'You'll want to return to Cardona. I'll organise—'

'There's no rush.' She looked at her hands then up at him. 'I can work here. I could stay on.'

Another man would say yes. A man who could give her more.

But Fotis knew his limits. He'd already pushed beyond them, dangerously far. He wanted Rosa to have everything she deserved, everything she desired, and suddenly he knew, from the hope in her eyes and the tension in her body, that she wanted more than a fling.

Even then, he knew a moment's weakness. It would be easy to let her stay, enjoy what they shared a little longer. But that would make parting more difficult.

'If that's what you'd like, you're most welcome. But,' he cleared his throat, 'I'm needed in Athens. Some important projects I need to oversee.'

There were always important projects and he'd set up his business so that he could work where it suited him most of the time. But she didn't need to know that.

She folded a page of her notebook, fingers working busily. 'You're going to Athens?'

He looked away, to the coast and the village where only yesterday he'd experienced such joy. Iron bands wrapped his chest, constricting his lungs, hampering his breathing.

'Initially. Then the USA and Asia.' The trip wasn't strictly necessary. But he needed to put distance between them. 'I'll be travelling for a while.'

'You're eager to get rid of me?'

The hurt in her voice brought instant denial to his lips, but he kept it in. 'Not eager, Princess. But our time's up. We have to return to our real lives.'

Fotis sensed her dismay but, true to type, only her agitated hands and rapid pulse betrayed her. And that invisible connection between them. He *felt* her shock, her hurt.

'You haven't called me Princess in over a month.'

He shrugged, ignoring the pain shrieking through taut muscles. 'If the shoe fits.'

'What if I said I don't want to go? I want to stay with you.'

'That's not possible.'

'It's not impossible, it's a choice. Yours and mine. You're saying you don't want me with you? What we share means nothing to you?'

'What we shared was beautiful.' He locked his jaw for a second, needing to ensure she couldn't read his inner struggle. 'Now it's over. It's time to return to our own lives.'

Her gaze held his and despite everything, he didn't want to look away. He was in so deep the prospect of separating hurt. Which reinforced the necessity to end this immediately.

Her soft hand covered his, stroking the ball of his thumb. 'I disagree. I want to stay with you. I love you, Fotis.'

CHAPTER FOURTEEN

IN ROMANTIC STORIES *I love you* was the catalyst for an answering declaration of love. The cue for a happy ending.

Good thing you're not really a romantic, isn't it?

Because instead Fotis stared, his mouth dropping open, before he shot to his feet and stalked away. Any faint hope that her announcement would prompt a similar one from him died.

He spun around, scowling down at her, that furrowed brow a perfect match for the dragon she'd drawn. Yet he didn't look angry so much as perplexed. Stunned.

'You really didn't know?'

She wanted to stand and face him as an equal but her legs were wobbly, so she was stuck here, staring up at him.

Just as well. If you were on your feet you'd reach for him.

Would he feel that spark of passion ignite now? Rosamund had always believed it was something they shared equally. But could it be one-sided, like her feelings?

'It's not love, Rosa. It's sex. And liking. You've been through a stressful time. Your emotions are—'

'Don't try to tell me what I'm feeling, Fotis.'

She loved him but he tried her patience. Was he wilfully blind? Did he *really* not feel this?

She forced her breathing to slow. 'I mean what I say. I'm not prone to romantic dreams. Remember, I grew up knowing the reality behind the fairy-tale fantasy. Then my teenage love affair cured me of such yearnings.'

Or so she'd believed.

Rosamund read the sharp planes of his face—they looked harsher than usual—and felt herself melt. Even angry with him, she didn't want him hurting. She stifled a desperate sob at the inanity of that. *She* was the one in mortal pain.

'I didn't mean to fall in love with you, but I have. It's real, what I feel for you.'

He raised his hand to stop her words. 'But I told you. I made it clear that I don't do long-term relationships. I can't.'

'You did make it clear and I agreed because that was all I expected. I wasn't looking for love.' Her voice cracked. 'I thought that was for other people, not me.'

She'd never said it before, even to herself, but she'd felt she didn't deserve love. It was only with Fotis that she'd realised, despite her outward confidence, at heart she'd never felt good enough.

That was part of the reason she loved him. He'd made her feel strong and confident as no one had since her mother. He'd challenged her, fought with her, then cared for and supported her. He didn't belittle, he expected her to shine. He raised her up until she felt she *could* take on the world as she'd always told herself. Look how he'd just engaged with her about her work. He'd encouraged her, yet all the time…

Her throat jammed as pain overtook her. Finally she found the strength to surge from her seat.

Instead of closing the gap, she planted her feet, grounding herself as waves of anguish battered her.

'Emotions can't be controlled by rules, Fotis. My feelings for you sneaked up before I realised what was happening. I didn't *intend* to love you, but I do.'

He shook his head. 'I'm sorry, but—'

'I'd love you even if we couldn't have sex again, though that would be tragic. I love the person you are. Complicated and intriguing. I love your loyalty. When you give your word, you mean it. I love your kindness and your drive. That sneaky sense of humour I didn't think existed at first. I even love it when you go haughty as if your way is the only way, because I know that underneath—'

'Enough!' he barked, stepping back as if repelled.

That stole the air from her lungs. Rosamund stood tall but inside she felt herself shrivel. It had been an incredible risk, admitting her feelings, but being with Fotis had made her courageous, willing to put her pride on the line and more importantly, her heart.

Now her certainty faded. Not about her own feelings, they were immutable, but about his. How had she been so wrong? She'd looked into his eyes, felt his tenderness, and believed he felt the same.

He looked at her, aghast, as if she'd turned into a stranger. 'I'm sorry, sorrier than I say. But I don't feel the same.'

'Because you won't let yourself?' She angled her chin. 'Or do you really feel nothing for me?'

He scrubbed his hand around his neck, his scowl deepening. 'I didn't say that. I'm not a robot. Of course I feel. I like you, Rosa. I admire you and I'm deeply attracted, you know that.'

'But not enough.' Her voice was flat. He *liked* her.

She'd thought she understood him. This had begun as an affair but over time it had grown into so much more. She'd been *sure* his emotions were engaged too. Perhaps it wasn't love for him but, she'd believed, it had become something strong and undeniable.

Maybe he had a voracious sexual appetite, lots of lovers, and he made them all feel…special.

She pressed a palm to her stomach as nausea welled.

'I don't want to hurt you, Rosa.'

Her gesture cut off his words. He hadn't hurt her. She'd hurt herself, she realised abruptly.

What was it with her and self-sabotage? In her teens she'd fallen for a charming guy who wanted to get into her pants because it was a way into the royal family. Now she'd fallen for someone incapable of loving her.

Even so, she had to be absolutely, completely sure. 'I see us together, Fotis, helping each other through the tough times and celebrating the good ones.' In her mind she'd imagined lots of good times, lots of celebrations. 'Building our lives together.'

But his closed expression confirmed her worst fears. 'Weren't you listening when I talked about my past? There are reasons I'm a solitary person. I need to be alone.'

Except for occasional sex.

All this time she'd imagined a growing bond but all he felt was the pressure to satisfy his libido. To be fair, she'd accepted those terms but then everything had transformed, for her at least.

Rosamund sucked in a shuddery breath and turned to the view, past the sun-baked plain to the village and glittering sea beyond. Above hung the vast blue sky, a reminder that she was merely a tiny speck on an immense globe.

She didn't need the reminder. She felt herself shrinking, becoming smaller and smaller, wishing she could disappear.

Of course she knew about Fotis' past. But, dazzled by her feelings, she'd managed to shuck off a lifetime's insecurity and think she could help him move on. That they'd have each other's backs so together they could cast away the shadows of the past.

That *she'd* be enough for him as he was enough for her.

What were you thinking, girl?

The contemptuous voice was her father's, the sneer as vivid as if he stood there, glowering at her.

Her life had been a series of lessons in not being good enough. She'd never been able to satisfy her father's high standards. As for having a man *love* her...

Fotis said something, his voice low, but she didn't hear it over the rush of blood in her ears. She folded her arms tight around her body, failing to hold in the pain.

She wouldn't have thought it possible but she felt worse than she ever had. Worse than her father had ever made her feel, or her first, deceitful lover. Worse than when the press portrayed her in the worst possible light. She felt as bad as when she'd lost her mother.

Because no one could inflict hurt as severe as someone you loved.

That's why Fotis doesn't want a relationship. He doesn't want that pain.

She understood, but he had no right to make her feel like this. And yet she loved him. Loved, and at this moment almost hated him.

Rosamund turned, surprised to find him so close, hands dropping to his sides as if he'd been reaching for her.

Even now her imagination tried to paint the picture she wanted instead of facing the truth.

'I had you wrong.' Pain prompted the words. 'If someone asked me for a word to describe you, I'd have said strong. But you're not, are you? You're a coward. You want to stay in your eyrie, cut off from people because you're scared of loving. Do you think your father and brother would have wanted that?'

His head rocked back as if from a slap. He looked dazed, then his eyes narrowed to slits of blistering fire and his nostrils flared. 'Don't bring my family into this!'

'I—'

'Don't talk to me about fear and hiding. You're proud of living the life you say you want, but are you *really* doing that?' His voice was unrelenting. 'That last day in France we went out to lunch so you could show the world you were unfazed by the attack, enjoying yourself with your boyfriend at your side. You were so concerned about projecting an image you didn't even give yourself time to recover from the shock of the attack. Time you needed. You're not in control, you're running scared.'

His expression softened to something that looked almost like pity. Her stomach spasmed. She didn't want his pity.

'*You're* hiding, Rosa. Letting your dead father and the press dictate how you live. You worry about the image you project instead of living your life. You'd rather let the world think you're a dilettante, living off the royal purse, than tell people about your work.' He paused. 'But you're strong, when you choose to be. You don't need me to lean on.'

For the longest time she was incapable of speaking.

Never, in her wildest dreams, could she have believed today would see them hurting each other like this, ripping away protective layers and inflicting such pain.

She shoved her hands into her pockets where he couldn't see them shake. 'Don't worry, Fotis. That's one lesson I learned a long time ago. I don't need a man to lean on.'

Couldn't he see this wasn't about propping herself up but about wanting to share and build together?

'I don't *need* a man at all.' Particularly one who didn't want her. She wanted to say it had been a mistake, she didn't love him, but couldn't do it. Her unrequited feelings were too deep to pretend.

She shoved her feet into her discarded sandals, gathering up her gear. But even with her heart crumbling, she couldn't leave him like this.

'Take a hard look at your own life, Fotis. You're not responsible for your brother's death. It wasn't your fault. As for believing you can only survive as a recluse...'

She gestured towards the village. 'You're not alone. You've been forging connections, real connections with other people. Dimitria Politis and her grandfather. Tassos and his wife think the world of you. So do the other villagers.'

Before he could interrupt she continued. 'Not because you've spent money improving the island's infrastructure. I heard them talk about you.' Everyone had anecdotes about his quiet acts of kindness, how he got things done, how he listened. Even rare examples of his dry sense of humour. 'They respect the way you roll up your sleeves and help work. They *like* you. You're not alone, Fotis, whatever you tell yourself. You've got people you care about and who care about you. That makes you stronger, not weaker.'

'Rosa…' His voice was rough with warning.

She met those ocean-coloured eyes and knew they'd haunt her dreams. Stark emotion welled and she felt that telltale prickle behind her eyes. She'd never see him again.

'Goodbye, Fotis.' She spun away. 'I'll arrange my own transport.'

'Rosa!'

She kept walking. There was only so much a woman could take. She'd reached her limit.

CHAPTER FIFTEEN

FOTIS' STRIDE SLOWED as he negotiated the throng. He'd known this renowned European book fair attracted crowds, but the vast complex teemed.

Impatience rode him, adding to the potent mix of anticipation and fear churning inside.

In the ten days since Rosa had left, his life had turned on its head. He'd let deadlines slide or alternatively micromanaged projects to the extent that he'd almost lost one of his best staff, unable to work with his suddenly interfering ways.

Fotis couldn't get the balance right. He'd thrown himself into work because for years that had been his prime focus. Since Rosa's departure it filled the empty hours. That and long workouts.

But nothing worked. He was strung out, jittery and operating on too little sleep.

He couldn't banish the memory of Rosa's dazed eyes when he rejected her. Or her gallant courage when she confronted him, forcing him to hear things he didn't want to hear, even as he read the hurt she tried to conceal. He'd never felt so emotionally stripped bare.

She loved you and you pushed her away.

He'd told himself it was the right thing. He couldn't give her what she craved. He couldn't be the man she wanted. He hadn't dared hope she was right and he could reach out and grasp the sort of happiness she promised.

Was he a coward?

He'd rejected her words the instant she said them. Because he always faced the truth about himself. He knew he had feet of clay. He'd failed his brother. In the past he'd picked himself up and kept going, even when it felt like he'd lost everything.

But as time went on her words had gouged deeper, eating through his certainties, leaving him in darkness.

Until yesterday when he'd heard she was appearing at the book fair. Not in her royal capacity but as the author of the Princess Lily books. The surprise announcement of her identity had taken the world by storm.

He'd been stunned when he'd looked them up the night she'd left. They were a worldwide phenomenon, translated across the globe.

A unique talent...wonderful world-building...engaging and utterly authentic...a humorous but honest voice for today's young readers.

He'd burned with pride at the praise. Her stories blended a lush fairy-tale world with a relevance to today's society that hooked children and adults. Her fans had gone wild when her identity was announced.

Fotis was sorry he hadn't been with her to tell her how proud he was, of her work and of claiming her place as the author of the much-loved books.

But she wouldn't want to hear from him. What right had he to offer praise after what he'd done?

Yet circumstances had altered when he'd learned she was appearing here. He'd contacted Leon, ostensibly to discuss progress in their lobbying, but Leon had seen through that ruse. He'd complained his sister had accepted the barest minimum security arrangements for her appearances. He'd also tried to quiz Fotis about their time together.

Fotis shouldered his way through the throng, quickening his step. He'd brought in top security staff to blend in with the crowd but wouldn't be happy until he saw she was safe.

Ricardo might be locked up but there were some dangerous people out there.

He slammed to a stop as he rounded a corner and saw her at a desk, dwarfed by the queue of people waiting have books signed. Others clustered, taking photos. Behind her two images filled the wall, a book cover and a photo of her, light dancing in her eyes.

Air backed up in his lungs as the noise faded. It was like the first time he'd seen her. That moment of absolute shock because he recognised this woman at a cellular level, knew her in the way of a man recognising his mate, though he hadn't realised it then.

The longing was just as fierce now, worse, because he knew he'd destroyed his chance with her.

Forcing himself to breathe, he moved in.

Rosa's hair was loose around her shoulders, its glow drawing him like a beacon. He hated that her face was pale against her cornflower-blue jacket, though her smile was bright as she chatted to a pair of teenagers.

She'd always been good at putting on a public face. Was she doing it now? Or had the thrill of connecting with her readers pushed aside the pain he'd inflicted?

Maybe she's already moved on.

Maybe she realised it wasn't love. Perhaps she's relieved to have left. She's embracing a new life that doesn't include you.

You're in her past, Mavridis. She won't thank you for pushing into her life now.

He noticed the woman standing between Rosa and the queue. His breathing eased. He'd employed the woman, hoping Rosa would be more comfortable with her than a man whose presence screamed *bodyguard*. Scanning the area, he saw other guards, incognito. At least she had some protection.

The teenagers moved on. Rosa flexed her fingers as if they were stiff and suddenly her gaze met his.

Everything in him stopped. Her eyes widened, the corners

of her mouth lifting. Her smile speared him. He felt blood flow from the wound as his breathing and pulse kicked in again.

Then her half-formed smile died. She looked away, mouth firming. The woman beside her said something and Rosa turned to the next person in line.

Fotis was gutted. She'd wanted to see him. Until she remembered what he'd done.

Still, he wasn't going anywhere. Not until he'd spoken with her. That was non-negotiable.

For the next couple of hours he watched, feeling the too-heavy thud of his bruised heart against his ribs. In all that time she didn't look his way.

That tells you all you need to know.

Yet he stood his ground, until finally staff erected a sign stating that the signing had ended for the day, setting up a cordon.

Fotis moved in, nodding to the security staff. Rosa was talking to a woman he recognised as her agent. They were at the rear of the space, backs to him, yet Rosa sensed him approach. Her shoulders rose, spine stiffening. She turned.

'I'm afraid the signing's over,' the other woman said. 'You can come back tomorrow.'

'Rosa?' Still she said nothing. This close, he read her fatigue. Despite the smile she'd worn for the crowd, her eyes were dull. Exhaustion from the signing or something else?

Beads of sweat prickled his nape as he moved nearer and the agent stepped in front of him.

'It's okay, Carlotta. I know him. I'll join you soon.'

You don't even deserve an introduction. Do you really think she'll listen?

Fotis ignored the voice, shoving his hands deep in his trouser pockets. Because it took everything he had not to reach for Rosa, wrap his arms around her and pull her in tight.

Rosamund had plumbed the depths of despair since leaving Greece, telling herself things would get better as she moved on with her life. Now she learnt she'd been wrong. The anguish of seeing him again, realising separation hadn't diminished her feelings, almost tore her apart.

His severe features had never been more starkly compelling. It had taken all her control not to look at him for the past couple of hours, though she knew he hadn't taken his eyes off her. She'd felt his gaze through every greeting, every new reader, every conversation.

She swallowed but stood her ground, hating the way she devoured the sight of him. The way her pulse quickened as familiar excitement stroked her. She was famished for the sight and sound of him. For his touch, his warm, spicy scent.

'We need to speak. Let's go somewhere private.'

She shook her head. They were in clear view of anyone walking by and that suited her. Being alone with him could only bring more heartache.

'There's nothing more to say, Fotis.'

Despite the passers-by, they were out of earshot, if they kept their voices low. Carlotta hovered several metres away, talking to one of the staff, darting concerned glances. Bless the woman for wanting to protect her, but she could handle this.

'I need to talk with you alone. It's important.' His voice was a velvet rumble that threatened her resolve.

'This is as alone as we get. If that doesn't suit, there's somewhere else I need to be.' She reached for her bag.

'Congratulations on your success, Rosa. I'm happy you stepped out of the shadows and claimed your place. That took a lot of courage.'

'Thank you.' Later she'd appreciate those words. For now, it was agony being close to him. She had to escape. She turned away.

'There's something else, Rosa.'

To her deep despair, the way he said her name still undid her. Tense muscles loosened and her insides unravelled.

'No! There's nothing. You think I don't know the so-called

publishing assistant over there is a bodyguard? Or that you arranged for others? I know you have strong protective instincts but I'm not your responsibility.' She saw his lips part, knew he'd argue, and couldn't bear it. 'I don't want a *minder*,' she snapped, whipping up anger as a defence. 'I want a *man*. One who's strong enough to believe in himself and in me. Now, it's time I left.'

She'd taken a step away when a single word stopped her. 'Please.'

She froze, hearing something in that one syllable she'd never heard from Fotis. Desperation. Longing. Something more, so powerful she drew the sound deep inside, holding it, afraid of what would happen if she let it go.

'You're absolutely right.' His voice was hoarse, as if his throat had constricted like hers. She was sure hers was lined with sandpaper. 'You deserve so much more than I offered. I'm ashamed, Rosa. I was a coward, all the time telling myself I was doing the right thing, pushing you away to protect you from even worse hurt, but all the while I was protecting myself.'

Slowly she turned back. Beyond him everything was a blur. All she saw was him, hands open by his sides, wearing an expression of such pain that answering grief stoppered her throat.

How could a man with such innate strength look suddenly so gaunt? Haunted? His cheeks hollowed, those bright eyes dimming as if he were a shadow of the person she knew. It killed her to see him that way.

'I came to say you were right. About me. I've been scared since I was a boy, scared of caring too much and losing what I cared for. Terrified of connecting, much less loving.' His chest rose on a deep breath and she saw a pulse race at his temple. 'It was easier to cut myself off. But I did yearn for more. For community. Friends. Love.'

His words reverberated between them, dying away into thickening silence.

She'd been hurt too many times. It had taken all her strength to walk away last time and now...

Rosamund shook her head, torn between excitement and fear. Her flesh was cold but scorching heat radiated inside. She blinked as fire burned the back of her eyes.

Instantly Fotis was there, so close she had to angle her head up to hold his gaze. And suddenly there was fire in his eyes too, blazing down at her, holding her in thrall. He might be haunted by past pain, but he was strong, a survivor, willing to learn from his mistakes.

'I was terrified, Rosa, because with you I wanted everything. I wanted us to continue as we were but I wanted so much more, things I'd never considered. I want you body and soul. I want to laugh with you, share with you, build a future with you.'

His words stole the air from her lungs, because she could see, feel, that he meant every syllable. The air crackled between them, her fingertips tingled as hope ghosted along her spine and settled near her heart. When he spoke like that...

But this time caution, the product of past hurts, stopped her. 'I...' She shook her head.

'It's all right, *asteri mou*. I know I'm another man who let you down when you deserved better. I know you need time to think. I won't crowd you.'

He raised his hands and stepped back. Part of Rosamund went with him.

'I love you, Rosa.'

Again her heart seemed to stop, before taking up a rackety, excited beat. Had she heard him right?

'I didn't know it at the time, but I suspect I loved you from the moment you went toe-to-toe with me that day in Paris, when you put me in my place then strutted off the plane. But what I feel for you is deeper than attraction. It's something I'll carry all my life, whether you forgive me or not.'

He smiled then, a rare, crooked smile that hooked her heart.

Who was she kidding? Her heart had been hooked from the first.

'You need space,' he said. 'I respect that. I'll go now and—'

'You're not going anywhere.'

One winged eyebrow rose. 'I'm not?'

'If you loved me, would you really go back to Greece now?'

'Who said anything about Greece? I'm trying to be reasonable, not pressure you. I've booked a suite in your hotel. I'm going to invite you to breakfast tomorrow when you've had time to think. I'm going to work on convincing you to forgive me, then I'm going to woo you properly.'

So, far from accepting defeat and retreating, he had a plan to coax her out from behind her defences. Or wear her down. Or perhaps seduce her into changing her mind. Anticipation rippled across her skin and eddied in her womb.

That was the man she'd fallen for. Powerful, clever, single-minded.

It was just as well she loved him the way he was.

Despite the gravity of the moment, her mouth twitched. 'Wooing? That sounds very old-fashioned.'

His eyes narrowed as if he read her changing emotions. 'My intentions are of the old-fashioned variety. I want to marry you, Rosa.'

Shock compounded on shock, but somehow each one was easier to take. She was learning to like the surprises Fotis offered today. Love. Wooing. A future together.

From the corner of her eye she saw heads turn in their direction. They'd forgotten to keep their voices down. She didn't care, and nor did Fotis, given his expression.

Nevertheless, she stepped closer, close enough to slip her hands beneath his jacket and plant them on his solid chest. The steady throb of his heart eased the last ache in her chest.

'Yes, please. I still love you, Fotis. I always will.'

His arms went around her, pulling her in as he groaned deep in his throat and kissed the top of her head then peppered kisses over her face. 'I don't deserve you, Rosa. I was petrified you'd changed your mind.'

'Never,' she whispered as she lifted her mouth to his. 'I want to spend my life with you. I've been so miserable—'

'Sh, *asteri mou*. I was a blind idiot but I'm going to make it up to you. We're going to be so happy.'

She slid her hands up to clasp the back of his neck, luxuriating in how good they felt together. In the impossible excitement of knowing this was only the beginning. 'I know.'

Then the globe's most reclusive billionaire and the world's most talked-about princess kissed passionately, ignoring the gathering crowd and raised phones.

They were in love and didn't care who knew it.

EPILOGUE

THE HUGE CHRISTMAS TREE twinkled with lights. Rosamund stifled a laugh as her toddler nephew stood at its base, wonderment in his eyes as he looked up to where it almost reached the frescoed ceiling. He craned his neck so far he lost his balance and abruptly sat on the floor, beaming.

'He really is the jolliest little boy,' she murmured, watching her sister-in-law, Susanna, scoop him up and carry him over to Leon.

'You want one like that?' Fotis' voice was like liquid velvet in her ear. His arms came around her, pulling her back against his tall frame, hands possessively smoothing her baby bump.

She sighed and relaxed against him. 'A child who laughs more than he cries? That sounds wonderful. But,' she covered one of his big hands with hers, 'whatever our baby's like, I'll love him or her.'

They were so lucky, to have each other and soon, a child. Beneath their joined hands the bub moved and, though she knew it was coincidence, Rosamund couldn't help imagining it was communicating with them.

'Didn't I tell you she'd be a footballer?'

Rosamund shook her head. What was it about men and football? 'He could be a chess player or a mathematician.'

She shivered as Fotis kissed her neck, his words tickling her skin. 'Or a world-famous author.'

'Sorry to intrude.' Leon appeared, comfortably holding the

heir to the throne, who grinned and drooled over his jacket. 'But can I borrow you for a few minutes, Fotis? It's about the children's services initiative I'm planning.'

'You'll need to consult Rosa too.'

'I already gave my thoughts when you were out for a run.' She stroked her nephew's soft cheek, overcome by the idea *their* baby would be here soon. She straightened and turned, realising Fotis was thinking the same thing. His expression made her melt. All that tender protectiveness and anticipation. 'Don't be long, you two. I know what you're like when you get your heads together over a project.'

Fotis' slow smile made her wish they'd already had Christmas dinner and were heading to their suite.

'I promise to be back soon.' He kissed her cheek, sending ripples of delight across her skin.

Rosamund moved to the group around the fireplace, chatting with relatives and family friends. Laughter rang out and she turned to see Dimitria Politis and Susanna's younger brother grinning together. Old Mr Politis was deep in discussion with Rosamund's elderly second cousin. Knowing both, they were either righting the world's wrongs or planning a new business venture.

Fotis and Tassos had spent ages planning a fireworks display back in Greece to see in the new year. Her family—her *family*!—would all travel from Cardona to Greece after Christmas and stay with them over New Year's to share the celebration.

How things had changed.

Her sister-in-law stopped beside her. 'What are you looking so happy about? Might it have something to do with a fascinating, dark-haired Greek?'

Rosamund shrugged. 'What can I say? I'm a lucky woman.'

'We both are.' Susanna slipped her arm through Rosamund's. 'I'm so glad you and Leon are spending more time together. That means you and *I* get time together too.'

Rosamund leaned closer, smiling at the glow of belonging she felt. 'I feel the same.' Leon's wife was a wonderful woman. 'I was just thinking how much fun it is to have two family celebrations. Did I mention there'll be a huge fireworks display on the island?'

Susanna looked past her, eyes dancing. 'I don't think you'll have to wait until next week for fireworks.' She slipped her arm free. 'I'd better check the meal's ready. But…' Her voice turned mock-stern, 'don't go getting distracted.'

She strode off, just as a warm hand captured Rosamund's. 'Have I told you, *asteri mou*, that you look gorgeous in silver? No other woman holds a candle to you.'

She grinned and cupped Fotis' jaw in her palms. 'You have, but I never tire of hearing it.'

'Excellent.' His head dipped, gaze fixed on her mouth.

A voice announced, 'Dinner is served.' Seconds later Susanna murmured beside them, 'That includes you two.'

Fotis lifted his head, mock-frowning. 'She's bossy.'

Rosamund pressed a quick kiss to his lips. 'Just as well you like strong women.'

He threaded his fingers through hers. 'Absolutely. And you like challenging men.'

They shared a secret smile then turned and followed their family into the dining room, hands linked and hearts full.

* * * * *

Did you fall head over heels for
Forbidden Princess's Billionaire Bodyguard?
*Then you're certain to love these other intensely
emotional stories from Annie West!*

Signed, Sealed, Married
Unknown Royal Baby
Ring for an Heir
Queen by Royal Command
Stolen Pregnant Bride

Available now!

MILLS & BOON®

Coming next month

SECRETLY PREGNANT PRINCESS
Lorraine Hall

Evelyne saw Gabriel's eyes widen. She tried to recover, but it was too late. He'd seen.

He pointed at her—at her stomach. 'What is that?' Gabriel demanded.

She had dreamed of this in her weaker moments. Telling him that he was to be a father. In her fantasies, she was calm, casual, disdainful almost. She did not give him the satisfaction of thinking that she needed him, wanted him, or was afraid of being alone.

She was determined to make fantasy a reality.

So, she beamed at him, made sure she sounded cheerful. 'In the States they call it a baby bump.' She ran her hands over the roundness, moved to give him a profile view. Refused to let the nerves fluttering through her show—she'd had ample practice at hiding those. 'Isn't that cute?'

He said nothing. Didn't move. She wasn't sure he breathed.

When he finally moved, it was with clear-cut precision. 'Explain yourself,' he said quietly, dangerously.

She chose to maintain her flippancy. 'Is it not self-explanatory, Gabriel? I am pregnant.'

Continue reading

SECRETLY PREGNANT PRINCESS
Lorraine Hall

Available next month
millsandboon.co.uk

COMING SOON!

We really hope you enjoyed reading this book.
If you're looking for more romance
be sure to head to the shops when
new books are available on

Thursday 15th January

To see which titles are coming soon, please visit
millsandboon.co.uk/nextmonth

MILLS & BOON

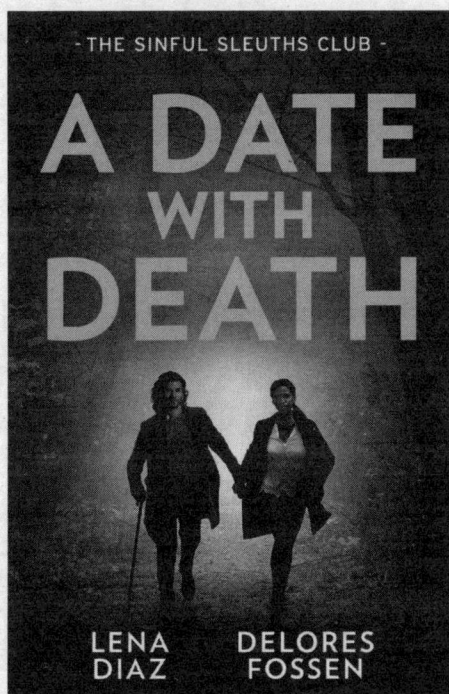

LET'S TALK
Romance

For exclusive extracts, competitions
and special offers, find us online:

(f) MillsandBoon

𝕏 @MillsandBoon

(O) @MillsandBoonUK

(♪) @MillsandBoonUK

Get in touch on 01413 063 232